Knotted

THE BOYS OF BISHOP MOUNTAIN
BOOK THREE

LEXXI JAMES

Knotted: The Boys of Bishop Mountain
Copyright © 2024 Lexxi James
www.LexxiJames.com
All rights reserved. Lexxi James, LLC
Independently Published.

With Grateful Appreciation to
KE
Autumn Gantz of Wordsmith Publicity
Jaime Ryter, The Ryter's Proof Editing Services
The Lexxi James Beta Readers

Cover by Book Sprite LLC in collaboration with Melody Barber

No part of this publication may be reproduced, distributed, or transmitted in any form or by any means, including photocopying, recording, or other electronic or mechanical methods, without the prior written permission of Lexxi James LLC. Under certain circumstances, a brief quote in reviews and for non-commercial use may be permitted as specified in copyright law. Permission may be granted through a written request to the publisher at LexxiJamesBooks@gmail.com

This is a work of fiction. Names, characters, places, and incidents are the product of the author's imagination. Specific named locations, public names, and other specified elements are used for impact, but this novel's story and characters are 100 percent fictitious. Certain long-standing institutions, agencies, and public offices are mentioned, but the characters involved are wholly imaginary. Resemblance to individuals, living or dead, or to events which have occurred is purely coincidental. And if your life happens to bear a strong resemblance to my imaginings, then well done and cheers to you! You're a freaking rock star!

Introduction

KNOTTED is a standalone romance in the Boys of Bishop Mountain series.

For fans of the Alex Drake Series, this book takes place long before the love story of Alex and Madison.

Brian

Here's the deal—I need a woman.

Not just any woman. Someone I can trust, who understands boundaries.
A 60-to-90-day fiancée arrangement.
She'll live her life, I'll live mine.
Business, plain and simple.

INTRODUCTION

And I know the perfect candidate.

Sweet Juliana Spenser.
Jules to her family. Ms. Spenser to me.
The proud introvert who believes social media is the devil.
She also happens to be the baby sister of a guy I served with.
The bad news? She hates me.

As a matter of fact,
she hates me a lot.

CHAPTER 1
Brian

From the age of four, my fate was sealed.

I mean, with the backyard being Gotham City, and the living room sofa transformed into the ultimate battlefield every afternoon—weekends, too—my future was crystal clear.

I was Iron Man—armed with sheer determination and an indomitable will. Some call me stubborn. Often my mom.

And since my best friend Mark was Batman, and his brother, Zac, perpetually switched gears between a half dozen evil villains, our battles were epic.

And usually ended with one of us in the ER on a monthly basis.

As if childhood games could foreshadow reality.

My foundations are built on a long line of heroes. My grandfather served in the legendary 101st Airborne Division, earning him a Silver Star and a Purple Heart.

My father was a Green Beret, leading missions that were the stuff of legends.

When it came to me, being a soldier wasn't just in my blood—it was my destiny.

From the moment I enlisted, I thrived. A bold statement, especially for the guy who was voted both prom king and most likely to end up in jail.

The drills, the discipline, the camaraderie—it all resonated with me. I excelled at executing missions with laser precision, each one building my confidence and arrogance in equal measure.

But airborne operations spoke to me like nothing else ever could. Leaping out of a perfectly good plane and hurtling toward the earth at breakneck speeds, relying on nothing but a thin piece of fabric to save my life—it was pure adrenaline.

A terrifying thrill that both scared me shitless and set me absolutely free. It gave me purpose. Defined me like nothing else before.

Like the kid who dashed around in his underwear and bedsheet cape, I felt invincible. All it took was one mistake—a sudden shift of the wind, an immovable cluster of trees—and my perfect world came crashing down around me.

That small twist of fate shattered everything I knew. My body broken, my spirit teetering on the edge, I clung to the one thing that could hold me together: pain.

Raw and unforgiving, I leaned into its cold beauty. And it kept me alive, transforming me from hero to someone tipping over the edge until I've become a man no one recognizes.

Playboy.

Asshole.

Sinner.

All while wearing five-figure suits and watches that cost more than cars.

I doubled down on being the worst side of me, doing whatever it took to dull the ache and keep the demons at bay. Because the real battle isn't in the field or the sky.

It's being haunted by all the mistakes I made, wishing to my core I could make just one right.

"I'LL DO IT," I SAY, MY VOICE SLICING THROUGH THE room's thick tension. For the past hour, I've watched Mark wrestle with his dilemma—caught between planning a six-week dream honeymoon for him and his blushing bride—aka, my baby sister—and the looming threat of four major accounts slipping through the cracks if he's off in Fiji, New Zealand, and Australia. These are all places Jess has fantasized about visiting since she was a kid.

With his former stand-in, his brother Zac, trading his suit and tie for a perpetual lumberjack ensemble, The Centurion Group is at a major crossroads, and I'm stepping in to play traffic cop.

Mark blinks, clearly taken aback. "You'll do . . . what?"

"I'll take the reins," I say firmly, meeting his gaze. "I'll stand in as the acting suit until you return."

"He knows the operation as well as we do," Zac says, rubbing his ever-growing scruff. His contemplative eyes shift to me. "But you do realize you'll hate it, right?"

I shake my head. "For the most part, this place is a well-oiled machine. You're just looking for a front man to be the face of the campaign for a month. I think I can handle it."

"Six weeks," he corrects. "And it's not the work you'll hate," Mark interjects. "It's the women."

"And women are a bad thing?" I ask, confused.

"They are when you've just landed on Manhattan's Top 10 Most Eligible Bachelor list."

"I can handle myself around women," I say, confident and assured.

"You think that now," Zac says. "As a hero in jeans and a T-shirt, you're catnip. In a suit, you're crack cocaine."

I scoff. "Having copious amounts of women clamoring for my attention? I think I'll manage."

Mark steeples his fingers, his gaze piercing. "No pressure, but you realize there's $300 million on the line this month. We have four separate contracts with high-profile clients who don't like too much attention."

I rub a hand through my hair, staring at my reflection in the mirror. "I am the king of covert."

"Is that why you're preening?" Zac asks, eyebrow raised. "Practicing to be more covert?"

Mark crosses his arms, his gaze drilling into me. "Everyone will know who you are. If you sneeze, you're on your deathbed. If you forgot your wallet, you're declaring bankruptcy. If you even fart, they'll record it."

"Lucky for us, I'm a champion clencher."

His jaw tightens, frustration rolling off him in waves. "I'm canceling the trip. Jess will have to understand."

I spin around, locking eyes with him, my voice razor-sharp. "One"—I hold up a finger—"my sister will never understand.

It's like you don't know Jess at all. And two"—I raise another finger—"I nearly died saving a dozen men and women, and you nearly died saving me. For fuck's sake, carpe diem already. Let me help."

I can tell by the look on his face he's still not convinced, so I throw one more argument his way. "Besides, you and Jess have been through enough. We're not letting the media win this one. Not on my watch."

Mark's eyes narrow, a storm brewing in his gaze. I can see the conflict warring within him, his jaw clenching as he weighs his options. Finally, he lets out a heavy sigh, his shoulders slumping in reluctant acceptance. "Fine. But don't say I didn't warn you."

Zac sucks in a breath. "Worst-case scenario, I guess I could shave my beard and come back to the office." He strokes his scruff thoughtfully, frowning.

I glare. "For your information, I do not need a safety blanket."

"You're a living, breathing PR nightmare in the making," he counters.

"I'll just lie low. Avoid headlines."

Mark reclines back in his chair, hands casually laced behind his head. His smirk is all arrogance as he drops the bombshell. "Really? Because one of your first orders of business is an interview with Roxana Voss."

Oh, fuck.

The one woman who's been a thorn in my side since day one. She's a bombshell, all legs for days and curves that could make a man forget his own name. But her obsession with me? She's got more red flags than a parade.

The last thing I need is for her to proposition me—again—about moving in and "helping me around the house." In the nude, no less. And she's dead sure I'm *the one* and can't wait to share a toothbrush with me.

Big, blaring warnings on every level. I mean, who the hell shares a toothbrush?

Yeah, hard pass. I prefer my crazies at arm's length. Or whatever's detailed in a court-mandated restraining order.

"Right," I say, forcing a casual tone. "I'll figure it out."

"You'll need to *figure it out* sooner than you think," Mark says, barely glancing up from his phone. "The Herald's been chomping at the bit for an interview, and PR can't blow them off any longer. I suggest you get a professional to help you with what to say."

I stare at him, incredulous. "To talk with Roxie Voss? First of all"—I hold up a finger—"she's a gossip columnist, not *60 Minutes*. And second"—I raise a second finger—"she's been trying to get me into bed for years." I lean in, my voice dropping lower. "I think I can have a simple conversation without a handler."

Mark's eyes flick to mine, a smirk tugging at the corner of his mouth. "You also thought indecent exposure would get you a slap on the wrist, not a mug shot. Face it, a guy like you needs a script. Everything you say won't just be used against you—it'll be a meme before you can even blink."

Zac leans against the wall, his grin widening. "Oh, I can see it now. *When he calls you baby but can't remember your name*, with a confused Travolta meme plastered right next to it."

Mark's chuckle turns into a full-on laugh. "Or how about,

When she asks for a commitment and his brain short-circuits, with Homer Simpson disappearing into the bushes."

Zac, barely holding back his laughter, raises his hand. "And how about Leonardo DiCaprio from *The Wolf of Wall Street* stumbling out of his car with the caption: *When he thinks he's God's gift to women, but tequila has other plans. Can someone say mug shot?*"

Mark doubles over, struggling to catch his breath between laughs. "For indecent exposure."

"Twice," Zac gasps, wiping tears from his eyes.

I roll my eyes, but the grin tugging at my lips gives me away. "You guys should really consider stand-up. You're killing me."

Mark claps me on the shoulder, his smirk widening. "Just looking out for you, buddy. You've got to be careful out there."

Zac nods, still chuckling. "Yeah, man. The internet never forgets."

I sigh, shaking my head. "Noted."

"Trust me, your image will be everywhere." Zac rubs his beard. "There's a reason I'm incognito. You can't be the face of The Centurion Group and stay behind the scenes. Keep things low-key. Practice discretion now."

I point at Zac. "You focus on growing that thing to Paul Bunyan levels."

"More like Jason Momoa," he says, stroking the shag with a smirk.

"And you"—I jab a finger at Mark—"focus on wining and dining my baby sis. If the media wants my rugged good looks plastered out there like I'm the next Calvin Klein guy, be my guest."

Zac shakes his head with a sigh. "I don't think you understand what you're in for."

I step closer, planting my foot on a chair, drawing attention to my newest prosthetic—sleek and damn near bionic. "I've been on the front lines, stared down war, and walked away with this little trophy." I flash them a cocky grin. "Trust me, I think I can handle one little date."

"This isn't a date," Mark bites out, eyes narrowing. "Call it that, and Roxie Voss will expect the world. Any rejection and she'll go nuclear. The last thing any of us need is to see your name headlining that disaster. This is professional. A meeting. Do not flirt with her. Do not charm her. And for god's sake, don't fuck her."

"As if I need a warning. I've had my share of stage-five clingers, so believe me, I know the drill."

Fool me once, shame on you. Fool me twice, and I'll be dodging round-the-clock texts and surprise late-night visits for months. Thanks, but no thanks. If I wanted a life of perpetual covert ops, I would've stayed in the military.

"I said I've got this," I repeat confidently.

Mark rolls his eyes, exasperation etched in every line of his face. "Famous last words."

CHAPTER 2
Jules

"Juliana Spenser?" the woman calls out.

The lobby is packed with thirty or so wannabe writers. Some clutching sleek MacBooks and attachés, others more classically grungy with spiral notebooks and a faraway look like they're conjuring their bestselling novel while they wait.

I hop to my feet, the electricity of wanting this job so badly I can taste it springing me to action. "Jules," I say, flashing a smile.

She returns a kind smile and leads me down the hall to a cramped office at the end. "Jules Spenser," she announces, handing my résumé to a man halfway through a sandwich.

Honestly, I'm hungry enough to ask if he's going to finish that.

The interviewer adjusts his thick glasses and straightens his slightly askew bow tie, scrutinizing my application with the intensity of a detective piecing together a crime scene.

Casually, he motions for me to have a seat. I do.

A nameplate on his desk reads Mr. Winston "Wyld"

Richards, but it's the blown-up photo of him at a wax museum with *quote-unquote* "*Prince*" that catches my eye. Mostly because right behind them is Marilyn Monroe and a yeti.

My nerves turn me into a babbling mess. "I've been crafting community stories and local news content for years. Mostly from behind the scenes"—by choice—"and my best work is with heartwarming pieces."

"Like the piece about the town's infamous squirrel whisperer?" he asks, flipping the page.

"Exactly."

"Riveting." His voice is flat, disinterested, but the slight raise of his brow tells me he's intrigued. My phone buzzes in my pocket, but I don't dare look away from his intense gaze. "What else?"

This is my moment. Time to claim a sliver of the credit I've been silently earning. "I, um, also ghostwrite."

That catches his attention. He leans in, his eyes narrowing as they study me with renewed interest. "The author behind the author, huh?" A smirk plays on his lips as he rubs his chin, clearly amused. "And, let me guess, you can't tell me who for."

I shrug, feeling the overbearing weight of the contract I've signed. "I'm bound by a nondisclosure agreement," I admit, hating how those words sound.

It's not about the fame, but damn, just once, I'd love to see my name on something that's actually mine.

He exhales sharply, as if making a decision. "What's your handle?"

I blink. "Huh?"

"Instagram. What's your handle?"

My answer comes out quieter than I intend. "I don't have one."

"Facebook? TikTok? Anything?"

"I don't do social media."

His eyes narrow as he studies me, a bead of sweat trickling down the back of my neck under his scrutiny. "An aspiring journalist who doesn't do social media and trapped herself into an iron-clad contract," he muses, clearly baffled. "Why am I not surprised?"

The opportunity is slipping through my fingers like the last rays of a California sunset. I can't let it disappear. Not like this. "Please, just one chance. That's all I'm asking."

He leans back in his chair, hands steepled, fingers tapping together with the precision of someone already dissecting my every word. "Who's been the biggest influence in your life and why?"

Heat rushes up my neck like an out-of-control wildfire, scorching everything in its path. I should have an answer, someone inspiring, someone who makes sense. But I don't. Because the only name that blazes through my mind is the one I keep buried deep in the closet of shame.

My mind teeters on a tightrope, balancing between landing my dream job and tumbling into the abyss of soul-crushing, minimum-wage gigs that threaten to snuff out every last spark of creativity.

I glance around his office, a chaotic mix of relics and memories. A battered copy of *Treasure Island* sprawls across his desk, its pages dog-eared and falling apart, a sight that tugs at something deep inside me. On the wall hangs a signed guitar, probably from someone famous, though the signature is a scrawl I can't quite place.

It's obvious that canned answers won't get me anywhere with this guy. Wyld is after something raw, something real. He's searching for the fire that sets someone apart from the sea of faceless, would-be journalists.

He needs to see that spark, the drive that fuels me, not the quiet girl who prefers Saturday nights curled up on the sofa with fuzzy socks and a shifter romance.

I take a deep breath, ready to blurt out someone impactful and timeless like Oprah or Christiane Amanpour. But then, the truth cuts through like a streaker, leaving me stammering as a Greek god with a dimpled smirk and glacier-melting eyes hijacks my thoughts.

Out of nowhere, he points at me, almost accusingly. "You're thinking of them now, aren't you?"

"I am *not* thinking of him," I lie, feeling flames burn my cheeks.

"Aha! It's a him!" he exclaims, snapping his fingers like he's cracked the code. Oh, this guy is good. His unkempt brows do a little dance, waggling like crazy caterpillars "So, who is he?"

God, do not do this to me. He's the last person I want to talk about. "Nobody."

Unblinking, he stares, as if he's perfectly content to wait me out.

"Just a—" I choke down the knot in my throat, "high school crush." And the bane of my existence.

"Well, Mr. Nobody makes your cheeks rosy, your eyes bright, and your pulse practically leap out of your neck." He clasps his hands on the desk. "Does the high school got a name?"

"Nope."

"Nameless?"

"Yup."

It's not as if *he's* the right answer for this Spanish Inquisition of an interview. Or anything else, for that matter. No way am I landing this job by crediting *who I am* to my mortal enemy.

Do people even have mortal enemies?

Dismayed, I shake my head. Apparently so.

"Look, kid. I've got dozens of candidates banging down my door for this job—people with more degrees, more experience, and social media followings that could fill a stadium. But"—he exhales sharply, eyes locking on to mine—"you're interesting."

"I am?"

He shrugs, a half smirk tugging at his lips. "In a weird, trainwreck sort of way. A writer with no social media—seriously, that's almost unheard of. Especially for a looker like you."

I sit up straighter, trying to decipher the mix of words he just threw at me. I'm pretty sure there was a compliment buried in there somewhere.

"And anyone who cranks out work as fast as you do without ever using your real name"—he points a finger at me, eyes narrowing with a mix of curiosity and suspicion—"there's got to be a story there. I can smell it."

"There's no story," I reply, keeping my voice steady, even as my pulse quickens. "I just prefer my privacy."

He tilts his head, eyes sharpening with interest. "No worries, kid. I can definitely work with someone who shies away from the limelight. And everyone knows the juiciest stories are dug up out of the shadows." He leans back, considering. "But you'll need a pen name."

A swarm of butterflies kicks up in my gut. This is it—the first time I'll be putting myself out there, even if it's under a an alias. "How about Sydney?"

"It's a guy's name."

"It's unisex, like Jordan or Taylor." And, for the record, it was the name of my teddy bear, circa years three through six. "Let's be real, women don't get half the respect men do in this industry."

He lets out a dry chuckle. "Untrue. I pay all my writers equally—the same shitty rates across the board. And what about a last name?"

I keep my tone casual, but inside, I'm buzzing so hard, the name comes out before I can stop it. "How about Bryan, with a Y?"

He holds his hands to his temples, as if conjuring knowledge from the other side. "And let me guess, Mr. Nobody's first name is B-r-y-a-n."

"His name is not B-r-y-a-n," I say, spelling it out as well. I don't bother telling him that my nemesis's name is Brian with an *I*.

"Let me guess. Brian with an *I* not a *Y*?"

"What are you? A mind-reader?"

"No," he says with a cocky grin. "I'm the owner of a newspaper with a Pulitzer in investigative journalism and a knack for reading people. Ms. Spenser—or should I say Mrs. Brian . . . *what*, I wonder?" His smirk sharpens, eyes gleaming with challenge as he dares me to fill in the blank.

I tense, the words digging up memories I'd rather forget. As a kid, I must have written it a hundred times—*Mrs. Brian Bishop*—scribbling it mindlessly until one day, my prince charming morphed into a dark, evil knight, shattering my fairytale into pieces.

Ugh, all those wasted adolescent hours I spent obsessively scrawling *Mrs. Brian Bishop* when I should've been daydreaming about being Mrs. Henry Cavill or Mrs. Insert-Your-Favorite Hemsworth. Hours I'll never get back, and for what? A childhood crush that turned into a nightmare.

"Brian what?"

Geez, Mr. Richards is a dog with a bone. When I hesitate, he leans in, eyes narrowing. "Spill, and you're in. Or clam up and holler 'next' on your way out."

My options are slim, and while lying seems like the easy way out, it's also the dumbest. True, I'm a writer and someone who often spins the world not as it is, but as it could be.

But lying to a news bloodhound? The man has the power to end my career with a single viral post—one scathing TikTok rant, and I'm done.

Meanwhile, my phone won't stop buzzing in my pocket. Taylor's relentless messages are pinging me like a toddler on a sugar high. It's driving me nuts, grating on my nerves until I can practically feel the hives creeping up my skin.

"You look a little green, kid. Purge," he says. "Unburdening the spirit always feels better."

Really? I exhale sharply, bracing myself for what's coming. The name that's been buried for a decade claws its way to the surface. "Fine. It's Bishop."

His eyebrows shoot up. "He's a bishop? Like a man of the cloth?"

"No!" I snap, frustration bleeding into my voice. "His name. It's Bishop." I pause, the weight of it pressing down on me as I force out the words. "Brian Bishop." His name escapes my lips like a secret I've held onto for far too long, barely more than a whisper.

You know how they say that if you speak the name of the devil, he appears? I nearly brace. After a decade and hundreds of miles I'm still trying to untangle myself from the mess he twisted my life into.

"Brian . . . Bishop?" he asks, and I can't be certain, but he sounds thoroughly underwhelmed.

I'm not sure what he was expecting, but I feel the need to brush it off. "He's nobody," I say, almost apologizing for how painfully ordinary my life is—even my nemesis is nothing to write home about.

He watches me for a long moment, his gaze too sharp for comfort. "When's the last time you stalked this Brian with an *I*?" He stretches out the name, milking every bit of smug satisfaction.

"Never." The word slips out, thick with disbelief and a touch of horror at the very idea.

"Never, huh?" Mr. Richards raises an eyebrow, then abruptly stands, snagging his coat from the back of his chair with a decisive movement and grabbing his cup of coffee. "Well, I've got an interview with the mayor uptown." He's already halfway to the door when he adds, "You start in three weeks."

"Three weeks?" The words come out sharper than I intend.

"I was really hoping for a job now." And, let's be honest, a paycheck.

He pauses at the doorway, flashing me a cheeky grin. "And I was really hoping to be sandwiched between Sofia Vergara and Margot Robbie."

"But you said I was *interesting*."

"Not that interesting," he says with a shrug. "The person you're replacing still owes me a headliner, and it's a doozy. A big Manhattan company is playing shuffleboard with its execs. And you know how these things go—first story wins. Besides, this gives you time to set up your accounts."

"My what?"

"Your social media accounts." He holds up two fingers. "You won't cut it as a reporter unless you get in the game. Two accounts, two weeks. Tag yourself in. Oh, and it'll give you time to get your homework done."

"Homework?" Just the sound of that makes me nervous.

"First, Sydney is fine. Bryan is out. Figure out the name you want, and make it count. Something that when you see it in print, you'll hold your head high."

Okay. Sure, as homework goes, that doesn't sound so bad.

"Then, attach that name to two social media accounts and start your first investigative task."

Why does this feel like the Wizard telling Dorothy to fetch the broomstick of the Wicked Witch of the East?

He shakes the coffee cup in his hand, eyes glinting with something between amusement and a dare. "Tell me how Mr. High School likes his coffee."

"What?" My voice pitches higher. Oh, my God. He wants

me to go full creeper mode, following around some guy I haven't seen in ten years, while wearing a trench coat and dark, oversized Jackie-O glasses, and sniffing after him to see if the sweetener in the trash is real sugar or some artificial sweetener.

Because the universe would be doing me a solid if he was balding sugar-addict with a beer belly and rotting teeth.

But Lady Luck has the nasty habit of bitch slapping me whenever it comes to the oldest Bishop brother, and sadly, I can totally see the former gym jock going full tilt on the sugar-free lifestyle just to keep those abs chiseled.

Knowing him, those biceps are probably as ripped as ever and just as overinflated as his colossal ego.

Before I can object, or even come up with a decent excuse, my phone buzzes again—Taylor, no doubt.

I fumble to find the right words. "But how—"

"A reporter is nothing if not resourceful."

I barely have time to protest because Mr. Richards is already halfway out the door. He glances back, all business. "Take it or leave it, kid."

I swallow hard, my heart racing. "I'll take it."

Then, he's gone, leaving me with my unsettling tasks and my phone buzzing like a vibrator.

> **TAYTAY**
> 9-1-1 already.
> I swear.
> This.
> Is.
> An.

> Emergency.

Shit.

CHAPTER 3
Jules

I race back to the shoebox of an apartment Taylor and I like to call home.

Technically, it's in Brooklyn. It's not the glossy, high-rise dream of Manhattan that's so far out of reach it might as well be on another planet, but let's be real—neither of us could dream of affording to live in the city. Hell, there are some months when even Brooklyn is a stretch.

But the moment we saw it, we both fell hard. It's like a rugged guy with just the right amount of scruff—rough around the edges but impossible to resist. Here, Taylor's got the walk-in closet she's always wanted, and I've claimed the oversized window that's become my writer's haven.

And it's got that old-school Brooklyn grit. The creaky floorboards and arched doorways whisper stories in my ear. This isn't just an apartment; it's history, alive and breathing, wrapping us in its worn, familiar embrace.

Plus, it's a quick, cheap subway ride from the heartbeat of New York. Or if things get desperate, a cab.

Like today.

Which is good because, at the moment, all I care about is getting through the door.

"Taylor?" I shout as I burst inside, my heart still pounding from the sprint up the stairs.

"In here!" Her voice floats back, calm as ever.

I rush to the bathroom and find her standing front and center, glued to the mirror.

She's fussing with her honey-gold hair, not even glancing my way as I practically crash into the doorway. She takes her sweet time, painting her lips with a rich cherry-red lipstick, each stroke precise. Finally, she turns to me, her big blue-green eyes locking onto mine—those eyes that tend to make men go insane. Fortunately, they have no such effect on me.

Emergency, my ass.

"Why am I here?" I ask. Taylor was ringing my phone like a damn alarm, and now, it's as if she never texted at all.

She bats those impossibly long lashes at me and flashes a pleading grin.

It's a grin I know all too well. The one that says I'll regret ever returning her call.

I roll my eyes, cross my arms, and brace for the inevitable. "That wasn't a rhetorical question, Taylor. I was in the middle of an interview."

She spins around, eyes wide with excitement. "Did you get the job?"

"Barely, with my phone going off like crazy. I'm pretty sure at one point, he thought I left my vibrator on. But I start in three weeks as a no-kidding, real writer."

She squeals and hugs me, nearly knocking me off balance.

"You're going to be a famous! In no time, you'll be cranking out stories and supporting your bestie in the lifestyle I'd like to become accustomed to."

"Simmer down," I say, untangling myself from her grip. "I have a lot of work to do before I begin. But back to you. You said this was urgent, and last I checked, getting glam isn't an emergency."

"But this *is* an emergency," she insists, her voice tinged with that familiar mix of drama and frenzy.

"Like the time you locked yourself out of the apartment while dog-sitting your boss's Rottweiler, and he ended up eating your shoes?"

"Those shoes were couture."

"Couture chew toys. Or the time you mixed up your laundry with our neighbor's and made me retrieve your bright red lacy lingerie from him?"

"He's sweet on you," she counters.

"He's eighty-three," I deadpan. "Old Mr. Grange still gives me the stink eye every time I pass him in the hall. He swears I turned his tighty-whities pink."

"He really needs to let that go."

"Taylor!"

"All right, all right . . ." She takes a deep breath as if transitioning to serious business. "I need someone to cover a few of my shifts."

"Why?"

"Because I've got a gig. In Milan. With my future husband."

"Another one? What is there, a hot guy vending machine around the corner?"

"Even if there was, you'd miss it because you're too busy

face-planting into the romance book vending machine right next to it." She points to my ever-growing pile of paperbacks. "They're not better than the real thing." She smirks.

No, but they're *safer*. I roll my eyes, trying to steer the conversation away.

"Leave my hot military mountain men out of this." It's not like my dream job starts anytime soon.

Besides, I like Bernadette. She owns a quaint little mom-and-pop restaurant and lets me have all the food and brownies I want. They're only open for breakfast and lunch, Monday through Friday, so she and her husband can escape to the mountains on the weekends.

"Fine. I'll text Bernie and let her know. Which day this week did you need me to cover?"

"Actually, it's not at Bernie's." She waves a black apron with "Salvatore's" stitched across the front, her eyes wide with faux innocence. "And it's tonight."

Here we go again. The last time I covered a shift at *Salvatore's*, I endured the hell of a double shift . . . during a bachelor party. The guys kept calling me "sweetie," pawing at me every time I walked by. And did I mention . . . worst tippers ever? I swore, never again.

"No," I say flatly.

"But you have to."

"Not happening."

"Come on," she pleads, her voice turning syrupy sweet. "You're my only hope. This guy is a Hemsworth-Cavill-Michael B. Jordan mashup. Don't make me miss out on having the most beautiful children ever because I had to sling spaghetti. And besides, you owe me."

I do owe her, but shouldn't there be an expiration date when someone saves you from stupid high school crap a million years ago? I give her a flat stare. "Salvatore's is an hour away."

"More like ninety minutes with how the subway runs," she says with a helpless shrugs.

"Taylor!" Seriously? Three freaking hours on public transportation?

Before I can say *no* or *hell no*, she's already slipped the apron over my head and cinched it around my waist. "Look, you said yourself that you don't start at the paper for three weeks, which means you need the money." She gives me that stare, and I know she's right. "Ghostwriting isn't exactly paying the bills."

She's got a point. One I hate. All my efforts barely pay for my morning dose of caffeine, let alone the rent.

She sees my disappointment and shoves me in front of the mirror, diligently adding mascara to my makeup-less face. "You're so talented, Jules. Soon, you'll be headlining major articles in the—"

"*Herald*."

"*The Herald!*" Taylor practically squeals. "Juliana Spenser, kickass journalist for *The Herald*."

"Yup. In a few short weeks, I'll be writing as myself. Well, sort of."

Her brow furrows as she looks at me through the mirror. "What do you mean, sort of?"

"Writing for myself was always the dream," I admit, feeling the words stick in my throat. The idea of it—the exposure, the scrutiny—it's all a bit too much. "But the thought of having my name and possibly my face out there for the world to dissect is so . . ."

I trail off, suddenly hyperaware of how dry my mouth is. "I'll be writing under a pen name."

"Like Dr. Seuss?" Taylor teases, raising an eyebrow as she continues to fuss with my hair.

"Hey, don't knock it," I shoot back. "He's in every bookshop around the world. The man's a global icon of children's lit."

She smirks, clearly enjoying herself. "Total respect to the ultimate brand ambassador of cats in hats and . . . foxes in . . . Sockes?" She stumbles over the last word, laughing.

"I believe the plural is socks," I correct, giggling.

"All I know," she says, pausing to twirl a section of my hair through the curling iron, "is that if I had that kind of reach, I'd be running the Milan fashion show instead of just styling models and vlogging about it."

I watch her in the mirror, her fingers moving with practiced ease, and an idea starts to take shape. "How many followers do you have on social media?" I ask.

She shrugs, not missing a beat as she curls another strand of my hair. "I don't know, a few hundred thousand, I guess?"

My eyes widen. "A few hundred thousand?"

Taylor just shrugs, like she hasn't just casually dropped a number people would trade their left kidney for. "A couple of well-timed TikToks and Reels, and it basically builds itself."

I try to play it cool. "You know I hate social media."

"Like a werewolf hates silver," she says, completely matter-of-fact.

I sigh. "Okay, how about this—I'll cover all those dreadful shifts while you're off gallivanting in Malta—"

"Milan," she corrects with a smirk.

"And in return, you help me get my social media off the ground?"

Unfazed, she adds another coat of mascara, though the glint in her eyes gives her away. "Be your social media fairy godmother for the next PoshBody award winner?"

"I think you mean Peabody," I correct with a smirk.

"Then the answer is yes!" she agrees, a grin spreading across her face. "And I'm taking every ounce of credit. Styled by @TheRunwayByTay. Starting with your official photo shoot."

The blood drains from my face. "What photo shoot?"

"Oh, honey, you can't have just an average picture if you're going to be front-page news. You need to be ultra-glam."

"I'd rather be incognito. Maybe a cute cat image with heart-shaped glasses on."

"Crazy cat lady? I think not." She grabs my chin, holding me steady as she paints cherry-red lipstick on my lips with precision. "What's your handle going to be?" she asks, tousling my hair with a playful glint in her eyes.

"What do you suggest?" I ask, my voice wavering slightly.

She pauses, a thoughtful look crossing her face before she grabs a dark pair of sunglasses and shoves them up the bridge of my nose. "We'll figure that out later," she says with a wink, sending a ripple of apprehension through me, a tingle of pinpricks along my arms and neck.

She picks up a scarf and a wide-brimmed black hat, weighing them in her hands, then slaps the hat on my head and tilts it slightly to one side. With the finesse of a fairy godmother —if Cinderella's fairy godmother was the creative director of Moulin Rouge—she transforms me. My lips are full and pouty, my hair styled into wild, untamed waves.

"Isn't this a bit much for serving spaghetti?" I mumble, barely recognizing the vamp staring back at me in the mirror.

"Say cheese," she sings.

"What?" I turn just as she snaps the shot. She shows me the image, and I'm speechless. She's right—I barely recognize myself. It's stunning, no doubt, but is this me?

I toss off the hat and glasses, ready to wipe off the lipstick, but she stops me with a firm hand. "What if your future husband walks in tonight?"

I scoff. "My future husband isn't the type to swagger into Salvatore's, flaunting a sports car and flashing a fat wallet."

She arches an eyebrow, still holding her ground. "They're not so different from Bernie's crowd," she challenges, daring me to reconsider.

I shake my head, fighting back a smile. "You couldn't find two more polar opposite places if you tried. Bernie's is a mom-and-pop burger joint. The lunch crowd there? They're real. Regulars without a pretentious bone in their bodies. I know their names, their stories, and they know mine."

Taylor's eyes narrow, her tone cutting. "You mean the story where you're still bleeding words in the shadows while someone else basks in the limelight that should be yours. That story?"

"The point is," I continue, "Bernie's isn't packed to the brim with social climbers or Insta-stars. It's not flashy—just genuine, easygoing comfort."

"Shoving past your comfort zone is exactly what you need. Besides, it's high time you started living like you mean it—with intention," Taylor says, dramatically flipping her hair over her shoulder. "A little wisdom from my Inner Harmony group."

I roll my eyes, trying not to laugh. Taylor's always joining some new group to meet men. "Let me guess, hot guys galore at your *a cappella* group?"

She narrows her eyes at me, all serious. "For your information, it's a profound and enlightening circle of kindred spirits focused on self-awareness and manifesting our best lives ever, thank you very much."

"Uh-huh. And I'm sure Hottie McHotStuff is just there to guide you through the wilds of self-discovery," I say, leaning back against the wall, a smirk tugging at my lips.

Taylor shrugs, unfazed. "Look, if things don't pan out with this future husband, my Inner Harmony guru is definitely helping me explore some uncharted energy fields. Maybe even go deep into my aura. Balls deep." She winks, and I lose it, bursting out laughing.

"Nice," I say, shaking my head.

She holds up a jade green dress, then a blush pink one, letting them skim her curves. She glances at the mirror, then back at me, raising an eyebrow. "You need to stop hiding away like a hermit crab and dive into life already."

"What's so bad about being a hermit crab?" I mutter, yanking the green dress out of her hands. I sigh, nodding toward the pink one. "The pink one—men go wild when you wear it."

Beyoncé's "Run the World" blares from Taylor's phone, the beat pulsing with pure energy that fills the room. Her eyes light up.

"What's that?" I ask, raising an eyebrow.

She bites her lip, giving me that mischievous look she's perfected over the years. "My alarm. You'd better get moving, or you'll be late," she says, her voice laced with urgency. Instinctively, I check my watch.

"Wait. Salvatore's doesn't open for a few more hours. What time is your shift?"

Her sheepish smile gives her away before she even speaks. "About the time you get there... if you leave right now."

"What?"

"They're opening a little early. Just to start catching the pre-Broadway show crowd, I think."

"Taylor!"

She clasps her hands together, giving me her best pleading look. "Do this, and I swear you'll have the best social media presence since the Kardashians. After all, you've been my best friend since third grade—"

"Second," I correct her, gripping the gorgeous jade green dress with a bit more force than necessary. "Fine, but I'm keeping this as payment."

"You really should. It's totally your color. And maybe, I don't know, go out in it. Like, with a real, no-kidding guy. On a date. That dress is too stunning to be wasted on the alphas lining your nightstand."

I don't bother telling her that those alphas are the only men who'll be anywhere near my nightstand for the foreseeable future.

A spark catches in her eyes, quickly spreading into a wildfire of excitement. "Ooh, you could wear it next month."

"What's next month?" I ask, confused. I know it's not her birthday—which she celebrates with more fanfare than the Fourth of July—or mine, which I quietly take in with homemade snickerdoodles and a pint of caramel ripple fudge.

Her smile stretches wider, practically glowing. "The Media Excellence Gala. It's the talk of New York. Journalists from everywhere are descending on our backyard. Awards, connections, the whole nine yards. And we are *not* missing it."

"And you're in the know because . . . ?" I arch an eyebrow, half-expecting some wild tale.

A triumphant grin spreads across her face as she tilts her phone toward me, revealing an elegant invitation. "Because I knew you'd nail the job, and I got us on the list." She taps the screen. "Plus, I've been keeping tabs on that hunky Jimmy Denton from the local news."

"Already ditched your emergency of a future husband?" I tease as she nudges me toward the door.

She shrugs, her grin turning playful. "A girl's gotta have options."

CHAPTER 4
Jules

"Excuse me?" a man's voice hollers, laced with just enough arrogance to grate on my nerves. Then he snaps his fingers like I'm some kind of servant. Or a dog.

I glance up, already knowing this guy is going to be a nightmare. Mr. Drunk and Belligerent is in a suit that probably costs more than my college tuition, and his smirk is the kind that makes you want to take a shower after just looking at it.

"Yes?" I ask, trying to keep the *I hate you* out of my voice.

"I'll take a blow job," he says, like he's delivering the punchline to a joke only he and his douchey friends find amusing.

"Of course."

I'm about to walk away, when he adds, "Could you repeat my order? I'm not sure you'll remember it."

What are we, at a bar? Or in eighth grade? I blink at him, fighting the urge to throw the nearest bottle at his head. He's seriously expecting me to say, *"One blow job, coming up?"* As if.

I smile sweetly. "I've got it."

"I want to be sure, baby."

And now he's calling me baby.

Rather than stroke his ego, which is exactly what Taylor would do, I decide that whatever tip he's hoarding over my head isn't worth it and go with my inner snark. "Your order. I don't exactly recall the name, but I know it's made of amaretto and Irish cream, extra whip on top, and is about the size of a shot glass." I pinch my fingers together. "Like, this big. Right?"

I skip away. He says nothing. His friends say nothing. And I feel the very real possibility I might get fired. But when I return with the drink, all his friends are suddenly gone.

He barely glances at it before sliding his phone across the table, and I already know where this is going. Discretely, I tap my phone but keep it in my pocket.

"Ready for the check?" I ask.

"Give me your number," he insists.

"I'm afraid I can't. It's against policy," I say with a smile so tight it could snap. Translation: *Go fuck yourself*.

He jerks my hand, hard enough to bruise. "Be nice, and maybe I'll let you lick this drink off my dick," he growls, low enough so no one else can hear.

I yank my hand free and take a step back, keeping my composure despite my erratic pulse. No scene, no drama. I just place the check in front of him, forcing a smile. "If you could just sign, sir."

He stares at it, almost confused, before finally slipping his credit card into the sleeve. "Do you know who I am?"

God, those six words—nothing screams entitlement louder. It's right up there with *I'll have your job* and *My daddy owns this place*.

I blink, feigning innocence. "No."

"Trent Mercer."

He drops his name like I should be impressed, and yeah, in any other setting, I might be fawning over him, begging for a job. But today? Not happening. "Doesn't ring a bell."

"Of Mercer Media." He says it with all the smugness of someone who thinks it's his birthright. And honestly, it's impressive. One of the biggest publishing houses in the country, with over two hundred bestsellers and offices in five major cities. Pissing him off would be career suicide.

But I calmly take the check and his card, settling the bill like I'm not mentally crafting the most bulletproof pen name in history.

When I return, he leans in, his voice low and sharp. "Mercer Media."

I know I should play ball here. Give him the ego stroke Taylor's perfected—bat my eyes, *ooh* and *ah* while I act impressed. But he's such an ass, I just can't do it. And before I can rein it in, or help myself, my superpower comes out, full force: the power to be the biggest smartass ever.

I pretend to think. "Still nothing," I say, deadpan. He signs the check, not bothering to look at me. "Stop fucking around and give me your number, or I'll have you fired."

Yup, saw that coming a mile away. Because when an a-hole's charm doesn't work, they resort to bullying and threats. God, give me strength.

"First of all, touching your phone would likely require a tetanus shot. And second, if this is how you tip, hard pass."

He's about to say something, maybe threatening, maybe to get the last word in, and instead of taking it, I walk away with his signed tab. I head past the kitchen to the manager's office. Marty's on shift tonight.

I pop my head in. "Taking five."

He nods while on the phone taking what looks to be a VIP request. "Private dining?" he asks, then adds, "Absolutely."

I chuckle and roll my eyes. They always say yes to a private dining room because what are people going to do? It takes a week to get a reservation, and if they're splurging on this place, they're not getting in anywhere of this caliber faster.

They're stuck, and the managers all know it.

I head out back and sit on the plastic milk crate and take in a breath. The air is crisp and cool as I gaze up at the stars.

It's clear tonight, and my heart squeezes. It's the kind of night my sister Angi would've waited until I looked away, then smacked my arm with a, "Did you see that? Shooting star? Quick, make a wish."

I shut my eyes, trying to escape the ache.

But then, out of nowhere, a pair of Bishop-blue eyes slice through my mind, uninvited, tearing through my thoughts with all the subtlety of a wrecking ball. My pulse kicks up, and all I want is to know what he looks like now.

Without thinking, my hand dives into my apron pocket, pulling out my phone like it's the only thing grounding me. My finger hovers over the B on the keyboard, itching with a dangerous need and slowly peeling away my resolve.

When the door swings open, I'm snapped back to reality. Dave and Lisa walk over, sharing a plate of fries like it's their last meal. Dave's got his usual rocket fuel in hand—an iced double cappuccino, zero sugar, extra strong. The kind of drink that could jumpstart a dead car battery.

"I don't know how you drink that stuff," I say, eyeing the cup like it's straight-up diesel.

Lisa answers before he can, a wicked grin spreading across her face. "Simple. The man's clearly burned off all his tastebuds and needs more hair on his chest."

He nudges the plate toward me with a grin. "So, was that guy as big of a dick as he looked?"

I chuckle, shaking my head. "Bigger." I hit play on the recording from my phone. His voice is even more cringy on repeat. *"Do you know who I am?"* We all burst out laughing as the whole ridiculous encounter plays out.

"Damn, that's gold," Lisa says, crunching down on another fry, her eyes gleaming with amusement. "You've got the crown tonight." She waves her phone at me, a wicked smirk curving her lips. "All I've got is some woman who reminded me six times she has a gluten allergy, then ripped me a new one for forgetting her bread."

Dave chuckles, shaking his head. "The best I've got is some guy insisting that his steak be medium-rare—no blood, no pink, just . . . somewhere in between." He smirks. "Pretty sure he'd have eaten anything, considering he inhaled the entire plate, parsley and all. Speaking of which, what's the difference between pussy and parsley?"

My face contorts, and I bury it in my hand just as Lisa blurts out, "What?"

Dave's grin widens. "No one eats parsley. Well, except the guy at table eight, apparently."

Lisa shakes her head, laughing. "So, where's Taylor? I heard she's off being wined and dined by some guy whisking her away to Ibiza."

Dave, with his mouth half full of fries, chimes in, "I think it's pronounced *'Ibitha.'*"

"Is that really how you say it? Ibitha?" Lisa asks, eyebrows raised.

"Sí," Dave adds with a wink. He takes another sip of his unfiltered swamp water, and Mr. Richards's words come back, full force.

Find out how he takes his coffee.

To him, it's just another task for the rookie, but the idea of Brian Bishop and coffee?

"What's on your mind?" Dave nudges my arm, pulling me out of my spiraling thoughts.

"Hypothetically," I start, trying to sound casual, "if I wanted to find out how someone takes their coffee, how would I do it?"

Dave's lips curl up like he's savoring the thought. "Depends. Hypothetically, are we above stalking?"

"Probably not," I admit, the idea churning in my mind. "But full-on dumpster diving? That's a hard pass. I'm not that desperate… yet."

"Is he hot?" Lisa asks, her curiosity piqued.

I haven't seen him in a decade, but the answer slips out, automatic and sure. "Yes."

Lisa's lips curl into a wicked smile. "Then I'd fuck him into a coma and ask him in the morning."

My mind goes straight to the gutter, picturing him fresh out of the shower, skin slick and glistening, those ice-blue eyes locked on mine like I'm a triple fudge sundae and he hasn't eaten in a week. The thought of him handing me a cup of coffee before dragging me back to bed to fuck me senseless almost undoes me.

Jesus, Jules, pull it together.

The door slams open, and I barely have time to react before the boss storms out, cigarette already lit. "No, seriously, don't bother getting up. Let's all pretend we're in kindergarten and take our breaks together. What's next, nap time?"

We trudge back inside, like kids caught with their hands in the cookie jar. Dave, being Dave, can't resist poking the bear. "Don't take it out on us just because you're stuck peddling fake private dining experiences. Maybe hand out some virtual reality goggles to smooth things over."

Marty doesn't even blink. "Keep it up, wiseass, and I'll make sure you're stuck serving every VIP reservation we've got. Permanently."

Dave's smirk falters. "All right, all right. No need to go nuclear."

The rest of the shift drags on, each minute feeling heavier than the last. By the time I'm on the subway, I'm too exhausted to even care that I'm standing. I finally make it home, drop onto the couch, and do the unthinkable. I pull up the only photo I have of Brian.

Graduation day. Not mine. His.

Three rows down, the *B's* straight in front of the *S's*. I zoom in, focusing on his face, but my eyes drift to the right, and there she is—Angi.

It's like a punch to the gut every time I see her. The memories hit me in waves, the good ones tangled up with the bad, until I can hardly breathe.

If you can describe a disastrous storm as bright and beautiful, it was Angi.

My phone buzzes, and the screen lights up with a familiar face, her dark brow quirked in that signature way. "Hi," I answer, bracing myself.

"Hi? That's all you've got?" My mother's voice blares through the speaker, riding that fine line between annoyed and thrilled. "Why am I the last to know you landed a job?"

"It's just an entry-level position, Eomma. I don't even start for a few weeks."

"Your dream job, Juliana," my mom says, her voice softening, laced with that familiar undercurrent of pride that threatens to sweep her into a full emotional riptide.

I'm not sure why landing a job makes Eomma so emotional, but considering my mom tears up over everything from Disney movies to Hallmark commercials, I'm not about to rock the boat.

"Remember how you used to interview everyone?" she asks. "And that piece you wrote on Mrs. D.? She still has it framed on her wall."

A smile tugs at my lips. Mrs. D. As in Mrs. Delilah Donovan, the legend of the Adirondacks. She started as the local mom who could whip up a feast from scratch and ended up a celebrity chef with her own YouTube channel, turning Donovan's from a cozy mom-and-pop spot into a nationwide sensation.

She's not just a mentor; she's family in the way that matters most. Mrs. D. didn't just open a door for me—she threw it wide open, offering me my first interview, my first job. She gave a quirky, awkward girl with thick glasses and a mouth full of braces a chance—a place where she finally belonged.

And because she's Mrs. Claus to everyone, she also gave Brian his first job, too, unknowingly setting the stage for the epic disaster of senior year.

A beautiful disaster I can't seem to shake.

She continues, her voice brimming with excitement. "I'm whipping up a batch of my prize-winning kimchi for Mrs. D. She's trying some Asian-fusion concepts, and you know how much she loves it."

To the untrained palate, kimchi is not to be trifled with. Should it be part of an asian-fusion cuisine? Hell yeah. And my mother's kimchi is the best. When she says prize-winning, she's not kidding. It took first at the *Annual New York Kimchi Contest* during Korean Culture Week—a victory that brought her a $500 cash prize and bragging rights for life.

"Angi would be proud of you, too, Juliana."

Her words linger, stretching the tension between us until it snaps under the weight of a million unsaid words. The pain is sharp, real, like a wave crashing against jagged rocks, only to pull back and leave the emptiness of a hollow ache.

But then her voice shifts, determined and light, sweeping away all the remnants of the moment as if it never happened. "So, what's your first story going to be?" she asks, charging ahead with a forced brightness.

I open my mouth to respond, but then it hits me, like a lightning bolt cutting through the dark. Wyld Richards's voice echoes in my mind, *A good reporter uses her resources.* And really, could there be better resources than the cunning wiles of two formidable mothers?

Oh, I think not.

I mull it over for a split second, the pieces clicking into place. The Donovans and the Bishops—two families intertwined in a history that runs deep, maybe as deep as Bishop Mountain itself. And if anyone knows how Brian Bishop takes his coffee today, it's Mrs. D.

This is too perfect. "You're seeing Mrs. D. soon, right?"

"Sunday," she confirms.

"I might need a little favor."

"A source? For your story?" Her excitement bubbles up before simmering to a cool, conspiratorial whisper. "Anonymously?"

I stifle a laugh. Could there be a better partner in crime than a die-hard Gillian Flynn fan? "Definitely."

CHAPTER 5
Jules

There are a few things I hold dear. Family ranks at the top, followed closely by my books and the precious privacy I cling to like a raccoon with a half-eaten taco.

Which is why, on Sundays when I'm not schlepping plates and forcing smiles at patrons of a restaurant, I'm right here—immersed in the comforting chaos of home.

Pots bubbling away, something savory crackling on the stove, and the air thick with the irresistible garlic, soy sauce, and bickering.

And, like clockwork, the scene unfolds. Mom and Halmeoni—my sweet, fiery grandmother—are back in the kitchen, deep in their weekly battle over the *perfect* recipe.

This time, it's bulgogi. A savory symphony of thinly sliced beef, marinated and grilled to perfection until it's melt-in-your-mouth tender and bursting with flavor. But the debate could just as easily be about something as extravagant as shrimp scampi or as humble as homemade mac and cheese.

Their motto might as well be: Have stovetop, will squabble.

And as much as we cherish our deep Korean roots, our father's American heritage runs just as deep. We kids straddle both worlds effortlessly—*tteokguk*, the traditional rice cake soup that promises good luck and a fresh start, is a non-negotiable on New Year's.

Frankly, if Angi, Colby, and I get our way, we're firing up the grill for a good old-fashioned burger burn with bacon, cheese, and thick-cut fries. Both worlds colliding into a spectacular display of fireworks—who we are, right on our plates.

Dad, ever the diplomat and the smartest man I know, wisely steers clear of the kitchen. I find him comfortably hiding in the den, the Yankees game on low enough not to draw attention, eyes darting between the *Times* crossword puzzle and the screen.

I lean over his shoulder, instantly spotting the mostly blank spaces for twelve across.

Gradual build-up of romantic tension, often found in contemporary novels (8 letters).

"Need some help with that one, Dad?"

"Hey, kiddo." He wraps an arm around my waist for a side hug. "I knew your reading habits would pay dividends in the future." He looks up at me, blinking in that way he does when he's trying to piece something together. "It's something about romance. Starts with S-L."

I crash onto the cushion next to him. "Slow burn," I say deliciously.

"Slow . . . burn? That sounds painful. Is that because love hurts, like when your mother insists, after twenty-five years of marriage, that if I give her kimchi just one more try, it won't numb my tastebuds?"

I grin. "It's not about pain, Dad. Slow burn is when the romance takes its time, builds up all this irresistible tension before anything happens. You know, like in a Colleen Hoover book."

He furrows his brow, clearly trying to connect the dots. "So, like in *The Hunt for Red October*? The way Tom Clancy makes the tension slowly burn from distrust to a tentative alliance between Captain Ramius and Captain Mancuso?"

I can't help but laugh, shaking my head. "No, nothing like that. Not unless Ramius and Mancuso discovered their undying love for one another and it led to a hot, steamy *mano-a-mano* shower scene."

Dad deadpans, leveling me with a look. "First of all, *mano* means hand, not man. And second, I backpacked El Camino for months. That is definitely not what *mano-a-mano* means," he chuckles.

"In male-male romance, it is," I counter, grinning.

He arches an eyebrow, unamused. "I'm not even going to ask how my sweet, innocent youngest daughter knows that."

"Probably best that way," I say. "Then, think more like Edward and Bella from *Twilight*."

He blinks, completely lost. "Who?"

I sigh, patting his arm. "You stick with Clancy. I'll tackle the romance."

I shove my hand into a bag of chips he's miserably trying to hide in the corner of the couch. That's when I notice his notepad.

One glance at it, and my stomach tightens. Angi's name is

scrawled across the page, along with a date, time, and location: midtown.

"Has she called?" I ask, the lightness of banter evaporating into thin air.

Dad exhales a heavy, frustrated breath, rubbing his temple as if he can massage away the tension. "No, but she tried withdrawing five hundred bucks from my account." He points a stern finger at me, his eyes pleading despite the tough exterior. "Don't tell your mother."

My heart sinks, a familiar ache settling in my chest. It's her pattern—Angi's go-to move when life backs her into a corner. Once again, she's drowning and has nowhere else to turn.

But Mom's been firm, unwavering—no money until she comes home and checks into a program. Something, anything, to get her on the straight and narrow path to sobriety.

But knowing she's still out there, struggling—it's like a punch to the gut. The weight of it all presses down on me, but I nod, swallowing my worry, because what else can I do?

And no matter how much I try to keep it together, it tears at me little by little.

And for a former Marine, Dad is all soft teddy bear with a marshmallowy center—sweet, easily forgiving, and always the first to offer a second chance.

But by the way he's about to rub all the skin off the back of his neck, even he's at his wit's end. Ghosted for months, only to be tapped for cash from the Bank of Dad? It's wearing him down.

"Did you give it to her?" I ask, already knowing the answer.

He shrugs, his expression a mix of resignation and worry. "I cleared two hundred. Though if I had five I would've given it to her. The thought that she might be out there, who knows where, doing who knows what . . ." His voice trails off, the weight of it all pressing down on both of us.

I lean in, close enough that our shoulders touch, offering silent support. "I know." I pull out my phone, showing him the screen. "I text her every night with *I love you to the moon and back*," I say, adding, "Totally plagiarizing Sam McBratney for her."

"You also pay her phone bill," he adds, giving me that paternal look that makes me shrink a bit in my seat.

"I don't want her without a phone. In case of an emergency."

He boops my nose, a small, affectionate gesture that pulls a smile from me despite everything. "You're mighty responsible for the youngest," he says, then quickly shifts gears, trying to lift the mood. "And I hear you have a new job."

"I was going to tell you, but if Mom knows, you know. And technically, I haven't started yet."

He drops the paper, mutes the TV, and turns fully toward me, his eyes bright. "I want details, and now that I'm retired, if you need a sidekick, count me in. I've got a trench coat and hat, and I'm a self-appointed expert in Clancy and all things espionage. I'm well-versed in the necessary three-letter agencies: FBI, CIA, MI6—and I can crack codes like it's my day job." He waves the crossword puzzle in front of me with a flourish.

I give him an appraising look, playing along. "Your credentials are pretty solid. But what about your rates?"

He leans back, that satisfied grin spreading across his face. "The usual family discount."

"So, free?"

"Exactly," he replies with a wink. "So, what's your first story, boss? Political scandal? Wall Street corruption?"

If only. Telling him I'm digging into the scandal of my past would have him hunting down Brian Bishop like a bloodhound, kicking down doors, and either giving him a piece of his mind or wrangling him into a headlock.

Rather than overcomplicate things, I flash a grin. "Let's go with investigative."

"Atta girl," he says, his voice swelling with pride.

Mom's voice echoes through the house like a dinner bell. "*Bap meokja!*" Translation: Let's eat.

Dad jumps up, grabbing the bag of chips and disposing of the evidence into the trash with a guilty grin.

With his arm draped over my shoulders, we step outside, and the world shifts. The evening air is crisp, laced with the scent of pine and the hint of mountain laurel. It's the kind of sanctuary that makes you forget there's a city at all.

Out here, it's nothing but green grass, towering trees, and the soft rustle of leaves. It's like pure oxygen, a breath of fresh air that centers my soul.

We all take our seats as the Adirondacks rise majestically in the distance, the peaks bathed in the soft glow of the setting sun. In less than an hour, the light will vanish, but Mom's already prepared. Half a dozen tea candles flicker around a small vase of wildflowers that Halmeoni likely gathered on her morning walk.

"I tried something new," my grandmother announces, holding up a bottle of convenience store cologne. With a dramatic flourish, she spritzes it into the air, and we all burst into laughter. It's the kind that smells like a mix of Old Spice and too much aftershave.

Mom takes the bottle, slips on her reading glasses, and shakes her head with a smile and tsks. "This is for men."

Happily, she nods. "I like it," she insists, her chin lifting in defiance. "It reminds me of Harabeoji."

Her words hit me with a wave of nostalgia. My grandfather, with one of us nestled in his arms, rocking in his chair as he hummed softly, his eyes fixed on the TV, watching anything from baseball to nature documentaries.

Halmeoni's hand pats mine. "Juliana, *jal hago ittda*," she says, her Korean wrapping around me like a warm blanket on a cold night. Translation: *You're doing well, Juliana.*

I nod, forcing a smile, though the weight of her words barely loosens the knot of doubt in my chest. News of my new job has spread like wildfire.

When I first started as a waitress, she called me a manager-in-training, destined to run the place with charm and authority.

Now, as an entry-level writer still proving my worth and praying they don't find a reason to fire me, she probably thinks I'm on the fast track to editor in chief.

"I'm just starting out," I say, my voice meek and as small as I feel.

"You are a Sun," she reminds me, her tone gentle but oh, so very firm. "Your grandpa would be so proud." Her hand cups my cheek, and this time, a genuine smile lifts my lips, chasing away some of the doubt.

Mom, ever the realist, swallows a bite and adds, "We all start somewhere."

Dad sips his beer, his voice carrying that familiar, militant tone. "All you need is hard work and direction. And a few hundred sit-ups," he teases.

"And a name," I murmur, feeling my shoulders slump under the weight of it all.

He arches a stern brow, his gaze cutting right through me. "Is there something wrong with Juliana Grace Spenser?"

I shake my head. "I mean a pen name. My editor sort of insists."

"Ah," he says, leaning back with a knowing nod. "The old Richard Bachman/Stephen King conundrum."

Mom chimes in, shaking her head. "More like Marguerite Annie Johnson and Maya Angelou."

Then Halmeoni jumps in, because of course she does. "Or Anne Rice and Howard Allen Frances O'Brien." We all freeze, confused as hell.

Casually, she snags a wonton with her chopsticks. "It's true. She was named after her father. But the second she got bullied at school, she switched it to Anne." We all just stare at her, and she points her chopsticks at us, daring us to question her. "True story."

I'm inclined to believe because Halmeoni's insatiable love of vampire romance means she knows everything there is to know about Anne Rice.

When our band had a competition in New Orleans, it was Halmeoni who gave us haunting details about the house Anne Rice owned, including the so-called "blood-red room" where she was rumored to write her most chilling scenes—though whether that was true or just folklore, no one could say.

Needless to say, I've learned not to trivialize my grandmother's vast knowledge of Ms. Rice and her coven of the undead.

Eomma refills my glass, her eyes soft but serious. "It should be something that fits, something that carries a piece of who you are."

I swallow back the lump in my throat, nerves dancing in my stomach. "I've decided on a first name. Sydney, with a Y."

"Isn't that a boy's name?" Mom asks, her brow furrowing.

"You sound like my editor."

Dad grins, giving me a knowing look. "After Sidney Sheldon? Or your old teddy bear?" He nods, approval clear in his eyes. "Either way, I like it. It's playful but mature. And it could easily be a girl or a guy, which is the point, right? No one knows who you are." He makes an ominous noise, wiggling his fingers in the air like he's casting a spell.

Halmeoni taps a finger on the table, the sound sharp enough to cut through the noise in my head. "What did I tell you just moments ago, Juliana?"

I pause, her words pulling me back down to earth. "That Grandpa would be proud of me... and..."

"You are a Sun," they all say together, the words ringing out like a chorus.

And they're right. It's my grandfather's name. It's our legacy.

"Sun," I repeat, letting the word roll around in my mouth, testing the weight of it. It's like something inside me clicks, a key turning in a lock I didn't even know was there. "Yes. I'm a Sun." My eyes widen as it hits me, and before I can stop myself, I'm throwing both arms around her in a fierce hug. "I love it."

That night, after the kitchen is cleaned and the house has settled into its familiar quiet, and rather than swim upstream back to the city, I find myself back in my old bedroom, sinking into the comfort of my childhood bed. My cell casts a soft glow in the darkness.

With my social media primed and ready, Taylor's been bombarding me with words of affirmation all day. Little nuggets of wisdom popping up on my phone like fortune cookies from a best friend who knows exactly when to push.

Poignant thoughts like *Carpe Diem* and *The only way out is through*. Or my personal favorite: *I swear by all that's Chanel, one post won't kill you.*

But the one that had me snort-laughing in the middle of dinner? *Go big or go home*, paired with a photo of a ridiculously big, brawny baker holding the biggest baguette I've ever seen. And, of course, he's holding it right at his crotch.

Trust Taylor to nail that twisted blend of motivational imagery and uncensored, full-throttle porn.

My breath hitches, a swarm of butterflies tickling through my insides, and my fingers itch to dive into my account. But, what to write?

With a deep breath, I open Instagram, shove aside the anxiety that's always waiting to devour me, and step into the creation of something that's entirely mine.

My future.

This pen name isn't just a name—it's a declaration. A way to carry my heritage, my family, into this new chapter of my life, and finally leave the baggage behind.

The words begin to spill out, each one peeling away another layer of fear and the need to be perfect. I'm just being me.

I pick a photo from dinner, the vibrant spread of dishes that Halmeoni and Eomma crafted with so much love, and pair it with a shot of the Adirondacks at sunset—enduring, like the mountains themselves.

Then, I push my avatar into the spotlight. The image Taylor and I decided on. Me with thick, dark Audrey Hepburn *Breakfast at Tiffany's* glasses, my hair down, my lips red, and a pen poised at my lips, the very picture of deep thought.

"Truth might be a wallflower, but every story deserves its moment to shine on the dance floor. And the best stories? They're the ones that steal the spotlight when you least expect it and leave a mark on your heart."
#NewJourneys #WritingWithHeart

I sign off **@SydneySun** and it feels so good, I hit post, and just like that, I'm out there.

No turning back.

CHAPTER 6

Jules

Be in my office. 9:00 a.m. Sharp.

Huh?

I blink away the last traces of sleep, my vision clearing as I read the email. Mr. Wyld Richards, in all his demanding glory, wants me in his office in a few hours.

Of course, I'm already awake because I'm the daughter of a former Marine who cursed me with being an early riser.

Yawning, I read the email again. Mr. Richards must've fired off this message just after I sent him my Instagram handle and the details of how Brian takes his coffee just before I passed out.

I have Eomma to thank for that, and Mrs. D.

I glance at the time. If I skip breakfast or a shower, I have just enough time to hop on public transportation, but it'll be close. Hmm. Shower? Breakfast? My brain does a quick calculation.

Before fully committing, I crack open my bedroom door, and the scent of bacon and freshly brewed coffee hits me like a wave. My smile is wide. Dad's on breakfast duty, which settles it, hands down.

I throw on some clothes, drag a brush through my hair, and barely glance at the mirror before rushing downstairs.

Sure enough, there's bacon, and not just that—an entire box of pastries from the local bakery. Usually, this spread would signal a special occasion, but I'm not complaining. And it's not just the usual half dozen, but a full dozen of those soft, melt-in-your-mouth bites, which means I can snag a few for the road.

As I reach for a random K-cup from the assortment, Dad steps in and hands me a steaming mug. "Try this," he says with enough of a smile, I can't say no, though I eye the cup warily. His coffee skills typically result in motor oil in a cup.

But this time, the caramel color and enticing aroma are too tempting to resist. I take a sip, and it's a revelation. "Mmm. Did you get a part-time gig at Starbucks? Because if so, keep it up."

"I thought you'd like it." Dad chuckles, clearly pleased. "In a hurry?"

"My new editor wants me in his office in a few hours."

He nods thoughtfully. "Well, you can't take the train and subway and make it on time. So sit back and relax. I found you a driver."

I narrow my eyes. There's no way I'm letting my dad trudge through that insane drive, especially since he insists on driving like we're permanently stuck behind a school bus.

And, wait a minute. "I'm sorry, did we change our last name to Gates? Since when do we have a driver?" I ask, stuffing a bite of peach fritter into my mouth.

"Since now," a voice booms from behind.

I turn, and there he is—a dark mop of hair, dimples in full

effect. That's when it hits me why Dad picked up so many donuts. Colby's back.

Without thinking, I throw my arms around him, hugging him tight. I didn't realize just how much I've missed him, or how fiercely I'm squeezing until he gasps, "Must. Have. Air."

"You can suck it up for one more minute," I insist, before finally letting go. "That's what you get for being gone so long."

"Not exactly a choice. A little thing called military commitment."

"Yeah, whatever." I give him a playful nudge, but my fingers find that spot on his side where he's ticklish. He jerks away, and I can't help the grin that spreads across my face. "Seriously, how do you live in Germany, surrounded by beer and bratwurst, and still manage to keep that 1 percent body fat? If it were me, they'd need a forklift to roll me out of there."

Colby smirks, throwing in a flex like he's in a damn fitness commercial. "When my sister finally lands her dream job, my ass is back stateside, ASAP."

"Wait, what? How long are we talking?"

His smile falters, uncertainty shadowing his eyes. "I'm not sure yet."

A cold knot tightens, sliding from my chest to the center of my gut. Young, healthy men don't just come home on a whim. I narrow my eyes, trying to read him. "Is everything all right?"

"I'm fine." His tone is too quick, too smooth.

"He's fine," Dad cuts in, his voice calm as he finishes preparing a second mug of coffee. "He's just at a crossroads, is all." Dad grabs both mugs and heads out of the kitchen. "Let me wake your mother and earn some brownie points with your coffee recipe." He pauses, pointing at us both like he's delivering a command. "Don't eat all the donuts."

"No promises," I mumble around the last bite of my fritter, washing it down with a sip of coffee.

The flavor hits again, stopping me mid-sip. My dad's coffee usually tastes like it could fuel a tank, and Colby's brew? Well, that's pure caffeine on steroids. But this . . . this is paradise, warm and soothing and just a hint of decadence. "This is your recipe?"

He shrugs, casual as ever. "Not exactly."

There's a strange pause, heavy with something I can't quite place. Then he nods toward the mug in my hand. "Dark roast, shot of espresso, two pumps of vanilla, and a dash of cinnamon. The Bishop special."

Dad pops in, his protective radar pinging off the charts. "The what?"

Uh-oh. Cue the internal alarms.

It's one thing that Brian torched my reputation and forced me into seclusion. But I'm still Daddy's little girl. Dad always warned me away from Brian—probably because of Angi—and I'm fairly certain that if the two of them were within a mile of each other, one of them wouldn't make it out alive.

And by one of them, I mean Brian.

Given that Mom swore on a stack of Ina Garten cookbooks that the name Brian Bishop would never leave her lips in front of Dad, I know she didn't say a word. Except, apparently, to Colby.

Colby steps in, casually fixing his own cup of coffee as if this conversation isn't teetering on the edge of disaster. "Relax, Dad.

No need to sharpen the pitchforks. It's just a TikTok thing. Named after some coffee fanatic bishop."

Dad narrows his eyes, clearly not buying it. "Is that so?"

"Absolutely," I chime in, trying to smooth things over. "It's as legit as yetis doing *Magic Mike* routines and that woman who claims she's a raccoon whisperer. If it's on TikTok, it's gospel. Hashtag verified."

Dad's gaze shifts between us, suspicion lingering in his eyes. "The two of you seriously need help."

"One of us does," Colby quips, jerking his chin in my direction. "I'm not watching stripping sasquatches."

"You, young lady—" Dad's stern brow levels right at me "—I'm going to pretend my youngest daughter thinks Magic Mike is a magician."

I roll my eyes. "I'm twenty-five."

He drops a kiss on my head, unfazed. "And still my baby." Then, with a devilish grin, he swipes the last éclair.

"Hey!" I object.

He wags it teasingly. "Consider this your penance for inheriting all your mom's spunk." He takes a bite, eyes flicking to his watch. "And you two better get going unless you're planning on making a grand late entrance for your new boss."

Colby fixes two fresh Bishop Specials in to-go mugs, and we rush out the door with Mom, Dad, and Halmeoni trailing behind us like we're off to win a war. Grandma gives Colby a light tap on the chest. "Drive safe, and don't worry. I'll have some hot *dakgangjeong* waiting for lunch."

Great. Now I'm going to be thinking about my brother devouring that crispy, sweet, and sticky Korean fried chicken instead of me. She tucks a delicate pink flower behind my ear and pats my cheek with a gentle smile. "Come back soon, Juliana."

"I will," I promise.

We're cruising down the road when something catches my eye. I do a double-take. "Is that a tattoo?"

He blinks, then smirks. "Yep. My fifth." He flexes, showing off the ink—a bold black serpent coiled around his bicep, its eyes glinting, daring to be messed with.

"Do I even want to know where the others are?"

He grins that infuriating, cocky grin. "Nope. I'm surprised you don't have one. I could totally see you with something like a feather or an infinity symbol."

"I always thought it should be deeply personal. Meaningful."

"Or just plain fun. I bet Angi's got a tattoo or three."

The mention of Angi shifts the air, the lighthearted banter giving way to something heavier. "Why are you really back, Colby?"

He sighs, the humor draining from his face. "Angi. She stole my identity and racked up charges on my government credit card. When my commanding officer flagged it, I knew something was seriously wrong. I have to find her and sort this out, or . . ." He trails off, the weight of what he's not saying swooping in like a dark cloud.

"Or what?"

"I don't know. Get out, I guess."

"Get out? I didn't think you could just quit the Army."

"Technically, it would be a dishonorable discharge."

The words slam into me like a bat to the chest. "Colby, a dishonorable discharge? Are you serious? They'd just kick you out? How much money are we talking here?"

His hands grip the wheel, knuckles white. "Fifteen thousand dollars."

Panic seizes me, my breath catching. "Could that mean jail time?" The silence that follows is deafening. "You can't let that happen, Colby."

"You think I don't know that?" his voice snaps, frustration boiling over, cutting through the air like a whip. "Angi's been digging herself deeper, and I'm not sure she can claw her way out this time."

"So, what? You're just going to let her drag you down that rabbit hole with her?"

His breath hitches, anger simmering beneath the surface. "It's not like I have a fucking choice." He pauses, jaw tight, eyes locked on the road ahead. "I'm on administrative leave without pay for thirty days. That's why I'm back—to find her, clean up this mess, or face the fallout on my own."

I reach out, my hand gliding across his arm, a pathetic attempt at comfort in the middle of this shit storm. "You're not alone, Colby. We'll figure this out together."

The words hang between us, and despite the suffocating tension in the air, his hand smoothes over mine.

An eternity of miles later, Colby leans in, his voice dropping to a rough whisper. "Word on the street is my sister's been stalking one of my Army buddies."

A flush creeps up my face. Mortified, I scramble to explain. "My editor gave me an assignment to—"

"To what? Rip open an old wound and watch it bleed out?" He shakes his head, eyes fixed on the road.

"N-no," I stammer, flustered. "Just . . . I don't know. Conquer a few demons, reclaim myself, prove I'm not some hack who needs to hide away like a mouse afraid of its own shadow."

"Hiding and healing are two different things."

Curiosity gnaws at me until the question burning a hole in my brain rushes out of my mouth. "You said Army buddies? As in you and Brian Bishop served together?"

"Yeah. A few times, actually. But that was before . . ." His voice trails off as he checks the GPS and takes a sharp right. "The thing is, if you lined up a hundred guys and asked me to pick out the asshole, I would've ranked him dead last. Shit, you're gonna hate me for saying this, but I wish I could've served with him longer before he bailed."

The words spill out before I can catch them. "He left the service?"

He gives me a look of pure disbelief. "Wow, you really have been living in a cave. How do you not know?"

"Know what?"

He pulls up to the curb, parking right in front of the building. "Listen, I gave you his coffee order. My stint as your secret spy ends here. Now, get your snooping butt in gear and be the investigative journalist you've always wanted to be. I've got a manhunt to tackle."

I'm a little disappointed, but I hop out anyway. "I think you mean a woman-hunt, and when it comes to Angi, start with Dad. She just used his credit card."

He lets out a relieved breath. "So, she's alive. Great. Just in time for me to kill her."

CHAPTER 7

Jules

The newsroom is a pulsating heart of activity, a dizzying mix of rapid-fire conversations, sharp heels clicking on the polished floor, and the rhythmic tapping of keyboards. It's sleek, modern, and exudes just the type of cold efficiency that says, "Produce or you're fired."

This is where globs of content are plucked, sculpted into something glossy, and shoved into the world for story junkies, hungry for their next fix.

I step inside, trying to blend into the polished chaos, but to no avail. Mr. Richards catches me in an instant. He is a shark over all he surveys, cutting across the sea of writers in headphones, sipping coffee.

His eyes flick to his watch, then back to me, a smirk playing on his lips—a silent warning that says, *Test my patience, and I'll grind your ambitions into dust.*

"Sydney Sun," he says, his tone sharp and efficient. It takes me a good ten seconds to realize he's talking to me. "Right on time. Unlike some people."

From across the room, someone shouts, "We heard that!" Laughter ripples through the space, and a smirk plays on Wyld Richards's lips as he hands over a ball cap and a badge, both emblazoned with *Manhattan Herald*.

I'm not even kidding, I will worship these like backstage passes to a Taylor Swift concert.

"Good job on most of your homework. And his coffee?"

I stand taller. "Dark roast with a shot of espresso, two pumps of vanilla, and a pinch of cinnamon."

He nods, and I catch the faintest trace of approval in his eyes. But before I can let that sink in, he hits me with something that knocks the wind out of me. "So, what else have you learned about that high school crush of yours?"

I freeze, my mind scrambling for something—anything— that won't make me sound like an idiot. "Uh . . . not much," I stammer. *Play it cool.* "He was in the military. The Army, actually."

"Tell me something I don't know."

I'm not even sure what that means, but I trudge through. "And he's . . . different now. Though I can't exactly put my finger on why." Yeah, dying here.

Richards gives me a look—part amusement, part calculation—that makes my stomach twist. "Barely scratched the surface, huh?"

"Digging too deep could be seen as invasive," I counter, trying to regain some composure.

He tsks, shaking his head slightly. "You sure you're cut out for investigative journalism?" Hands on his hips, he assesses me. "Aren't you even a little curious?"

I hesitate, then pinch my fingers together, letting out a breath. "Maybe . . . a little."

His smirk widens, a knowing glint in his eyes that makes me suddenly nervous. "Don't worry, kid. We're about to satisfy that curiosity in ways you haven't even imagined."

What the hell does that mean?

A young man grabs his attention. "Shit, I need to deal with this." He points across the room to a corner that's about as far away from sunlight as possible. "Your seat is over there. Get settled, introduce yourself, snoop around, and find the kitchen and bathroom, then check your email."

He heads off as I weave through the maze of desks, my eyes darting from one cluttered workspace to the next. Some are neat and organized, others look like the aftermath of a tornado, but all of them scream one thing: This is where the magic happens.

Or the mayhem, depending on your perspective.

I spot the empty desk near the back, nestled in a quad with a decent view of the room. Just as I'm about to make it mine, a voice calls out from behind me, laced with playful warning. "Take that seat at your own risk."

I turn to see a guy with thick glasses and a grin that looks permanently etched on his face. He's lounging in his chair like he's got all the time in the world, hands casually behind his head, an amused glint in his eyes.

Suddenly wary, I give the chair a once-over, scanning for anything that screams trouble—coffee stains, ink splatters, or something worse that would make me cringe just thinking about it.

"That was Roxie's seat," a woman with platinum blonde

hair and fuchsia streaks chimes in, a teasing edge to her voice. "We're pretty sure it's cursed."

"Roxie?" I echo, pausing as I take in the desk. It's not as empty as I hoped—a half-drunk coffee mug with blood-red lipstick smeared on the rim, a few pens scattered like afterthoughts, and a notepad with the first few pages aggressively torn out. It still feels... lived in.

"As in Roxana Voss," an older man with wire-rimmed glasses adds, his grin a mix of warmth and something a little more twisted. "The one and only—famous for *Spilling Tea with Roxie V*."

"Roxana Voss," I repeat, the name turning bitter on my tongue.

Her last story? A brutal hit piece on a teen pop star—unflattering photos and all. Word is, she staged the whole thing up, paid off some lowlifes to spike the girl's drink, then had her photographer capture the meltdown.

"She's—"

"Legendary," a cute guy with dark, wavy hair corrects, leaning in like he's about to share a dirty secret. "And an absolute nightmare to work with."

"I'd call her infamous," the woman interjects. "And lethal. Cross her, and she will eat you alive in the press," the woman with rose-tinted hair says, her smile sweet as she shakes my hand. "Anabelle. I handle fashion, style, and the occasional restaurant review if they're really desperate."

Glasses Man extends a hand. "Alfred Walsh, but everyone here calls me Scoop. I live for research and digging into all the hard-hitting investigative pieces."

"Felix," the wavy-haired guy says as he grabs a bright blue

Post-it, scrawling something on it. "I'm the unlucky bastard stuck covering all things sports—which I hate, by the way."

Confused, I ask, "So, why do you do it?"

He shrugs casually. "Because I get to interview all the hottest men in town," he purrs, handing me the note with a smirk.

I look down: *Fortuna audaces iuvat.* I can't help but smile. "Fortune favors the bold."

"Exactly," he says, his smirk deepening. "Words to live by."

Anabelle giggles. "See? The two of us are flanked by looks and brains."

"So, what happened to Roxie?" I ask.

Anabelle leans in, lowering her voice just enough to make it feel like we're sharing a secret. "She was just linked to a high-profile divorce. Word is, she wasn't just reporting on the affair—she *was* the affair."

"Thank God she's gone," Felix chimes in, rolling his eyes. "If I had to hear that fake sultry voice one more time . . . 'Oh, *Mr. Richards*,'" he huffs, mimicking her in a raspy tone.

My stomach drops as I catch a glimpse of Mr. Richards striding away, his presence looming even from across the room. "Her affair was with the boss?"

"Can anyone say home wrecker?" Anabelle rolls her eyes, her voice laced with disdain. "Rumor has it, if Wyld Child doesn't pull off a big story soon, this paper's going to disappear faster than Houdini."

My pulse quickens, the space around me shifting from opportunity to quicksand. "That could really happen? Seriously, I just got this job."

Scoop waves a hand over the desk, dark amusement dancing

in his eyes. "Hence why we call the desk cursed. You're the fourth one to sit there in as many years."

Felix pats my hand with a sympathetic smile. "Be brave, girl. I'll grab some sage at lunch." He nods toward my laptop. "And for the love of God, make sure that thing works. Roxie blamed it for every missed deadline and crappy piece of work she churned out."

Taking a deep breath, I finally sit down, powering up the laptop that's staring me down like it knows I'm already in over my head. The screen flickers to life, and I dive into my email using the code they gave me at orientation.

The first email is the usual welcome schpiel, but the next subject line stops me in my tracks: *Assignment*. There it is, clear as day, in black and white. My first official writing gig addressed to *sydney@herald.com*.

My heart flutters, a rush of nerves colliding with pure excitement and just enough fear to keep me grounded. This is it—it's happening—I'm about to take Manhattan by storm. One irresistibly charming human interest story at a time.

All right, *Sydney Sun*—

Let's see what you've got. Start with your man crush's coffee recipe, and write me a human interest piece about him. Not the *real him*. An imaginary version of him so I can see your writing chops.
Make him the perfect man with an *oh-so-obtainable guy-next-door* vibe. Irresistible.

Give in to your dark side, kid. And have it on my desk by ten.

Wyld Child

Seriously? He really goes by that?

I glance at the clock and—shit. Forty-five minutes. My fingers drum on the desk, the image of Bishop's piercing blue eyes and that infuriatingly sexy smile flash through my mind. And instead of fighting it like I usually do, I do the opposite.

This time, I give in.

I've devoured enough scorching romance novels to know exactly what makes a man irresistible. Rugged good looks, pecs that practically rip through his shirt, that perfect mix of sexy yet cuddles with kids and brings you breakfast in bed.

I'm not sure if I'm crafting every woman's fantasy or just indulging in mine, but for this little exercise, Brian Bishop is about to become pure Alpha porn.

And not the total a-hole he is in real life.

My fingers fly across the keyboard, driven by my imagination on overdrive and a few vivid memories of him. There's no time to waste, no hesitation—just pure, unfiltered creativity pouring into every word.

Reimagining Brian as the man he should be is both cathartic and, oddly enough, a turn-on.

A wicked little smile tugs at my lips as I hit send, feeling a thrill I didn't expect.

Eat your heart out, Wyld. Hot and cocky, at your service.

CHAPTER 8
Brian

I keep a brisk pace as I weave through the bustling city streets, my heart pounding in sync with the first half of my eight mile run. Breaking in this new prosthetic hasn't just kept me moving; it's lit a fire under me, driving me to push harder, to see just how far I can go.

With every stride, I'm not just running—I'm charging forward, testing the limits, daring the fucker to keep up.

I smile and wave to a few folks on the bench who've stopped feeding squirrels to watch as I whip past. I'm no stranger to curious looks when I charge through—my left leg, a sleek blade of metal, flashing in the sunlight.

It used to eat away at me, exposing that missing piece of myself for the world to see. I'd bury it under breathable sweats, trying to dodge the inevitable pity in people's eyes. But over time, I learned to own it. Every scar became a piece of armor I wore with pride.

Now, it's my go-to conversation starter. It breaks the ice with battle-hardened vets who've faced the unimaginable and kids in wheelchairs who refuse to let life pin them down. Strength that lies in all of us. Sometimes, you just have to wade through the bullshit to force it to the surface.

So, when a few more pedestrians stare, their gazes feel . . . different. They're watching me with wide smiles and something like awe, as if I'm the quarterback who just scored the winning touchdown at the Super Bowl.

Women seem extra friendly this morning. Unnervingly so. My spidey sense is all sorts of confused, like predators who've caught the scent of prey.

And I am not imagining it. They're whispering, giggling, some blatantly staring. And maybe it's my imagination, but I'm pretty sure some are sneaking photos.

I slow my pace, threading my way through a cluster of ladies waiting for the bookshop to open. Out of nowhere, a chorus erupts. "It's him!" and "Are you Brian Bishop?" and, "Oh. My. God!! You!"

I blink, momentarily stunned. And before I can think or curse or say anything remotely meme-worthy, suddenly, too many camera phones are thrust in my face to count.

I hustle out of there and pick up the pace, heart pounding as I try to escape the frenzy. And, I'm not even kidding when I say that some of them actually chase me. And they are both determined and freaking fast. In heels.

I speed up and eventually manage to put some distance between us. Two more miles uphill, and my lungs are on absolute fire.

I round the corner and nearly crash into a small coffee shop, my legs threatening to give out. The line isn't long—thank God —so I slip inside, craving a moment of peace.

As soon as I step into the queue, the whispers start, sharp and cutting. Glances follow, eyes dissecting me with every passing second.

But the line moves quickly, and running isn't an option. Seriously, I'm one deep breath away from puking up a lung. So, I do what any battle-hardened soldier would do: jam my EarPods in, lower my head, and avoid eye contact like it's a game of dodgeball.

The barista gasps the second her eyes land on me, then instantly vanishes into the back.

When she returns, her smile is wide, and she has two others in tow. "Good morning, Mr. Bishop," she chirps, sliding a perfectly crafted drink across the counter. The other two hover nearby, their eyes wide with awe and barely contained excitement.

I pull out an AirPod, my smile tightening in confusion. "What's this?"

She hands me the cup with a knowing grin. "Your favorite, right? Dark roast with a shot of espresso, two pumps of vanilla, and just a dash of cinnamon."

My gut clenches. How the hell does she know that?

I chuckle, but it's forced. "Thanks." I move to pay, but before I can pull out my card, a woman behind me chimes in. "I've got his drink."

"No, I do," another one snaps, practically elbowing her way forward.

I take the cup, but before I can get out of there, they're going at it—right there in the coffee shop over who gets to pay for my damn drink. It's as if I've been yanked into the spotlight of a reality show . . . in the freaking Twilight Zone.

I snatch the cup and back away, watching in disbelief as they girl-fight over who gets to pay for it. It's ridiculous, but before I can even process what the fuck's going on, another woman steps up, asking for my autograph.

"Huh?"

And then—what the hell—someone's hand lands on my abs. Which is my cue to get the hell out of there.

Everywhere I look, there are women—too many, too close, their eyes locked on me like I'm the main course. My apartment might be a stone's throw away, but there's no way in hell I'm leading this pack of deranged stalkers to my doorstep. No matter how much I need a shower.

Sweet but psycho is so four years ago. Fool me once . . .

My jog takes on a full-blown sprint as I head for our headquarters. There's a small crowd formed at the entrance of the building—some of the paparazzi I recognize, though up until now, they've never recognized me.

There's a swarm of them—dozens of women. One of them even has a sign that reads, *I want Brian Bishop's baby*. I run a hand through my hair.

What the actual fuck?

"There he is!" one of them shrieks, and before I can react, they're on me like I'm the last Birkin on earth.

Considering I'm a foot taller than them, I remain calm, figuring I can talk my way out of this. Firmly, I hold up my hands, trying to reason with the crowd though I'm forced to take a step back. "Look, ladies, I think you've mistaken me for someone else—"

"Did you really save that dog from drowning?"

Bruiser? My damn goldendoodle? The fact that they know about him is just plain creepy.

Another woman chimes in, her voice dripping with sticky sweetness. "It's adorable that you eat chocolate chip cookies for breakfast, Bri."

Bri? Since when am I Bri?

"Tell them we're getting married, baby," another one purrs, her hand reaching out to brush my arm like we're already a couple.

All right, that's it. Loon meter officially pegged. I'm out.

Just as I turn to make my exit, I feel a hand grab my ass. *What the—?*

I spin around, ready to set one of these nut jobs straight about looking with their eyes, when the movement throws me off balance. My prosthetic skids, throwing me off balance

I stumble, crashing headfirst into a stack of newspapers at the stand. Papers scatter as I lie there, half-buried in tomorrow's headlines, when I feel massive hands haul me up.

"We've got you, sir," Dean says as several guards swoop in, clearing a path and ushering me into the building. I swear, I'm doubling the salaries of every last one of them.

We make it through the lobby and to the elevator where Ames has it waiting. We rush in, and the doors slide shut.

I slump back against the wall, trying to catch my breath.

"That's, uh, quite the fan club you've got," Ames says, eyeing me with a mix of amusement and concern.

"Har," I mutter, pressing the button for the twelfth floor repeatedly—corporate gym. My eyes drop to my favorite running shirt—now soaked in coffee, with two fresh tears marring the vintage Batman logo. Perfect.

Ames sniffs the air. "Do I detect a hint of cinnamon?"

"No." Ames shakes his head. "More like two pumps of vanilla if you ask me."

I blow out a breath. "What? Is there a billboard or something?"

"Nope." One of them shows me his phone.

And there it is, splashed all over social media—like a headline straight from hell:

Get Up Close and Personal with the Iron Man of Manhattan.

My picture is plastered across the front, and not my good picture. Like, shit, my DMV photo.

"Iron Man," Dean says with a smirk, his gaze dropping to my leg. "It's got a ring to it."

"Childhood nickname," I start, trying to brush it off. "Mark was Batman, I was Iron Man, and Zac . . . Dean just raises an expectant eyebrow, clearly waiting for more. I open my mouth to explain, but then give up with a sigh. "Never mind."

How does anyone even know about that? Did my mom start a fan club or something?

Before I can dwell on it, Ames chimes in with a grin. "Great interview, by the way. That story about you and the dog—"

Oh, for fuck's sake. Irritation bubbles up. "I did not do an interview. And if that whack job publicist we hired went rogue, I'll—" My words falter as my eyes land on the photo.

A tiny image of breathtaking beauty, full red lips tucked beneath oversized shades and a wide-brimmed hat, stares back at me, and suddenly, my brain short circuits.

I want to know everything about her—what makes her laugh, what keeps her up at night, what she's thinking behind those mysterious glasses. How she takes *her* coffee in the morning.

Instantly, I scan the byline. Hmm, *The Herald*. And—

"Who the hell is Sydney Sun?"

Ames and Dean both shrug, clueless. Ames checks his phone. "Uh, boss? Your secretary's trying to find you. Something about a finance meeting. Texting her now."

"What?" I blink. "That meeting starts at ten." I glance down at my wrist, and then it hits me like a wrecking ball.

My watch. It's gone.

Goddamnit.

Jess gave me that watch a millennium ago when she and Mark were still bitter enemies. She saved up for months, scraping together every spare penny she could find. Some days, she even skipped meals just to make sure I got it.

That's how much it meant to her—and to me.

And even though it's chipped and only keeps time if I wind it twice a day, that watch has been with me through deployments around the world—a silent witness to my brightest moments and my darkest hours. Now, the closest thing I have to a family heirloom is MIA.

I can already picture my baby sister's reaction. Jess won't waste time crying over spilled milk. No, she'll be too busy tightening those slender fingers around my throat.

The elevator doors slide open, and we spill out. I drag a hand down my face, groaning. "I'm about to take the fastest shower of my life and pray soap hits all the right places. Dean, stall the board. Ames, get anyone available on the team to start tracking my watch."

They scatter while I storm down the hallway toward the locker room. The second the hot water hits my skin and I lather up, the buzzing under my skin sharpens. I have the sudden urge to deal with a certain plump-lipped beauty—maybe teach her a lesson . . . over my knee . . .

Not. Now!

I shove the impulse down and rinse off. I've got bigger fires at the moment.

Little Miss Sydney Sun will have to wait.

CHAPTER 9
Jules

The moment I step through the glass doors into the office, every head swivels in my direction. Which is bad. Anxiety slams into me, tightening its grip around my chest. It's like senior year all over again. Except without the neon-colored braces or unfortunate perm.

My pulse pounds in my ears, each step slower than the last as I try to make sense of the sudden attention. And then it happens—they break out in applause. Clapping and cheering and... What. The. Hell?

Panic surges through me like a tidal wave. I speed up, desperate to reach the relative safety of my cubicle and Anabelle, Felix, and Scoop. "What's going on?"

Anabelle's face is lit up like Christmas morning. "You're viral!" she squeals, practically bouncing in her seat.

The commotion dies down as Felix shoots me a glare, half teasing, half envious. "Ten thousand likes, bitch?"

What's he talking about? My brain struggles to keep up. "There must be some mistake."

"Oh, there's a mistake all right. And here I thought you were low-key when you're the queen of trending. Ten. Thousand." He scoffs. "I busted my ass for weeks and barely scraped one thousand." He blows a kiss dripping with drama. "Hate you, love you."

Scoop leans back, arms crossed, a satisfied smirk on his face. "Well done, kid."

"What exactly is going viral?" I ask, my voice barely a whisper. Do I even want to know?

They turn their screens toward me, and my world stops.

Get Up Close and Personal with the Iron Man of Manhattan.

My stomach drops. No. No, no, no.

My article—the one I thought was just a fictional exercise for Mr. Richards—is plastered across every monitor. The headline is bold, glaring, and 100 percent published.

Online.

For the freaking world to see.

My heart slams into overdrive. "This cannot be happening."

I scramble to read it, my heart racing, praying—*begging*—this is some kind of sick joke. But no, it's all there. My words. My thoughts. My name, or rather Sydney Sun's name, plastered right at the top.

"I can't believe you know Brian Bishop," Anabelle says, practically bouncing with excitement.

"Huh?" I snap my head up, confusion swirling. "You know Brian Bishop?"

"Duh," Anabelle replies with an eye roll that screams 'get with the program.' You know what? I don't want to know.

Suddenly, several pings cut through the air. "What's that?" I ask, feeling like I've just stepped into a minefield.

"Likes," Felix says with a smirk, as if it's the most obvious thing in the world.

"Oh, my God." Panic surges through me, propelling me out of my chair and straight to Mr. Richards's office.

Having lost every last shred of my mind, I burst through the door without knocking, adrenaline in high gear. "What the hell, Mr. Richards?"

He looks up, completely unfazed, even with a sandwich in his hands. A slow smile spreads across his face. "Great job, Sydney."

"No," I snap, my weak attempt at firmness dying on the vine. "It's not a great job. It's fiction. You have to pull it back. Now."

He leans back in his chair, completely at ease. "Too late, kid. It's already out there."

"But you said it wasn't real!" My hands ball into fists at my sides, trembling as I try to keep it together.

He shrugs, infuriatingly casual. "Yeah, I lied. But hey, speaking of lies, is anything in there completely made up? Like, totally fabricated? Because the last thing you need is a lawsuit."

He takes another bite of his sandwich, as if he just tossed a grenade at me. The room tilts, spinning wildly out of control. Lawsuit? Seriously? Why the hell would I get sued?

Oh, right, I know why. Because I wrote the damn thing, and my name is all over it.

I'm on the verge of hyperventilating, mentally replaying

every word, every detail. Did I lie? No. But exaggerate? Well, yeah, that's another story.

Maybe I did embellish a bit on his herculean muscle tone—broad shoulders, chiseled chest, washboard abs. But news flash: It's not like I've seen the man in ten years. How the hell would I know what he looks like now?

"I don't think so," is all I manage to choke out.

Mr. Richards waves it off like it's no big deal. "Then you've got nothing to worry about. Oh, and your next assignment is in your inbox."

"My next . . . assignment? Like an actual journalist piece, or should I keep churning out Harlequin novels?" I throw in a half-hearted fist bump for effect.

He shrugs, utterly unfazed. "You said you do human interest."

I stare at him, too stunned to even argue. "Can't you just tell me what it is?"

With a blatant disregard for manners, self-respect, or good hygiene, he picks something out of his teeth with a paperclip. "Nope."

Frustration bubbles up, but I know when I'm outmatched. I've got two choices: quit on the spot or stomp back to my desk and at least see what this so-called assignment is.

He's about to take another bite of his sandwich when he looks up, clearly annoyed. "You're still here?"

Argh.

Frazzled and doing my best to ignore the curious glances from my coworkers, I make my way back to my desk. As promised, the email is sitting there, taunting me. I open it with a mix of dread and a solid dose of what the actual fuck.

Assignment: The Secret Lives of Billionaires

Dumbfounded, I gape at the screen.

Billionaires? What do I know about billionaires? Maybe I'll catch one grabbing a mocha frap at Starbucks. Or wedged uncomfortably close to me on the subway. Because, aside from knowing they exist—thanks in part to my Harry Potter obsession—I'm totally out of my depth.

My phone buzzes, jolting me out of my daze. The name TayTay flashes on the screen, paired with a photo of her, mime-like and dramatically mimicking *pick up the phone*.

I answer, trying to sound normal with my heart lodged in my throat. "Hey, Tay."

"Okay, I only have a second, so don't hate me."

"Hate you?"

"My flight got delayed, and I know I said I'd be back today..."

Translation: she hooked up with some guy and is now measuring his cock to see if he's true husband material.

Brimming with excitement, Taylor's going on and on, speed-talking a mile a minute, while I'm barely catching half of it. "So, I should be back soon..."

And I should be listening. I really should. But my eyes fly to a new email that just landed in my inbox.

"Taylor, I have to go."

"Wait! Can you cover one more shift for me? Please?"

"Sure," I mutter, still reeling. "When?"

"Tonight. Salvatore's. Thanks, girl. You're the best!" She hangs up before I can even respond because... well, shit.

Between my insane assignment and Taylor's relentless

pursuit of dick, I guess I'll be spending the evening scouting for billionaires while serving *pappardelle al ragu* and asking if they want extra breadsticks.

Could this day get any worse?

Oh, right. It can. And it just did.

Because the email staring me down is from the last person I ever expected to hear from. Ever.

Brian fucking Bishop.

My finger hovers over the screen, my heart pounding like a war drum, before I finally gather the nerve to open it.

Four words, straightforward and to the point.

We need to talk.

CHAPTER 10
Brian

"As you can see," Morrison, the finance guy, says, "we're counting on these four major clients to catapult next quarter's earnings projections. It's the difference between keeping the company private or having to go public. Which would mean a hundred times the scrutiny and far less control." He clears his throat. "Any unfavorable publicity could certainly tip the outcome."

I feel the weight of two dozen anxious faces landing on me at once. Probably because last night, I sent Mark and Jess on their way to breathtaking Fiji. And now, a small part of me wishes I'd gone with them.

I blow out a breath and force a smile. "Why are you all staring at me?"

Morrison shifts uncomfortably. "You're the heart of a *Herald* article."

"A favorable one," I add, having caught up on it during the more boring moments of this meeting.

"And now, you're having dinner with Roxana Voss," one of the attorneys says. "Tonight, correct?"

I am? Shit, is that tonight? I was going to go on a city-wide search for my watch tonight.

I clench my jaw. "How do you know that?"

He flashes a grin, annoyingly upbeat. "Your calendar's an open book, boss. That's why you're pulling in the big bucks."

Perfect. Technically, I was supposed to confirm, which I haven't. Mostly because after my dumpster fire of a morning, I'm dreading it.

Roxana takes stalking to an Olympic-level sport. For the poor bastards who don't play along, she's got a talent for writing scathing articles that can ruin reputations. Her takedowns of the rich and powerful are legendary. And that's the last thing The Centurion Group needs right now.

They continue to stare, eyes wide with expectation. I lean back in my chair, exuding calm confidence. "It's not a date. It's a meeting. A professional meeting."

"Then why is it at Salvatore's?" he asks.

A few light snickers ripple through the room, and, fuck, why is it there? It was supposed to be here, at the office.

I let the moment settle, then add with a measured tone, "It's under control. Let's stay focused. We've got work to do."

By mid-afternoon, just as the dust finally begins to settle, I stand by the office window and lose my gaze in the street below. Most of the morning's chaos has cleared, but a few die-hard stragglers still linger, refusing to let up. What a mess.

A knock sounds at my door. "Come in."

Imani steps in, her smile warm and all business. "Just a quick reminder about the *thing*." Imani isn't just Mark's assistant—she's more like a team coach, handling everything from scheduling meetings to smoothing over any looming disaster, like the one she's nudging me about right now.

That *thing* would be my meeting with Roxana Voss. "Why is it at Salvatore's?"

Imani shrugs helplessly. "She insisted."

I loosen my tie, feeling the noose tighten at the mere thought of the evening ahead. "Great."

"Don't worry. Salvatore's is a great place for a meeting. I have standing instructions with Mark, so I called ahead and ensured a good, quiet table for a meeting."

She hands me a Post-It. "The place isn't far from your Upper East Side digs. The maître d' is expecting you. Private dining room. Dinner at eight."

"Private dining room?" I echo, arching a brow. I've been going to Salvatore's on and off for years, mostly for business because pretentious and overpriced isn't exactly my thing. But a private dining room? Never noticed one before. And noticing shit *is* my thing. Along with surveillance, reconnaissance, and dragging skeletons out of closets.

I take the card, shaking my head. "It's bad enough I'll be seated across from a piranha. Is the private room really necessary?"

Imani shrugs. "The good thing is if there are no witnesses, it never happened."

I chuckle. "Good point."

Two sharp knocks sound at the door. Then it flies open without waiting for a "come in."

A tornado of kids rush past Imani. Connor, the teenager, strides to the floor-to-ceiling windows, his eyes going wide as he takes in the sprawling view of Central Park. "Whoa," he breathes, completely entranced.

Ollie, the eight-year-old, makes a beeline for my desk chair, sprawling out with a comic book like he owns the place.

Then there's adorable little Snooki-Pie, all of five years old, who gives Imani a quick hug before dragging her over to the bookshelf. Nowadays, with Zac comes Hannah, and with Hannah comes her brother Harrison and his brood of kids.

Snook starts scrutinizing books with the serious air of a pint-sized librarian. Jess had thoughtfully placed several books at her height, including her all-time favorite series like, *Pinkalicious, Amelia Bedelia,* and any and every book with princesses, fairies, and, of course, unicorns.

Their father, Harrison, chuckles from the doorway, a warm, amused glint in his eyes as he watches his kids invade the space. "Don't mind them. They're just making themselves at home."

I nod, a smile tugging at my lips. "As they should." Having Harrison and the kids meld seamlessly into our Bishop Mountain fold has been so natural, it's as if they've always been there.

"This one," Snook says, handing it to Imani to read to her. "I've never seen this one before."

That's because I only just added *The Care and Feeding of Unicorns* to the library yesterday. "Careful," I caution her. "You know what happens if you make a unicorn a pet?"

Two big eyes look over to me. "What?"

"You have to clean up all the unicorn poop."

"Ewww."

Imani takes a seat on the floor next to her. It's not public, but Imani is a few months pregnant with her own little one on the way, and will happily take a few minutes out of her day to read to Snook.

I pull a new comic from my drawer and toss it to Ollie. His eyes light up as he catches it, an excited grin spreading across his face. "Finally! I've been waiting forever to see what happens to Dark Avenger since the last issue!" he exclaims, eagerly flipping through the pages.

Then, I grab the military-grade binoculars from the shelf and hand them to Connor. He takes them with a look of pure fascination, inspecting every detail. "These are insane! I bet I can see people in planes with these," he asks, already lifting them to his eyes to peer out the window.

When Mom and Dad passed, the torch fell to me to care for Jess and the boys. Which wasn't easy, but it taught me the fine art of keeping kids busy. Tossing around distractions like confetti is second nature, and it gives Harrison and me a chance to catch up.

"We all had to see you in a suit and tie to believe it," Harrison teases, a grin stretching across his face as he takes a seat and hands me a brown paper bag. "Here," he says, chuckling.

The savory aroma wafts up, making my mouth water.

I open the bag and peek inside, my stomach instantly growls in response. Inside the bag are a double cheeseburger and fries from my favorite spot in the city, along with a dozen giant homemade cookies from Hannah.

I bypass the burger and shove a cookie into my mouth, moaning in pure delight. "That is incredible."

Harrison chuckles, his eyes crinkling at the corners. "That's her latest creation—Chocolate Sea Salt Paradise. She's been obsessing over it for months." He pats his belly with a satisfied grin.

The cookie is a masterpiece. Rich, gooey chocolate chunks melt into the chewy dough, the sprinkle of sea salt cutting through the sweetness with just the right balance. The edges are perfectly crispy, providing that satisfying crunch, but the center —*mmm*, the center—is soft and buttery, dissolving in my mouth with every bite.

I'm about to shove another one in when I pause, holding it up in offering. "Do the kids want some?"

Harrison shakes his head, smirking. "They've been at them all day. And I'm pretty sure Snooki's stashed away a secret hoard somewhere. Like a little squirrel, saving them for later."

"Jess used to do that." I laugh, remembering her cookie phase all too well. "Then she'd be up all night with tummy aches, regretting every bite." I take another bite, savoring the flavor. "You're a lifesaver."

Harrison's grin widens. "Your sister told mine that if I didn't bring you some, you might just starve to death."

"Thank God. I was feeling faint," I reply, shoving another cookie in my mouth and worshiping it for the glorious indulgence it is, considering it's the only thing I've eaten all day.

Harrison leans back, watching me with amusement. "You know, seeing you in that suit, I almost didn't recognize you. But hey, you clean up nice."

I swallow, smiling back. "Thanks, man. Just don't get used

to it. I'd pick my BDUs over this corporate getup any day." I take another bite, then glance over at Harrison. "So, how are you adjusting to life with the kids? Away from back-to-back deployments?"

Harrison's expression softens, a shadow of loss flitting across his features. "There are days I ache for it," he murmurs, his voice barely above a whisper. His gaze shifts to the kids playing nearby, and a deep sigh escapes him. "Then there are days when I wonder if I was out of my damned mind, leaving them behind for as long as I did." He falls silent, the unspoken grief of losing his wife settling between us.

I reach over and clasp his shoulder. "I'm here for you, man."

He nods, a smirk tugging at his lips. "Likewise. But tell me, why am I here bringing you food when you're about to go on a date with the infamous Roxana Voss? Is it because women like Voss don't actually eat? They just push their food around, hoping it'll magically turn into gold."

"It's not a date."

"Uh-huh."

"And that vampire doesn't need food; she feeds on words. She'll suck the blood from your neck and spit it out in print that reads like a damn indictment." I shake my head, frustration and fatigue gnawing at me.

"Have you seen her legs?"

"Yeah, and trust me, the woman's a walking nightmare," I grumble. "But with Mark and Zac gone, it's time I buckle down and, well, take one for the team."

Harrison scans the room, making sure the kids are out of earshot before leaning in, his voice dropping to a low whisper.

"And by 'take one for the team,' what exactly are we talking about here?"

"Exactly what you think it means," I mutter, shoving a few fries into my mouth.

He rolls his eyes, letting out a groan. "So, that's where we're at now? Martyr sex?"

I nearly choke. "What? No! Are you out of your damn mind? Roxie's been trying to spider-crawl her way into my bed for months. Pretty sure that would end with me on Page Six and a restraining order on speed dial. We're having dinner. One professional dinner."

"Ah." Harrison leans back, a smirk tugging at his lips. "So there's someone else."

Instantly, an image of full red lips and jet-black hair comes to mind. Which reminds me, I have an email to send. "No," I finally reply. "No one else. No one in months, actually." Or a year, but who's counting?

"Well, if she's the living terror you say she is, you'll need an escape plan to ditch her before dessert."

I look up, a sliver of hope slicing through the dread. "You've got one?"

Harrison's grin sharpens. "Oh, I've got three."

Harrison glances over at Connor, Ollie, and Snooks, their faces all innocent and sweet.

I chuckle. "Bringing the kids on a date? That sounds like a catastrophe in the making." I pause, letting the idea sink in, then shake my head. "It'll never work. She's got my stats—eternal bachelor, no kids. There's no way she'll buy that they're mine."

"What about a last-minute babysitting crisis? You can't just leave them alone, right? And if things go south, oh well. Your calendar is packed, and by the time you can reschedule, Mark and Jess will be back."

A slow grin spreads across my face. "Think they can fake being 'sick' on command?"

Harrison laughs, tipping his chin in their direction. "Getting out of school with a little cough and a well-timed sniffle is sort of their superpower. And if Ms. Voss is as high-maintenance as you think she is, she'll run from children like they just rolled out of a radioactive swamp."

"Or fingerprinting day at school," I add.

Harrison nods, confident and assured. "My kids? They were born for this. Toss in some Comic-Con tickets, and their performance will be Oscar-worthy."

"Comic-Con?"

Harrison points the cookie at me. "They'd fake a cough for free. But I've been wanting to take them there for years. It's the upside of being their dadager."

"Dadager?"

"Dad-slash-manager."

I glance over at the kids, satisfied that my secret weapons are as innocent-looking as they are absolutely nuclear. Shaking my head, I can't help but grin. "Selling out your kids—pure evil genius."

Harrison laughs, giving me a solid clap on the back. "One team, one fight, brother," he says, his eyes already locked on the bag.

"And maybe one more cookie."

His hand dives in. "Only if you insist."

CHAPTER 11
Jules

We need to talk.

How can four little words flip everything upside down? Brian Bishop emailing me is bad. Really, really bad.

Those words shouldn't have this much power, but they do. Because Brian isn't just anyone. He's the guy who ripped through my life like a hurricane, leaving my world in shambles.

Brian was the rebel—the one who thrived on breaking rules. And the only person who could keep up with him? My sister, Angi. The two of them lived on the edge where the sky was the limit and there was no room for anyone else.

It's wild when you think about it. Angi and I are only eleven months apart. Close enough to share the same grade, but polar opposites in every way.

Where I'd pause, she'd plunge headfirst. I was cautious; she was reckless. I'd map out every detail, and she'd blow through life like a storm.

Slow to trust, always overthinking—you might as well carve that on my gravestone. Angi? Living, breathing chaos, pulling everyone into her vortex and leaving you scrambling just to keep up.

And then Brian came along, and suddenly, I was the awkward third wheel, watching from the sidelines as she spun out of control while he chased her like wildfire.

Seeing his name pop up after ten years sends a sticky cocktail of anxiety and anticipation through my veins. It's like my body can't decide whether to panic or get excited, and honestly, that terrifies me most of all.

How close was my article to the Adonis I remember? I'd kill to find out he's gone bald and flabby, maybe with a side of halitosis and a hairy back. The universe finally serving up the ass-kicking he so richly deserves.

But what if he's still . . . him? All lean muscle, sun-kissed skin, and those ridiculous dimples that could disarm you with a single smile?

And then there are those eyes. Bishop Blue, as everyone used to call them. Deep, oceanic blue that could look right through you, stripping away all your defenses until you're left feeling exposed, vulnerable.

God, I hope he's changed. But what if he hasn't?

What if he's still the same guy who could tear my world apart with just a look? Would he still call me that stupid pet name?

The thought sends a wave of anxiety crashing over me, which I try to control with a few slow, meditative breaths. My fingers drum impatiently on the desk, but it's no use.

Finally, I've had enough. "I'm going home," I mutter to no one in particular, because, fuck it. I grab my laptop and purse, and without another word, I'm out the door.

By early afternoon, I'm sprawled on the couch, wrapped in sweats and leggings, my butt perfectly molded into the well-worn groove that practically has my name on it.

Right now, it's just me and my two favorite men—Ben and Jerry. They're busy seducing me with thick Caramel Sutra while I scroll through Netflix, hunting for the perfect distraction.

Then my phone pings with a text. I glance down.

TatorTot

> 9-1-1 already.

I roll my eyes, but a smile tugs at my lips. I type back quickly.

ME

> You really need to reserve 9-1-1 for no-kidding emergencies.

> What is it now, drama queen?

Her response is almost instant.

TATORTOT

> More like runway queen, and this IS an emergency.

> I'm pretty sure my BFF has taken every inch of the lumpy couch hostage and hogged the two most important men in my life.

My phone rings, and it's a FaceTime from Taylor. I answer, narrowing my eyes. "Is there a nanny cam installed that I don't know about?"

"Hey," she says, her voice softer than usual, with the glow of twinkling city lights behind her. "I heard about the article."

My pulse spikes. "From where? Milan? Ibiza? How on earth did you hear about it?"

"Paris, actually. And word travels fast when you're the full-time manager of every last one of @SydneySun's social media accounts." A tender smile tugs at her lips. "Want to talk about it?"

Do I? Not really.

But will Taylor let it go when she can clearly see me in my finest frump gear, spooning ice cream like it's the only thing holding me together? Not a chance. I scoop another spoonful into my mouth and shrug.

"You never did tell me what happened with Brian 'The Total Bastard' Bishop."

I laugh, feeling the tightness in my chest ease just a bit. I keep forgetting Taylor was gone most of senior year, jet-setting off to start her modeling career. "Fine," I say, letting out a sigh. "But no judgment."

She nods, leaning closer to the screen, fully invested now. "May Ben and Jerry oversee our sacred no-judgment zone."

"Remember that scholarship from Ma Mabel's Wicked Good Sweets?"

Taylor's brow furrows as she thinks. "I remember they were offering something ridiculous, like work there every weekend for a month for a chance to win five grand."

I point my spoon at her, smirking. "Try every weekend for the entire school year. And I was desperate. So yeah, I was there, in a giant lollipop outfit."

"What?" Taylor's eyes go wide before she bursts out laughing. "You? A giant lollipop mascot? What flavor?"

"Peach."

Taylor's laughter bubbles over, and I can't help but join in. The absurdity of it all—me, dressed as a peach lollipop, waving at cars like my life depended on it—somehow feels lighter now that I'm sharing it with her.

"Please tell me there are pictures," she begs.

Pictures. My laughter fades to a frown. But I try to make light of it. "I burned every last photo."

"I bet your mom has some," she muses absently before asking, "And what exactly was your job?"

"The hell if I know. Drum up business. Show up and look ridiculous. And everything was going fine until"—I let out a long breath—"Brian showed up."

Taylor blinks, confused. "You dated him?"

"No! Me, he ignored," I say, the frustration still bubbling up even after all these years. "But Angi? Wherever Hurricane Angi went, he would follow. Chased her down until they were practically attached at the hip. Meanwhile, he made it his mission to remind me just how ridiculous I looked. He and his friends would hang out at the ice cream shop across the street, watching me like I was some kind of freak sideshow."

"Classic jerk move," Taylor mutters.

"It gets so much worse." I take a deep breath, bracing myself to spill the rest. "Every Saturday, I'd rush to the candy shop, change in the back, and slip into that damn lollipop costume. Those things were like portable saunas, and that winter? It was unseasonably warm. I was roasting alive in that suit, so I kept it simple—tank top and shorts. But somehow, someone managed to snap a photo of me mid-change."

Taylor's face falls, concern flooding her eyes. "Naked?"

"Not technically. But it might as well have been," I say, the memory tightening my chest. "The way the picture was taken, exposing my back. My hair was in pigtails, I was glancing over one shoulder, and with the angle and everything . . . I *looked* naked. The next day, that picture was plastered all over social media like I'd hired a publicist. And Monday morning, when I went to my locker, hundreds of peach lollipops spilled out, like some twisted joke."

"Oh, God."

I swallow hard, the weight of that humiliation still heavy even after all these years. "It was a living nightmare, Tay. Every time I thought it couldn't get worse, it did."

Taylor's eyes widen with a mix of horror and disbelief. "Please tell me you at least got the scholarship."

"Ha, right. The wholesome candy shop giving five grand away to 'scandal girl?'" A lump rises in my throat, and I swallow back the tears threatening to spill. "From then on, I was Peach Pop."

Taylor's mouth drops open. "And Brian did that?"

"Oh, he did," I say, the memory still sharp and raw. "Before I got fired from being the worst-paid employee ever, I dug up the receipt. Three hundred peach lollipops, courtesy of Brian Gabriel Bishop."

Taylor looks genuinely horrified. "Jules, I'm so sorry. I can't believe I missed all this. I could've been there for you."

"Trust me," I say with a bitter laugh, "if I could've been off jet-setting with you, I would've. In a New York second." I try to joke, but there's an edge of truth there that I can't quite mask.

Taylor's expression hardens, her voice sharp. "You don't have to face him alone, you know. I'm here, and I will absolutely carve *asshole* into the side of his car for you."

"Promise?" I ask, swiping at a tear that slips free.

"Hell, yeah," she says, with the kind of conviction that only a true friend can muster. "And if you don't want to work tonight, I'll find someone else to cover. You don't need to deal with this right now."

Her words are like a balm on every last one of my frayed nerves, and for the first time in a long while, I feel like I might actually be able to breathe again.

I shake my head. "It's fine. I need to do something tonight other than drown in the next pint in the queue—Half Baked, I believe."

"You sure?"

I nod, more to convince myself than her. "It's been ten years. It's definitely time I moved on with my life."

"Hell fucking yeah, it is." Taylor pumps a fist in the air, her fierce energy radiating through the screen. Her confidence is infectious, the kind that makes you believe you can take on the world. And right now, I almost believe it.

For the next hour, we lose ourselves in an episode of *Bridgerton*, escaping reality just long enough for me to hear Taylor's soft snores. I whisper a quiet goodnight and disconnect, turning my attention to the laptop waiting patiently for my next move.

It's time to face this demon head-on. I fire it up and reread the screen.

We need to talk.

Funny thing is, I don't feel anxious or intimidated reading his name with those words. At this very moment, I feel rage. My fingers fly across the keys.

You want to talk, then let's talk.
Anytime. Anywhere, Asshole.

Which feels so good, but I instantly delete it.
Then I start typing:

I need to speak to you like I need bed bugs and a scorching case of herpes.

But considering this is my first real writing gig and my editor's already throwing around words like *lawsuit*, unless I'm ready to torch my career on the spot—and frankly, that douchebag has already cost me more than enough in this lifetime—that's not happening.

Delete, delete, delete.

But here's the thing—I'm not that scared little girl anymore. I'm Sydney Goddamn Sun, and it's time to erase Brian Bishop from my life for good.

He wants to talk? I want a peach pop crammed up his a-hole so it wags when he's excited. But I simply type four little words.

When hell freezes over.

CHAPTER 12
Brian

Confused, I read the email again and again while I lean against the car and wait.

When hell freezes over.

Wow. Clearly, Sydney Sun has some serious issues. Or maybe I'm the one with the issues because I've never been so confused yet turned on by a woman in my life. And I don't even know her.

The front door to Harrison's house swings open, and out marches Connor, looking suspiciously green around the gills. Literally. I squint at him. "What's on your face?"

"Dad's camo paint. Does it make me look sicker?"

I tilt my head, taking it in. "You've nailed that 'I just crawled out of the grave' aesthetic."

"Cool." He grins and hops into the front seat.

Ollie trails behind, already perfecting a raspy cough, while Little Snooki-Pie arrives cradled in Harrison's arms, her big eyes wide and innocent. She looks at her father, all sweetness and light. "Do we get ice cream if we do a good job?"

"Only if you get Uncle Brian out in under an hour." Harrison kisses her on the forehead, and I open the back door as Ollie and Snook slide in, hacking up a storm.

"No acting on the road," Harrison reminds them, his voice stern but eyes full of mischief. "Save it for the restaurant."

I shut the door and flash him a grin. "I'll have them back in a few hours. Want anything from Salvatore's?"

He shrugs, a smirk playing at the corners of his mouth. "Sure. Surprise me."

AS WE STEP INTO THE RESTAURANT, THE MAÎTRE D'S nose twitches like he just caught a whiff of something that doesn't quite belong in his five-star establishment.

His gaze lands on the kids, sniffling and coughing like they've been cast in a flu medicine commercial. The guy looks like he's debating whether to call security or a hazmat team.

"Can I help you?" His tone is as warm as a New York City winter.

"Reservation for Bishop," I say, keeping my voice casual.

He frowns, checking his system. "I only have one reservation for Bishop, and it's a VIP table for two. Unfortunately, we're fully booked. We won't be able to seat you tonight."

I smile, catching sight of the half-empty restaurant behind him, and lean in. I tap his screen with a casual confidence. "Yes, you have a table for Bishop. Me. And it was for two, but now it's for five. Private dining."

His horrified eyes flick back to the kids, who are doing their best impressions of a grand arrival at death's doorstep, then back to me.

"And we'll need kids' menus," I add with a smirk.

Bewildered, he stammers, "W-we don't have kids' menus."

Why am I not surprised?

I mean, come on. It's an Italian restaurant. Pasta, butter, cheese, and breadsticks—this place practically *is* a kids' menu.

I give him a grin that's all teeth. "I'm sure you'll figure it out."

He exhales sharply, nodding like a man about to walk the plank. "Right this way."

CHAPTER 13
Jules

For the record, I'm so over people.

I trudged all the way here on the subway, sandwiched between a guy picking his nose and a woman with her earbuds in, belting out her own private concert, completely unaware of how loud her banshee screeching actually was.

By the time I reach the restaurant, the stench of sweat and cheap cologne clings to me like a bad decision. My skin feels sticky, my hair's a disaster, and my clothes have somehow absorbed an extra layer of grime.

Taylor better be off picking wedding venues with her future husband, because I am never, ever taking another one of her shifts again. Unless, of course, I decide to quit the *Herald*—a thought that makes my stomach turn, considering it's my first official writing gig, and I've only been at it for, oh, no time at all.

I slip on my apron and glance at the board. Next to my name are a few table numbers and the dreaded initials: V.I.P. I let out a long, deflated breath. With my luck, I'm in for a night of Very Important Pricks.

Peeking out the door, I spot two VIP tables. One is blissfully empty, but the other is surrounded by a group of rich, entitled jerks. I don't need to guess—they made it obvious when Lisa walked by, miming obscene gestures like grabbing her ass and licking their lips.

The sight of them makes me want to run straight to the shower. I can already hear Taylor's voice in my head, reminding me to be on time or risk getting stuck with the worst tables. Which is exactly what's happened.

Not my fault. Five measly minutes late because the subway doors refused to open, and now this is my punishment. What was I supposed to do, kick down the doors? Though, honestly, I was tempted. And I might've even cheered on the booger guy who actually tried to.

So, thanks to that fiasco, I'm now stuck serving the biggest snobs in the city. Lady Luck, you're a ruthless bitch.

The eight of them are loud and obnoxious, snapping their fingers for attention and bombarding me with questions.

The guy with slicked-back hair and a Rolex taps his menu. Let's call him "How's the medium-well steak? Pink, or too pink?" he asks, his eyes narrowing as if sniffing out some deep, dark steak secret I'm hiding.

"Pink," I reply confidently, forcing a smile.

Then there's the woman with perfectly manicured nails and trendy designer clothes—I've mentally named her Chanel. She wrinkles her nose. "Is the lobster fresh?"

"Yes," I reply, because honestly, it's all subjective, right?

"How fresh?" she demands, as if I should personally assure her that I, myself, plucked it from the coast this very morning.

I'm not sure what the right answer is here, so I go with, "Fresh as a TikTok trend."

Which is when Mr. Trust Fund with the preppy sweater draped over his shoulders asks, "Is it organic and cage-free?"

"Cage-free? The lobster?"

"Yes," he says like a duh. "The lobster."

I barely manage to keep a straight face on that one because, yeah, it's definitely cage-free now—freed straight from its captivity to land on your plate.

"The chef assures me it is," I say, delivering the line I've been mercilessly trained to recite.

After an hour of enduring their endless demands and haughty attitudes, half the dishes come back untouched, with the lot of them insisting on refunds. Fine by me—those plates become the ones we all snack on because management is too cheap to comp our meals.

And no matter how much their snooty expressions and dismissive waves make my blood boil, I let it roll off me like glitter off a preschooler. The food here is freaking divine.

I snack on a few truffle fries, feeling that familiar nervous anticipation as I finally check the tab. In an industry where tips are everything, this is the moment of truth—the deciding factor on whether I can restock my stash of Ben and Jerry's or go without for the next week.

Instead of a tip, these yahoos scribbled, *"Buy low, sell high"* on the receipt.

Ya know, I don't like wishing bad things on people, but I wouldn't mind if their expensive Italian loafers crossed paths with a little gum. Or better yet, a steaming pile of dog poo.

By the end of my shift, my nerves are fried, and my feet feel like they're about to fall off. I'm beyond ready for this to be over. I grab my bag and make a beeline for the door.

"Jules!" It's Massimo, the manager.

I pretend not to hear him and hurry to the exit when he suddenly jumps in front of me, blocking my path. "You're not leaving, are you?" There's a hint of desperation in his voice—a certain pleading quality that I've fallen for too many times before.

I pause, biting back a grin as I knot my coat tighter. "Massimo, my shift is over. You'll have to beg someone else this time."

"I have a mega-important VIP, and three waitresses are practically at blows over who gets to serve them."

I glance back, and sure enough, three girls are locked in a frenzied standoff, their faces flushed, postures damned near feral. It's like watching a pack of rabid fans vying for a chance to slather sunblock on their favorite ripped celebrity.

One girl clutches a bottle of champagne to her chest like it's a lifeline, her eyes wild. "I saw them first, Becky! You always get the good tables!"

Becky, practically bouncing on her toes, grabs the other end of the bottle and tugs. "You already had your chance. Remember the *Esquire* model?"

"That was months ago," the first one snaps, tightening her grip as they start a full-on tug-of-war over the bottle.

The third, hands on her hips and glaring daggers, steps in closer. "Both of you, back off! The customer is always right, and he smiled right at me!"

I watch the three of them wrestling with the champagne, barely holding back a laugh. "Sheesh. Who's coming?"

"Roxana Voss is doing an interview with some exclusive VVVIP in the private dining room—Brandon something, I think—and if I let those three at him, they're liable to serve him his food on their bare-naked asses."

Their voices are rising, and the air is thick with the tension of a gladiator-level girl fight about to break out.

Unfazed, I pat Massimo on the shoulder. "Looks like you've got more than enough help for one table. I really don't see a problem."

"I'll give you half off your dinner," he pleads, desperation practically seeping from his pores.

Half off? He'd crap a brick if he knew we all had our fills of the last VVVIP's leftovers. "Polite pass," I say and breeze past him.

"If you don't do this, you and Taylor are both fired."

I stop dead in my tracks and whip around to face him. "You can't do that."

"Desperate times," he replies, his tone a mix of apologetic and firm.

Oh, this guy. Me getting fired is one thing, but I can't get my best friend fired. And despite her current jet-setting lifestyle, for the most part, Taylor actually needs this job.

I let out a frustrated sigh. "Fine. One last table," I grumble, reluctantly shrugging off my coat.

"Table 23. And hurry, they've been waiting."

Table 23 is technically the private-though-not-so-private dining room. It's more like a slightly elevated platform two steps up from the main dining area, with full view from the kitchen.

He yanks the champagne bottle from the girls and thrusts it

into my hands. "This costs a thousand dollars a bottle. Don't drop it."

Don't drop it? I'm a total klutz. Has he met me?

I clutch the bottle tightly and head toward Table 23, mentally prepping for whatever awaits. But then I see the VIP in the flesh. There she is—Roxana Voss, and she's not alone.

Hmm. Massimo mentioned a table for two. Funny, because I count two adults, though all I can see of the man is his back, plus one, two, three kids. And another chair. Not sure if they're waiting on someone or if there's a dog in that oversized purse, but whatever.

As I close in on the table, I can already sense it—this guy is going to be the Very Important Prick of the century, and I haven't even seen his face yet.

His voice cuts through the restaurant, loud, demanding, and grating on my last damn nerve. "Can we get some water here, please?"

Seriously.

With the bottle in one hand, I grab a pitcher of water with the other and head over, mentally counting to ten. I let out a long, meditative breath, reminding myself that Taylor is definitely fired if I dump this pitcher of ice water all over Mr. Personality's enormous head.

CHAPTER 14
Brian

I approach the table with the kids in tow, and I see it—the split-second where Roxana's flawlessly composed mask slips. Her eyes dart to the kids, and there it is—a flicker of fear, quickly buried beneath a tight, controlled smile. It's almost impressive how fast she recovers, but I catch it.

"Sorry about this," I say. "I completely understand if you'd prefer to reschedule."

Connor coughs on cue, and Snook wipes her nose with her sleeve in a move that's equal parts adorable and disgusting. And then there's Ollie, who decides to stick a finger in the water glass. It wasn't part of the act, and I'd normally correct him for it, but right now? I roll with it.

Her tight smile doesn't budge. "No, no. We're here. Let's have dinner," she says, her voice threaded with that iron determination that screams she won't be outdone by a bunch of kids.

Amused, I almost chuckle. Roxie's in way over her head.

There are three chairs at the table—one for her, one for me, and one, apparently, reserved for her ostentatious and enormous purse.

"Can I sit with the fancy purse?" Snooki asks, her eyes wide with excitement.

Roxie scoots her along. "No. My purse needs a chair all its own," she says, and every fiber of my being wants to chuck it across the room. But I don't. I've got three kids with me who need a role model, not the Hulk.

"But you can sit next to it," I insist despite Roxie's really obnoxious pout.

"Where?" Ollie asks, eager to get this show on the road. And, of course, the maître d' has vanished like a fart in a hurricane.

Roxana's response is instant, her fingers snapping like she's summoning an army. "More chairs," she barks, her voice sharp enough to cut glass.

My patience instantly severs. I've seen the type before: rude and entitled. But that's not me. Not now, not ever.

I grew up in Donovan's Restaurant, same as everyone in my family. My first job was scrubbing dishes until my hands were raw, serving tables while biting back every retort, and bartending when I was finally old enough to mix a drink. That place was a crucible, forging work ethic and respect into every damn one of us.

Before the waitress or anyone else can go out of their way, I cut in. "We've got this," I say.

Without missing a beat, the boys and I each grab a chair from a nearby table. I motion for Snook to take the waiting seat, and she hops up with that angelic smile of hers.

Connor and Ollie move in sync, just like we planned—

Connor flanks Roxie on one side, and Ollie takes the other, boxing her in.

But, of course, that doesn't dissuade her. Roxie clasps her hands, elbows sliding to the table like she owns the place, literally elbowing the boys aside. "So, Brian," she purrs, eyes narrowing as if she's got me all figured out. "When did you get so paternal? I don't recall you having kids."

"Babysitting duty," I reply, keeping it short.

"For an acting CEO? How curious." She doesn't miss a beat, pulling out a pad and pen from her purse and scribbling down a note like she's documenting a crime scene.

Fine. If she's dead set on keeping this meeting, I've got a few questions of my own. "So, you're still at the *Manhattan Herald*?"

Her answer is clipped, no-nonsense. "Yup." She scurries along to another topic. "I've taken the liberty of ordering champagne."

"Can I try some?" Conner of the living dead asks as Roxana finally notices his ghoulish complexion and scoots to the far edge of her seat.

I blink and give him the same line Mom and Dad gave me when I was his age. "Maybe after you balance your checkbook and pay your taxes, sport." I take my time helping Snook with her napkin, then steer the conversation where I need it to go. "So, tell me more about Sydney Sun."

Roxie's expression shifts, her brow furrowing as if I've just thrown her a curveball. "Sydney Sun?" she repeats, drawing out the name, confusion clouding her face.

"You know her, right? From the *Herald*."

"Right. What exactly do you want to know?"

God, what don't I want to know?

I want to know the scent of her and how long it lingers in a room long after she's gone, haunting and unforgettable.

I want to know how she sounds when she laughs—really laughs—the kind that lights up her whole face and makes everything else fade into the background.

And damn it, I want to know what her lips taste like after she's had that first sip of coffee in the morning, when the world is still quiet, and it's just her.

I swallow hard, trying to push those thoughts away, but they linger, stubborn as the day is long.

Sydney Sun is more than just a name to me now. She's a total stranger who knows me more intimately than any woman alive, and I need to know how . . . one intoxicating detail at a time.

Before I can even get a word out, Snook tugs at my sleeve, her little face scrunched up in discomfort. "My tummy hurts," she whispers, voice tinged with uncertainty.

"Pipe down, sweetie," Roxana snaps, her irritation cutting through the air. "The grown-ups are talking."

She did not just say that.

I know I promised Mark and Zac I'd handle this. And I'm fully aware Roxie's got both the vindictiveness and memory of an elephant to make me pay for this in the press for years.

But screw it. This interview is over.

I'm about to unleash on Ms. Roxana Voss when Snook suddenly slumps heavily against my arm. Alarm bells go off in my head as my hand instinctively touches her forehead.

Is she warm? Maybe. Nothing serious, but enough for a ball of lead to settle deep in my gut.

"Hey, kiddo," I say, concern lacing my voice as I gently lift her chin to meet her eyes. They're a little glassy, and that's all it takes for me to act.

I look up and call for the waitress, maybe a little louder than I intended. "Can we get some water here, please?" Because there are still only two glasses at the table. One is empty, and Roxie's had Oliver's finger in it.

"Your water, sir."

The waitress's voice barely registers, a soft note on a breeze compared to the thud in my ears. She rushes through pouring several glasses, though I only need one. I look up, and—fuck.

Jules.

Her hair falls in soft black waves, framing a face that's always stopped me dead in my tracks. And that mouth . . . God, that mouth. But there's a fire in her eyes now, a blaze I know well.

She's pissed.

By the black apron, I'm guessing she works here. And from her expression, she's not especially impressed that I used my best Training Instructor voice to get her attention.

But for one brief, glorious second, our eyes lock. And everywhere I look, she's stunning. I notice the light freckles on her nose, the full lower lip she just licked, and the subtle shift in her expression—irritation melting into something else.

What is it? Disbelief? Recognition? It's like she's seeing a ghost.

She blinks, her lips parting slightly as she breathes out, "Brian?"

I can't help it—a goofy grin spreads wide across my face. "Peach Pop."

She gasps.

Uh-oh.

My little term of endearment lands like a turd in a punchbowl. Instantly, her expression shifts from curious surprise to a full-on death glare.

Before I can say another word, or get kicked square in the balls, it happens.

Little Snook hurls.

Right into Roxana Voss's fancy-ass purse.

CHAPTER 15
Jules

Peach Pop?

He actually said it.

The words slip out of his mouth, and before I can even think about telling him off or flicking him in the forehead, the little girl's face crumples as tears well up in her eyes. "Sorry," she whispers, her voice trembling.

Without hesitation, Brian scoops her up in his arms, holding her close like she's the most precious thing in the world.

I catch her eye and offer a reassuring smile. "Hey, it's all right. We've all been there. We just need to make sure you're okay."

She leans against Brian's broad shoulder, and for a fleeting moment, all I see is my high school crush—gorgeous, grown-up, and smiling so tenderly at me that it melts my heart.

I'm about to offer her a little soda and bread when Roxana's shrill voice slices through the air, sharp enough to shatter glass. "Goddamnit! What are you, a moron? Of course, I'm not okay. My purse is full of vomit!"

The room freezes, the shockwave of her words rippling through the air. Everyone's attention suddenly snaps to me.

It's the point where Brian 'The Butthead' Bishop returns, full force, because, of course, he says nothing. No apologies, no explanations, just him bolting for the door, his little girl in his arms, with two boys at his heels.

The psycho waitresses elbow each other as they charge after them, chasing the man like he's the last margarita in Mexico. They shove past me, one slamming into my shoulder with enough force that I nearly hit the floor.

I somehow keep my footing, but the champagne bottle isn't so lucky. It slips from my grasp, practically falling in slow motion before smashing against the marble with a deafening crash. Which, like all things under enough pressure and at their breaking point, erupts like a geyser.

Golden, bubbly spray goes everywhere, splattering across the floor and drenching Roxana Voss's pristine designer shoes in thousand-dollar brut.

Massimo rushes over, face pale, his words tumbling out in a panicked rush. "Ms. Voss, oh, my God, are you all right?"

But Roxana's focus is locked on me, her eyes narrowing to serpent slits. "You," she hisses, her voice cold enough to freeze. "You did this."

"What?" The word slips out, barely a whisper, as every gaze in the room pins me down, the weight of their judgment crushing. I can feel the sting of tears burning at the edges of my eyes, but I fight to keep them at bay. "I had nothing to do with any of this."

"You dropped the champagne," Massimo says, his voice low,

almost apologetic, like he wishes he didn't have to say it. "I saw you."

My heart twists painfully in my chest, the desperation clawing at my throat as I struggle to make him understand. "They bumped into me. It wasn't my fault."

Roxana steps forward, her expression icy, her lips a thin, unforgiving line. "My Manolos and purse cost four thousand dollars."

"Purse?" My voice cracks, frustration and disbelief mingling into something raw and jagged. "I am not responsible for your bucket o' puke, and your shoes were an . . . accident."

Roxana leans in closer, her voice like a cold blade slicing through the air. "If you fire her now, I'll settle for half."

The words hang in the air. I see the turmoil in Massimo's eyes, the way he avoids looking at me. The tension in the room builds, and I know what's coming, but it doesn't soften the blow when he finally speaks.

"You're fired, Jules."

I stand there, sucker punched and dizzy, as Massimo goes back to fawning over Roxana. "Ms. Voss, we're truly sorry. Please order whatever you like. To go. And we'll settle the difference from their paychecks," he says, each word a nail in the coffin.

"My paycheck?" I choke out, my voice trembling with disbelief and hurt. "My paycheck barely covers the cost of this ridiculous champagne!"

Massimo doesn't flinch, doesn't even acknowledge the unfairness. "Which is why I need to dock it from both yours and Taylor's pay."

My stomach lurches. "You can't do that!" At this point, whatever fight I have crumbles to a plea.

Massimo's hand lands on my arm, a weak, useless gesture against the tidal wave of humiliation crashing over me. The heat of everyone's stares burns into my skin, intensifying the shame coursing through me.

I see phones rising, recording my downfall for all the world to see. Again.

I can't breathe. The room spins, heat wrapping around me in suffocating waves. Massimo delivers the final blow. "Taylor can keep her job if you leave now. Quietly. Before I have to call the cops."

CHAPTER 16
Brian

For an hour, I've been pacing the hall, grinding the carpet down to threads. Guilt claws at my insides, prickly and relentless, refusing to let up.

I never should have brought the kids tonight. The thought of little Snooki being sick because I was desperate to dodge a date with Roxie Voss crushes me with every step.

When Harrison finally emerges from Snooki's bedroom, closing the door quietly behind him, my nerves stretch to the point of snapping. "Is she okay?"

"She's fine. And she's definitely learned her lesson about downing six cookies before dinner."

Relief floods through me, and I let out a breath I didn't even realize I was holding, dragging a hand through my hair. "Perfectly good cookies . . . wasted on Roxana's purse."

We head to the kitchen where we can talk without waking the kids. "Beer? Something stronger?" Harrison offers.

"After tonight? The strongest you've got. Maybe a notch just below jet fuel."

He grabs two tumblers from the cabinet and a bottle of whiskey, pouring a generous amount into each glass.

"Thanks," I say, accepting the drink with a grateful nod. With one satisfying sip, the tension melts away.

Harrison leans back against the counter, his eyes studying me over the rim of his glass. "So, what's the story with the woman?"

I pause, caught off guard. "What woman?"

"The nice lady Snooks told me about. The one you were making, and I quote, 'googly eyes' at."

I groan, rubbing a hand over my face. "Googly eyes? Obviously, Snooki-pie was deliriously ill. I'm a grown man." I stand taller. "Grown men do not make googly eyes."

"Not for just anyone. So, who is she?"

"It's . . . complicated."

"Complicated?" He raises an eyebrow, swirling the whiskey in his glass. "Try me."

Relenting, I sigh. "Peach Pop."

"Peach Pop?" Harrison's interest is piqued as he swirls the amber liquid in his glass. "Who's that?"

"Juliana Spenser. Jules to her friends. Ms. Spenser to me." His eyes widen with intrigue. "She was at the restaurant tonight."

"Snooks said she was beautiful. Like a princess."

I hesitate, the words sticking in my throat as I search for the right way to say it. "Beautiful isn't the half of it. I've been head over heels for that girl since high school. The problem is . . . I may have briefly dated her sister."

Harrison winces, sucking in a breath. "Yikes."

"Yeah," I mutter, the guilt creeping back in. "I knew it was a mistake. Especially when she stole and maxed out my first credit card. But I let it go on for way too long."

"Why?" he asks, studying me as he waits for the rest.

But the truth is lodged so deep in my chest, it takes everything I have to pry it loose. I down the rest of my glass, the burn of the whiskey nothing compared to the ache of what I'm about to admit.

I force myself to say it out loud. Tell the truth for once. "To be close to Jules."

For a long moment, we sit in silence; the only sound is the soft splash of whiskey as Harrison refills my glass.

He finally lets out a low whistle, crossing his arms as he leans back. "So, you've got it bad for the baby sister, huh? So, when are you going to see her?"

I huff out a dry laugh, shaking my head. "If it's up to her? About the time hell starts welcoming polar bears."

Harrison raises an eyebrow, a knowing smirk tugging at his lips as he sets the bottle down. "And if you have your way?"

My wide grin answers for me.

YAWNING, I JAB THE ELEVATOR BUTTON AND SLUMP against the wall, exhaustion setting in like a lead weight. Harrison and I spent the entire night chasing one irritatingly elusive ghost across the World Wide Web.

We scoured every corner of social media—Facebook, Instagram, Twitter, even the depths of LinkedIn—and came up empty. It's like she's vanished into thin air. Or got abducted by aliens.

How the hell does anyone disappear in this day and age?

I even stalked her family, which felt a lot like prying. It reopened a door I'd closed so long ago, I'd forgotten it existed.

Angi's still pouting for the camera, her Instagram wall packed with selfies. Not a single one with family—no surprise there.

Eomma's account is a vibrant gallery of food and mystery books. I make a mental note to check out her latest recommendation—an intriguing suspense she swears by.

Her dad's profile is practically untouched, with a few random memes tossed in—like a picture of him in sunglasses, holding a grill spatula, with the caption: "Grill master by day, meme master by night."

And Halmeoni's account? It's a garden of flowers, from bright pink roses to big, blue balloon flowers. It's the rich-colored marigolds that make me smile. Jess's favorites.

And then there's Colby. My brother in arms. His most recent post is a video of the Statue of Liberty at dusk. It tells me two things: One, his drone maneuvering is as precise as ever. And two, he's home.

After a split-second debate, I shoot a message to his account.

In NYC? Want to shoot some hoops?

His reply is instant.

Need your ass kicked that bad?
Name the time and place!

I laugh and shoot him the time and address, along with a little note.

Bring it, punk.

The elevator dings, and the doors slide open. Imani is there to greet me, a steaming mug of coffee in her hand, like she's been waiting just for this moment.

"You're a godsend," I say, graciously accepting the cup and taking a sip, letting the warmth chase away some of the morning's tension.

"I know," she replies with a warm smile. "It's why Mark keeps me around. And I got your text. The security team is on the hunt for your watch."

Her smile falters, and I know what she's thinking. It's a long shot, but if anyone can find it, my team can. "Thanks," I murmur. "And clear my calendar for later this afternoon. I've got a meeting with the *Herald*."

"Do they know that?"

"Nope."

Her eyes widen, concern flashing across her face. "Ms. Voss?"

"God, no."

"Maybe Ms. Sun, then?"

A guilty grin tugs at my lips.

"Ah." Her expression softens with understanding. "Well, there's someone waiting in your office."

That's never good. "Care to clue me in?"

"Can't. Sworn to secrecy."

"Traitor." I smirk, shaking my head as I walk past her. She giggles as I push open the door.

There, lounging comfortably at my desk—formerly his desk—is Zac.

His size 12s are kicked up, and his beard, that untamed jungle, looks even wilder. A newspaper is sprawled out in front of him. He looks up, amused. "If you wanted me back, you could've just asked," he says, voice dripping with enough sarcasm, I know it can't be good.

I close the door behind me, hands sliding into my pockets. "What happened?"

"You're making headlines again."

I'm not sure I want to know, but I ask the question. "How bad is it?"

"Four—count 'em, one, two, three, four—major accounts have called me this morning alone." He presses a hand to his ear. "If you listen really hard, you can hear the sound of three hundred million dollars going down the drain."

Fuck. Mark and Jess nearly canceled their honeymoon when Zac stepped down, and they deserve one uninterrupted month without me crumbling Mark's empire to shit overnight.

"I've already demanded a meeting with Ms. Sydney Sun." Her response was less than encouraging, but Zac doesn't need to know that. I've already cleared my schedule to drop by her office today.

"This isn't about Sydney Sun. It's about Roxana Voss."

"What?"

"You know, that *thing* you were supposed to handle? Well, she also called me," Zac says, tapping his fingers on the desk, his tone a mix of frustration and amusement. "Did you seriously bail on her?"

"I didn't bail," I say, straightening my cuff. "Snooki was sick."

Zac blinks. "You brought Snooki?"

"And the boys," I admit, rubbing the back of my neck, already regretting where this conversation is headed.

"On a date?"

I point a finger at him. "It wasn't a date, remember? It was a professional business meeting."

He deadpans. "You were trying to get out of it, weren't you?"

I stay silent and admit nothing.

Zac lets out a low chuckle. "And what the hell happened to her purse?"

I can't help but stifle a grin. "No comment."

"Well, hell hath no fury like a reporter scorned," he says, reaching for a newspaper on the desk. He slides it across to me, the headline glaring up at us. "Here she is, handing you your ass on a platter with this mockup and an invitation to quote-unquote chat."

I pick up the newspaper, my heart sinking as I take in the headline.

Eternal Bachelor & Billionaire F*Boy Destroys An Empire, One Woman at a Time

I snatch up the paper, my eyes narrowing as I skim the headline. "Can she even say that? It's a public newspaper!"

Zac shrugs, leaning back with a smirk. "It's just a mockup. The real thing will probably be so much worse."

I skim the article, my blood boiling with every line. "The fact that this woman works at any paper is staggering. Misspellings all over the map. Chock full of lies. First off, those insane women who chased me and the kids to the car were not my dates. And second, no matter how she paints me, I am not a fuckboy. Just ask Sydney Sun. She paints me as a hero."

Which is weird, considering she won't even talk to me.

"There are no less than three dozen women parked downstairs just waiting to get a glimpse of you." Zac blinks, then points to the window with a casual wave. "*You* know you're not a fuckboy. And *I* know you're not a fuckboy. Mostly because if you were, things would go a hell of a lot smoother with Ms. Voss. But they"—he motions wildly toward the window—"your adoring fans, very much think you are."

"Can I help it if I'm irresistible man candy?" I mutter under my breath.

Zac rolls his eyes. "Don't make me gag."

I pause, letting the weight of the situation settle in before tossing the paper into the trash. "Speaking of gag, what now? Do I sic the lawyers on her with a gag order?"

Zac snorts, shaking his head. "You'll have better luck gagging her yourself."

I glance out the window at the sea of bodies below. My hand instinctively smooths over my left wrist, the absence of my watch burrowing an ache deep in my chest.

Dismayed, I shake my head, a tired grin tugging at my lips. "I never thought I'd say this, but I think I need a break from women." Honestly, it's not much of a stretch. This dry spell?

It's been dragging on for a while. "Maybe I should have *Off Limits* tattooed in all caps on my ass."

Zac sidles up beside me, admiring the crowd below. "Tattoo or get hitched."

Out of nowhere, an image of a feisty, dark-haired beauty with full lips and a fire in her eyes flashes through my mind. A woman who despises me with every fiber of her being. "I'll fix it."

"How?" He pats my back. "By going cold turkey?"

"Yup."

CHAPTER 17

Jules

I sit at my desk, twirling a pen between my fingers, my gaze catching on the shiny new nameplate in front of me:

SYDNEY SUN, REPORTER

It's all too surreal, like a dream I've been chasing forever and somehow managed to catch. But the longer I stare at the blank screen in front of me, the tighter that suffocating feeling wraps around me.

Getting fired from Salvatore's shouldn't sting this much when I've got a cushy safety net like this job, but it does. It's like ripping open an old scab, the wound still raw underneath.

And what if I fail at this job, too? That fear gnaws at me as I nibble my lip, staring at the same seven words that have been mocking me for the past hour:

Up Close and Personal with a Billionaire

"Holy shit," Scoop mutters from across the room, snapping me out of my thoughts. Anabelle and Felix immediately pop their heads up, eyes locked on the front of the room.

"Don't even think about it," Anabelle declares, her tone playfully threatening. "He's mine."

"I don't see your name on him," Felix purrs, his voice dripping with catty dismissal.

Anabelle's eyes narrow, a wicked grin spreading across her face. "Well, when you see my tongue on him, consider him claimed."

"Huh?" I look up, and my heart slams to a stop.

Striding down the hallway, right next to Mr. Richards, is Brian Bishop.

The fitted blue suit he's wearing does nothing to hide the fact that beneath it lies pure, lickable perfection—broad shoulders, tight abs, and everything in between sculpted to perfection.

Every inch of him radiates confidence and power, and if he wasn't the biggest dick on the planet, I'd be right there with Anabelle and Felix, fighting to stake my claim.

But as those ocean-blue eyes sweep in my direction, my pulse skyrockets. Panic surges through me, fast and fierce, and with him closing in and my shiny new nameplate practically screaming "Sydney Sun," I make a split-second decision.

I slide off my chair and duck under my desk. "Cover for me!" I beg, my voice barely an audible squeak.

Felix drops down next to me, eyes wide. "What the hell are you doing?"

"I'm . . . shy," I mutter, curling into myself, trying to disappear completely.

"You're insane," Anabelle whispers, peeking under the desk. "Do you know who you're dodging? Manhattan's newest billionaire."

Newest what?

Before I can even process that, Mr. Richards's voice grows louder as they approach. "Mr. Bishop has graciously agreed to give an exclusive interview," Richards says, practically beaming with pride. "To Sydney Sun."

My heart plummets. Oh, my god, is he serious?

"Lucky girl," Anabelle purrs, her tone dripping with syrupy sweetness. "Maybe you could wait around."

"Or not," Scoop cuts in, amusement threading through his words. "You know how reporters are—always chasing a story."

I can practically feel Brian's smirk through the desk as he replies, "Has a knack for disappearing, does she?"

"Her loss," Felix says, teasingly trying to coax me out. "But she could be back any second now."

Yeah, right. There is no way I'm popping out from under this desk like a freaking birthday cake.

Mr. Richards grumbles, "Your call, Bri."

Good Lord, he called him Bri. I smile wide. Brian hates that almost as much as pistachio ice cream and chick flicks.

Brian makes a long, drawn-out sound that tells me he's weighing his options. I silently pray to every god out there that he has something—anything—better to do.

Finally, he sighs. "I, uh, actually have another engagement."

Richards snaps to attention. "Understood. When she returns, remind her that this interview is her top priority."

Anabelle replies, all earnestness and glee. "Of course, Mr. Richards. The second she returns."

I stay hidden, holding my breath until I finally hear their footsteps retreating. I release all the air in my lungs and slowly climb out from under the desk.

Cautiously, I peek out, only to be met with the amused, curious stares of my colleagues.

"Thanks," I mutter, crawling back into my chair, my face burning with embarrassment.

Scoop flashes a wide grin. "No problem, Sydney Sun. How about we work on that shy streak of yours?" He rubs his hands together like he's about to unlock my chakra. "All right, deep breath in."

I follow his lead, inhaling deeply, filling my lungs to the brim.

"Long breath out," he continues, his voice soothing, almost hypnotic.

I exhale slowly, feeling a tiny sliver of tension slip away.

His hand lands on my shoulder, his eyes kind and steady as they meet mine. "Now, ready for that interview?"

My pulse spikes like a shot of adrenaline. "Not even close," I mutter, still rattled.

He pats my shoulder. "We'll keep working on it."

We all settle back into our seats, but I can't let it go. My gaze snaps to Anabelle. "I'm sorry, did you just say billionaire?"

CHAPTER 18

Brian

The Centurion Group's private gym is nothing short of luxury wrapped in state-of-the-art design.

Colby steps onto the court, giving the place a once-over. With the polished hardwood floors and sleek, high-end equipment, he smirks. "Damn, look at you—fancy digs and all. When you said hoops, I was picturing cracked pavement and a rim with no net. What's next, gold-plated basketballs?"

I chuckle, tossing him the ball. "I was thinking stealth," I tease.

After a quick bro hug, he checks out my prosthetic, eyeing it down to the classic Air Jordan at its base. "You shouldn't be playing in those." He points to the shoes. "They should be mounted on display."

I yank the ball back with a grin. "If I own it, I wear it." I dribble once, twice, then nail a shot with precision. "Two points."

He flips his cap backward, his expression shifting to something more serious. "Oh, game on."

A few rounds in, and it's clear—if either of us thought we'd take it easy, we were dead wrong. The game is intense, just like old times. Winded and out of breath, we keep pushing, neither of us willing to back down.

He blocks my next shot so effortlessly, it's almost insulting. With a cocky grin, he spins the ball on his finger like we're back on base. "Ready to give up, *harabeoji*?"

"Grandpa?" I pant, barely catching my breath. "I'm only three years ahead of you, man." I dribble the ball under each leg, flashing a grin. "Catlike reflexes. Sharp as a tack. And yeah, your elder, so now that you mention it, I could use a breather."

"Hey, your Korean is still intact."

"After two tours in-country, I try to keep it fresh. I actually managed to watch *Parasite* without subtitles."

Colby nods and says, "*Insangjeogine*." Impressive.

We grab towels and some bottled water from the sleek fridge, then collapse onto a bench at the side of the room. Colby takes a long swig, then waves the glass bottle in my face. "Fancy stuff for one of Manhattan's Most Eligible Bachelors."

I cringe. "You saw the headline?"

"Only because one of the guys posted it in the Facebook group. Got a ton of hearts from the ladies. And a few from the guys, too."

"Nice," I mutter. "Just what I need. More unwanted attention."

"So, what's going on with you, man? When did you trade in the dog tags for designer suits?"

"Not long after I realized I wasn't going back. Had to do something with my time, right? And the monkey suit? Temporary. I usually run security. We're always on the lookout for kickass talent."

"Food for thought." I wipe the sweat from my face, feeling the familiar burn in my muscles. "How long are you back for?"

Colby's grin fades, his easygoing demeanor slipping. "Not sure."

A knot forms in my gut. "Did something happen?"

He looks at me, his expression unreadable. "I'll give you one guess."

"Sounds like Hurricane Angi." I catch the ball, my heart sinking. "How serious?"

"Hard to say. She stole my identity, ran up my government credit card," Colby says, his voice low and tight. "I've got a few weeks to find her."

Shit. This isn't just a slap on the wrist. This is a full-blown military criminal offense—dishonorable discharge, a career in shambles, maybe even time in the brig. It could destroy everything Colby's worked for.

My mind races, trying to process the gravity of what he's just said. "If it's just a matter of being paid back—"

"It's not," he cuts in, his tone hardening. "Dad already tried. He was ready to refinance the house if it came to that. But the problem isn't just the money. It's what she did with the card. The charges are tied to illegal activity—not classified, but enough to raise red flags."

Of course, they are.

"The thing is, if I don't have that card physically back in my hand to give to my commanding officer, they'll nail me for negligence and refer her to the DA for criminal prosecution."

He shakes his head, frustration simmering beneath the surface. "If I don't find her, I'm screwed."

"You realize the chances of finding her are slim to none, right?"

He shoots me a look like I've lost my mind. "Thanks for the vote of confidence."

"Which is why I'm saying *we* find her. You've got me and my entire team backing you up. Seasoned recon men and women at your disposal."

His eyebrows lift, surprised. "Really?"

"And if push comes to shove, I'll pony up a reward."

"No. No reward," he insists, shaking his head. "Dad would have a cow."

"Only as a last resort," I say, giving him a reassuring pat on the chest as he snags the ball. We start up again, and, of course, he sinks the first hoop. Damn kid's gonna kill me.

Ignoring the sharp pain in my knee, I grab the ball with a smirk. "Payment in exchange for some intel."

Colby nods, dribbling before attempting a three-pointer. It bounces off the rim, frustration flickering in his eyes before curiosity takes over. "What kind of intel?"

I go for a layup, the ball swishing through the net with a satisfying thwack. "How's Jules?"

He catches the ball. "And you're asking because . . . ?"

"Because I am," I say, adding, "And this is the part of the conversation where you *give* intel. No questions. Just answers."

A knowing grin spreads across his face. "Fine. She's okay, I guess. Pretty much hates your guts."

Tell me something I don't know, though I'm still not entirely clear why.

I mean, yes, technically, I dated her sister. Briefly. Not even first base. "What's she up to?" I ask, trying to sound casual, like I didn't just see her last night.

"She was working at this fancy schmancy restaurant—Salvatore's. But she lost her job, thanks to some dickhead and his barfing kid."

The grin evaporates from my face, replaced by a tightening in my chest.

Fuck.

Colby tosses the ball back with sharp, quick force, and it bounces off me before I catch it, the impact jolting me back to the present.

He watches it rebound away, then nods as he jogs after it. "Right. Catlike reflexes. Sharp as a tack."

This time, when he snaps it at me, I catch it midair, but my chest tightens. I got her fired?

His gaze sharpens, the teasing gone. "Something going on with you and Jules?"

I hesitate, swallowing a ball of lead in my throat. "Nope."

CHAPTER 19
Jules

Taylor's voice bounces off the walls before the door even finishes closing. "Jules?"

"In the kitchen," I say, leaning against the counter, a glass of wine cradled in my hand. Second glass. Or maybe third.

She bursts in and pulls me into one of her signature bear hugs. "Miss me, bitch?" she teases, grabbing the bottle of wine on the counter. "Wow, St. Émilion Grand Cru. The good stuff. We celebrating something big?"

"Not exactly."

She catches the look on my face, and her smile fades. "What's wrong?"

"Massimo fired me."

"What?"

"Lisa and Dave smuggled this to me as a quick parting gift. For a red, it's remarkably smooth. I was tempted to finish the whole thing myself. But since you're here, I guess I'll share."

"You're damn right, you'll share," she says, grabbing the bottle and studying the label, her perfectly arched brows lifting in appreciation. "This is a four-hundred-dollar bottle of premium red. No way you're keeping all this to yourself." She takes a deep breath, savoring the scent from the cork like it's pure oxygen. "And let's be real, you hated Salvatore's anyway."

"I know. But still." I take another sip, the frustrations from last night seeping into today, settling deep into my bones. "I needed something—anything—to take the edge off, and we were out of tequila." I swirl the rich purple liquid in my glass, staring at it for a moment. "It was awful."

"Then I quit, too."

"Taylor, no. You need that job. I can't let you do that."

"Oh, thank God. Because after this trip, I really do need that job." She grins, taking a sip from my glass before handing it back. "Come on. You get the blankets; I'll grab the snacks."

We shuffle out to the balcony, our little slice of vintage Brooklyn. The rustic fire escape, once all rust and practicality, has been transformed with faux wooden floors and a sleek metal railing, turning it into our cozy perch.

Three floors up, we swing our bare feet like kids, imagining the passing cars below as part of a parade. On particularly tipsy nights, we might've even thrown in a royal wave or two.

Taylor drops a silver tray between us—one of the many vintage treasures she has a knack for finding. It's piled high with pretzels, mixed nuts, and marshmallows—every bit of comfort food she could scavenge from the pantry.

Wrapped in blankets softened by time and way more fabric softener than anyone recommends, we settle in. The jagged skyline of old brick and steel stretches out before us as Taylor launches into a story about her latest almost-fiancé.

"I had to give him the '*it's not you, it's me*' speech, because what could I say? I can only make a square peg fit in a round hole for so long."

I laugh so hard, I nearly shoot a mouthful of expensive French wine out my nose. "No one should jam a square peg in anyone's round hole ever."

She clinks her glass against mine. "Amen, sister." We sit in companionable silence for a moment before she suddenly tosses a peanut at my face. "All right, miss 'drunk after half a glass,' spill it. What got you fired? Drunk and disorderly?"

I take another swig and slump back against the cool brick, the warmth of the booze crawling up my chest. "Butthead Brian happened," I mutter, letting out a sigh that feels like it's been lodged in my throat for days.

"Oh, my God," she says, chomping on a pretzel. "Did you get caught making out with him in the bathroom?"

I blink. What on earth? "No." I shudder at the thought. "And why would I? That bathroom might look clean, but I know the guys who mop it—they're mostly just smearing the urine sprinkles around."

"Ewww," she snorts, cringing and laughing as she scrunches up her nose.

I stare at her, genuinely wondering where she comes up with this stuff. Who is this person?

I continue and steer the conversation back on track. "Brian Bishop is the reason I'm fired. Apparently, he's not just good-looking—he's obscenely rich, has three kids, and hangs out at places like Salvatore's. Drinks thousand-dollar champagne, barks orders, kills careers, and drools over beautiful women like Roxana Voss."

Her eyes go wide, and that goofy smile spreads across her face. "Someone sounds jealous."

I gasp. "Jealous?"

"You have nothing to be jealous about. You're way prettier," she says, topping off our drinks like it's no big deal.

I snap, narrowing my eyes. "I am not jealous." Am I?

"You did say he was hot. And rich," she reminds me playfully.

"It's Brian. He's also arrogant, immature, tackles womanizing like an extreme sport, and is a colossal capital D. As far as I'm concerned, he can suck it. Even if he came crawling back on all fours, begging for forgiveness for every last dish of crap he's ever served me, it'll be a sub-zero day in hell before that happens."

"Is that so?" a deep, gravelly voice calls up from the street below, "What if I fed you lobster Thermidor and a chocolate soufflé?"

Taylor and I look down, and there he is—Brian Gabriel Bishop himself. He's leaning against a shiny black Mercedes, wearing a smile a mile wide, jeans that fit too well, and a T-shirt that clings to his broad shoulders and biceps in a way that should be illegal.

In his hand, he's holding a large picnic basket. Standing next to him is a man who gives us a casual salute. Must be his driver. Because, of course, Brian and his kind would have a driver.

"Hello, Jules," he says, his voice smooth as velvet.

"Ms. Spenser," I correct instantly, tossing another nut into my mouth. "And I hate prissy food."

"That's right. You do," he says, tossing aside a red-and-white-checkered handkerchief. "Then perhaps something more along the lines of barbecue chicken, green beans, mac and cheese, and cornbread."

Mrs. D's barbecue dinner. My favorite.

But he doesn't stop there. "I don't have three-layer chocolate cake, but a friend made dark chocolate cherry brownies."

God, he's playing dirty. Brownies are my kryptonite, and throw in berries? I'm completely defenseless.

I stiffen my posture. "I'm not hungry," I lie, though my stomach betrays me with a growl loud enough to wake the dead —like a bullfrog strapped to a megaphone, of course, at the worst possible time.

Then, clear as day, I hear him say, "I just want to fuck."

"What?" I snap out of my expensive booze fog, heart racing.

"I said I just want to talk, Ms. Spenser. Just. Talk."

And the way he says "Ms. Spenser" sends a phantom finger trailing down my spine, making my pulse stutter and my knees go weak. Suddenly, dinner is the last thing on my mind. I'm picturing him wrapping a fist in my hair, bending me over a desk, and demanding to know if I've been naughty.

I eye the fancy wine. The good stuff really should come with a disclaimer: *May impair hearing and trigger X-rated fantasies.*

"Come on up!" Taylor cries out, her voice full of cheer.

What?

"It's my place, too," she says, all coquettish and smug.

The room tilts a little as I stand and watch her buzz them up. Before I can protest, or walk a straight line, there's a knock at the door.

"Aren't you going to get that?" Taylor teases, nudging my body in the direction of the door.

"No," I grumble, reaching for the bottle in her hand. She keeps it just out of reach, grinning like she's won the lottery. "Not until you let my future husband in."

A flicker of jealousy ignites. Her future husband is—"Brian?" I ask, completely thrown.

"What? No. The hunky guy downstairs. I'm telling you, he's the one." She sets down the bottle and clasps her hands together, pleading. "Please?"

I roll my eyes, exasperated. "Ugh, fine. But don't blame me when his freakishly big square peg doesn't fit in your round hole."

She squeals, smoothing my hair like a toddler.

Reluctantly, I crack open the door.

His stupidly gorgeous face greets me with a wide smile, just the right amount of scruff to catapult his heat factor to scorching. "Hi," he says, his voice low and rumbly.

I fuss with the blanket, trying to hide my body's betrayal—flushed cheeks, hard nipples, and a molten heat pooling between my thighs.

Still, I don't budge. "What do you want?"

He raises the basket. "Dinner. And an offer."

"An offer?"

He nods, his eyes locking on mine. "Hear me out, Ms. Spenser?"

With his Calvin Klein looks, aroma of food, and my inebriated state way beyond tipsy, I'm in way over my head.

And don't even get me started on that chiseled jaw. And those ocean-blue eyes—any woman would drown in them.

My mouth opens just as my brain completely shuts down. "Fine."

CHAPTER 20
Jules

Both men come in as introductions kick off. Brian nods toward the tall, rugged guy standing next to him. "This is Logan."

I raise an eyebrow. "Your chauffeur?"

The two men exchange a contemplative look, the kind that speaks volumes without a word. "I guess I'm whatever the boss needs," Logan says, his tone smooth.

Brian claps a hand on his shoulder. "Mostly combat support since the article."

"Combat support?" I echo, suddenly concerned.

Logan's lips twitch into a smirk. "Yeah, keeping the crazed fans off the boss has become a full-time job. Ever since some wackadoo of a journalist turned him into a Marvel superhero, the attention's been relentless."

Smug as the day is long, Brian chimes in, "I prefer to think of her as a mad fan."

Mad fan? I am not a fan. In fact, I'm the polar opposite of a fan and want to set the record straight, but all I squeak out is, "Oh."

I play dumb, taking refuge in another sip of my wine, trying to mask any hint that the wackadoo in question is me.

Brian jumps in. "And he only drives when my leg gives me trouble. Usually later in the day."

A flicker of concern snakes up my throat, spilling out before I can stop it. "What's wrong with your leg?"

Brian looks at me with an expression I can't quite pin down—maybe surprise, maybe something deeper.

Then, with a subtle lift of his jeans, he reveals the gleam of metal where muscle used to be. "Me, 2.0," he says, his voice carrying a challenge, daring me to feel sorry for him.

But I don't.

So much stirs inside me, but pity isn't one of them. What's a day in his life really like? When he's not being an insufferable ass, that is.

Every person carries a story, and I'm drawn to his like a curious moth to an irresistible flame. It's like standing before a masterpiece I'll never paint, yet I'm compelled to understand every brushstroke.

I want to see more of Brian Gabriel Bishop—the man that all the bruised parts of me are desperate to forget but somehow can't seem to ignore.

Taylor elbows me, breaking the spell.

I clear my throat, trying to shift gears. "Um, we don't exactly have a big place. The kitchen table's tiny, but we've got some fold-up chairs in the closet."

Brian steps into the kitchen, and it's like the air shifts—his presence filling the room, commanding attention, and leaving no space unnoticed.

His eyes lock on to the nearly drained wine bottle. "St.

Émilion," he whistles, clearly impressed. "Nice. But it looks like it's on its last leg."

"Sadly, it is," I say, downing the last drop in my glass.

Brian's lips curl into a grin. "Funny thing, I brought the exact same bottle."

The last thing I want is for him to think I'm pretending to be someone I'm not—or worse, that I need expensive things to feel complete. "Mine was stolen."

"Same here," he says, flashing that infuriating grin. "I left an IOU with Mrs. D."

I can't help but smile. He used to pull that stunt all the time. We all did—grabbing food and leaving her IOUs like they held real value. And if any of us tried to make good on one, Mrs. D. just opened a drawer, shook her head, and insisted it wasn't there. If it wasn't there, nothing was owed.

I love imagining Mrs. D. with a secret stash of those IOUs hidden away in a secret warehouse—or better yet, tossing them into the fall bonfire every year, savoring her own fancy glass of wine as they burn to ash, a satisfied smile on her face.

"If I remember correctly," Brian says, "one leg, one thigh, a quarter plate of green beans, another quarter of mac and cheese, and honey butter on the cornbread." He hands me the plate, his voice casual but his eyes sharp.

By the time dinner winds down, I'm so stuffed I'm not sure I can even move.

The entire evening has been light and easygoing, full of laughter over memories I haven't visited in so many years, I forgot they were ever there.

Like the time he taught Mrs. Thompson's parrot to say

"Pluck Off" and "Kiss my Big Beak" so she'd stop bringing it to church.

Or the time he convinced the evil math teacher that all the thermostats were voice-activated. The poor guy spent a week screaming at the thermostat. It wasn't until he shouted, "Warm up, damn it!" loud enough that the principal heard and finally set him straight.

My stomach aches from laughing so hard, a feeling I haven't had in what feels like forever. I'll give the credit to both Brian and my fourth glass of wine.

And then, without thinking, I open my mouth. "Why did you do it, Brian?"

Brian's expression falters, the bright ocean blue light in his eyes dimming to a stormy sea of gray. But I wasn't asking about that—about my epic waterslide crash into the nickname Peach Pop. No, that's a conversation definitely reserved for straight liquor.

I quickly scramble to cover. "I mean, why did you join the military?"

He shakes his head as a faraway look settles in his expression. "It was all I ever wanted to do. My dad and grandpa were both vets. Plus, it helped transform me from the hellraiser I was into something more..." He struggles to find the word. "Manageable?"

Logan cuts in with a grin. "Or into someone who's only slightly less of a pain in the ass."

Brian lets out a small laugh, then shares a look with Logan—one that seems to be Logan's cue to leave. "I need a little air." He stands. "Care to join me?" he asks Taylor.

Taylor practically lights up, her excitement barely

contained. "Absolutely! I'll just grab a sweater." She darts off, returning in record time, beaming as she links her arm with Logan's.

They head out, leaving the room quieter, more charged. Brian's gaze locks on to mine, studying me like he's searching for something.

Before the blush heating my neck can hit my cheeks, I jump in. "You said something about an offer?"

He leans back slightly, his tone casual, but his eyes are razor-sharp. "I heard you were fired."

I can already see where this is headed. The guilty rich boy wants to ease his conscience. So I do it for him.

"At the risk of denting your overinflated ego, the world doesn't revolve around you." His head tilts slightly, those sharp eyes of his softening. "Roxana Voss got me fired, not you. And honestly, I never liked the job to begin with."

He pauses, as if considering his next move, then nods and reaches out, smoothing a hand over mine. The touch is electric, a current that feels too natural, too right.

It scares the hell out of me, so I pull away, shaking off the lingering sensation. "How's your little girl?"

He sighs, the weight of whatever he's carrying pulling down his shoulders. "She's fine. But she's . . . not mine."

"Huh?"

"The kids. They were, uh, sort of on loan," he admits, the words falling out awkwardly.

By this point, I'm pouring the last of the wine into his glass. A Roxana Voss story? Now, this, I have to hear.

He takes a generous gulp, and flashes a shy grin. "I needed

an excuse to cut my meeting with the vampiress short, and their father had this idea and, well, sort of volunteered them."

I shake my head, a smirk pulling at my lips. "Using kids as a shield? And you call yourself a soldier."

He chuckles, the sound low and rough, cutting through the tension, but it doesn't ease the knot in my stomach. I can't dodge the elephant in the room any more than I can ignore the intensity in his gaze or the way his damn aftershave lingers in the air between us. "Why did you really come here, Brian?"

He lets out a slow breath, as if he's figuring out what to say. And for a second, I think he's about to stand up and walk out. But then, he shifts, kneeling down in front of me, his hand gently wrapping around mine.

His eyes find mine, and when he speaks, his words hit with the force of a Mack truck, head-on. "Because I need a wife."

CHAPTER 21
Jules

Stunned, I wriggle my hand free from his grasp, my heart pounding like a drum solo at a halftime show. Calmly, I set down my glass, trying to convince myself I'm hearing things again. "You need a what?"

"Wife," he says, his voice clear as a church bell. "As in matrimony."

"Matrimony," I repeat, my head slowly nodding as I slide his glass of wine just out of reach. He's obviously had more than enough.

He smirks, completely unfazed. "I'm serious."

"Really? Because I'm pretty sure you're drunk. And insane."

"I've had one glass of wine. Drunk? Not even close. Insane? Debatable." He shrugs with that casual confidence that drives me crazy. "I need a wife, Jules," he repeats, layering on that maddening charm as he tacks on the word, "temporarily."

"A temporary wife? Like a prostitute?"

"More like a business arrangement. Though I'm not exactly opposed to . . . more."

What the actual fuck?

I narrow my eyes, studying him.

And then it clicks. The real reason he's buttering me up with food, wine, and that damn scruffy charm. "So that's why you're here," I say, letting out a disappointed breath. "Another practical joke, is that it?"

I stand abruptly, my chair scraping against the floor. At which point he stands, too, towering over me and the tiny furniture like it belongs in a dollhouse.

"It's not a joke," he insists.

I glare at him. "You saw me at the restaurant, rich jerk that you are, and thought, hey, this'll be fun. Same old asshole—maybe with more muscles and swagger, but an asshole all the same."

He smiles wide. "So, you noticed my muscles and swagger?" He waggles his brows and, damn it, I didn't mean to mention that, but they're right in my face, impossible to ignore.

Argh. I push past him and move toward the door, forcing a polite smile. "Thanks for the meal, *Bri*. Time to go."

"Not until you hear me out, *Peach Pop*."

"Ugh!" I shove him aside, frustration bubbling over. "Stop calling me that."

I bolt for the door, but he's quick for an ogre, stepping in front of me and blocking my path again. "Just listen. You need a job—"

"Not that goddamned bad," I snap.

Before I can push him away, he presses a finger to my lips. The touch is electric—a slow burn searing through me, making my breath catch as his finger brushes along it just long enough to leave me aching when he finally pulls back.

His voice drops, low and raspy, the heat radiating off him in waves. "As I said, I need a wife. A billboard to the throngs of women stalking me around the clock showing that I'm off the market. And Logan wasn't bullshitting. I've been pinched, grabbed, robbed . . ." He lifts his wrist, showing me the pale line where a watch once sat.

"You poor billionaire," I retort, my tone dripping with sarcasm. "Lost another Rolex, did we? Too bad. Go cry in your pile of money."

I spin around, hand on the doorknob, fully prepared to kick him out, when his next words stop me cold. "It was a gift from Jess."

I freeze, my heart squeezing. He might be a total wad of used toilet paper, but his love for his family? It's the one thing we actually have in common and hits too close to home.

His voice grumbles in my ear, raw and laced with an emotion that pins me to the spot. "When Mom and Dad died, it was hard. On all of us. Tough on me, but roughest on Jess. Before my second deployment, she saved up everything she could to get me that watch. I've only taken it off when I had to. It's cracked across the face and keeps its own sense of time, but it means more to me than a thousand Rolexes. And now it's gone."

I turn slowly, suddenly face-to-face with him. The heat between us feels like lava below my skin, melting me from the inside out.

For a long, drawn-out moment, I just stare at him, caught

between the urge to rip him apart for everything he's done to me and the strange, unwelcome need to actually hear him out.

"Why me?" I whisper.

He swallows, drawing way too much attention to his neck. "I need someone I can trust," he says, his voice almost vulnerable. "Someone who won't see dollar signs when they look in my eyes. And considering you once rode your bike an hour and a half out of your way to return a book Angi stole, you're the first person I thought of."

"Two hours." The memory gets me thinking of Angi.

He shakes his head, frustration seeping into his voice. "There are hundreds of millions on the line. Do this, and you can name your price. Anything you want."

"Anything?" I ask, amused.

He spreads his hands, a hint of resignation in his eyes. "Feel free to screw me over six ways to Sunday."

"Oh, you'd love that," I bite back.

He shrugs, smirking. "I'll take Peach Pop any way I can get her." Then his expression shifts, more serious. "I mean, Ms. Spenser."

Our eyes lock, and everything I've kept buried rushes to the surface in a messy swirl of sharp, jagged pain. "You don't get it," I say, my voice trembling with hurt. "This isn't just about that nickname. That photo cost me everything."

"Photo?" The word rolls off his lips, slow and confused. "What photo?"

"What. Photo?" I sneer. "The one that captured me from behind, just enough skin showing to make me look naked. And my face turned just enough for everyone to know it was me. The one that went viral overnight. Ring a bell?"

The look on his face is unreadable. Then, he stammers out, "It was . . ." He hesitates, like he's trying to find the right word. "Art," he finally blurts out, and it's like a punch to the chest.

"Art?" My voice screeches, the floodgates threatening to burst. "I lost everything. Every friend I had except Taylor. And my scholarship."

His face falls as if for the first time in his life, the weight of what he's done is actually starting to sink in. Then he says what I never thought he'd ever say. "I'm sorry. I didn't know," he says quickly, almost desperately. "I deployed right after graduation."

"And since graduation, I've been hiding from life," I falter out, the sting of tears burning my eyes. "Terrified that anything I do will end up plastered for the world to see."

And then, despite everything, he reaches out. And when his hands cradle my face and his thumbs brush away every last one of my tears, I lean into it. And I hate myself for it.

"I know a little something about having my world crumble around me and crawling my way back," he says, his voice softer now, laced with an unexpected pain.

When my eyes flicker to his leg, he shakes his head, stopping me. "That's not what I mean," he adds. "I lost my parents. Mark and I nearly died. Trust me when I say I'm not the man I was. Not by a mile." He reaches out, tucking my bangs behind my ear, his fingers lingering a moment longer than they should. "I really have changed, Jules. I'm not asking for your forgiveness. But do this, and let me make it right."

For a long moment, I stand there, trying to process his words. I can't believe I actually ask it, but the words slip out before I can stop them. "How temporary?"

"A month. Two tops." He flashes a shy grin, and there's that weird quirk—a dimple that suddenly appears, like he's holding on to some kind of hope.

I sniffle. "I still hate you," I say, my voice wavering as I try to keep my composure, the cracks in my armor barely holding.

"And the more you hate me, the better this works," he replies, his tone almost too casual. "Quickie wedding, quicker divorce."

"Thirty days," I mutter, thinking it through.

"Could be sixty. Ninety tops."

I need a little power in this bizarre exchange. I stand taller and clear my throat. "You can't humiliate me. Ever. No women traipsing around if you and I are hitched. Even if it's not real."

"Agreed."

The speed of his response almost throws me. Just like that, no hesitation. So, I go for the one thing that feels impossible to ask—a silver bullet in the dark. A sliver of hope.

"Here's the thing, Brian. I need to find Angi. Like, yesterday. And it's not just for me. Colby needs this," I say, my words tumbling out faster than I can control. "Angi messed up—bad. If we don't find her, Colby's fucked." I look at him, desperation creeping into my voice. "I wouldn't ask, but Colby mentioned that the two of you served together. I know it's a big ask, but someone like you . . . you have the resources, the connections to track her down . . ."

"Hey." He steps closer, his hands finding my shoulders, steadying me. "That's family. You don't even have to ask. I'll do that no matter what your answer is, no strings attached." His fingers tilt my chin up, and I'm suddenly trapped in the depths of those darkening blue eyes, intense and unreadable beneath his thick brows.

My mind spins, trying to process his words, the wine humming through my veins, making my pulse race.

Him.

This offer.

And a marriage proposal—fake or not—means being bound, ball and chain, to the *Iron Man of Manhattan* himself.

Suddenly, I can't breathe. The air feels too thick, too heavy. When I finally manage to speak, my voice is barely a rasp. "I don't know."

His gaze drops to my mouth, and I can't help but lick my dry lips. "What do you want out of this?" His voice is soft, like a feather along my neck, down my spine. "Something just for you."

After another awkward beat where I'm definitely staring at him way too long, the stupid billionaire assignment and the *Herald* flash through my thoughts.

Why not go for it? Ask Brian for an interview. He practically rolled out a red carpet at my feet—well, at Sydney Sun's feet—handing me a shot at an exclusive. But then I'd have to explain that *I* am Sydney Sun and dive into the tangled mess of why I wrote a story that opened him up to a flood of psychos.

One of whom stole his sister's watch.

And seriously, what the hell? Did Wyld Richards know who Brian was when he handed me this story? Because it feels like I'm the only one who missed the memo.

Brian trusts me. He said so himself, and whether I like it or not, I can't carve him up for the world to see. It's just wrong.

"Well?" he prompts, snapping me out of my thoughts.

That's when I realize I've been standing here, zoned out,

staring at a small cluster of scars on his neck I never noticed before.

I dodge the tension with a smirk. "What do I want? Well, for starters, I expect you to keep me in the lifestyle I've become accustomed to."

He glances around the room, his eyes lingering on the lumpy couch and the lived-in vibe that clings to the place. "If you insist."

"And a prenup," I throw in, challenging him.

"Come again?" His smirk shifts, curiosity piqued.

"You might be a bazillionaire or whatever, but you said it yourself—there's hundreds of millions on the line. My meager pennies might not be much, but they're still mine, and I'm not about to let them sink with the Titanic."

"Fair enough."

"And no expectations of, *um*, consummation."

His full lips twitch, barely containing a grin. "I'll never force you to do anything you don't want to do." He leans in close, his voice dropping to a whisper that skims my ear. "No matter how much it tortures you, Peach Pop."

I burst out laughing. "Ha! No women for months on end? Yeah, that's got 'torture' written all over it. The infamous *Fuckboy of Bishop Mountain* going celibate? Perfect. Desert droughts for everyone."

He chuckles, the sound a deep, steady rumble that vibrates through his chest. He takes my hand, his grip firm and steady. "Deal."

Then, before I can say another word, he guides me to the center of the room, drops to one knee, his firm grip wrapped my hand.

"Juliana Grace Spenser," he begins, his voice dropping to a dangerously seductive octave, "will you do me the honor of becoming my wife? For the next thirty to sixty days? Ninety max? To hate, torment, and . . . let's say tolerate, for as long as you avoid murdering me in my sleep?"

A small smile lifts, and I don't know if it's the wine, or the fact that he actually knows my middle name, but I well up.

I blink through tears. Am I seriously contemplating doing this? Getting married? To my worst enemy?

And just then, as if on cue, Logan and Taylor burst through the door, arm in arm, giggling like school kids.

Taylor's eyes go wide as she takes in the scene. "What the fuck?"

CHAPTER 22
Brian

Shit.

Worst timing ever.

Logan's apologetic look is met with my eye roll. What's a cock block called when it's a proposal? A rock block. Well, maybe if I'd actually bothered to present her with a ring. It's the least she deserves under the circumstances.

Jules answers before I can. "Oh, nothing. Brian Bishop was just proposing."

Taylor's eyes go wide, and she gasps, both hands flying over her mouth. "And what did you say?" she demands, her voice low and urgent. Like if she doesn't know soon, her head will explode.

I trace gentle circles over my would-be fiancée's knuckles. "She's still considering it," I say, keeping my tone from sounding too annoyed. I mean, I could ask any number of women for this exact arrangement, and they'd be falling over themselves to say yes.

But it had to be Jules.

Why?

The hell if I know. But every time I pulled out my phone and scrolled through my contacts—a long list, by the way—my mind kept drifting back to the one woman who wasn't in there.

And I wasn't bullshitting earlier. When it comes to women, it's been a blur of meaningless sex and bad decisions. Ten years' worth, to be precise.

My eyes lock onto those questioning doe eyes. And for reasons I can't explain, I need this. "Come on, Ms. Spenser. Mutual benefits."

Taylor leans over to Logan and whispers, "Did he just say friends with benefits?"

Which sends my little Peach Pop into a tailspin. "Oh, my God, no. First of all, it would be *enemies* with benefits, and that's not happening. Like, ever."

Wow. Could she be any more offended at the thought of sleeping with me?

She tries to slip her hand from mine, a feeble effort at best. Then she swallows hard, her voice softening. "A business arrangement, right?" I can practically see the wheels turning behind those beautiful dark brown eyes, and I know I'm close.

"Yes, a business arrangement. One that the world believes is real and everyone in this room is sworn to secrecy on."

I turn to Taylor, giving her a pointed look.

"What? I can keep a secret," she insists, her voice a little defensive.

"Not really," I say because I'm pretty sure Taylor's been the town crier since grade school—spilling every secret from who kissed who behind the bleachers to who got caught cheating on the math test.

Which I did not appreciate, by the way.

Jules flicks a glance at Taylor, probably hoping for some backup—or hell, maybe just clarity on an answer. God, please don't let it be the latter.

If she's still the same old Taylor, she'll take an hour just to decide on pizza toppings—never mind the life-altering shit.

If Taylor's calling the shots, I'll be stuck on my knee all fucking night.

"Do what's best for you," she finally says, her words full of care. Then, with a sudden shift, she turns to me, her eyes narrowing. "But if you hurt her, I'll cram my thickest six-inch stilettos straight up your worthless ass."

Given the fact that this girl has a thing for wearing spiked-heel ankle boots, I can't help but clench a bit. "No one's getting hurt, especially not me. I'm not about to take one for the team in the bunghole."

Their laughter rolls through the room like a warm breeze, and Jules finally gives in, a smile tugging at her lips as the tension melts away. "All right, fine. Brian Gabriel Bishop, I accept you as my test drive, try-before-you-buy hubby, but only for three months, max." She tilts her head, that familiar spark gleaming in her eyes. "So, when do we kick this off?"

"As soon as possible."

"As in this weekend?" She's trying to keep it together, but the way her pulse flutters along the curve of her neck, I'd say Jules is already teetering on the edge and forty-eight hours from sobering up and backing out.

I cut through all her doubts with a single word. "Tomorrow."

CHAPTER 23
Jules

Last night was a blur of reckless decisions and impulsive promises. The, *sure, I'll marry you, Brian,* quickly followed by us plunging headfirst into wedding plans and venue hunting—a dizzying whirlwind that sends anxiety slithering up my neck like a nest of angry bees.

When ideas like Vegas and Paris are tossed around, I catch myself scratching at my neck, the reality of *till death do us part* pushing me dangerously close to the brink of an official runaway bride.

Then Brian brings up the one place we can both agree on.

Donovan's.

A haven—breathtaking, secluded, a perfect escape from the world.

No media.

No paparazzi.

Just us.

By the stroke of midnight, Brian leaves—surprisingly superstitious for a big, gruff military man. Either that, or he's afraid of turning into a pumpkin. "Eight p.m. sharp," he says, all dominant military man. "Make sure she shows up, Taylor. In a gown. I'll tackle the rest."

Then, like only the desperate or borderline delusional would, he hands Taylor his black card, with strict instructions. "Make her happy."

Taylor's eyes light up. "Can I make me happy, too?"

He sighs, giving in. "As long as you avoid anything that involves pink slips or deeds."

And from the time I wake up, it's a whirlwind, with Taylor dragging me all over town, swiping that card like it's the Olympic sport she was born to dominate. Driven around by Logan, no less.

The ladies at the bridal boutique practically roll out the red carpet the second Taylor flashes it. By the time I'm slipping into the sixth gown—after countless glasses of overflowing brut, fresh berries, and bite-sized cupcakes that are too adorable to eat, not to mention the endless selfies—I'm done.

"No matter what, the next one I try on, I'm taking," I declare, half-joking, half-serious. "Maybe I'll end up serving burgers and fries in it at Donovan's."

Taylor giggles, her eyes bright. "Remember when we thought we could serve twice as many people on roller skates?" She snorts, and I nearly collapse, a wave of uncontrollable laughter hitting me as the ridiculous image of us wobbling around with trays full of drinks and food floods back.

It's all so perfect. Too perfect. And that's when my phone starts blowing up.

First, a text from Colby.

> COLBY
>
> Is there something you want to tell me?
>
> About you.
>
> And
>
> Brian Bishop???
>
> WTF—Over???

Next, the name Eomma lights up the screen.

"Shit." My eyes go wide as I glance at Taylor. "It's my mom. What do I do?"

She shrugs. That's not exactly reassuring. "Answer."

I swallow the knot of nerves tightening in my throat and pick up. "Hello?"

"Hello? Is that all you've got to say?" Eomma's voice leaps from mildly annoyed to full-blown panic. "Juliana Grace, are you getting married today?"

"What? Where'd you hear that?" I try to keep my tone light, playing innocent, but my heart's pounding wildly, a trapped animal desperate to break free.

"It's all over Facebook. And Instagram. And don't even get me started on TikTok."

"TikTok? What?"

My eyes snap to Taylor, who's already swiping through her phone.

She flips the screen toward me, and there it is—pictures of Brian and me splashed all over social media. The hashtags #HighSchoolSweethearts and #Billionaire&Bride are spreading like California wildfire.

This is definitely not how I wanted to handle this. But

before I can even process her question through the champagne still buzzing in my veins, Dad's voice barrels through the line. "Are. You. Getting. Married? Yes or no, Juliana?"

"Um . . . Yes."

"Seriously, Juliana? You're going to marry him. The guy you've hated for years."

I want to explain, but there's a sales associate lurking in the room, and probably the one who leaked this to the world in the first place. I shoot daggers at her while Taylor hustles her out. "Dad, it's not what you think—"

"Young lady, you listen to me. I don't care how old you are or what's going through your head. You're still my little girl. Period. If my little girl is getting married, I will be walking her down that aisle. End of story. And you will not deprive me of the pleasure of threatening that Bishop boy within an inch of his life if he even thinks about breaking your heart. Am I clear?"

My response is automatic. "Yes, sir."

He exhales, the sound long and heavy, like a dam about to burst with all the parental patience he has. "When is this blessed event supposed to take place?"

"Eight tonight," I mutter, sheepish.

"Fine. We're heading there now."

"But you don't know where it is."

"The entire world knows where it is, Jules," he snaps, his voice edged with frustration. "It's at Donovan's. We just didn't know when. And before you even think about dodging this all-in family affair, your mother is bringing Korean honey cookies, and Halmeoni is picking your bouquet from the garden now."

Then the line goes dead.

I'm still breathing through the tightening in my chest when I look up, and Taylor's already dialing, her fingers moving fast.

"Who are you calling?" I ask, my voice more strained than I'd like.

"Logan."

"Is this really the time for that?"

"I think so," she says, not missing a beat. "Logan said if anything came up, he'd cover our six. Whatever that means."

True to his word, within minutes, Logan is at the door, all business, flanked by another guard who seems to have materialized out of thin air. "We'll take care of everything," he says, as the other man gathers my belongings and quickly ushers Taylor and me into a waiting SUV, with an identical one shadowing us like a ghost.

"I just need to pay for this dress," I stammer, looking back.

"I took care of it before we collected you."

He did?

We take off just as swarms of paparazzi descend like vultures on roadkill. "What a nightmare. Is this what Brian deals with all the time?" I ask, more to myself than anyone.

Logan glances back in the rearview mirror, his eyes meeting mine. "Unfortunately, yes. Since the article came out. But he'll make sure you're protected." His words cast Brian in a new light for me—*protector*. Then Logan adds, almost offhandedly, "Beautiful dress."

"Thank you," I murmur, forcing a smile up my lips, still processing it all. Brian—the guy whose only way out of this media storm is me. The same girl who threw him into the spotlight in the first place.

My phone rings, flashing an UNKNOWN CALLER ID. I'm

about to ignore it when Logan says, "I gave the boss a heads-up about the situation. That's him."

Oh.

I pick up, and Brian's voice comes through, soft and full of regret. "I'm so sorry, Jules. This isn't how I wanted things to go down. I had a plan and, hell, I don't even know what the plan was anymore. I just thought I'd have more time to get ahead of this. If you want to back out—"

"No," I cut him off, my voice firmer than I expected. "I can handle it." I have to. I caused it to begin with.

"It won't last long," he promises, steady and reassuring.

"How can you be so sure?"

"Because the media thinks we're just high school sweethearts. It's the kind of 'nothing to see here, folks' story that they'll drop in no time. Are you sure you're all right?"

"I am, but you might not be."

A pause. "What do you mean?"

"Um, my family's coming to the wedding."

"You told them?"

"No. Social media did. Pretty sure they were tipped off by the lady at the bridal shop."

He inhales sharply, then lets out a low chuckle, nerves and amusement threading through his voice. "On a scale of *all good* to *your dad is picking out headstones*, how worried should I be?"

"Considering Mom's busy making *Yakgwa*, you'll live at least long enough to eat. And in case you didn't remember, *Yakgwa* are—"

"Sweet, gingery cookies, deep-fried to perfection, then soaked in honey syrup, traditionally served at special occasions. Like weddings. And let's not forget they're one of your favorites

—heaven help anyone who tries to snag one before you do, because you're liable to bite off their hand. I remember."

"You do?" If I wasn't already sitting down, I might've swooned.

"I remember everything about you, Jules." My heart skips a beat, and yeah, I'm definitely swooning. "See you at eight."

CHAPTER 24
Jules

Stars glimmer above, like shards of glass scattered across the velvet sky I've known since childhood. The crisp scent of pine mingles with the smoky warmth of a distant bonfire, and the cool Adirondack breeze plays with the hem of my gown.

I step out of the vehicle, my feet finding familiar ground on the sprawling east side of Bishop Mountain. A strange sense of nostalgia washes over me.

I'm home.

Or, at least, the place that feels most like it when I think back to growing up—skinning my knee on dozens of trails, swimming laps in the lake, and that first, hopeful wish on a falling star. The one I've tried to forget.

That one day, Brian Bishop would fall in love with me.

In my defense, he and his pain-in-the-ass self were always around, impossible to avoid. And sure, no one's exactly tossing around the L-word. But there's something about being here that tugs on my heartstrings.

It's as if the mountain itself holds on to every wish I've ever made, whispered back and forth between the earth and the stars.

"Ready?" Taylor asks.

Not even close. "Ready."

Mrs. D. greets Taylor and me and wraps me in one of her signature warm hugs, the kind that smells like fresh-baked cookies and feels like a sweater in fall. "Look at you," she beams, her eyes crinkling with genuine joy. "I always knew you and Brian were meant to be."

Her words sink in slowly, like a stone dropping to the bottom of a pond, rippling out through me until all I feel is the weight of the lie.

The more she gushes, going on about how perfect we are for each other, the more I feel my stomach twist. It's like watching a train wreck in slow motion, and I'm the one driving.

First, I'm lying to my parents, and now to Mrs. D., a woman who's practically family. The guilt gnaws at me, each word solidifying how I'm all paid up on that timeshare in hell.

Taylor, standing beside me, gives my hand a quick squeeze, her silent support a lifeline in this inky-black sea of deception.

"Brian Bishop won't know what hit him when he sees you in that dress," Mrs. D. says, brushing a stray hair from my face. "Your family is inside, and Brian will be waiting for you in the garden with the pastor. He's the one with the tux and that goofy grin of his." She winks.

I think I'm going to be sick.

We all make our way inside, and my eyes land on Dad and his tall, steady presence in a tux. It's slightly rumpled, and just a hair snug. But it's the most dressed up I've seen him in, oh, ever.

The moment his eyes meet mine, his expression softens, and

that familiar, reassuring smile plays at the corners of his mouth. He crosses the room with purpose, his strong hands resting gently on my shoulders, grounding me in the whirlwind of emotions.

"It's not too late, kiddo," he says, his voice steady but filled with a tenderness that only he can offer. "I've got the engine running outside. We can still ditch this whole thing and head to your favorite ice cream shop." He pauses, his smile widening as he adds, "My treat." Then, he asks, "You love him?"

And here's the thing. I can't lie to my dad. I end up stammering to the point of near hyperventilation and break out in hives like no tomorrow.

"Mr. Spenser!" Taylor wraps him in a big hug. "It's so great to see you. Where's Mrs. Spenser and Halmeoni?" she ask, her voice steady.

He chuckles softly. "Outside. My wife's bawling her eyes out on Brian's shoulder like it's the stampede scene of *The Lion King*, and Halmeoni's busy picking flowers from the garden—something about bringing two gardens together for luck."

"I'd better go find them."

I move to walk off when a big, familiar hand hooks my arm. "You didn't answer my question, young lady." Dad narrows his eyes, a living, breathing parental lie detector. "Do you love him?"

I take a breath. "Dad, only nut jobs and pathetically hopeless romantics marry when they're not in love."

Then Taylor adds, "He handed me his credit card and insisted I use it to make Jules happy. If that's not a testament of love, I don't know what is."

My dad wrinkles his brow, a teasing glint in his eyes. "Could be love. Could be lunacy."

I can't help but giggle as he leans in closer, his voice dropping to a conspiratorial whisper. "By the way, the ice cream shop just got in your favorite—Peach Cobbler Crunch."

"Rain check, I promise." Before I know it, he's pulling me into one of his big, comforting hugs, pressing a kiss to the top of my head.

Just then, Mom and Halmeoni appear, wrapping their arms around us, turning the hug into a full family embrace.

Dad hands Mom a handkerchief to avoid drenching my gown, and Halmeoni, beaming with pride, presents me with an enormous bouquet of flowers that smell like home.

It's a masterpiece—a few soft peonies in blush pink and cream nestled alongside delicate sprigs of Queen Anne's lace and lavender. Each flower carefully plucked from the gardens back home. The greens of eucalyptus and ivy, gathered from the base of Bishop's Mountain, weave in and out, binding the bouquet together like a thread of memories with roots that run deep.

I choke up. I know she spent hours making it and it's the most beautiful gift I've ever seen.

"*Uri gajok-ui sarangi yeogi itda,*" Halmeoni says. Translation: *Our family's love is here*.

We step outside, greeted by the gentle strains of a harp mingling with the soft hum of a small string quartet. Fairy lights twinkle around the old oak trees, casting a soft, golden glow over the gathering.

When we step into the garden, there he is—Brian. He's in the middle of a lively conversation with Colby, probably catching up on their time serving together. Brian's animated, gesturing as he talks, his face lighting up with that easygoing charm that's always been second nature to him.

The sight of him in that classic tux, all sharp lines and effortless allure, makes him look like he's just stepped out of *The Great Gatsby*.

He's always had that timeless, magnetic charm, the kind that feels like it's woven into his very DNA, effortlessly drawing anyone in. But I have to remind myself—just like in Fitzgerald's tragedy—this isn't some grand romance.

Letting myself get caught up in the moment, in him, will only end in more pain, more heartache. Haven't I been hurt enough by him?

It's a business arrangement, Jules.

Nothing more.

But damn, why does he have to look so good?

The tux fits him like a second skin, molding to his broad shoulders and tapering effortlessly down to his trim waist. Every inch of him radiates that cool, measured restraint, like he's never ruffled, always in control.

His wavy hair, tousled to just-fucked perfection pairs seamlessly with a steady, unyielding stance that radiates military dominance. He commands attention without even trying. A control freak to the end.

And no matter how many times I've looked at him—tried to ignore him, forget him, or outright hate Brian Bishop—the truth is always staring me in the face.

He's under my skin so deep that not even an exorcism could get him out.

Then he turns, and our eyes meet.

There's something in his expression that makes me stop cold. It's not the cocky, self-assured grin I'm used to, the one that says he's always got the upper hand.

No, this look is different.

There's a flicker of something else—something raw and unguarded.

For the first time, there's uncertainty in his eyes, a flicker of doubt that makes my pulse race. Is he reconsidering this whole thing?

Am I?

But before the thought can take root, the music shifts, and the opening notes of "Here Comes the Bride" fill the air, snapping me back to the whole reason we're here. With my family.

Dad appears at my side, his presence solid and reassuring, and my hand slides naturally into the crook of his arm. "Showtime, kiddo," he murmurs, a soft smile playing on his lips.

Showtime. Right.

I let out a long breath as we take those slow, deliberate steps down the aisle. Part of me is still half-expecting this to turn into some god-awful prank, but I kick that thought under the rug and focus on the rhythm of our steps, the steady grip of my father's arm, and not tripping in these insane heels Taylor picked out that were not meant for grass.

The pastor waits until the strings fade away to begin. "Who gives this woman to be married?" And for a split second, time seems to freeze.

"No one does," Dad says, his voice firm, almost defiant. My heart skips a beat, mortification clawing at my throat as I brace for impact, and just before my mother has an outright heart attack, Dad adds, "Instead, we take Brian Bishop into our fold."

That's my dad—always giving tradition the middle finger.

Brian steps forward, extending his hand. "I'm honored, sir." My dad takes it without hesitation, their handshake firm, a silent agreement passing between them.

As Dad turns to me, tears glisten in his eyes. He kisses both my cheeks with a tenderness that catches me off guard, a lump forming in my throat.

He places my hand in Brian's, his grip lingering just a moment longer, as if he's trying to say everything he can't put into words. Then, with a final nod, he steps back and returns to his seat.

"Hey," Brian says, his voice low and steady, almost reverent.

"Hey," I manage to reply, my voice trembling despite my best efforts to keep it together.

Before I can gather my thoughts, Brian says, "Before we begin, I have a small surprise."

If it's Peach Pops, he is so dead.

Brian gestures subtly, and suddenly, the fairy lights are extinguished. Every candle is blown out except for the few surrounding us. The garden plunges into darkness, leaving nothing but the mountains, the starlit sky, and a single candle burning beside us.

Then, as if on cue, fireflies begin to dance around us, their tiny lights flickering in the night, casting a magical glow that feels almost otherworldly.

I feel tears prickling at the corners of my eyes. Because we both know this is just an act, right?

I lean in closer, my voice a soft whisper meant only for him. "Why are you doing all this?"

His answer is quiet, but it takes my breath away. "Because

I'll never marry anyone else, Jules. I want it to be memorable. For both of us."

And under that endless night sky, surrounded by the gentle flicker of fireflies, we say our vows.

I become his wife.

To have and to hold.

In sickness and in health.

"To love and to cherish, for as long as we both shall live." He speaks the words with such reverence, such sincerity, that for a moment, I want to believe it.

But deep down, I know it's a lie.

It's all a lie.

Isn't it?

Colby hands over the rings. Brian's is a stately white gold band, understated and timeless, sliding onto his finger like it was made for him. It probably was.

But mine—mine steals the air from my lungs. A stunning solitaire, haloed in a delicate ring of diamonds, that catches the light and glimmers with every movement. It's not just perfect; it's so me it actually scares me.

"You may now kiss the bride."

He must catch the flicker of doubt in my eyes because he cups my face in his hands, his grip firm yet achingly gentle. "Kiss me, Jules," he murmurs, his voice low and electric, more command than request. I don't hesitate—I can't.

The moment his lips touch mine, soft and tender at first, a shiver races down my spine, igniting an inferno of emotion and heat. His arms wrap around me, pulling me in so tight that something inside me finally snaps.

I let myself go, kissing him back, exploring. A slow burn of tongues colliding, the rough scrape of his stubble against my skin, and the rhythm of his heartbeat pounding against mine.

The sound of applause cuts through the haze, and with one last taste, we pull apart.

His forehead rests against mine, his lips brushing mine with a possessive growl. "Torture," he breathes.

Holy fuck, am I in trouble.

CHAPTER 25

Jules

By the end of the evening, we hit that inevitable, awkward moment where the last guest has departed, leaving us with nothing but leftover cake and those "now what" expressions hanging between us.

"Logan can take Taylor home, make sure she's safe," Brian says, as if he's worked out a plan. "But I don't want you going back there, Jules. The Mach 5 media shitstorm means there's no way you can slip back there unnoticed, not with the vultures circling."

I think for a minute. Staying with my parents would completely defeat the purpose of the evening—dodging the inevitable questions leading up to a full-blown inquisition.

Brian runs a hand across the scruff on his jaw. "I have something in mind."

∽

THE ELEVATOR DINGS, AND THE DOORS OPEN.

"I have four rooms," Brian says, his voice casual. "You're welcome to any of them. All of them have toiletries, and I have some spare clothes from Jess. Pajamas. Robes. Anything you need."

"Thanks." I nod as we make our way through the penthouse.

"I'll make sure you have everything you need, Jules, to make your stay comfortable," he says, his voice a bit too tight, like the words don't quite fit. Then, with a hint of something almost like regret, he adds, "It's only temporary."

Just like me. *I'm* temporary.

The place is breathtaking, with floor-to-ceiling windows offering a panoramic view of Manhattan, the city lights twinkling like scattered diamonds below.

The upscale finishes are sleek and modern, with marble countertops, polished hardwood floors, and artful touches that speak to a life well-lived. Everything about it screams luxury, but in a way that feels lived-in, not staged, with black-and-white photos of family and friends everywhere.

Each room is a sanctuary of its own, complete with a private bathroom and a walk-in closet that could rival a boutique.

As I wander through one of the rooms, my eye catches on a book resting on a chair. I pick it up, curiosity piqued. "*Pinkalicious*?" I ask, glancing back at Brian.

He leans casually against the doorframe, a hint of a smile playing on his lips. "Yeah, that friend of mine with the three adorable kids you met . . ."

"The one who did a serious number on Roxana's purse?" I interject with a smirk.

He chuckles, nodding. "That's the one. They stayed here

for a bit while he was building a new home for them. It's not far from Donovan's, actually." He shrugs. "They're probably the closest I'll come to having kids around, so I soak up the time with them whenever I can."

He must catch the curiosity on my face because he adds, almost as an afterthought, "Eternal bachelor."

He's quick to steer the conversation away, leading me to another room that's more gym than guest suite. It's impressive: weights, a rowing machine, top-of-the-line equipment. But what really grabs my attention is the set of parallel bars and the other specialized gear.

"What's this?" I ask, pointing to the setup.

"Physical therapy," he says, his tone easy, like it's no big deal. "Three days a week. You'll probably see Cameron in and out of here."

My gaze shifts to a table tucked in the corner. "And that?"

He follows my gaze, then looks back at me. "That's a massage table."

I bite back the flood of questions suddenly swirling in my mind—like, who is Cameron? Is she attractive? Have you dated? Fucked?

Stop it.

"Massages?" I muse out loud before I can snap my big mouth shut.

He nods, a touch more reserved than usual. "I get the occasional massage when the knots in my leg tighten up to the point of pain."

"Pain?" In this moment, I hurt for him. God, I'm an insensitive idiot. "You've been on your feet all day. Are you in pain now?"

"I'll manage," he says with a reassuring smile, pocketing his hands with quiet resilience. "I'll get out of my getup once you're settled."

"I'll take whatever room is easiest," I offer.

"No, Jules. You'll take what you want. The way it should be." There's a flicker of something in his eyes—warmth, maybe a hint of something deeper—and holy hell, it's *combustible*.

Then he shakes it off, gesturing with a sweep of his arm. "Come on, I'll show you the rest."

We reach his room last, and I hesitate at the threshold, awkwardness cementing my feet to the floor. He notices, turning back with a teasing grin. "What are you, a vampire? Need permission to enter?"

"Try to wake me at the crack of dawn, and my fangs will definitely come out," I shoot back, trying to keep it light.

In one swift move, he grabs my hand and pulls me into the room, forcing me to get comfortable with the space. It's as if somehow, his presence alone can keep the tension at bay.

The moment I step inside, I notice the small retrofits— discreet bars along the bed, a bench near the shower. Everything is carefully placed, designed for function rather than form. Brian catches my gaze and speaks up, his voice steady. "If you have any questions, you can ask me, Jules."

"Is it uncomfortable?" I ask, motioning to his leg. "Being on it this long?"

He blows out a breath, the kind that carries more weight than he lets on. "Honestly, it's more aggravated than usual. Nothing a little ice and rest won't cure."

"I can help," I offer. "Ice is in the kitchen, right? I definitely remember the kitchen during the tour—two side-by-side built-in refrigerators and an oven big enough for the witch from *Hansel and Gretel*."

Before I can make a full-on sprint down the hall, he steps in front of me, blocking my path with an easy confidence. As he loosens his tie, it draws way too much attention to the strong line of his neck. "Relax, Peach Pop. I've got it."

He unbuttons two buttons of his shirt, revealing just enough to make my pulse quicken. And, of course, now I'm staring.

I blink, trying to snap myself out of it, reminding myself that straight-up gawking is rude, even if, on paper, this man is my husband.

"Okay," I say, glancing at the layout—the guest rooms in relation to his. My feet take me back into the hall, my mind made up before I can second-guess it. "I'll take this one," I say, choosing the room closest to his. Because, I don't know, I just want to be a little closer.

"Nice choice. Gorgeous evening views and minimal morning sun," he says, then makes a goofy vampire face, hissing playfully. Just when I think he's done, he leans in and, out of nowhere, pecks me on the lips—a quick, soft brush that catches me completely off guard.

"Goodnight, Peach Pop," he murmurs with a grin, leaving me standing there, heart racing, high and dry as the Sahara.

For twenty minute, I try—and fail—to unbutton this damned dress past the fifth button. At one point, I probably looked like a cartoon cat chasing its own tail. *Argh*.

Which means I'm stuck with exactly three options: sleep in it, rip it to absolute shreds, which would be a tragedy because this dress is too stunning to take scissors to, or swallow my pride and ask Brian for help.

I knock softly on the door, and after a brief pause, his voice comes through. "Come in."

I push open the door to his room and immediately freeze. Brian's lounging on the bed, wearing nothing but a pair of pajama bottoms, his hair still damp from the shower, glistening under the low light.

He's sprawled out in all his lickable glory, and for a second, I'm stunned silent, my mind going completely blank.

He notices me standing there, probably looking like I've forgotten how to function. "Everything all right?" he asks, his voice casual, but there's a hint of amusement in his eyes.

"So, so fine."

Quirking an expectant eyebrow, he waits. For me. To speak. Must use voice. "Oh, right. I need help getting out of my dress."

"Have you tried scissors?" he teases, a smirk playing on his lips.

"Funny," I shoot back, rolling my eyes.

He pats the bed beside him, and it's only then that I notice his prosthetic leg resting nearby, detached. My heart gives a little squeeze.

"Does it bother you?" he asks, reading the brief flicker of emotion on my face.

"What? No," I say quickly. "Grandpa Spenser had one, too, below the knee, just like you. For medical reasons."

"I forgot about that." His smile lifts a little as he scoots over, making room on the bed and patting the spot beside him. "Come here."

I rush to take a seat beside him, feeling the mattress dip as he shifts his weight. "Hang on," he says, and I hear the grin in his voice. "My hunting knife is in the top drawer."

"Use it and the next thing it's used on is your favorite vintage tee," I snap back.

"Feisty." He chuckles, but it fades as he reaches out, trailing a finger along the back of my neck, moving aside the last strands of hair.

His touch sends a shiver down my spine, making my breath catch.

Slowly, he begins unbuttoning the long line of tiny buttons, his fingers skimming my skin with each one. The dress loosens, inch by inch, until it nearly slips off.

"Thanks," I whisper.

"You're welcome." Hot breath flames across my shoulders and down my neck.

This is the point where I should be leaving. Standing up. Walking out the door. But I don't.

His touch, his caress, lingers on my bare skin, sending warmth spreading through me, settling low in my belly. It feels so, so good.

I turn to face him, ready to make my exit, but the moment our eyes lock, everything changes. Before I can process what's happening, he pulls me into a kiss. And it's not just any kiss—it's an *everything* kiss.

Deep. Breathy. Erotic.

When his tongue sweeps through my parted lips, it sends a shockwave straight to my core.

The kiss is so slow and desperate, it knocks all the air from my lungs.

One large hand grips my waist, pulling me flush against him, while the other tangles in my hair, his dominance drawing a soft whimper from deep within my throat.

But then his hand skims my thigh, and reality crashes all around. His words from earlier slam into me like a bat to the chest. *"It's only temporary."*

"Wait!"

The second the word slips from my lips, everything freezes. His hands fall away, releasing their hold, and I struggle to catch my breath against the rhythm of his hard, labored breathing. Our eyes lock—his ocean blue, clouded with something I can't quite decipher. "What is it?" he asks, his voice rough around the edges.

"This is all wrong. You. Me." I push myself to my feet, my heart beating wildly—a bird trapped in my chest, desperate to escape. He reaches out, but instinctively I back away, putting distance between us. "I hate you, remember?"

He swallows hard, his head dropping against the headboard in defeat. That enormous dick of his is still straining against his pants, ready to bulldoze its way through. "Yeah, I remember," he grumbles, sounding like a frustrated kid. "Just . . . don't go. I won't do anything. But I don't want you leaving. Not like this."

Like what?

Wound up tighter than a drum, ready to explode, because the thought of me riding the rough stubble of your mouth hasn't crossed my mind even once.

Not at all.

I catch my breath. "Sooner or later, I have to go." I remind him. "Temporary, remember?" He reaches out for me again, and I break for the door, rushing from the room.

"Torture," he hollers after me, and damn it, he's right.

This is torture.

My body's lit up like a Christmas tree, every nerve buzzing, and all I can think about is him.

CHAPTER 26
Brian

Are you trying to kill me?

I reread the text from Parker Adams, our head of PR.

For the record, I do not need this.

It's been a week since Jules moved in, and she's been avoiding me like roller food at a gas station. But, fuck me, she's so close that no matter where I go or what I do, I can't escape her.

Her light giggles hit me when I least expect it, and that scent —like peach blossoms and home with just a hint of citrus— follows her damn near everywhere she goes, lingering in every room she leaves just enough to taunt me.

And then there's the constant *click-click-click* of her fingers on a keyboard, a relentless drumbeat she's never without because she is always, *always* working on something. I swear, the way things are going, that laptop will get more hand action from her than I ever will.

But here's the thing—that doesn't actually bother me.

Jules has been chasing the dream of being a writer since eighth grade, starting with a blog about indie musicians and obscure bands she discovered before anyone else.

By fourteen, she'd scraped together enough money to swap pen and paper for a keyboard and never looked back.

And deep down, I know nothing makes her happier than pouring every last word onto the screen. It's her obsession, her escape. Her passion.

So, I don't complain. Not about any of it. But damn, every reminder of her—whether it's the way she bites her lip while she types or her perpetual fascination with my vintage running tees, which I know she's been stealing from the dryer to sleep in—the woman has me taking cold showers three times a day just to keep myself in check.

The truth? If I have her this close for much longer, every last ounce of my restraint and self-control will snap.

I step into my office. Instantly, Parker repeats her text, out loud. "Are you trying to kill me?"

I point a finger at her. "Attempted murder is a serious accusation, Parker."

She crosses her arms, utterly unimpressed. Parker's been with the company for years—a no-nonsense ball buster who takes no prisoners, ever. Her entire PR team is already gathered around my conference table, their faces drawn tight with stress.

I brace myself, expecting her to start with, *"You got married?"*

But instead, she flips open a stack of papers, revealing a tabloid with my face splashed across the front page.

The headline makes my head explode.

Brian Bishop:
Playboy Billionaire or Corporate Saboteur?

What the fuck?

Below it, there are pictures of me with Roxana Voss, looking way too cozy for comfort. It was taken at the restaurant, probably by a patron or one of the staff. The article insinuates everything from a love triangle to corporate espionage.

All I can think is thank God, none of the kids are in the shot. Harrison would have my balls hanging by a tight thread.

"This is bullshit," I growl, feeling my temper rise. "We're going to sue Roxie Voss and her entire company."

Parker's eyes flash with controlled fury. "There's just one problem. Ms. Voss didn't write this."

"What?" I flip to the byline, my stomach dropping when I see the name: Sydney Sun. Next to it, that damn vixen image that's practically seared into my brain.

First, she hero-worships me. Now, she vilifies me.

My blood simmers, rage bubbling just beneath the surface, ready to erupt. Because I've officially crossed the line from wanting to kiss her to wanting to crush her.

She could've said anything about me—call me a womanizer with a few depraved tastes, label me a commitment-phobe with a wicked one-hit-wonder streak.

Fine.

Whatever.

All's fair in love and war.

But this isn't just about me. It's about Mark's company. A family legacy I won't let her destroy.

"This ends now," I say, my voice cold and final. "I don't care how you do it, Parker. Just take care of it. Whatever it takes."

She holds my gaze, her expression hardening. "You're sure about that?"

I hesitate for a split second. "Yes." I handed Sydney an exclusive, and she used it to stab me in the back. So, fine—no more Mr. Exclusive. Our attorneys can start handing out lawsuits like fun-sized Snickers on Halloween.

But then I remember how much press our lawsuits usually attract and pull back. "No. Not whatever it takes. Just quiet it down."

I'll take care of Sydney Sun myself.

Parker nods, her jaw set with determination. "All right. We'll handle it. But just so you know, we're already putting out fires left and right," she continues, her tone edged with frustration. "Every day is a whole new frontier of damage control, so please, tell me you won't be adding more lighter fluid to the fire."

I blow out a breath, knowing what's coming. "I did happen to get married last week."

Her eyes widen, and I casually wiggle my ring finger. An annoyed smirk tugs at her lips.

"What?" I ask, feigning innocence.

"Nothing. Just that you didn't say a word." She pats my belly. "Does someone have a bun in the oven?"

I wish. "Definitely not."

"And that would've been useful information to help us get your legions of adoring fans off your back. Which coming from the guy who overshares every one-night stand, is weird."

She's right. It is weird.

The whole point of this sham marriage was to control the narrative, to mold the story exactly how we need it, and hit send. Publish it to the World Wide Web and beyond.

But instead of sticking to the plan, I buried it, locked it away.

Why?

Maybe it's because I know how much Jules despises the spotlight, mostly because of me. And yet, I'm about to throw her straight into the center of it. It's twisted—being both her villain and her husband.

But here's the thing: no matter which role I'm playing, protecting her is non-negotiable. Anything less is not an option.

"We'll get a press announcement out the door," I say, already feeling the weight of the decision.

The phone rings, and I switch it to speaker. "What?" I snap, irritation seeping through my bones. The last thing I need today is more shit on my plate.

"Do you accept a collect call from Fiji?"

I blink, momentarily thrown as Parker and the team start to leave.

"Yes," I answer, a grin tugging at the corners of my lips, brightening my mood instantly. "A collect call? From Fiji? Didn't know that was still a thing," I mutter.

"It is when Mark and I decide to go all 'unplugged' for our honeymoon." Jess's voice cuts in with that signature snark she's honed over the years. "We had to have someone translate the headline with your picture. Even half a world away, my 'keeping it low-key' brother is making headlines."

"And he got married," Parker blurts out, her voice echoing

through the room. I shoot her a warning glare, and she quickly ducks out, shutting the door behind her.

Chuckling with a groan, I rub a hand over my face, trying to muster the energy to deal with my baby sister going full throttle on me. "Good morning to you, too, Jess. Or is it evening?"

"Don't you 'good morning/evening' me," she snaps. "Do you have any idea how maddening it is to be lounging on a beach in Fiji, trying to unwind, only to see your cheesy grin splashed across every headline? And I'm too far away to flick your forehead or squeeze you in a bear hug?" She takes a breath. "And you're married?"

"Sort of." I don't bother mentioning it's temporary. Jules sucked it up with her family, so I'll do the same with mine.

I can practically hear the eye roll in her voice. "Right. 'Sort of.'"

Mark jumps in, "Like 'I sort of just put in the tip?'"

Jess adds, "Or 'we're sort of pregnant'? Wait, are you pregnant?" There's a strange excitement in her voice.

"Men don't get pregnant," I remind her, but she lets the question hang in the air.

The silence stretches, and something hollow expands in my chest until it deflates like a slow leak. "No," I finally say. Why I have to hide the slight shadow of disappointment is beyond me, but I do.

She lightens the mood with a quick shift. "And, by the way, I already knew you were hitched."

"How?"

"Mrs. D. finally got a hold of us this morning. Apparently, she's been leaving a ton of voicemails and emails on Instagram, not realizing that not only are we without our devices, but we never check our Insta messages anyway. It's usually full of Insta-stalkers making obscene offers to get with Mark." She sighs. "She said the wedding was beautiful. Just the Spensers and close friends."

"I'd intended for it to just be us, but then her parents caught wind," I admit, feeling a slight pang of guilt because I know Jess is hurt. "It was an impulse," I say honestly. "Hurting you was the last thing I wanted."

"Jess will be fine," Mark cuts in. "You may have had a wedding, but I've already gotten an earful about her plans for a mammoth reception, so start thinking of the guest list now."

If the marriage lasts that long. "Absolutely."

"Wait," Mark's voice cuts in. "The Spensers? There are two Spenser sisters, right?"

"Yup."

"And are you going to tell us which one? Or keep us in the dark?" Jess asks, and I can hear the curiosity practically eating her alive.

"Somehow, keeping you in suspense feels like Christmas morning."

She huffs. "Fine, at least give me a hint. Didn't one of them absolutely hate your guts?" Jess presses, a playful yet accusatory quality to her tone.

"Still does, pretty much. Guess my warm and fuzzy side did the trick."

Mark laughs, loud and booming. "Please, for the love of everything holy, spare me any mental images of your warm and fuzzy side. But you dated Angelina, right?"

A fact I wish people would let die. "No comment."

"And the other one is Juliana, right?" Jess asks. "Close to a year apart, but all three of you in the same grade?"

"Yes. And she goes by Jules," I correct, a little too quickly.

"And don't forget the third woman in his life," Mark adds.

Huh? "What third woman?"

They both laugh, and I can practically see Mark's grin stretching ear to ear. "One Miss Sydney Sun, the writer of that article we had translated. So, who the hell is she, and what exactly did you do to land yourself on her bad side?"

Question of the fucking day.

CHAPTER 27
Jules

The coffee shop is my refuge, the one place where I can fade into the background, sip my Americano, and watch the world spin without me. With the dark glasses Taylor gave me and baseball cap in place, I slide into my usual corner booth, the one with the worn leather seat and the perfect view of the city streets.

The barista doesn't even need to ask—being a regular has its perks—and soon enough, a steaming cup of coffee lands in front of me.

I take a sip, letting the warmth seep into my bones, and pull out my laptop.

Lately, writing about the secret lives of billionaires has felt like pushing a three-hundred-pound boulder uphill. Creativity is a temperamental diva, and my heart's just not in it.

Instead, I'm borderline obsessed with a new piece that has latched onto my brain and refuses to let go. *Everyday Heroes Among Us*, though I'm tempted to rename it *Secret Lives of the Guys Next Door*.

Just as I'm finally slipping into the zone, my Instagram messenger blows up like a pinball machine on overdrive.

What the hell?

I open my @SydneySun account, and my heart slams to a dead stop. Notifications are flooding in—tags, likes, shares—because, somehow, my story just went viral.

Brian Bishop:
Playboy Billionaire or Corporate Saboteur?

The problem is, I didn't write it.

I didn't write anything remotely close to it.

Whoever did not only hacked into my account and made me look like a total ass but also has the grammar skills of a middle school dropout. And the spelling? Don't even get me started. Seriously, who the hell spells "believe" without the 'i'?

A new message pops up. *Huh?* Who would be messaging me?

I tap it open, and there it is. The handle that feels like drumsticks on my heart.

@MountainBoyNYC

Brian Bishop.

Former jerkface.

Current husband.

The guy who makes gray sweatpants look like pure athletic porn.

His message is simple, direct, and dripping with that annoying trademark confidence.

@MountainBoyNYC: We need to talk.

I can almost hear his voice, smooth and commanding, the kind that gets under your skin whether you like it or not.

My heart does that stupid little flutter it always does around him, and I have to remind myself to stay calm. This is Brian Bishop we're talking about. No way am I letting him get the upper hand or know who I am.

My fingers fly across the keyboard.

@SydneySun: I'm super busy right now. How about next week?

Or, as Sydney Sun, how about never?
The reply comes back almost instantly, like he was waiting for it.

@MountainBoyNYC: If you wanted to know more about me, all you had to do was ask.

@MountainBoyNYC: When. Can. We. Meet?

My fingers hover over the keys, my mind spinning. If I tell him I didn't write the story, he'll think I'm full of it.

But admitting I did?

Not happening. One, it's a total lie, and two, the story is an affront to everything I stand for—personally, professionally, and grammatically.

@SydneySun: Sorry, super busy. Totally swamped, actually. Maybe next week?

@MountainBoyNYC: Busy? With what? Deciding on your next victim to slay? Or choosing which emoji to use in your next tweet? You know, for a writer, your punctuation is, um, let's call it flamboyant.

I didn't write that! But I can't exactly confess that to him, now, can I?

@SydneySun: I prefer the terms fun and frolicsome.

@MountainBoyNYC: I prefer the term schizophrenic and desperate for a dictionary. And since you're basking in the glory of your viral article, I'm sure you've got a few minutes to spare. Tell me where you are, and I'll stop playing hard to get.

Him playing hard to get? Yeah, right.

@SydneySun: Playing hard to get? Please. You chase women harder than a kid after an ice cream truck.

@MountainBoyNYC: At least I'm honest about it. You're in way over your head.

@MountainBoyNYC: Do not make me come after you, guns blazing.

@SydneySun: If your gun's blazing, maybe a doctor can help. A nice round of antibiotics should do the trick.

@MountainBoyNYC: So, you don't want to meet with me. What's the matter? Scared?

My heart stutters, and a rush of irritation follows. It's the same damn line he's been using since I've known him. And for me, it always manages to push the right button that sends me from zero to furious with something to prove.

It's how he got me into the lake to swim for the first time. Trying to skateboard down the biggest hill in town. Tasting *uni*, a Japanese sea urchin delicacy which, for the record, isn't bad, just not for me.

I narrow my eyes and type out a response, my fingers flying over the keys.

@SydneySun: Of you? Hardly. Of contracting a mystery rash from sitting on the same park bench as you? Definitely.

@MountainBoyNYC: Good. So, it's settled. We're meeting.

Wait. What?
No, we're not meeting. We are *not. Meeting*.

@MountainBoyNYC: Where and when?

I need to shut this down. It feels wrong, deceiving him like this. He might be my worst enemy, but he's still my husband, after all.

So, I do what any cornered spouse would do.

I hide.

@SydneySun: Meet me at the Statue of Liberty.

@SydneySun: Tomorrow. Noon.

@SydneySun: And bring lunch.

I only add that because, as much as I want to send him on a wild goose chase, I'm not heartless enough to let him do it on an empty stomach. The man barely eats right as it is.

His response is instant.

@MountainBoyNYC: I'm more in the mood for coffee. How about *The Grind House*? Ten minutes.

My pulse quickens as my eyes flick up, and there it is—the sign of *The Grind House* staring back at me.

How did he know I was here?

As if reading my thoughts, another message buzzes in.

@MountainBoyNYC: While you've been chatting with me, I've been homing in on your location.

@MountainBoyNYC: You really should turn that off. Security risk and all.

@MountainBoyNYC: See you in 10 minutes, and I'll take a—oh, wait, you already know exactly how I take my coffee. Make it that. On ice.

@MountainBoyNYC: PS: Don't even think of leaving. I will chase you down like a kid after an ice cream truck. And eat you alive.

Instantly, a million filthy images of him flood my mind—his face buried between my thighs, devouring me like I'm a melting creamsicle on a hot summer day.

God, I'm so screwed.

CHAPTER 28

Jules

I rush through my backpack, using everything at my disposal to look as least like myself as possible.

Dark glasses?

Check.

Hair in a high ponytail and baseball cap pulled low?

Check.

Dark red lipstick that Taylor keeps slipping into my purse?

Yeah, okay, fine. *Check.*

I find a new seat in the darkest back corner, the one farthest from the entrance, and try to steady my nerves.

With five minutes to go, my fingers drum on the table as I debate whether or not to order his drink. I mean, it's pretty presumptuous of him to have me order a drink for him. Arrogance personified.

But this is Brian, and the man acts like food is optional. I know he needs to eat. He knows he needs to eat. Screw it. I order it anyway, throwing in some extra protein for good measure and a turkey gouda croissan'wich because, damn it, the man needs looking after.

The door chimes, and in he walks—the living, breathing definition of suit porn.

His tailored jacket is loose and unbuttoned, the crisp white shirt beneath hints at the rippling muscles I know all too well. The silk tie he asked me to select this morning is perfectly knotted at his throat and somehow manages to deepen the sharp blue of his eyes that scan the room before locking onto me.

He's lethal in every way, owning every step, every move.

He spots me, and a slow, devastating grin spreads across his face. The closer he steps, the harder my heart slams against my ribcage.

His gaze sweeps over me from head to toe, analyzing me. Like any second now, he'll zero in on who's hiding beneath the disguise. Then, with deliberate slowness, he sits and straightens his tie.

"You got me lunch?" He sounds confused.

"I thought it was the least I could do."

I open my mouth to speak, to apologize, to explain this whole mess. Hell, maybe even tell the truth. But before I can get a word out, he raises a hand, gently cutting me off.

"Let me cut to the chase, Ms. Sun."

"Okay."

"I'm not sure why you wrote that article, but here's the bottom line. I don't care what you say about me or what fresh hell it brings into my life. Just leave my family and my company out of it." His ocean-blue eyes lock onto mine, a flicker of something deeper behind them. "Please."

"I can do that," I manage to whisper.

He takes a sip of his drink, a tired half smile tugging at his lips. "The thing is, I have a wife. She's been screwed over, and she deserves to be happy. And I won't be the one to fuck that up. So, I'll do whatever you want. An exclusive, a photo shoot. You name it. Just give me three months before you tear me apart."

I'm stunned silent as he tears into his sandwich, devouring it in just a few bites. And everything he's just said hits me. He's willing to sacrifice his own privacy for me?

My chest tightens, and before I know it, tears are welling up. I sniffle to hold it in. Which he notices, pausing mid-bite to hand me a napkin. "Are you all right?"

"Allergies," I lie, choking back the emotion. This is too much. I need to tell him the truth—at least that the article wasn't mine.

Just as I'm about to speak, his phone pings. "Shit. I have to go." He stands, holding out his hand. "Truce?"

I nod, swallowing hard. "Truce."

The moment my hand touches his, something ignites between us—static, electric, like a rush of champagne bubbling through my veins.

His grip is firm, commanding, and when his thumb brushes over my skin, goose bumps scatter up my arm. "I'd love to speak with you again, Sydney Sun," he murmurs, his voice low, almost intimate.

Without thinking, I say, "I'd like that, too."

He walks out, and all I can mutter is, "I'd like that too?" My head falls to my hands. Why the fuck did I say that?

I tear down the hallway, each step a thunderclap of fury.

"Everything okay?" Anabelle's voice floats my way, all concern and wide eyes.

"Peachy," I bite out, knuckles white from the death grip on my own rage.

Scoop hustles beside me, his steps quickening to match mine. "Hey, kid. I don't know what's gotten into you, but barging in on Mr. Richards right now? Not the best idea."

"Oh, I'm definitely barging in."

"You'll get fired."

"I'll take my chances."

Felix darts in front of me next, throwing up a hand. "Trust me, girl. Some things can't be unseen."

Huh?

I shoulder past him without so much as a second thought, and I don't knock. I just burst through the door, full force, ready to lay down the law.

And then, like a car slamming into a brick wall, I come to a dead stop.

Roxana Voss is sprawled on the desk, wrapped in a trench coat that barely conceals what I'm certain is nothing but skin underneath.

And Wyld Richards? He's buried in her chest like a dog sniffing for a treat.

Ugh. Thank God I skipped that croissant at the coffee shop, or I'd be decorating the floor with it.

Hastily, he straightens his tie, and helps her to sit. "Ms. Voss and I were just, uh, discussing your article."

Horrified, I shake my head. The idea that any article of mine is their kink is just wrong. "Actually, that article is what I came in here to discuss."

Roxana's eyes narrow, her lips curling into a smirk. "You mean barged in." Her gaze sweeps over me like I'm some lower life form she hasn't yet classified. "You're that waitress from Salvatore's, aren't you?"

Ex-waitress, thanks to you.

I ignore her and turn all my attention to Mr. Richards. "Can we talk? Privately?"

He leans back in his chair, the picture of nonchalance, despite his belt hanging loose. "Whatever you've got to say to me, you can say in front of Ms. Voss."

His hand curls possessively around her waist, and it's clear that their on-again, off-again romance is on again, like a bandage slapped over a festering wound.

"Fine. The article you published under my name."

"You mean under Sydney Sun's name," he adds.

Yes. Me. Sydney Sun.

I'm not exactly sure what he means by that, so I keep trudging forth. "That article's riddled with errors, bad grammar, and straight-up lies. I think my account was hacked, and someone used it to pass off their crappy works as mine."

How it even made it past editing and into print is beyond me, but I'm not here to nitpick his job. All I want is for it to be retracted so I can move on.

Roxana stiffens, her lips curving into a smug, almost predatory smile. "I can spell, you know."

My eyes snap wide, and realization slaps me hard. "Oh, my God, you wrote that? Why the hell did you put my name on it?"

She shrugs, dripping with false innocence. "My name isn't trending like it used to, so I borrowed yours. Sydney Sun—it really grabs attention, doesn't it?"

"It does. Because it's my name."

"Your pen name, you mean. And just so you know, it now belongs to the *Herald*—along with your laptop and email. So, if you want to keep your job and very steady pay, deal with it. But if not, there's the door. But anything that's property of the *Manhattan Herald* stays right here."

Her words land like an uppercut to the chin, knocking the wind out of me. Getting me fired was dirty, but this? This is toxic, one step below nuclear sewage.

I want to lash out, to wipe that smug smile off her face, but the bitter truth is, she's got me.

My mind spins because she's right. I did sign away the rights to my work the moment I walked through these doors, but my name?

Cold and indifferent, Richards piles on. "Read your contract, kid. If there's an issue, have your lawyer call mine. Oh, but wait—you're just a washed-up waitress with not one article to your name. Yeah, good luck with that. Now"—he straightens his tie—"get to work, or get out."

CHAPTER 29

Jules

I sink deeper into the couch, letting the cushions swallow me as Taylor paces like a hangry lioness.

She's fuming, practically crackling with enough energy to light up the entire city, and I've been silently thanking God that Brian's penthouse spans the whole floor. Seriously, the noise complaints would be nonstop with her shouting down the roof with every swear word in the book.

"That's fucking bullshit! They can't fire you for that!" She throws her hands up like she's ready to storm down there, picket sign in hand, and demand, "Justice Now! Justice Now!" in her leather mini and six-inch heels.

She punches the air for emphasis. "You point out her car. I'll slash her tires."

I giggle a little because this is why I love Taylor. She's always ready to rush in, full charge, straight into a class E felony without a second thought.

I try to shrug it off, pretend it doesn't matter. But it still stings. This was my shot—my no-kidding, real writer's job. And now, just like that, it's gone.

Taylor finally stops pacing and drops onto the couch beside me. "Do you want me to see if Salvatore's will take you back?" she asks, her tone softening, a hint of concern threading through her fiery outrage.

"No," I mumble, burying my face even deeper into the throw pillow, hoping it will somehow smother the disappointment gnawing at me. "At least, not yet."

The truth is, I'm so disillusioned with people right now, I don't even know what I want anymore. The world feels like it's spinning out of control, and I'm just clinging on for dear life, without the slightest clue where or how I'm supposed to land.

First, there's Brian. My walking, talking contradiction. He's everything I've ever despised and craved all rolled into one infuriatingly gorgeous package.

How is that even possible?

It's as if every time we get closer, we're on the verge of colliding—bright, white, and explosive. There's no middle ground—either we crash and burn, or we ignite.

And then there's the hand thing—what the hell was that about? He held it way too long for a guy who's supposed to be married. Fake or not, labels still matter.

And yet, here I am, using every trick in my Sydney Sun arsenal to convince myself that my sins of deception aren't nearly on par with his.

Then there's the *Herald*—my so-called dream job turns out to be nothing more than a sandcastle.

And the sand? Kitty litter.

"What do you want?" Taylor asks softly.

Brian.

Whoa, where did that come from?

I press my face into the pillow, trying to push the thought away. "I want to write," I mumble, my voice muffled. Then I lift my head, locking eyes with her. "But I want to write what I want to write."

Taylor nods like she gets it—like she always has. She's been my ride-or-die for so long that sometimes it feels like she knows me better than I know myself. "If it's any consolation, they can take your laptop, your email, and yes, maybe even your street cred, but they can't take your name."

"What do you mean?"

"I set up every @SydneySun account for you. Not them. You own it. Completely."

I blink, processing. "I do?" I chew on my lip, the thought of it sinking in. "But what if I don't want to be @SydneySun anymore? What if they start dragging her name through the mud?"

"If you ever want to change it, we can," she says, her voice all beautiful passion and rage. "We'll tell every last follower to jump ship to your new account. Say it was hacked or whatever. You pick the name. I'll handle the rest."

Her words are a lifeline, and even though today's drained me dry, I muster the strength to finally put an end to the Sydney Sun charade for good.

The fewer lies I have to unravel for Brian, the better.

I pull out my phone, eyes locked on the Instagram app, ready to say goodbye to @SydneySun, when a message from @MountainBoyNYC pops up.

It's like no matter which way I turn, Karma's always there, ready to have the last freaking word.

I click on the message, my heart doing a little flip in my chest like it always does with him.

@mountainboyNYC: "I need your help, Ms. Sun."

"Anything," I type back before I can think it through. He replies almost instantly.

@mountainboyNYC: "I'm missing a watch. It doesn't have a lot of street value, but it's been with me for years. A gift from my sister. I'd like to offer a reward for its safe return. Maybe a full-page ad in the *Herald*?

I straighten in my seat, resolve tightening in my chest. "Taylor, I want to help him. I do. That watch means everything to him. But—"

Before I can even finish, Taylor's fingers are already flying across the keyboard.

@SydneySun: I'm in.

"What the hell, Taylor?" Panic flares up, my voice edging into disbelief. "I can't pull this off! Did you miss the part where I quit the *Herald*? And I can't crawl back. I don't trust them. No way."

She glances up, her expression deadpan. "Oh, right." Then she pauses, thinking it over. "You don't need the *Herald*. Print papers are old-school. Great for a lazy Sunday with pancakes, but terrible for going viral. We need viral."

"Viral?" I echo, not quite catching on.

"Yeah. Videos. Of Brian. Asking for help. Possibly shirtless."

"Taylor!"

"What? Would it kill him to lose a button or two while he's at it?"

CHAPTER 30
Brian

"Hi." I clear my throat, the words sticking like glue. "I'm Brian. You've probably seen a lot about me in the press lately, but what you don't know is that I'm, uh..." Damn it, what the hell do I even say?

Taylor's waving her hand, urging me to keep chatting up her phone's camera.

Fine. *Sigh*. I give in. "Hi, folks. I'm a total dumbass whose watch was stolen. And my sister? She's a firecracker who'll kick my ass from here to kingdom come if I don't get it back."

"Cut!" Taylor shouts, like she's directing a full Hollywood production. "I need more heart, Brian. Deep, desperate—like you'd crawl through glass to get that watch."

I shoot her a look. "I'm not exactly auditioning for *The Bachelor*."

"Maybe lead with 'I'm filthy rich and offering a reward.'" Unfazed, she claps her hands like she's running an actor's boot camp. "Now, back to one, people!"

I lean in toward Jules, my voice a rough whisper. "There's literally just the three of us here."

"She takes social media seriously. Blink the wrong way, and she'll have you shirtless and greased up for the next shot."

Taylor squints at her iPhone, a smirk curling her lips. "Whoops. Forgot to hit record. My bad—I'm not usually behind the camera. So, what filter are we feeling? X-Pro II or Clarendon?"

"One where I'm not naked," I snap.

"Boo," Taylor pouts, scrolling through her options like she's selecting her next target.

I tug at my tie, rolling up my sleeves as I study the woman suddenly lost in a selfie spiral. "How exactly does Taylor know Sydney Sun?"

She hesitates, biting her lip in that telltale way she does when she's skirting the truth. "They've known each other for years. We all have."

"Is that so?"

"Yup."

I glance at Jules, sensing a disturbance in The Force. "No laptop today?" The absence of it hits me like a soldier without his weapon.

She bites her lip—again—and my patience snaps like a frayed wire.

I tug her closer, drop my voice low, and let it curl around her like a dark temptation. "Don't lie to me, Jules. Or I'll have to take you over my knee."

Her eyes widen, and the soft gasp that slips past her lips goes straight to my cock. And that blush blooming on her cheeks? A bright red flag to a pent-up bull.

I arch a brow, daring her. "Well?"

She swallows hard, and I can practically feel her pulse racing. "It wasn't mine. The person who owned it wanted it back. So, I gave it back. And my old one won't turn on because, ugh, I don't know. It's ten years old and identifies as a paperweight."

I study her for a moment, then shake my head with a smile tugging at my lips. Who borrows a laptop? "What happened to the credit card I gave you?"

"That's for emergencies," she said, so matter-of-fact that I know she's convinced herself it's true. Because why would her sworn enemy give her a credit card?

Just like I know Jules will never get it through that stubborn, beautiful head of hers that maybe, just maybe, I gave it to her because I wanted to.

Or maybe it's easier for her to avoid the risk of disappointment when our fairy dust romance inevitably ends.

By this point, with the scent of apple blossom shampoo teasing my nose, I don't know, and I don't care. I tilt her chin up, catching her uncertain gaze in mine, needling through the small crack in those walls she's built.

"No, Jules. That's for whatever the hell you want." I catch Taylor out of the corner of my eye and smirk. "Clear your calendar. After Taylor's done parading me around like a prized show dog, we're going shopping."

"First, I don't have a calendar. Only executives and Tiger Mom's have calendars. And second, you don't have to do that."

"Yes, I do. You're my wife."

The words slip out so naturally, it catches both of us off guard. The air between us shifts, heavy with the beating of our hearts and silent confessions, making the moment feel almost too much.

Too real.

Jules blinks, a flicker of something unreadable passing through her eyes. Then, she quickly brushes it off, as if nothing was said at all.

"Ready?" Taylor waves the camera at us, snapping us back to the task at hand.

I reach to straighten my tie, but Jules's soft fingers land on mine, stopping me in my tracks. The warmth of her touch lingers as she takes a good, long look at me.

"Don't," she says, her voice steady, flames playing in her eyes. "It's perfect. This is exactly how you should look."

"How's that?" I ask.

"Like the guy next door. But, undone."

A slow grin spreads across my face as I lean in, just enough to tease the distance between us. "Just fucked, it is."

CHAPTER 31
Jules

"I need something that heats up gradually but lasts all night," I say, my voice a soft, teasing whisper, laced with just enough allure to make him pause.

Brian looks at me, arching a brow. "All night? You sure you're ready for that?"

I let out a playful sigh, meeting his gaze with a hint of mischief. "Oh, I'm ready. Mama's got needs."

His breath catches, the mask of control slipping just enough to reveal a flicker of interest as he leans in closer. "I'm pretty sure we've got something that can meet your... demands."

I nod slowly, letting a coy smile tug at my lips as his gaze locks on to mine. "And it's got to be," I draw out the words, savoring every second, "big."

"Big?" He rubs his chin, pretending to consider it. "How big?"

I hold my hands about *yay* far apart, watching his eyes widen, curiosity piqued.

"You think you can handle that, Ms. Spenser?"

"I believe you mean Mrs. Bishop, and I can definitely handle it," I purr. "As long as it's packed with power, responds to every touch, and, no matter how intense things get, just won't quit."

My fingers linger on a sparkly one—the latest model, an upgrade of the last one I had, except this one comes with a blazing-fast processor, a stunning 4K display, and an ultra-responsive touchpad.

Brian's voice growls low against my ear. "Would the two of you like a room?"

I trace the sleek lines, already imagining the damage I could do with this baby, banging out my Pulitzer-worthy yet completely imaginary blog. "Put me in a room with this powerhouse, and I'll be there all night."

Just then, the salesman appears, all eager and chipper. "That's an excellent choice. The Quantum Elite Pro just launched."

My fingers pull back, my love for the machine warring with a good, strong dose of practicality. "How much is it?" I ask.

"Don't answer that," Brian says, cutting the salesman off as he slides his card across the counter. "We'll take it."

"I can't let you do that."

"And I can't let you mope around the house like you lost your favorite stuffed animal," he says, adding, "And throw in the latest digital notebook, the newest flagship phone, and anything else that'll make a geek girl's heart swoon."

The salesman's eyes light up with enthusiasm. "How about a glittery laptop case and some holographic I *Love Coffee* stickers?"

By this point I'm beaming like a kid about to slurp straight from Willy Wonka's chocolate moat.

Brian looks down at me as I blink up at him in wonder. Who is this guy?

He grins. "Sold."

AFTER A FEW MORE SHOPS AND MY STUBBORN REFUSAL to let Brian buy me anything beyond a cappuccino, we finally head home.

Well, *his* home.

Not mine.

Temporary, I remind myself.

I practically have to arm-wrestle Brian to let me carry any of the bags. In the end, he relents—barely—allowing me to carry just the laptop.

It's the first extravagant gift I've ever received, and I swear, I couldn't worship it more if Jessica Pressler herself handed it to me.

We get home, and I barely make it through the door before I tear into the box, excitement bubbling up inside me like I'm unwrapping the best gift ever.

"Like Christmas?" Brian asks.

"More like ten Christmases, birthdays, and Korean New Year's all rolled up in one," I reply, my grin widening as I finally get the laptop out and plug it in.

"Korean New Year's." Brian's voice softens. "*Seollal*."

"You remember?"

He pockets a hand, his gaze drifting into the past. "I

remember your halmeoni hiding treats around the house like Easter eggs. And you, tearing through the place, hunting down peach pops like a contestant on *Survivor*."

I laugh softly, surprised by a memory buried so deep it takes both of us to dig it out. "As much as I hate to admit it, they were my favorite."

He looks at me, his deep blue eyes locking onto mine. "Why do you think I left them alone and focused on the almond cookies?"

I tilt my head, puzzled. "I thought you liked them."

He shakes his head, a gentle smile tugging at his lips. "I've never really cared for almonds, Jules. I'm more of a chocolate chip kind of guy."

A frown creases my brow, confusion knotting in my chest. "But you ate them."

His gaze softens, a trace of something bittersweet in his eyes. "If I didn't, your halmeoni might not have invited me back. And I wanted to come back."

I move cautiously toward him until I'm knotted in intoxicating heat and the scent of dark spice and cedar. "Why?" I whisper.

"You know why."

My breath catches, and my heart freezes in my chest. Because I do know.

And yet, I don't.

I've loved this man for so many years, in so many ways—furious, terrified, pure—that anything less than love feels like a lie.

But I don't understand how he's managed to be both a

storm and a ghost, tearing through my life one minute, then vanishing without a trace the next.

All I know is when he's gone, his absence clings to me like the chill of winter—invisible and suffocating, all at once.

And Angi? Can I really brush aside that once upon a time, they were practically inseparable?

His fingers trace the curve of my jaw, and everything inside me just . . . stops. Then, he brushes the line of my lips, and goose bumps race across my skin, every rational thought dissolving into electricity pulsing between us.

My lips part, and when his thumb presses in, impulse takes over —I lick, then gently suck. The low, guttural moan that rumbles from his chest is raw, primal. Blue eyes darken, like a storm gathering over the sea, the heat in them so intense it has him trembling.

"Jesus," he breathes, his voice rough, thick with lust. "You're going to be the death of me."

His lips touch mine, and what starts as a soft, gentle brush quickly tidal waves into a crush of lips and tongues, sweeping me under, swallowing me whole, until I can't breathe.

Years of simmering emotions, of tension building, building, building, until we slam into the breaking point, boiling over and spilling out of control.

My belly clenches as his thick cock presses against me, leaving me breathless and desperate, clawing at his shirt. And dammit!

Why the hell are there so many buttons?

I swear, from here on out, this man is legally obligated to wear only T-shirts. And considering the way they cling to him like a second skin, it's sort of a crime not to. Win-win.

Argh!

Where the hell is that damn hunting knife?

The heat between us reaches a fever pitch, but then—his phone rings.

And rings.

And rings.

His jaw clenches, and he checks it. "Shit."

He pulls back, our breaths still mingling, panting hard. His forehead presses against mine.

It's as if the whole world is holding its breath as the moment slowly slips away.

He sighs, heavy enough to snuff out any last remaining embers between us. "I'm sorry, I have to go."

And then, he's gone.

CHAPTER 32
Brian

I step into my office—*my* real office, not the polished, picture-perfect front I use to keep up appearances.

This place is raw, all sharp edges with no trace of comfort—no windows, no sunlight. Just the hum of two walls filled with glowing monitors and high-tech gear. And right now, it keeps me right where I need to be—focused and in control.

This is the true heartbeat of The Centurion Group. Recon. Surveillance. Where movements of everything from people to money are tagged and tracked, and every threat is neutralized.

My team's already locked in. Harrison's running point, his sharp eyes and gut instincts making him the best damn asset we have, now that he's out of the service.

And Colby?

My brother-in-arms, and in matrimony, is here, too.

Between his keen eye and an arsenal of surveillance drones, the guy would've shown up no matter what. It's his sister we're looking for, and if it were mine, nothing would stop me either.

So, I didn't even try to keep him out—I rolled out the red

carpet. And now he's here, smirking like he knows something I don't, which is dangerous.

Colby's grin widens, and he points at my chest. "Sorry, did we interrupt something? Please say yes."

I glance down at my shirt—buttons mismatched, completely out of line. Damn it.

Well, considering I was just about to fuck his sister six ways to Sunday, I force my voice to stay even. "Nothing at all."

Smart ass.

I brush past him and zero in on Harrison, who's standing with his arms crossed, gaze fixed on the screen. All of New York City stretches out across the monitors, holding his attention like the *Queen's Gambit* chess board.

He doesn't need to look up to know I'm here. "What've you got?" I ask as I step beside him.

Harrison's focus doesn't waver, zooming in on a cluster of red dots. "Every place Angi's been in the last six days. With timestamps. You see what I'm seeing?"

My gut tightens. Yeah, I do.

I lean in, pulse pounding in my ears. Each red dot on the screen feels like a flick to the ear, taunting me, daring us to catch her if we can.

Then, I see the still shots on the other monitor, and my jaw clenches so hard I'm one second away from cracking a tooth.

Angi.

I shove my hands into my pockets, taking her in—head-to-toe leather, hair cascading down to her ass, a Hermès purse that's definitely stolen, and heels that make it clear wherever she's headed, she's not walking there.

She's still the wild, reckless girl she always was. Still lost.

Emotion slithers up my chest, coiling around me so tight, it's hard to breathe.

She's close. Too damn close. "She's coming home," I mutter under my breath, trying to steady the rush of nerves.

Colby steps forward, his features strained. "She's got a handful of places she holes up in. I'll start there." His tone is disciplined, almost militant, but I know him too well.

His future's hanging by a thread, and maybe not just his career, but his freedom, too. And finding Angi is his only way out.

I nod, placing a firm hand on his shoulder and squeezing. "I'll send a few teams to sweep the areas. We'll find her. Right, Harrison?"

Harrison's smirk deepens as his eyes land on my shirt. "What happened? Did the laundry win this round?" He chuckles, eyes gleaming. "Or maybe it's *someone* who's got you all twisted up like a knot?"

I clench my jaw, wedged between the hellcat woman on the screen, and her sister, the one tucked safely away in my house.

My wife.

I fumble with the buttons, fixing my shirt before steering the conversation in the opposite direction. "Speaking of twisted, got a bill in the mail for Roxana Voss's puke purse."

Harrison barks out a laugh. "Should I organize a taco sale? Or maybe a GoFundMe?"

I snort. "She'll get a dime from me when hell freezes over." My gaze narrows on him, voice dropping. "If you're here, who's watching the kids?"

Harrison smiles, pressing the buzzer by the door. The heavy metal slides open, revealing the panic room. The kids are sprawled out in the middle, surrounded by military-grade sleeping bags, lounging with snacks in hand, eyes glued to the latest Marvel flick on the big screen.

"Nice," I mutter, the corner of my mouth twitching with the hint of a smile. At least someone's night is all figured out.

BY THE TIME I GET HOME, IT'S LATE, BUT THERE'S still time to salvage the night. Unless, of course, Jules is tucked away in bed making love to her new laptop.

I texted her to let her know I was on my way, and not because she asked or because I'm pussy-whipped, though if there's any part of Jules's pussy that's involved, count me in. I did it because I wanted her to know. Being yanked away from her like that, hot and heavy and hard as fucking granite, only makes me more determined.

I want Jules.

I want her so much that in the few hours we've been apart, I've drifted in and out of physical pain.

Hell, I can still taste her on my lips from that kiss . . .

God, that kiss.

It's the kind that rewires your brain and wrecks any notion of moving along without her.

I step inside, instantly hit with signs of her everywhere—her laptop tossed on the sofa, phone abandoned on the table, and her favorite plush winky face emoji slippers, tossed haphazardly on the floor, a small reminder that she's here.

This is home now. Messy. Lived in. Happy.

A second later, her sweet voice drifts from somewhere in the house. *Hmm*. She must be on the phone.

The sound of her light giggles shoots straight to my dick, tightening low and deep, making me feel every damn inch of the want I have for this woman.

But then another voice cuts through the space, deflating me faster than a bouncy house rented by the hour.

I rush down the hall, following familiar laughs and voices until I step into the kitchen.

And there she is. My gut sinks like a stone, heavy and hard, when I see the last person I ever expected to find here tonight standing beside my Peach Pop.

Jess.

My sister.

The one who's supposed to be in Fiji. On her honeymoon. With Mark.

"What the hell are you doing here?" I ask, pulling her into a hug and forcing a grin that feels like it's about to crack. "You're not supposed to be back for weeks," I add, biting out the words a little too sharp.

Because just like that, everything I've been holding onto—this marriage, Jules—feels like it's about to crumble to dust.

And I'm not ready for that. Not yet.

"We came back early," she says, her voice light as a song. Jess's new tan and wide blue eyes beam at me, completely clueless that she's about to demolish every last brick of my well-laid plan.

Okay, so maybe I don't have an actual plan. But I have Jules, who's already twisting her wedding ring like it's suddenly strangling her finger.

Jess catches the shift in my expression and, in typical Jess fashion, blurts out, "The suspense was killing me. And there was a typhoon coming. Plus, I *had* to meet her—my new sister! Imagine my surprise when I find out you married Jules."

God, I love my sister, but can she please stop talking already?

Jess grabs Jules's hand, inspecting it closely, noticing how Jules is practically ripping the ring off her skin. "Couldn't you at least get her a ring that fits?"

"We were . . ." I fumble, my throat tightening as I scramble for the right words. "Impulsive. In a rush." The second the words leave my mouth, I know they're wrong. "It's just . . . temporary."

Shut up. Shut up. Shut. UP!

I glance at Jules, and it's like watching her heart shatter in slow motion. Her eyes wide, filled with uncertainty, doubt, and so much hurt it slices from her heart to mine.

She's already halfway gone, the need to run practically etched into every line of her face. But she covers it up with a fake smile and misty eyes that make it a thousand times worse.

"I'll let you two catch up," she says quietly, her voice small, distant, already out of reach.

She's trying so damn hard to hold it together, to mask the cracks splintering her apart, but it's all there—visible, raw. Breaking her in ways I never wanted to.

And all I can do is stand here, helpless, watching her slip through my fingers.

Because what else can I do?

I need to smooth it out with her. Talk with her. Maybe . . . I don't know, explain.

But if this is going to end anyway, then fuck it, let it end now. I need to rip the bandage off and bleed out, no matter how much it kills me.

Instead of running after her, I stand there, locked in place, making small talk with my sister about her damn honeymoon, gushing over the beautiful wedding she missed and how we *wished* she could've been there. All the while my heart burns like acid and my brain screams *this is wrong*.

Me, playing the role of picture-perfect husband, while my wife walks away.

CHAPTER 33
Jules

It takes all of twenty minutes to pack my suitcase because let's be real, it's over. Billionaire Brian Bishop doesn't need a wife anymore, and I'm not sticking around to hear him say it to my face.

Honestly, leaving now is probably for the best because, God, he told her. That casual, inconsequential word: *temporary*. That this means nothing. *I* mean nothing.

And if I don't get out of here now, I know exactly what's coming. I'll end up balled up, sobbing in the fetal position, drowning in a tsunami of emotions I'm not sure I'll survive.

I'm done having my heart smashed like Play-Doh every time he does something thoughtful. But it's even worse when he touches me. And the kisses? They destroy me.

The way he pulls me in, makes me feel *everything*, only to tear away and bail like he's snagged the last parachute on a crashing plane.

Ugh.

Why won't this damn suitcase shut?

Maybe it's just as exhausted as I am, overstuffed with too many emotions to keep inside.

I throw my weight onto it, bouncing with all my might. Even my luggage is so over this mess. But finally, it shuts.

I've already booked an Uber, courtesy of Brian himself. After that last bus ride when I nearly got eaten alive by paparazzi, he made sure I'd never have to deal with public transportation again.

So, being the rich boy he is, he prepaid enough Ubers to last me a lifetime. Like his credit card, I hadn't planned on using them, but his words stuck: *"They're paid for. Just. Use. Them."*

Turns out, it's pretty convenient when you're trying to duck out of a fake marriage without being noticed.

The sound of laughter spills from the kitchen as I slip toward the door. It's too much. His carefree voice, that low, gravelly laugh. And the dimple—*his* dimple, the one that always shows when he's happy from the top of his head to the tips of his toes.

Granted, it wasn't there when I passed him a moment ago, but I can picture it now, and it's unbearable. The tightness in my chest squeezes so hard I can't hardly breathe.

I'm almost at the door when—*dammit.*

What am I forgetting?

I've got all my clothes packed, along with a couple of his old tees that I'm pretty sure he won't miss. They're soft as angel clouds, and at this point, I consider them community property.

My eyes land on the other half of the cookie I was eating—some crack-cocaine-level treat his friend's sister makes called *salted caramel brownie bombs.* I can't leave it behind.

And not because I licked it and therefore it is mine, but because there is no shame in last-ditch stress eating.

As I reach for it, something else catches my eye, stopping me cold. The ring. That blinding spotlight of a rock, sparkling like it was a gift from the gods and crafted just for me. The most beautiful thing I've ever seen in my life.

And now, it's just a stupid, shiny reminder that this whole thing—this marriage, this life—was a sham. A devastatingly beautiful dream that, ready or not, I have to wake up from.

I tug it off, slow and deliberate, like each millimeter it moves is dragging regret along my veins. Then I leave it on the table as the flood of tears I've been holding back presses harder against my eyes.

I shove the cookie into my mouth, hoping the sugar can somehow plug the dam that's about to burst.

Without another glance, I make a break for the door and leave.

CHAPTER 34
Jules

"You are *not* going to believe this," Taylor says, practically diving onto my bed like she's announcing the apocalypse. Or a sale on Jimmy Choos.

I groan and pull the covers tighter over my head. Whatever it is, I don't want to know. Not today.

It's been a week since I slipped away, leaving nothing but my wedding ring behind. No goodbye, no explanation. And since then?

Nothing.

Not a single word. No text, no call, not even a damn smoke signal. Not even a whisper of regret.

I guess I shouldn't be shocked—fool me twice and all, but damn if it doesn't burn.

If I had an ounce of sense—or a shred of courage—I would've faced him. Looked him dead in his infuriatingly handsome, smug face and said, *"No, you're not doing this to me again."*

You don't get to wreck me twice.

But part of me feels like it's already done. Like there's not enough left to piece myself back together.

While you're laughing it up with your family, mister, I'm here, shattered, dreading how I'm supposed to break the news to mine. *"Yeah, Mom, Dad, Halmeoni—turns out it didn't work out with Mr. Asshole of the Century. Guess I didn't learn the first time when he tore my world apart."*

And the kicker? He never lied. Not once. He said it right to my face—the more I hate him, the better this works. Quick wedding. Quicker divorce.

But the real gut punch? I hate that I fell for him. Again. I wanted him. Wanted more.

And God, I hate how disappointed I am. Because somewhere, buried deep in the most vulnerable part of my heart, I actually thought he'd come after me.

Ha! Fat chance.

He told me from the start. Temporary. Torture. And damn it, he delivered. In spades.

He also promised, *"Till death do us part."*

Shut up, Jules.

And now bubbly Taylor's bouncing on the bed beside me, all sunshine and pep, promising that a little sunlight and fresh air will fix everything.

Will it?

I'm pretty sure that's the same horseshit they sold Dracula.

Taylor might be my best friend, but she's probably gearing up to tell me she's following her *latest* "future husband" to Scotland. Or Dubai.

And honestly? After a week of trying—and failing—to piece my heart back together, I can't be bothered to care.

Taylor rips the comforter off my head. "Don't make me steamroll you," she growls, then, without warning, flings herself on top of me like some overzealous pro wrestler, rolling back and forth until laughter I didn't ask for bursts out of me.

"Ugh," I manage between begrudging giggles. "I give, I give."

She releases me, victorious, as I sit up, clutching a pillow for dear life. Then, Taylor launches a full-blown assault on my hair, yanking through the tangles like a dance mom on competition day. Efficient, relentless, and completely merciless.

Her eyes catch on the shirt—worn, soft, roughly six sizes too big, with a faded Army logo that somehow still carries Brian's scent.

"Where'd you get that?"

"Amazon," I lie.

"Well," she plops down next to me, beaming, "your account is blowing up like the Eiffel Tower on New Year's Eve," she says, buzzing with excitement.

"What? Why?"

"Someone found the watch!" she squeals, clapping.

"That's incredible." I mean, yes, I care that the idiot gets his watch back. This isn't about us. It's about family. "So, they're getting it to him?"

"Slow your jelly roll. This is where social media ends and public relations kicks in."

"Public relations?" I frown.

She hits me with a deadpan stare. "You. You're public relations. You're still Sydney Sun on Instagram, and you need to make sure this person isn't a total weirdo before you go telling Brian where he can find his precious watch. Also, babe, it's two in the afternoon. Time to get up and rejoin society."

After a skin-scalding shower and a shave that finally rids my legs of their Yeti-level hibernation, I grab my phone and dive into my real obsession: investigating.

The beauty of being a writer with time to kill and a laser-sharp focus? I can snoop the hell out of anything or anyone like a free-lancer on a caffeine bender.

First, I pull up the source.

An Instagram account with the handle @BigDogCoach57 —because, obviously, big dogs need a life coach, right? His feed is flooded with shots of him, two retrievers, and enough little-league action to make you wonder if he's running for team dad of the year.

It's all suburban and harmless. But when I open the images he sent, something clicks. And for the first time in days, a real smile stretches across my face.

We didn't share every detail for a reason. The second a billionaire dangles a reward, every opportunist with a Wi-Fi connection comes crawling out of the woodwork.

Taylor, the social media queen she is, picked through the chaos like a kid fishing peas out of Sunday dinner, equal parts focused and fed up. And I have to hand it to her, when it comes to weeding out the crazies, the woman is a human spam filter in heels.

The pictures of the watch are a goldmine, all the proof I need. The face is chipped, cratered like the moon, and the strap shows the wear and tear of more than one deployment. But it's the inscription on the back that cinches it: *Our path may change as life goes on, but our bond is ever strong.*

That watch is Brian's. No doubt about it.

I'm buzzing with so much excitement that my fingers slip, fumbling with my phone as I accidentally hit the video call option—because, of course, me and social media? Not exactly besties.

A kid's face flashes across the screen. He's maybe ten or eleven, with a messy mop of dark hair and wide, innocent brown eyes that seem to light up the entire call.

He's wearing a battered baseball cap, tilted just enough to make it cool, and a jersey that's been through one too many games, hanging on by pure determination.

"Uh, hi," he says, a little awkward, fiddling with the brim of his cap. "Are you . . . Sydney Sun?"

"That's me. What's your name?"

"Max."

So few people know I'm Sydney Sun, and the fact that this kid does sends a strange flutter through my chest. I can feel a grin lifting sky high—wide and goofy. Must. Fight. Smile.

I'm just about to ask for his dad when it hits me—he knows my name. Then it clicks. "Wait, you're the one who sent the photos."

He bites his lip, glancing over his shoulder like he's about to spill state secrets. "So, uh . . . I saw that Brian guy on TikTok. And I found his watch."

My pulse skips. "Where?"

"The dugout."

"The dugout?" I repeat, a little thrown. From my little

league days, I know the only things left in a dugout are sunflower seeds, gum, and spit.

"Okay, fine." He groans. "I found it in my sister's backpack. She'll kill me if she finds out." He runs a finger across his throat for emphasis.

I smirk, leaning in like we're partners in crime. "Our little secret." I pretend to lock my lips and toss the key, sealing the deal with a wink. "How old's your sister?"

He rolls his eyes, exasperated. "Ancient. Like, nineteen."

I bite back a laugh. "Brutal."

He blows out a breath. "That Brian guy said there's a reward."

"There is." I lean in closer, my voice dropping to a conspiratorial whisper. "A big one."

"Good. We kinda need new uniforms," he says, full of hope.

A voice shouts in the background, "And bats!"

I raise an eyebrow, half-expecting his entire little league team to spill out from wherever they're hiding. I imagine half the dugout crammed out of sight behind the screen.

He brightens, his face lighting up with possibilities. "Yeah, and bats." He gives a casual shrug, testing the waters. "Maybe he could throw in a few gloves, too. And I promise I'll take good care of the watch 'til he picks it up."

I can't stop the grin pulling at my lips, my heart softening as I watch him, this little negotiator, completely clueless that Brian would probably hand him the keys to his dream sports car in exchange for that watch.

He hesitates, then asks, "Where does he live? I'm not allowed to ride my bike past Elmwood."

"Tell you what, Max. Make a list of everything your team

needs, and I'll make sure *that Brian guy* delivers—and picks up the watch."

A burst of excited cheers erupts from behind the screen, and I laugh so hard my body shakes, the weight on my chest lifting just a little.

It's been a while since I've felt this—something light, something good. It's like a shot of hope straight into my veins.

This whole situation is practically begging to be a story.

A Sydney Sun story.

When the call ends, I feel . . . different. A little less worn down, a little more determined, and yeah, maybe a little terrified. But I know what I have to do.

I need to reach out to him. Tell him about his watch.

And that from here on out, in my mind, Mr. Brian Gabriel Bishop will forever be known as *that Brian guy*.

The guy who will always hold my heart.

Even if he never knows.

CHAPTER 35

Jules

After a deep breath and a shot of tequila, I fire off the first shot across the bow.

@SydneySun: *It's your lucky day.*

Then I send him all the images of the watch. His reply comes in almost instantly.

@MountainBoyNYC: *That's... incredible. Looks like you're my guardian angel. How soon can I get it back?*

I stare at the screen, and missing him hits me from out of nowhere like a thunderbolt—fast, hard, and impossible to ignore. It's almost laughable that after everything—his insane proposal, the whirlwind wedding—this is what we've become.

Two strangers on Instagram, slipping into each other's DMs over a watch.

@SydneySun: As soon as you'd like. Just send over where you'd like it delivered.

Simple. Keep it professional. He doesn't even realize it's me.

@MountainBoyNYC: I can swing by and grab it. The Herald?

He wants to come by the Herald? My stomach does a full-on somersault. Of course, he wants to come by. He still thinks I work there.
Which . . . I don't.
I tap my finger against my chin, running through options.
Maybe I could meet him at a coffee shop.
But how? As Sydney Sun? I barely survived the first round with him, and the way this man scrambles my brain, with his blue eyes and stern brow, something is bound to slip. I know it.
There's no way I'm pulling it off twice.
Don't panic. Do. Not. Panic.

@SydneySun: I'm super busy, deadlines and all. I would ask Taylor, but she's—

Crap. She's what?
Think, think, think . . .
On a Paris runway?
In Mexico, chasing down future husband number 105 because this time, he's *definitely* the one?
My fingers start moving before I even realize it.

@SydneySun: —she's a little clumsy. This morning, she spilled an entire caramel macchiato all over her favorite pair of heels and blamed it on a ghost.

True story. Though, technically, it was last week.

@SydneySun: She's got her hands full. But what about her friend?

@MountainBoyNYC: Friend? What friend?

Me. Your wife, you idiot. *I'm* the friend.

@SydneySun: Y*ou* know. Gorgeous. Brilliant. The kind of woman a man would be a complete fool not to sweep off her feet and ravage mercilessly for three days straight.

Too much?
Delete, delete, delete.

@SydneySun: I think her name is Jules.

There's a long pause. Agonizingly long. Bubbles pop up. Then disappear. And it's. Killing. Me.

@MountainBoyNYC: I've waited this long for the watch. A little longer won't hurt. But I'd rather meet you. Just to talk.

Just to *talk?* I suck in a sharp breath. He wants to talk—to *me.* Not his wife?

Also me.

@SydneySun: Didn't I read somewhere that you were married?

I hit send without overthinking it, my heart racing as I stare at my phone. I shouldn't care.

I mean, we never said *I love you.* Never even made it to second base. But the idea of him moving on so fast? It's, ugh, infuriating.

And we did say vows in front of a freaking pastor.

And then his reply comes in.

@MountainBoyNYC: She left. Hates me, actually.

My eyes focus on the screen. *Hates?*

I mean, I did. I hated him with every fiber of my being. But the thing is, when it comes to Brian, I'm all out of hate. And what's left is this warm, unexpected feeling bubbling up—like a cozy fire on a crisp mountain night.

A few seconds later, more bubbles.

@MountainBoyNYC: She walked out. Didn't say a word. Took a cookie for the road and left the ring. Not that I blame her. It was a really good cookie. But still . . .

@MountainBoyNYC: If I'm being totally honest, I didn't want it to end like that.

@MountainBoyNYC: Not that she would believe me, but I didn't want it to end at all.

The tension in my chest tightens, refusing to let it go. I pick up my phone, my fingers moving on their own.

@SydneySun: You didn't?

@MountainBoyNYC: Maybe it's just a broken heart talking, but I need to talk to you. From that first article, it's like you know me better than anyone. Granted, you were a little rough on me with the second one, but I probably deserve it.

@MountainBoyNYC: Coffee?

I blink at the screen, my heart stumbling over itself. He's heartbroken? Over *me*?

I should tell him. I should come clean right now and admit it's me. That it's been me all along. That me and Sydney Sun are one and the same.

My fingers hover over the keys, ready to spill the truth, when another message pings.

@MountainBoyNYC: Tomorrow. Noon. Coffee shop. Or I'll hunt you down at the Herald.

I go to type a reply, but he's gone. Offline. Deliberately. A classic Bishop move.

One step ahead.
Always playing to win.

CHAPTER 36
Jules

I've been nursing the same lukewarm latte for what feels like forever. I'm tucked into a cozy table for two at the very back, but my eyes keep darting to the door.

Where is he?

I glance at my phone again and huff out a breath.

Twenty minutes late.

And military man Brian Bishop is *never* late.

No calls. No messages. Not even those stupid bubbles that give you false hope that someone's typing.

My foot bounces under the table, the impatience building. Maybe he's not coming. Maybe this was all some kind of twisted payback for leaving his ring behind. Or maybe he's still pissed that I ate his last cookie.

Or maybe, just maybe, without the hat, dark glasses, and red lipstick, he took one look at jeans-and-T-shirt, plain old ordinary me, and bolted faster than a New Yorker avoiding a subway rat.

Ugh.

That's it. I've had enough.

I move to stand, ready to bail. And then I hear it.

That deep, gravelly voice—the one that makes my knees weak and roots my feet to the floor. "Jules."

Slowly, I turn, and there he is. But this isn't just Brian standing in front of me. No, this is Mr. Take-Names-and-Kick-Ass Bishop. And damn, does he look good.

Too good.

It's the kind of good that hurts in all the wrong ways.

His dark suit is perfectly tailored, clinging to every hard edge of his body. The light blue shirt, unbuttoned at the collar, no tie—just the right amount of a casual tease.

His jawline is tense, sharp as cut glass, and those blue eyes...

So much colder than usual, with only the faintest flicker of warmth trying to break through. But in all his sex god glory, what hits me hardest is the wall—ten miles high, impenetrable.

Not that I blame him. My wall's so high it makes his look like a picket fence.

He leans in just close enough for his aftershave to cloud my judgment. "I thought I might see you here." His voice is too smooth, too calm, as he pulls out the chair for me.

That's Brian. Manners in spades. Or maybe it's just the control freak in him making sure I don't bolt.

I sit, crossing my arms. "Is that why you're twenty minutes late?" I mutter, not bothering to hide the annoyance simmering beneath the surface.

He settles into the chair, completely unruffled. "No. I emailed Sydney Sun to let her know. Sorry if she didn't get the word to you, but I was unavoidably detained."

Oh. Right. He sent her an email. Which would be perfectly reasonable, except all access to that account has been cut off. My heart stutters, but I force my voice to stay steady. "She no longer works at the Herald," I blurt out, the words tumbling over each other.

"She doesn't?" He looks genuinely surprised.

"She was probably too embarrassed to mention it, but she's been busy"—licking my wounds?—"figuring out her next move."

His gaze drops to my hand, lingering on my bare ring finger just long enough. I quickly tuck my hand under the table, feeling suddenly self-conscious and exposed.

"How have you been?" he asks, his voice low.

Before I can answer, the barista rushes over, practically glowing, eyes wide as if she's just spotted a unicorn. Or a Hemsworth.

"I added the dash of cinnamon just the way you like it, Mr. Bishop," she gushes, batting her eyelashes. "On the house. Anything else I can get you?"

Great. A fan. I roll my eyes.

His eyes shift to me, unreadable. "Would you like a top-off?"

"No," I reply flatly.

"Thanks," he replies, his tone stiff and distant. Polite, but nothing more. Then he adds, "My wife and I could use a little privacy."

"Oh." Her eyes go wide as saucers. "Yes, of course."

She hurries away, and what follows is an awkward silence so thick, it's suffocating.

He finally takes a sip of his drink, easing back into his chair like he's decided to settle in. "How are Taylor's shoes?"

I blink, caught completely off guard. Is he testing me? Or does he just assume I'd know because I'm her roommate?

I think it through and decide to play it safe—straightforward and honest. "She decided to dab them in straight coffee. They're . . . wearable. And look a little like a barista's dog marked its territory."

A soft smile tugs at his lips, enough of a chuckle escaping that I find myself laughing, too. But it fades quickly. "I hoped you'd be here," he says, his voice almost vulnerable.

Sure. A likely story. "You're here for your watch."

"I'm here for my wife."

His words hit me like a hammer to the chest, and before I can stop it, tears prick at the corners of my eyes. I blink hard, but it's no use. The cracks in my composure are all over the map, tearing apart, impossible to hide.

He pauses, his expression softening, and when his eyes meet mine, they're red and watery, too, like it's taking every ounce of strength for him to hold it together. Just like me.

"It killed me," he says quietly, his voice raw. "You, leaving your ring."

I choke on the words building in my throat, my voice tight, thick with everything I *can't* say.

Then he adds, "It's worth more than a cookie, you know."

"I know." My breath shudders as a tear breaks loose. "But you said *temporary*, and—"

"I meant the *fit*, not the ring." His voice is tight, like he's fighting whatever it is he wants to say. Then, as if balancing on the edge of a razor is too much to bear, he blows out a breath. "Dammit, Jules. I can't do this."

My heart crumples. I swallow hard, two seconds from bolting when he beats me to it, already on his feet.

I wipe away a tear as he reaches into his pocket, pulling out something small and familiar—*my* wedding ring. The one I left behind. The one I never thought I'd see again.

He circles around to my side of the table, sliding his seat next to mine until he's too close, too hot, too much. He takes a seat, and my pulse spikes, but I can't bring myself to move.

He holds the ring up, letting it catch the light as he studies it. "It should fit now."

My eyes search his, confused.

"It's why I was late," he murmurs. "I was getting it resized." He takes my hand, the warmth of his fingers against mine as he slips it on. "I want to try for real, Jules."

Speechless, I stare at him. This man, sitting here with so much emotion swirling between us, it feels like time has stopped, locking us in place.

"Say something," he whispers, his lips agonizingly close, his breath warm against my skin.

"You're sure? You're really sure?"

"I've never needed anyone more in my life. Say yes, Peach Pop."

"Yes," I whisper, and when our lips finally touch, it's soft and tender, until the walls between us melt away and nothing exists but us.

His lips sear a slow path down my neck, and without hesitation, he discreetly drags my hand to his length. And whoa, there's a lot of it. His voice drops, rough and possessive. "Can we get out of here? I'm two seconds away from showing you—and everyone else in here—just how much I need you."

Before I can respond, my phone buzzes, and a familiar freckled face with a mop of hair lights up the screen.

Brian pulls away just enough to glance at my phone. "Who's that?"

I smile, unable to help myself. "That, Mr. Bishop, is your one o'clock cock block."

CHAPTER 37

Brian

We're driving through what looks like the quietest suburban area just outside the city. The kind of place where everyone knows each other, lawns are modest but well-kept, and there's always a dog barking somewhere in the distance.

Jules is hunched over her phone, squinting at the map like it's written in hieroglyphics, refusing to let me take a look.

"Do you even know where we're going?" I ask, glancing at the winding road ahead.

She doesn't look up. "I've got this."

Sure, because Jules and directions go together like sushi and cereal. If this were Taylor? Hell, we'd probably be halfway to Vegas by now.

"Turn here!" she shouts, and I jerk the wheel, the tires shrieking as we skid onto a dirt road that looks like it hasn't been driven on in years.

Dust billows up around us, and just when I think we're heading into the middle of nowhere, it appears—a rundown baseball field.

The chalk lines are almost gone, barely ghosting the field, and the dugouts are hanging on by a thread, but the place still holds all its charm.

I can't help the chuckle that escapes. "It's been a while since I crushed you at baseball," I tease.

"In your dreams, Bishop."

We park and start walking around. "This could almost be a romantic stroll down memory lane—like that time I watched you totally lose your shit at the ump over a strike call."

"Strike, my ass." She giggles, her eyes lighting up.

That's my Peach Pop. Feisty and gorgeous. "If someone had told me what I was in for, I'd have brought a change of clothes."

"And spoil the surprise?" she fires back with a smirk.

I glance around at the field. With the look of these grounds, I could probably play just fine in my current prosthetic. But if push comes to shove, I've always got a blade tucked safely in the trunk—just in case Jules's competitive streak rears its Godzilla head.

And let's be clear, barring an alien invasion or biblical flood, there's nothing keeping me from racing around that diamond if she asks.

Before I know it, a group of kids rush from the dugout, like they've been waiting for this moment all day.

One of them, the kid Jules has been texting, sprints right up to us, breathless. "You're that Bishop guy," he says in awe.

"I am." I guess.

"Did you bring the list?" Jules asks, all business.

He pulls it from his back pocket, crumpled but intact, and hands it over. Jules motions to me, and I unfold the list. Uniforms. Bats. Mitts. And . . . a popcorn machine?

I arch a brow. "What is this?"

"Well, Mr. Bishop," Jules says, smirking. "You've officially entered ransom negotiations with Max here."

"For my watch?" I light up.

Max grins, pulling off his ball cap and letting the watch slip into his hand, still a little sweaty from being crammed in there.

Jules cringes. "Eww," she mutters, patting me on the back as if I'm the one who has to deal with it. "Promise to get them every last thing on that list, and the watch is yours," she says.

I don't even hesitate. "Sold."

He points. "What happened to your leg?"

Jules looks mortified, but before she can step in, I offer a warm smile, doing what I've always done with the curious and the innocently unfiltered. I roll up my pant leg, revealing the prosthetic, and let them have a look.

"It was an accident. The doctors saved my life, and this leg? It lets me keep doing everything I love."

They huddle around me, wide-eyed, asking a thousand questions. "Can you leap tall buildings?"

I chuckle softly. "Only when no one's looking," I say, pressing a finger to my lips with a playful *shhh*.

Another kid pipes up, eyes wide with curiosity. "Can you run faster than a car?"

I laugh, rubbing my chin. "Depends on the car. A Matchbox car? Hands down."

The kids giggle, their eyes wide with wonder.

I lose the blazer, roll up my sleeves, and switch prosthetics as I lose myself in their world.

I might have gone with the sneakers that are always in my

gym bag, but let's be real—the blade always keeps the kids interested.

One kid, Logan, challenges me to a race around the diamond, and for once, it's nice not to be the only one showing off.

Meanwhile, Jules has slipped into the game like a comfy pair of Uggs. She's posted up on third base, chatting with Max, probably negotiating another deal, when she suddenly breaks for home.

The kids scramble, hollering and screaming, trying to catch her, but she's fast—just as fast as I remember, if not faster.

I move before thinking, catching her just before she reaches the plate, lifting her clean off the ground and over my shoulder, giving the kids their much-needed victory. Cheers erupt all around us.

She squeals, half laughing, half complaining. "Hey! Put me down!"

I don't. Not until I feel her laughter vibrating against my shoulder, warm and infectious, spilling over into my chest.

And then, because I can't help myself, I set her down and kiss her right there, in front of all the kids.

My girl.

"Eww!" they groan in unison, hands flying up to cover their eyes.

Whatever. I'm standing here with a watch strapped to my wrist that spent some quality time in Max's sweaty ballcap. I have earned this.

Let this be a lesson to their kind: When a man spanks his wife at sports, kissing *will* happen.

CHAPTER 38
Jules

By the time we get home, we're dirty, sweaty, hot, and so worked up we can't keep our hands off each other.

Every touch, every breath between us is fire. We get to the bedroom, and he kicks the door closed. I'm already on him, tearing at the fabric of his shirt like the answer to where the Holy Grail is hidden is scrawled across his chest.

"We need a shower," I breathe between kisses and gasps for air.

"Yes," he growls, pressing me up against the wall. "We definitely do."

We stumble into the bathroom, high on laughter and drunk with lust. He turns on the water, and the steam rises around us, thick and hot, filling the small space.

In one swift motion, he tears off my shirt and jeans, leaving me exposed to two darkening eyes and the heat of the moment.

When he peels away my bra, revealing my full breasts and tight nipples, the world seems to stop, suspended in the tension between us.

"You're so fucking beautiful, Jules," he murmurs, his voice rough with need.

Then he drops to a knee, his breath hot against the fabric of my pink cotton panties. Slowly, achingly slow, he lowers them, his tongue following with a deliberate, tantalizing lick.

All it takes is one thick, deep lick, and my world spins out of control. "Oh, God," I gasp, my hand gripping his hair as I try to hold on to a shred of control, but it's impossible.

I'm unraveling like a ball of twine down a winding staircase, and my only option is to let go and ride this glorious fall.

His licks are hungry, ravenous, each one deeper and wetter than the last.

There's no apology, no hesitation—just raw, desperate need. Brian is relentless, like a man possessed, tearing the orgasm from me as if it belongs to him. And hell, it does.

It's so good, so ridiculously good, that I'm borderline addicted, craving more by the second.

I've wanted this—wanted *him*—for so long. And for the record, he was worth every second of the wait.

I've imagined it a thousand ways, but nothing could prepare me for the moment his fingers slide inside. I'm already widening my legs, the desperate plea tumbling from my lips like a prayer. "Please."

I'm riding his hand like it's the only thing keeping me tethered to the earth. The pressure builds and builds until there's no choice. I crash headfirst into a brick wall of an orgasm as my entire body shudders from the impact.

A guttural hum vibrates from his chest to his lips. "Mmm."

Before I can even catch my breath, he's stripping off his clothes, his mouth claiming mine, my taste still on his lips.

The world tips as I'm lifted up, the rush of hot water cascading along my back.

That's when it hits me. "Your leg—shouldn't we—"

"It's fine," he growls, cutting off any protests as his teeth graze my lower lip. He tugs gently, just enough to silence me.

My hands roam across his chest, fingertips tracing every ridge, every groove of his sculpted muscles. He pauses, letting my eyes linger, drinking him in like he's a masterpiece carved by the gods.

For the first time, I see him—all of him. The water glistens over his skin, exposing every scar and imperfection etched into him like constellations on a canvas, and I drink him in.

There are the parts of him I've loved without seeing—these parts—all of him. This man I will love until the day I die.

The moment my eyes lock on to his mouth—those full lips framed by rough stubble—I'm spun around, my back slamming against the cool tile.

Water pours over us as his kiss turns deeper, more demanding, like he's starved for it. His heart pounds against mine, his tongue teasing, taunting, until we're both breathless and panting and gasping for air.

"I've wanted you for so damn long," he murmurs, lips grazing the curve of my wet shoulder, the feel of his stubble sending a tingle to my toes.

He locks me in his arms, my legs wrapped around his waist, his hands cradling my ass as the thick head begins to press at my entrance.

His entire body trembles with barely contained restraint. "If we do this, there's no going back, Jules. You're either mine, or you're not."

"I'm yours."

In one desperate, searing thrust, he shoves in. And he's so big, so perfectly thick, that I swear I see stars.

There's too much of him for me to take at once, and he has to work for it, stretching me inch by delicious inch.

Deep.

So. Damn. Deep.

Every breath is for him. Every thrust is pure possession.

I've never felt anything like this in my life. He's everywhere, filling me up until I'm drowning in him—mind, body, and soul. It's too much and not enough all at once.

Like having him this way will never be enough. I crave more. And the more he gives—faster and harder—the more I need.

And damn, is he giving it to me. A lifetime of pent-up desire, unleashed all at once.

A few more impatient, punishing thrusts, and my world shatters into shards of color and light and breaths and moans.

And him.

CHAPTER 39
Brian

For a while, we just exist in each other's arms, letting the water pour over our skin, soaking in the quiet intimacy.

There's no urgency, no rush.

Just us.

We should be lathering up, washing off every trace of today. But the second either of us catches that look—the heat in our eyes, the unspoken longing—we're drawn back in, making up for lost time in fucking spades.

I carry her out of the shower, our bodies locked in a wet, tangle of limbs and kisses as we collapse on the bed. The cool air hits us, but it barely registers, not with the blazing heat between us still threatening to burn everything in its path.

It's like the world has vanished, and all that's left is this—the pulse of want and a primal need that fuels every breath and touch.

Slowly, she shifts me onto my back, her fingers trailing lightly along my skin—my side, my abs, down my thigh. Until she reaches the speed bump in the road, and hesitates.

When her gaze rises to meet mine, I see something that tightens my chest—tenderness and ...

Carefully, she undoes the strap, gently removing my steel-crafted limb with a care that damn near wrecks me.

It's like she knows the part of me that can't feel pain is the one that weighs on me the most.

It's a simple, practical act—its removal. But with Jules, it's pure torture and bliss all at once, as if she's peeling back every dark, twisted layer I've ever hidden behind.

Exposing the wounded beast. The broken soldier. And a man who would bleed his soul dry just to let her in.

She slides over me, our lips barely brushing, and suddenly it's not just lust—it's more. It's every hollow, aching part of me being filled all at once, overflowing.

My hands glide over her skin, soft as silk, my fingers tracing the fullness of her breast. I tease her dusky rose nipple with my lips and tongue, savoring the way her body responds to every touch.

Her back arches, fingers on my chest, taking me until I'm buried deep. We move together, perfectly in sync, and instinct thrums through me hard.

I flip her onto her back, my body taking over, relentless as I give her everything I have, both barrels.

With one swift move, I throw her leg over my shoulder and slam into her, a raw, guttural "fuck" escaping as I lose myself in her warmth, her slick heat pulling me deeper.

Even with the sound of skin slapping against skin, our ragged breaths echoing through the room, I hear it—soft, like a confession. "I love you," she whispers, her voice breaking through the haze.

It's all I need.

Whatever control I had left snaps, and we fall apart together, our bodies trembling as the world fades, completely undone in each other's arms.

With her wrapped around me, we drift into a deep, sated sleep, the words slipping out softly, effortlessly.

"I love you, too, Jules."

CHAPTER 40
Brian

I'm finishing up the last few tasks at the office when a soft knock snaps me out of my thoughts. Imani steps in, her hand resting on the barely there curve of her belly, a warm smile tugging at her lips.

"Off to the doctor," she says, giving her stomach a little pat.

I grin and nod. "Take the day off. You've been pulling double duty, as my admin and Mark's. But soon enough, I'll be out of your hair."

"Thank God," she teases, rolling her eyes dramatically. "But let's be real—you're just moving one floor down. I'll still hear your crazy love-struck humming."

"I do not hum."

She raises a brow. "Oh, you definitely do. *Can't Take My Eyes Off of You, Dancing in the Moonlight.* And what's up with this disturbing attachment to ABBA songs? *Take a Chance on Me* has been on repeat all day."

I shrug, trying to play it off. "Want me to switch it up? My mom was a huge ABBA fan." I crack my knuckles with a smirk.

"Their whole catalog's locked and loaded. I take requests. How about a little *Gimme Gimme Gimme*?"

She snorts. "A man after midnight? Okay, who are you, and what have you done with Grumps McGrumps? You're floating around here with that goofy grin, and Mark says it's really creeping him out."

Satisfied, I smile. "Mission accomplished." A chuckle escapes as I make a mental note to call him when he's knee-deep in meetings, just to leave obnoxious voicemails.

I think I'll start with *Dancing Queen*. Hell, I could turn it into a series—a different ABBA hit every time he ignores my call.

Imani heads out, and I turn back to my desk, ready to dive back into the last bit of work. One email in particular catches my attention. I read it, twirling the ring on my finger.

From: sydney@herald.com
Subject: Media Excellence Gala Invitation

I pause, my fingers hovering over the mouse before clicking it open. *Sydney Sun.* Didn't Jules say she left the *Herald*?

Mr. Bishop,

I'm inviting you to the Media Excellence Gala. It's the talk of New York this year, with true red carpet treatment for the rich and elite.

Journalists from all over the wurld will be there, and I'll be presenting an award for the Herald's 50th anniversary.

RSVP required.

*In a tux or out of a tux,
I need you.*

xoxo

I smile at the words, *Mr. Bishop.* So formal. *Ms. Sun.*

I reread it. Again. And again. I don't even know why. But my heart does this weird, fluttery flip, like it's been waiting for her to reach out to me like this.

Sydney Sun.

She always has this effect on me. And every time, I've brushed it aside. But this time . . . I can't.

She found my watch, and I can't keep sweeping this connection under the rug. It's there, whether I want to admit it or not.

Still, as I glance over her message, something doesn't quite sit right in my gut. I'm not the type who's into froufrou events. I'm more of a whiskey and warm fire kind of guy.

And yeah, *wurld* is misspelled, but we've all fat-fingered a text or ten. Guilty as charged.

But that's not what's gnawing at me. It's that last part—I can't shake it. *I need you.*

Those words tug at me in a way I can't explain. I have to go.

I type out a response, my finger hovering over the *Send* button, but I freeze. I just sit there, thumb up my ass, tapping my fingers on the desk, staring at the email like an idiot.

Why am I hesitating?

My eyes drift to the watch on my wrist.

That's why.

My watch.

Lost to the universe, and somehow, *she* found it. She didn't have to, but she did. So when Sydney Sun says she needs me, there's no way in hell I'm saying no.

Then, a thought slinks in—what if this is her swan song? Her last hurrah before she calls it quits. My wife said it herself—Sydney Sun is embarrassed, still figuring things out.

What if this is her way of asking for help? For a lifeline as she steps into the unknown?

I blow out a breath, and RSVP.

Bottom line: If she's asking, I'll be there. Every damn time.

CHAPTER 41
Brian

The early morning light filters through the blinds, casting soft, golden rays across Jules's luscious curves as she stirs in her sleep.

She's sprawled out on her stomach, her hair a mess of dark waves across the pillow, showing the soft lines of her bare shoulders. Her glorious breasts rise and fall with each breath, and all I can do is watch her.

She's breathtaking. Peaceful. Beautiful in a way that makes my breath hitch and my cock stir.

I want to touch her, but I won't. I know better. If I even so much as run my hand down the curve of her hip, there will be hell to pay.

Disturbing Jules on a lazy Sunday morning? I may as well kick a hornet's nest. A hornet's nest that transforms into ten Godzillas.

I can already imagine her glare burning through me, her sleepy wrath ready to pounce. And make no mistake, my little Peach Pop is evil. I wouldn't put it past her to throw a pillow at my head with the precision of a Navy SEAL, then roll over like nothing happened.

Is it my fault her mesmerizing body practically dares me to start a damn pillow war?

Because I've fought battles that were easier than going toe-to-toe with a cranky Peach Pop. Like when we were eight, and I told her she was too little to play WWE wrestling, thinking she'd pout and storm off.

Spoiler alert: she didn't.

The damn girl had me in a headlock five minutes later, her legs locked around my waist like a python, flipping me to the ground until I ate my words—and half a mouthful of dirt.

Which was weird, because I was talking about a video game.

In my defense, I was scrawny for eight. And Jules? She was a damn hurricane in sneakers. Came at me with all limbs flying. Some serious Greco-Roman wrestling shit. Her arms and legs locked in around me like a candy wrapper and—

Wait, why is this a bad idea?

Without opening her eyes, she mumbles, "We're closed."

I smirk. "Closed?"

"To that big cock knocking at my ass. Yeah, we're closed. Come back in an hour."

A grin tugs at my lips as I lean closer, my breath just grazing her hair. "I can't. In an hour, my dick will have shriveled up from sheer neglect. Blue balls will have claimed their final victim. And then where will you be?"

"Sleeping blissfully," she mutters, yanking the pillow over her head like a shield.

I chuckle, undeterred. "Plus, in an hour, we'll be hitting the road."

Her pillow shifts just enough for one eye to peek out. "You're coming with me?"

I'm not sure why she's so surprised. As if I could last an entire day without her.

I sigh dramatically, flopping back on the bed. "Yes, I'm coming with you. Even if impending dick death is on the line."

"How heroic," she says, kissing a line across my chest. "You make it sound like my problem."

"It *is* your problem. You're a certified sex maniac. And I'm warning you—if you don't feed him now, there will be hell to pay. You'll be desperate and horny, and there'll be nothing left for you to play with but a shriveled-up beef stick."

Before I can even blink, her hand snakes under the sheets, wrapping around me, firm and teasing. A sharp breath escapes me as she squeezes.

"He seems pretty plump already," she purrs, her voice like a warm shot of whiskey, and damn, I love it when we're like this. Fun and playful, and so hot I swear I'll lose all self-control if she keeps this up.

"Jules," I groan, gritting my teeth. "Get up here."

I want more. I *need* more. Coming in her hand? Polite pass. I can tackle that on my own.

My girl does what she does best. Tortures me. "What do you want, Mr. Bishop?"

"You." Always. Forever. "Up here. Now!"

But she just grins, sliding lower, her breath ghosting over me. "Shh," she whispers, her lips hovering just an inch from launching a full-on attack on my sanity. "You said it yourself—we don't have time."

I open my mouth to argue, but the second her lips wrap

around me, warm and slick, whatever words I have vanish. Along with my willpower. And every last brain cell. Thinking? Not an option.

Hell, it's taking every ounce of strength I have just to keep breathing.

Her tongue traces a slow, torturous line along my length, and I'm throbbing so hard I swear I'm on the verge of exploding.

Not just my dick. Me. Into a thousand pieces I will never recover from.

When she sucks, my eyes roll back in my head. My hands grip her hair as I groan. She hums in response, the vibration sending another shockwave of pleasure ripping through me until I'm on the edge, begging for it.

"Jules," I rasp, barely holding it together. "Fuck. Yes. Suck it harder."

Her hands grip my thighs as she sets a rhythm that's damn near euphoric.

The heat, the pressure, the way she moves—it's pushing me straight to the brink, and I'm barely hanging on.

Then her eyes flick up to mine—owning me in every way possible with just one look—and I'm done.

My body tightens, every nerve lit up like a fuse, and I'm gone. Completely at her mercy and loving every fucking second of it.

My whole body tenses with a guttural moan, and I'm done—completely undone, hard, fast, and so deep it knocks the wind out of me.

In pure Jules form, she doesn't stop. She milks every last drop of pleasure from me, relentless, until I'm left trembling, my breath coming out in ragged bursts, completely wrecked in the best way possible.

Finally, she pulls back, a self-satisfied grin on her face as she wipes her lips with the back of her hand. "On a scale of 1 to 10, how satisfied is he?"

"Ten thousand," I gasp, still trying to catch my breath, barely able to string a sentence together. "You overdid it."

Her brow furrows. "Overdid it? How?"

"You sucked him dry. He needs recovery time." I dramatically throw a pillow over my head, groaning. "Must. Sleep."

She snickers that evil little laugh of hers, before nuzzling her face into my neck. "I'm showering," she sweetly coaxes.

I don't move.

"Maybe I'll have a moment with the shower nozzle if you're too wiped out."

I fake a snore.

But the second I hear the water turn on, I'm on the phone.

Mark picks up on the first ring. "Hey, Brian, what's up?"

"It's Grandma Spenser's birthday, and I need a cake."

There's a brief pause before he laughs. "Last minute as usual. When do you need it?"

"An hour."

"An *hour*? Jesus, no pressure. All right, favorite flavors?"

"Halmeoni loves anything apple. And booze."

"Allergies?"

"Definitely not." I chuckle, shaking my head. "I've literally watched her eat everything from nuts to fruit, and even a mind-boggling assortment of wildflowers and weeds just to prove they weren't poisonous. The woman's practically invincible."

I can hear the wheels turning on his end, the familiar

sounds of him rummaging through his colossal pantry. "You're in luck. I'm fully stocked. If I start now, I can do a Tarte Tatin with a bourbon-soaked crust and buttery rum caramel glaze. Or are you aiming for a real showstopper? Perhaps an apple cake with bourbon cream cheese frosting."

"Surprisingly, she *does* have a thing for cream cheese."

"Fine. Done. But only if you cease and desist all ABBA karaoke on my voicemail. I still read the transcriptions during meetings." He pauses. "And let me tell you, reading 'You are the Dancing Queen' in the middle of a budget review is less than ideal."

I snort, trying to keep a straight face. "I bet it is."

"Not that I particularly mind being told I can dance, I can jive, having the time of my life. But do you have any idea how hard it is to keep from humming 'Dancing Queen' during meetings?"

I burst out laughing, doubling over, unable to stop the mental image of Mark trying to keep a straight face while humming ABBA in a boardroom.

"Do we have a deal?" he asks, deadpan.

I wipe away a tear, still grinning. "Deal."

I hang up, elated that the birthday girl will have a very special cake, and I can't wait to tell Jules. I slip on my prosthetic and head to the bathroom.

The steam clings to the mirror, and Jules is already under the water, her hair soaked. She catches me watching, her eyes dropping to my *growing excitement* with a teasing grin.

"Haven't you had enough?" she asks, playful as ever.

I move in behind her, wrapping my arms around her waist and pressing her back against my chest.

"Enough?" I murmur, brushing my lips against her ear. "When it comes to you, I'll *never* have enough."

CHAPTER 42
Brian

We pull up in front of the Spenser family home, and I'm already fighting the tension creeping up my neck. The place looks exactly how I remember it—warm and welcoming. For everyone but me.

She kills the engine and glances over at me. "You look worried."

I sigh, running a hand through my hair, avoiding her gaze. "Worried? Why would I be worried?"

Maybe because her father has me pegged as a dirtbag who ruined her life. You know, no reason at all.

I suck in a breath and remind myself that I'm not here for him. I'm here for her.

"It'll be fine," she says softly, but I hear the edge in her voice.

Once we're out of the car, cake in hand, Jules nudges me toward the door with all the gentleness of yanking a stubborn mule.

Then she shoots me a look that says, *Don't make this harder than it already is.*

We breeze past the kitchen, which is full of life—the chatter bouncing off the walls, mixing with the clatter of pans. I've learned to steer clear, or risk getting dragged into an impromptu showdown of who's *whatever dish* is better: Eomma's or Halmeoni's.

And we all know, there's no right answer.

On the patio are plates of colorful banchan lining the table—kimchi, japchae, pickled radish—and there's a platter of hot wings in the middle, most likely Colby's contribution.

I set down the cake and spot Jules's dad across the room, already frowning in my direction. Classic.

Leaning in, I murmur in her ear, "If they find me floating in the river, take care of my 1952 Mickey Mantle rookie card, will you?"

She deadpans. "You have a Mickey Mantle rookie card? And have not yet shown this to me? Wow, you're lucky I don't toss you into the river."

Innocently, I shrug.

She rolls her eyes, but a smile creeps in. "Just charm Eomma and Halmeoni in Korean, and maybe don't mention the card to Dad. He doesn't need another reason to throw you the hairy eyeball."

"For the record, I don't want him throwing his hairy anything at me."

"Just don't set him off."

"Got it. No mentioning to Papa Spenser how when his daughter's really fired up, she moans like a shewolf to the moon."

"Brian!" Her playful smack on my arm can't hide her giggles.

Halmeoni approaches, her smile wide as she shuffles over.

"*An-yong ha-se-yo, Hal-mo-nee*," I say, offering her a respectful bow. "Happy Birthday."

She beams, eyes sparkling as she reaches out and cups my cheeks with both hands. Eagerly, I lean down a little and grin. "You look so much like your father," she says, her voice thick with nostalgia.

I choke up, unprepared for the sudden wave of emotion. When my parents passed, people said things like that all the time —how I looked like my dad. It was just something to say when they didn't know what else to say.

But she means it. Halmeoni's not just making conversation. Our families were close. It's part of why I clung to the Spensers so hard. Her dad and mine were tight, and I wedged myself into their world, desperate for any shred of the family I lost.

I blink, swallowing the lump in my throat, and pull a small gift from my pocket—a delicate lavender silk scarf folded like a crane. I know it matches her favorite sweater.

Halmeoni's eyes light up when I hand it to her. She unfolds the scarf carefully, smoothing it out before knotting it delicately around her neck. "*Eotteoke boyeo?*" she asks, her voice light with excitement. *How do I look?*

"*Areumdawoyo.*" Beautiful.

Colby, spotting the teary, touchy-feely guy on the verge of a full emotional meltdown while chatting with his grandma, swoops in to cut the tension.

He wraps his grandma in a hug, flashing a wide, teasing

grin. "Come on, Halmeoni, you can tell me. How old are you? Twenty-nine, right?"

Halmeoni swats his arm, her expression playfully affronted. "Twenty-nine? Try *twenty-two, pungk-uh!*" she says, calling him a punk with a smirk.

We all laugh, the mood instantly lighter as her playful sass fills the room.

The day kicks off with a late lunch—easygoing and casual. Then it's team games like ping pong or corn hole, which inevitably get competitive.

After that, photos—lots of them.

Then Eomma has a small team come in for manis, pedis, and massages. The whole spa treatment, because of course, she does. Meanwhile, us guys are left to lug tables, set up decorations, and "man the grill."

Which is complete bullshit.

Hey, *I* could use a mani and a foot rub just as much as the next person. But nope, we "menfolk" are relegated to prepping for the after-dinner festivities. And with what Colby has planned, it takes the better half of two hours.

The evening descends in a wash of gold and purple, the sun dipping behind the mountain, casting long shadows across the yard as the last streaks of light paint the sky.

In the background, the football game hums, but no one's watching. The final hand of Texas Hold'em is down to the wire, and somehow, Halmeoni's winning.

We're letting her, of course—not that it's easy. The woman plays like she's never heard of poker in her life.

She'll call out "Go Fish!" and ask if we want to trade cards like kids do with properties in Monopoly. But it's her birthday, so, obviously, we do. Because on her special day, she *has* to win.

That's the rule.

When she scoops up her pile of chips, grinning from ear to ear, she looks around the table with a sparkle in her eyes. "I'm ready for Vegas."

Dead silence. We all freeze, eyes flicking nervously at each other, and Colby's eyes lock on mine, his expression practically screams, *She's joking, right?*

Her bright eyes say otherwise.

Then Jules breaks the tension with a nervous laugh, and soon, the rest of us are chuckling, too, because we know better.

If Halmeoni says we're going to Vegas, we're going to Vegas.

Jules's dad stands, pats me on the back, and gives a subtle nod toward the back door. "Let's grab some air."

Here we go.

We step outside, and the cool air slaps me in the face, a welcome reset from the tension inside. Jules's dad reaches into his pocket, pulling out a couple of cigars. He hands me one like it's the most natural thing in the world. "You smoke?"

I take it. "Every now and then."

He lights both, and we each take a satisfying drag. Silence stretches out like a wad of chewed gum. And after what feels like an eternity, he finally speaks. "Did you tell her?"

I shake my head. "I promised I wouldn't, and I won't. For now," I add. "What happened with Angi is ancient history." Not to mention, I have no idea how I'd even start to explain.

He lets out a long, relieved sigh.

Taking another drag, he blows smoke into the night air, his expression softening. "I'm surprised, honestly. The two of you being married and all. I figured my Jules would've mind-melded it out of you by now."

"I'm keeping it from her for now, not forever. First, we find Angi. Then either you tell her, or I will. Jules deserves the truth."

He lets out a quiet laugh, the sound almost bitter. "Angi always did know how to put the people closest to her through hell, didn't she?"

"That she did," I say, regret creeping into my own voice.

"And Colby?" His voice sharpens, cutting to the quick. "You're helping him?"

I don't even blink. "You're damn right, I am." I know he's caught between a rock and a hard place, but that's not my problem. He can hate me all he wants, but I'm not picking Angi over Colby.

Not today. Not ever.

His frustration tightens. "What happens if you catch her?"

"What happens if I don't?" I shoot back. "Colby's career is on the line. His whole future. Yeah, she needs help, and I get that you've done what you can. But I'm not letting her drag him down with her just because she decided to take him along for a joyride on the Titanic."

And I see it in his eyes. The moment he gives up. "You've got the resources now. The connections. If you're set on finding her, I can't stop you." He pauses, glancing at me. "Just don't be too hard on her. Please. I know how she always gets under your skin."

"Yeah. Like a damn spider."

After another stretch of silence, I pull out my phone, scrolling through the places Angi's been spotted recently. "Do you want to see what we have so far? Where we think she's heading?"

He hesitates for a moment before his eyes soften with worry. "All right," he says quietly, voice almost fragile. "Where's my little girl?"

I hand him the screen, watching as the weight of it sinks in. A map of bad choices, one after another. The anger's gone, replaced by something deeper—fear. He's just a dad now, wanting his daughter home safe and sound.

The door creaks open, and Jules steps out, her voice cautious. "Everything okay? What's going on out here?"

When the awkward silence settles over us, I pocket a hand and stay silent. I wait for her dad to say something—anything—because it's not my place to display the family skeletons. It's his.

Just as her dad's about to speak, Colby swoops in, grabbing his dad's cigar like he's been eavesdropping the whole time. "What does it look like? Man-time. No girls allowed."

Jules rolls her eyes, unfazed. "More like caveman time." Her gaze softens as she turns to me. "You ready?"

I nod. "Five minutes."

She heads back inside, and the air shifts between her dad and me, a quiet understanding passing without a word. Colby leans against the railing, grinning. "Do you two need a moment? Or a room?"

"Smart ass," his dad mutters, yanking the cigar back. He gives me a pat on the back. "Well, boys. Let's light 'er up."

Jules's mom gently guides Halmeoni to her seat, while Jules watches me, her eyes dancing in the soft glow of the evening. And with no makeup and hair in a ponytail, she's breathtaking.

"Do the honors," her dad says, handing me the lighter with a grin and a nod toward the fireworks setup.

Right. Because nothing says *Fire Marshall nightmare* like three guys with zero pyrotechnic experience and a handful of YouTube tutorials.

Fuck it. Here goes nothing.

I light the fuse with my cigar, stepping back as the sparks fizzle and sputter down the line.

We all wait, staring at the dark sky, holding our breath. A beat passes. Then another. Then . . .

Nothing.

We're all about to give Colby hell when *boom*—a million colors explode across the mountain sky, lighting it up like the universe just birthed a Technicolor star.

The bursts of reds, blues, and golds reflect off the peaks, to the point where the world is magic and light.

Jules slides under my arm, her head resting on my shoulder as we watch in awe.

A perfect end to a perfect night.

It's late, past midnight, and I'm wide awake.

Something about that email from Sydney Sun keeps poking at my brain like a sharp twig, refusing to let me rest. So, I sit alone, in my den, sipping rye and reading her email again and again until the words blur together.

When I blink my eyes open, there's a new email sitting in my inbox.

A small smile tugs at my lips before I glance at the door.

Is Jules asleep?

I'm tempted to go to her when curiosity gets the better of me, and I click it open.

From: sydney@herald.com
Subject: Media Excellence Gala Invitation

Thanks for the RSVP.
See you at the gala.

xoxo

A knot tightens in my chest. *See you at the gala.*

No mention of going together. Is that what she wants? Separate entrances, separate . . . everything?

And the email. A *Herald* email. So why would Jules say Sydney's no longer with them?

Confusion twists in my gut as I shut down the computer and drain my glass. For a long while, I don't go to my wife, and I don't email back.

I simply sit in the quiet, letting the darkness wrap around me, and I think.

CHAPTER 43
Brian

"Two weeks, Captain." The voice on the other end of the line is sharp, unyielding, like the steel of a cannon. "That's your deadline. If you can't produce the family member you claim took your card, the facts speak for themselves. Your card. Stolen money. We can all do the math."

Colby's jaw clenches so tight I can almost hear his teeth grind, frustration pouring off him.

I jump in, trying to keep things from boiling over. "Sir, with all due respect, two weeks is nowhere near enough. We *are* making progress. If we just—"

"Frankly, Mr. Bishop, the only reason you've even gotten this far is because your daddy called my daddy," he spits, the word *daddy* dripping with contempt. What he really means is my congressman pulled strings with his chain of command.

I know better than anyone that pulling a move like this is the equivalent of firing a flare gun at a grizzly bear. To be done when you're out of options and as a last resort because the backlash will be brutal.

And by the sound of his voice? Oh, yeah, he's definitely pissed.

"You've been dragging this out long enough," his voice snaps. "In two weeks, if this Angelina Spenser isn't standing in front of me, *you* will be appearing before the military tribunal. Is that clear?"

Colby and I respond in unison, voices tight. "Yes, sir."

The line goes dead with a sharp, emotionless click.

"Shit." I rub my temple, the pressure building. "Where exactly is your XO located?"

Colby exhales, trying to keep it together. "Iceland. Secure as hell. Three military jets and a chopper just to get there—and that's if we travel straight through."

"Fuck," I mutter under my breath. "This is a goddamned nightmare."

Colby leans back in his chair, deflated. "I'm screwed."

"No, you're not," I insist, though every tick of the countdown echoes in my head.

Why Uncle Sam won't just take the damn money and call it a day is beyond me. Instead, they'd rather make an example out of a decorated soldier like Colby.

Is there any universe where this makes sense?

My phone buzzes, vibrating against the desk. Logan's name flashes on the screen. He's got strict orders not to bother me unless something's on fire, blown to pieces, or royally fucked, so I answer.

"What?"

"That tux appointment. The tailor called. Need me to cancel it?"

Right. The tailor. The one who would've come to me, no

problem, but I didn't want to make a fuss. I glance over at Colby. "I can cancel."

"Don't cancel," he says, shaking his head. "Everyone's been working around the clock, and you've been burning every spare minute on this. You have a life, too."

"I'm still working on this."

"I know you are. Your entire team is. It'll be okay," he says, but the half-hearted tone makes my gut sink. It's killing him, and it's killing me, too.

The second I'm out of earshot, I will be doubling the team on this. And offering the reward I held off on.

"We'll find her," I say, but the words feel thin.

Colby nods, but the weight of it all hangs heavy, like it's slowly chipping away at whatever hope he's got left.

By the time we step outside, he forces a grin, trying to lighten the mood. "So, a tux, huh? Hot date?" he teases.

I shrug, keeping it vague. "Something like that."

I'M AT THE SHOP, STANDING IN FRONT OF A THREE-way, full-length mirror as Irving, my go-to tailor for years, pins and tugs at the tux. His fingers work with practiced precision, and he's muttering something about the fabric and shoulders, his Brooklyn accent lending authority to every word.

Not that it matters. I trust him implicitly, which is good, because my mind is a million miles away.

"My, my, my. Don't we look good enough to eat," a voice purrs like sticky sweet saccharine.

I don't need to turn around to know who it is. I see her in

the mirror—the last person I wanted to deal with today. Roxie Voss.

The nightmare of a reporter. And the woman who got Jules fired.

My patience? Instantly razor thin.

The tux suddenly feels too tight, and I can almost picture myself lunging for her throat.

And where the hell is Logan? The one guy who can shield me from the masses—and, more importantly, shield them from my wrath? Gone. Out for coffee because, like the idiot I am, I sent him off to "stretch his legs." Rookie mistake.

Now I'm trapped here, in a room with Roxana Voss, Bloodsucker Extraordinaire, the woman who somehow always manages to make me regret not bolting the door behind me.

"Tracking me down like a bloodhound on a still-warm corpse?" I say, turning to face her, my voice flat with irritation. "Whatever it is, you're wasting your time."

She smiles, slow and deliberate, like she's got the secret of Oak Island safely tucked away. "Well, I hear the Excellence Media Gala is going to be *the* event of the year."

Of course. She's here to weasel her way into that. Always scheming, always calculating. Always day drinking way too much if she thinks she's getting so much as a press badge from me.

Not today, Satan. Not today.

"I'm sure you'll find a way to crash it," I say, deadpan, hoping she'll get the message and leave.

But Roxie? She's like a cheap wine stain that just won't come out—persistent, insidious.

"Oh, darling," she croons, stepping closer. "I don't crash events. I create them."

I stare her down, not even sure where this is going. "And?"

"And I'm giving you one last chance."

"For?"

Her smile sharpens. "You promised me an exclusive."

I smirk, unbothered. "So, sue me."

Irving glances at me, awkward and fidgety, his eyes darting between us like he's silently asking if he should bail. I give him a quick wave, letting him know he's not going anywhere.

If anyone's leaving, it's definitely her.

Roxie crosses her arms, leaning against a counter. "Either you give me the exclusive, or you'll be making headlines anyway."

Really? A threat? Why am I even surprised?

I shake my head, "Fire away, Ms. Voss. Because you're not getting jack shit from me."

Logan strolls in, two coffees in hand, his eyes immediately narrowing at the viper in the room. "You need to leave," he says, tone sharp and unflinching.

Even though he's got a solid foot and at least a hundred pounds on Roxie, the look on his face says he's one snide comment away from yanking her by that overpriced Birkin and drop-kicking her scrawny ass straight out the door.

Roxie's smile stretches, slow and wicked, her eyes clinging to me like a leech sucking the life out of its host.

"I was just leaving," she says, sauntering to the door with the confidence of someone who knows she's left a bomb ticking in the closet.

She pauses at the threshold, glancing back with that same smug, self-satisfied grin. "See you at the gala," she sings.

And it's disturbing—like watching a creepy clown grin from the shadows, hunting you down with a red balloon. It's not just that she showed up here, uninvited, or even the way she casually tried to blackmail me for an exclusive.

It's those words.

See you at the gala.

Five simple, harmless words. Except they're the exact same ones at the end of Sydney Sun's last email.

Coincidence? Maybe.

Unease twists in my gut, the gnawing thought that Sydney Sun and Roxie Voss are somehow . . . connected. But why? My brain spins like a mouse on a wheel, running fast but getting nowhere.

"You all right?" Logan asks, breaking through the haze.

"Hmm? Oh, yeah. Just thinking."

"Dangerous," he smirks, handing me my coffee.

I take a sip, but it does nothing to shake the unsettled feeling that something's off. And for whatever reason, all I want is to talk to my girl.

Scratch that. I *need* to talk to her. I'm on edge, prickly, and the urge to check on Jules is clawing at me from the inside out.

Plus, a few words from her is all I need to smooth away all the wrinkles in my day. And right now, Roxie Voss is a big fucking wrinkle that I need gone.

I pull out my phone and hit dial.

On the second ring, Taylor picks up. Of course, she does. She's the one who snagged Jules the gala invite in the first place, and if I know Jules, Taylor probably had to drag her, kicking and screaming, out of her jeans and into a dress.

"Wait until you see her," she squeals, skipping the hello entirely.

And now, with Taylor gushing over how great my Peach Pop looks, everything seems strangely . . . normal. I'm not even sure why I called.

Still, my spidey sense doesn't ease off. "Can I talk to Jules?"

"Nope. She's in the middle of hair and makeup. We're lucky she hasn't bolted yet. If the glam team can't keep her still, they'll have no choice: horse tranquilizer."

I exhale slowly, pinching the bridge of my nose. "Fine. So, everything's . . . okay?"

"Yup."

"So . . . I guess I'll see you there."

"Uh-huh," she says, her tone casual, like she's barely paying attention. Probably too busy admiring her reflection in her freshly manicured nails.

Now me calling is just getting weird. I'm not even sure why I'm still on the line. "Great. See you two there," I mutter, feeling ridiculous as I hang up.

CHAPTER 44

Jules

I hug the corner of the room, soaking in the spectacle—the glittering sea of celebrities and journalists, all decked out like they've stepped off the pages of *Vogue*. It's the kind of event where hiding feels like survival.

But even in my little cocoon of anonymity, the deep rumble of a voice cuts through the hum of conversation.

"Ms. Spenser."

I turn, and all breathing stops.

Standing before me is a walking god in a panty-melting tux. Tailored to perfection, it hugs every muscle, every hard line, in all the right ways. His wavy hair is the right level of just fucked, and that light stubble? My fingers itch to run across it.

And those eyes—normally ocean blue, but right now darkened to the midnight sky—hint to just the kind of night I'm in for.

But it's the way he says "Ms. Spenser," in that low, gruff tone like he's tasting every syllable that makes me lose a little more of my mind.

It does things to my insides.

Sinful, criminal things.

And I love it when he calls me that, even though technically, I'm his wife—Mrs. Bishop. But when he leans in and gets all "Ms. Spenser" on me, I know I'm in for one hell of a night that'll leave me wrecked and breathless, and barely able to function by morning.

It's a fantasy we regularly slip into.

He looks so good, I'm damn near on the brink of begging him to rip this dress and throw me against the nearest wall.

I'm in awe, but I pretend I'm not. "You clean up pretty good, Bishop."

"As do you, Ms. Spenser. I'd love to clean you up with my tongue. Starting with that pretty pussy of yours."

I flush, suddenly feeling naked in my spaghetti-straps dress that hugs every curve like cellophane. I tug at the straps, praying my nipples don't make a bid for freedom and take out an eye. "Down, boy," I mutter below my breath. "It took the glam squad three hours to get me looking like this. You can't ruin all their hard work right off the bat."

"Three hours?" His brow shoots up, surprised.

I shrug, a smirk tugging at my lips. "It takes a village . . ."

He fakes an exasperated sigh. "Then I guess I'll bide my time. Maybe work the room." His hand slips into his pocket as he glances around casually. "I hear Sydney Sun is on the agenda."

Wait—what? *She* is?

"After her last few emails, I'd like to say hello."

I blink, confused. "She's on the agenda?" I ask. And what emails?

A slow smile spreads across his lips. Brian leans in, close enough for me to catch the warmth of his aftershave and the heat radiating from his chest.

My pulse spikes, and for a second, I almost think he's about to say something suggestive. I brace myself, already anticipating how it'll make my knees go absolutely weak.

But instead, his voice drops to a whisper. "You haven't seen her, have you? Sydney Sun? We've been emailing for a while now."

What?

My brain goes into a tailspin. A full-on death spiral. *Sydney Sun—emailing him?*

And he's emailing her back?

And . . . he likes her.

A group of people drifts past, and he steps in closer. The heat of his brick wall body against mine. "She's done so much for me, especially with my watch and all. I'd love to show her what she means to me. How deep our connection is. Since I have a few hours to kill . . ."

What the actual fuck?

Because three hours is too long for him to wait, and his dick needs an appetizer?

What the hell did fake Sydney Sun even say to him? Were they sexting? Sending photos?

Is this why he plans to *work the room?* He's horny?

My chest tightens painfully, anger wrapping itself around something deeper—something raw and ugly. *I'm hurt.*

He wants her.

I can feel it in the way his voice drops to that low, breathy tone, in the bedroom eyes he's flashing, and holy shit—the bulge in his pants isn't exactly subtle.

Argh!

Focus, Jules. Bigger issues at hand.

Sydney's on the agenda.

Sydney's been emailing him.

But *I'm* Sydney.

Only . . . I'm not.

Shit, shit, shit. I can't tell him off without telling him the truth. And if I tell him now, he'll know I've been lying to him this entire time.

Not outright lying, I guess—I never said I *wasn't* Sydney Sun. But we texted, we talked, and I had so many chances to tell him, *"Brian, I am Sydney Sun."*

And now, it's all unraveling. One second, we're on solid ground, and the next, the earth is crumbling beneath my feet, everything I've built with him about to be ripped away, slipping through my fingers like it never even existed.

I open my mouth to speak, but it feels like sand in my throat. Nothing comes out. *I could lose him.*

Or maybe I've already lost him. With the way he fawns over Sydney Sun, like if he doesn't have her soon, he'll die—he isn't mine.

My pulse thuds loudly in my ears and drowns out the world.

She's not Sydney Sun. I am. But does that even matter anymore? Whoever he's been speaking to, whatever connection they've made, feels . . . real. And it's killing me.

But it's also a lie, and this tight, suffocating ache in my chest, knowing I need to tell him the truth—I know I'll be taking a blowtorch to everything we've tried to rebuild until there's nothing left but rubble and ash.

I have to tell him. Now.

My lips part, the confession clawing up my throat, ready to be unleashed. But before I can say a word, a man interrupts, casually clearing his throat. "We're ready for you, Mr. Bishop."

"Ready?"

"Yes, from your RSVP. You'll be introduced in a minute to present the Trailblazer Award for Journalism."

"There must be some mistake."

The man checks his clipboard. "That's what I have here. If you'd like, I can have you speak with the production team."

Brian gives an impatient nod, then leans in, pressing a quick kiss to my cheek—*my cheek*. "I'll be right back."

And just like that, he's gone, slipping through the crowd, leaving me standing there with my heart tossed carelessly back at me.

Stunned, I stand there, rooted to the spot like an idiot as I fight tears.

"Well, if it isn't little miss waitress," a voice sneers beside me.

I turn, dazed, staring blankly at a man with a three o'clock shadow and a lime in his gin and tonic. He looks vaguely familiar, but my mind is too scrambled to place him.

Honestly, the man could be the Easter Bunny, and I wouldn't blink. My gaze is still locked on Brian, watching his every step as he disappears into the crowd, heading toward the stage.

Then, with a crooked smile and a ridiculously oversized watch that practically screams, *I'm important,* he says, "You should've fucked your way into my good graces when you had the chance."

His words hit like a hard slap, knocking the wind right out of me. My pulse skyrockets into overdrive, and I realize who he is and how much I despise the guy.

It's him. The sleaze bucket from Salvatore's. The one who couldn't stop dropping his name like bird crap, splattering it all over our very brief conversation.

Trent Mercer. Of Mercer Media.

And right about now, another helping of his shit is the last thing I need. Especially with my heart in shambles over Brian.

I spin on my heel, ready to walk away, to put as much distance between us as possible. But his hand snaps out, looping around my arm, his grip iron tight.

"Not so fast, Ms. Spenser. Or should I say Sydney Sun?"

CHAPTER 45

Jules

What the hell is going on? Has everyone lost their minds tonight? If this guy thinks he can manhandle me at the Excellence Gala, he's in for a nasty surprise—and a swift kick to the balls.

I jerk my arm back, ready to let him have it, but he raises his hands, sloshing his drink in the process, eyes wide with panic. "Hey, I'm sorry. I didn't mean to, *fuck*—"

The alarm in his voice makes me pause. And I can't just walk away. He knows who I am, heads and tails of my Spenser/Sun identity crisis, and I need to know how.

My voice drops to just above a whisper. "Why did you call me Sydney Sun?"

He blinks, genuinely confused. "Because that's who you are." When I glare, waiting for more, he sighs and adds, "I do own a global media conglomerate. People talk. Especially the ones from our latest acquisition, the *Manhattan Herald*."

The weight of his words sink in.

He lets out a long, weary breath, and by the heavy bags

under his eyes, it's clear he's about to offload a burden that's been wearing him down. "Look, I'm in a twelve-step program." His voice wavers, cracking under the pressure. "And I'm botching this all to hell, but I'm trying to apologize."

My eyes immediately dart to the glass he's clutching like a lifeline.

He follows my eyes, lifting the glass with a faint, self-deprecating smile. "Gin and tonic. Sans the gin. I keep the lime in there so people stop trying to buy me drinks." He takes a sip, grimacing. "Tastes like piss, by the way."

"Is that why *I should've fucked you when I had the chance*?" I scoff, crossing my arms.

He winces, the smirk wiped clean off his face. "That was . . . a crude attempt at humor. I don't usually have to try. People kiss my ass, laugh at my jokes, all without me lifting a finger. Except for you . . ."

His words trail off, and realization hits me like a truck. This isn't about power or manipulation. There's no game here, no strategy. It's raw, messy, unpolished remorse—laid bare.

Straightening his suit, he clears his throat. "I'm sorry."

"You should be," I quip back, a little sharper than intended. But then I soften. "And you're forgiven." I step closer, lowering my voice. "And you've got this. *One day at a time.*"

His eyes search mine. "You know about addiction?"

I nod, my throat tightening. "A little. My family thinks I'm oblivious, that I don't know my sister's an addict. She'll do anything for a hit. We call her Hurricane Angi because she'll damn near destroy everything and everyone to get what she needs. I've volunteered with NA for years."

Slowly, he nods, a flicker of understanding crossing his face.

"I'm so desperate for a drink right now that if you spilled your glass, it'd take everything in me not to lick it off your shoes."

"If you ever need someone to talk to . . ."

He arches an eyebrow. "On or off the record, Ms. Sun?"

"Off the record, definitely. Officially, I'm not Ms. Sun. The *Herald* kept my account and screwed me out of my name."

He tilts his head thoughtfully. "Which articles were yours?"

"Just the first one."

He nods, acknowledging the weight behind those words. "Business is business. And brutal. But that article was good. You've got real talent. I'm sure we can come to some kind of arrangement if we can persuade you to come back."

I shrug, noncommittal at best. "I'm not sure the *Herald* is my passion anymore. I'm more of a hometown news girl at heart. Maybe I'll stick to ghostwriting. Or try freelancing."

"Here." He hands me his card, his expression unreadable.

It's not the same card he gave me before. No *Mercer Media* on it. "Excelsior Media?"

"My new global conglomerate. Twenty-three countries and counting. I'm shifting my focus international." His smile lifts, just barely. "The good thing about sobriety—it clears the head. Bigger margins. Fewer sewer rats."

He gestures subtly toward Wyld Richards, who's got his arm draped around Roxie's waist. Good to know I'm not the only one who thinks the guy is a walking roach turd.

He takes another sip, wincing. "*Bleh*. I need to take off. It's not easy, staring at Roxana Voss and being damn near ready to French kiss that vampire just for a taste of her martini."

We both laugh, his wink adding a dash of charm before he

heads out, vanishing across a sea of people just as the announcer's voice booms through the speakers.

"Ladies and gentlemen, please take your seats. Presenting our first award—the *Trailblazer Award for Journalism*—is Mr. Brian Bishop, Manhattan's own Bachelor of the Year. And with him, the recipient of this prestigious honor . . . Ms. Sydney Sun."

Wait—what the hell?

CHAPTER 46
Jules

Brian strides to the center of the stage, a woman's hand locked firmly in his. And she's beautiful. Watching him with the living, breathing doll of Sydney Sun is almost too much to bear.

Her long, dark hair cascades the full length of her back as she casually adjusts the Jackie-O sunglasses higher on her nose, like it's all part of her mystique—which it is. The plunging red dress matches that infuriatingly perfect shade of cherry-red lipstick. Her smile spreads, polished and precise, cutting through the room like royalty.

And what do I do? I stand there like an idiot and watch with everyone else.

I should be furious. I should storm up there, shouting up a storm that she's a fraud and that I'm Sydney Sun.

The real Sydney Sun. But I can't.

The louder the crowd claps, the harder my chest tightens.

She's not just beautiful—she's a flawless reflection of my alter ego, the image I once dreamed would come to life.

And now, it has.

Just not for me.

My heart slams against my ribs as Roxie's wolf whistle slices through the noise. And then, in slow motion, everything snaps into place. Wyld's first job offer. The carefully crafted identity. The job that seemed too good to be true.

And the assignment: Brian Bishop—billionaire.

A hand-picked journalist, molded to draw out the one man no one could get to.

"You all know her," Brian says into the mic, flashing that smile as a hush falls over the crowd. "The woman whose first article captured me in a light that was both rich and heartfelt, and won over not just my heart, but America's, too. I'm beyond honored to present the Excellence Gala Trailblazer of the Year award to Ms. Sydney Sun."

Thunderous applause erupts, and their hands rise together. It's like watching the tide crash in, wiping out the beautiful castle I'd built.

Then she kisses him. Full on. Deep. So deep that the crowd loses their absolute shit as my heart shatters. The world blurs, and my chest collapses on itself until I can't breathe.

I should say something.

Tell him the truth.

Tell everyone the truth.

That's not Sydney Sun. I am.

But I can't.

I'm too busy wiping away the tears to do anything else.

"You need to take a seat, miss," a woman says, her voice breaking through the haze.

But I don't sit. I can't.

My feet unlock, and I rush to find Taylor. By the time I

reach her, she's already at a table on the other side of the room, wrapping me in the biggest, tightest hug.

"You won!" she squeals, excitement bubbling over. "I saw you in that killer red dress, and—"

Her voice falters as she pulls back, her face twisting with confusion when she sees I'm still in the emerald dress I came in. "What's going on? And . . . why are you crying?"

"We need to find Brian." The words come out in a choked sob. "I have to tell him the truth."

By the time we make it backstage, he's gone. My doppelgänger's gone. And most of my hope is gone with them. Then I call. And Taylor calls.

Nothing.

For the next hour, we push through the crowd. My mind spins, emotions crashing into one another like waves in a storm—rage, fear, regret. It's all too much, but I can't stop. Not now.

Brian first. Breakdown later.

Then we split up, and I stumble onto Wyld and Roxie. They're practically wrapped around each other, limbs tangled like two cozy wolf spiders caught in a web. And my last shred of my sanity snaps.

I lunge for Roxie, fury blazing through me. "You've had your fun. Where is he?" My voice cracks, but I don't care. I'm past that.

She shoves me back and straightens her dress, her smirk deepening. "Don't you mean *they*?" Her voice is syrupy, mocking. "And shouldn't you know? You're his wife, after all."

She pulls out her phone, scrolling leisurely, dragging out the moment like she's savoring it. "Must've been awkward, right?

Watching him kiss another woman while you just stood there, letting him."

Then she shoves the phone in my face, the screen blaring with the shot. Brian and *Not-Sydney Sun*, kissing. And raw pain hits my chest all over again.

And the next shot?

It's me. On the verge of tears, my reaction captured in brutal clarity.

By this point, I'm so done. Either I'm getting charged with attempted murder, or I'm leaving.

With fury boiling beneath my skin, I storm off, ready to let the social media chips fall where they may. Let them post. Let them speculate. I don't care.

Except I really do. It's public and horrible and the heartbreak of Brian Gabriel Bishop all over again.

Her voice slices through the air. "I believe he's whisking her away for the weekend," she calls out, the smugness dripping from her words. Her hot pink phone is already pointed directly at me. "Any comment?"

I whirl around, fury pulsing through my veins. "You want a comment? You've got one. Go fuck yourself."

I know I've just handed her exactly what she wanted—perfect footage, a juicy headline—but at this point, I don't care. Not anymore.

All that matters is Brian.

What if she slips into his life, prying open his deepest, most vulnerable secrets? She could twist everything—his wounds, his strength—turn him into a shell of the man he is, laid bare for the world to see, his hidden scars and the weight of his past exposed.

I call two more times, and when that doesn't work, in one last desperate attempt, I text him.

The woman you're with isn't Sydney Sun.

Minutes crawl by, each one heavier than the last, until my phone finally pings with a reply.

I know.

CHAPTER 47
Jules

It's been two days, and I'm a wreck. Barely functioning. My picture has been all over the news, and Brian's been MIA.

But when there's a knock at the door, I nearly bulldoze Taylor out of the way to answer it.

But it's not Brian.

It's Trent Mercer.

"Can I come in?" he asks, looking less like hell warmed over and more put together. Polished. Professional. Like he's here on business.

Meanwhile, I'm standing there, woefully underdressed in my unwashed sweats, heart on my sleeve and barely holding it together.

I shrug, numb to just about everything right now. So, sure. Why not?

I step aside, letting him in just as Taylor barrels out of her room.

"If that fuckface is here, I'm about to tear him a new one for breaking your heart and—" She halts mid-ass-kicking, her eyes widening in realization. "Oh, sorry. I thought you were her husband."

He nods, like being mistaken for someone's cheating husband is just another Tuesday for him.

Then, like a switch flipping, Taylor shifts gears into hostess mode, looping her arm through his. "You're Trent Mercer."

"Yes. All-around asshole and recovering alcoholic," he says dryly, his eyes locked on mine. "Can I have a moment alone with Ms. Spenser? Or is it Mrs. Bishop?"

Barely hanging on, I choke out, "Just Jules."

Taylor glances at me for permission, and with a quick nod, she retreats to her room, leaving me to face whatever the hell this is, head-on.

Trent's gaze flicks between the lumpy sofa and the rickety chair, his rich-boy discomfort barely hidden. Then, he frowns. His eyes fall on the wine bottle on the table.

I wave it off. "It's empty," I say, trying to sound more composed than I feel.

"It's not that," he says, his voice low, steady, but heavy with something unsaid. "That was the wine they served at my wedding." He pauses, glancing down as if the memory stings just enough. "My wife left a few years back, and it's these little reminders from the universe that keep me sober."

Slowly, he settles into the chair, as if his weight might collapse it.

I clear my throat. "What are you doing here?"

He pulls out a hot pink phone and tosses it my way. I catch it with one hand, my stomach tightening in a heavy knot. "This is Roxana's."

He nods. "I confiscated it from her. Right before I fired her."

I force a smile, trying to push down the storm of emotions. "Thank you."

He leans back, his tone casual but direct. "I killed her story. No guarantee she won't try to sell it somewhere else, but it won't be with me, so . . . I figure you owe me."

I narrow my eyes, the tension lifting just slightly. "If jerk face Mercer is back, I swear I'll flick you in the forehead."

He smirks, shaking his head. "Look, I don't know what's going on in your life, but I was thinking you could use an escape. And now that I've fired Roxie, I happen to need a reporter."

"I told you, my heart's not in investigative reporting." Not anymore.

"Did you?" He arches a brow, leaning forward, elbows resting on his knees. "Well, that's a relief because I'm not looking for an investigative reporter."

"Then, what are you looking for?"

"Connection. Did you know in Singapore, they give tax incentives to families who live close to each other? It's their way of encouraging connection, keeping loved ones together."

I shake my head, not even trying to fake it. "I had no idea."

He gives me a soft smile, but there's a spark of excitement behind it. "And in Korea, they have this beautiful tradition called *Chuseok*. It's like their Thanksgiving, but it's more than just a holiday. It's about gathering, honoring ancestors, sharing food, memories, and, more importantly, time."

I nod, tucking a strand of hair behind my ear. "That, I knew."

His words come out more animated now. "That's what I'm offering you! A chance to be somewhere different, to really experience life, and to write about what brings people closer. This isn't just a job or a headline—it's about in-depth pieces, one major story at a time."

I fight a grin, trying to keep my excitement in check, but I can't help it.

My mind is already running with the picture he paints. Trekking through foreign cities, tasting new foods, meeting people whose stories I'd bring to life. It's the adventure of a lifetime, but I don't want to get too ahead of myself.

I fell for the dream job once, and look where I am.

I bite my lip, keeping my words calm and sedate. "How in-depth are we talking?"

"For starters, six months."

"Six months," I repeat, thinking it through.

He dives into the details, and I'm all ears. "You get to clear your head, escape the chaos, and immerse yourself in a whole new world. While I get a reporter who writes hometown stories like no one else. Premium salary, all expenses covered. Traveling across Asia, experiencing the culture firsthand. And a whole new handle that you own."

Each word pulls me in deeper, my mind already wandering through the possibilities. That is, until he says, "But there's a catch."

My heart stumbles. "What?"

"I need you on a flight first thing in the morning," Trent says, his voice calm but full of promise. "You'll be following the story of a rising athlete—Sora Kim. All the big media outlets are eager to cover her journey as she climbs toward

Olympic status, but her family isn't looking for flashy headlines. They want someone who can show the heart of their story—the way they work together, the sacrifices they've made to reach this dream. I showed them your work, and they loved it."

My smile is instant, and somehow, I feel lighter. "They did?"

"We're still finalizing the details with your in-house social media manager, but everything else is ready to go."

From the back, Taylor bursts in, "She comes with full social media management!" Clearly, she's been hanging on every word.

I laugh, shaking my head at her perfect timing, and Trent holds out a hand. "Say yes."

The man is a hell of a salesman. And maybe it's the exhaustion talking, or the fact that this feels like the perfect way to lick my wounds and finally reconnect with the one person I lost in all the chaos—me.

So, I agree. "Yes. On one condition. I won't be Sydney Sun. I'll be using my real name."

"I wouldn't have it any other way," he says, taking my hand in his as we shake on it, sealing the deal.

For the next hour, we go over the details, and when we're done, I step back, feeling lighter than I have in days. "I'd better start packing," I say, as Taylor silently waves me off with a grin.

I find myself lingering because, for once, it's my turn to eavesdrop. She walks Trent to the door, but there's something different—she's genuine. No playful banter, no flirty quips, just real curiosity. "Didn't you start a nonprofit to create safe spaces for artists and models during their travels?"

I hear him chuckle, his voice low and amused. "Ironic, with how I treated Jules when we first met. You're an artist?"

Taylor replies, her voice light but sincere. "Intermittent fashionista. But when I landed in the country broke, I stayed at Château Bellemont in Paris, and being that far from home in a strange country? I felt safe. It really helps." She pauses for a moment, then casually adds, "If you're free sometime, maybe we could grab dinner."

I'm on pins and needles, waiting for his response. What most people don't know about Taylor is that her dad is a recovering alcoholic—twenty years sober now. She knows the terrain, the rough patches that lie ahead, and she's never been one to back down from anything. It's why we're best friends.

"The most beautiful stained-glass windows are made from shattered glass," she always says.

It's not just a line. It's how she sees the world.

When he hesitates, she quickly adds, "I was thinking of blowing off some steam. Arcade World. Vintage games, junk food, zero booze. And spanking you at Pac-Man."

His smile spreads, confident and easy. "I'd love to."

I NOD OFF, THE FRAY OF NERVES AND SADNESS FINALLY surrendering to sleep. And for the first time, I'm not running from something. I'm running toward it.

A new life. As me.

CHAPTER 48
Brian

I wipe my lips on my sleeve, still tasting the smudge of Angi's lipstick, pretty sure nothing will get it off short of paint thinner.

Colby gives me a sharp look. "What the hell are you doing?"

"Trying to get this damn lipstick off. You got a belt sander?"

Angi's quiet for once. Peaceful, even. It's what happens when the high fades and you come crashing down. The aftermath of a storm, and the eerie calm before the next one.

The XO's office is a symphony of rustling papers. He's flipping through Angi's file, shooting her glances like she's a ticking time bomb. She's passed out cold on the cot, handcuffed to it like they expect her to wake up swinging.

"Angelina Spenser," he reads aloud, his voice clipped. "Arrested since eighteen. Coke, meth, possession, intent to sell." The list goes on, the words tumbling out as if they don't carry the weight they should. "Multiple suicide attempts. Recommended psych watch." He pauses, staring at the scars on her wrists before his eyes flick back to me.

I clear my throat. We don't need a full history lesson. "She's here now. Three military flights, one helicopter, and a fight I won't forget anytime soon. You asked for her. And here she is."

Which, by the way, is more than I can say for my phone, currently sinking somewhere in the Atlantic after Angi came at me like a banshee for the third time. And Colby's phone is so smashed to hell, I'm not sure why he's still holding onto it.

"What more do you want?" Colby asks, his nerves frayed but with enough military bearing he's holding it together.

The XO doesn't flinch, his gaze like granite as it shifts between me, Colby, and finally lands on Angi, who's starting to stir on the cot. "I need assurance she hasn't compromised national security. When she wakes, we'll interrogate her."

"You'll question her," I snap. "With one of us in the room."

His lips twitch, the barest hint of a concession. "Fine. We'll question her. If and when we're satisfied, she'll be remanded back to civilian custody." He leans back in his chair, expression unreadable. "Unfortunately, there's a bench warrant out for her arrest."

"Of course, there is." Welcome to Angi's world. One problem solved, and five more take its place.

Colby folds his arms, jaw set like stone. "Well, at least she's consistent."

"Is Captain Spenser cleared?" I ask, the words coming out more forcefully than I intended.

The XO sighs, rubbing his temple before letting his eyes fall back to the file. "Considering she took down half the MPs and all five-foot-three of her trashed a jeep on her way in . . ." He shuts the file with a decisive snap, the sound cutting through the room like a knife. His gaze meets mine. "If my little chat with your sister pans out, yes. You're cleared, Captain Spenser."

He stands abruptly, his chair scraping against the floor. "I've got a meeting with JAG to prepare for our 'questioning' session." He throws up air quotes, his voice dripping with disdain. "I'll be back."

"Can I use your phone?"

He deadpans. "No."

With that, he strides out, leaving us in the heavy silence of the office.

I blow out a breath, feeling the tension in my shoulders ease just a hair. But it's not over—not by a long shot. With Angi, nothing ever is.

Colby shakes his head, the weight of Angi's latest shitshow pressing heavy between us. "I'm sorry about all this."

I clap a hand on his shoulder, firm to ease the guilt clouding his eyes. "Don't be. When your dad first hired me to keep an eye on her, I didn't think I'd still be chasing after her ten years down the line."

A tired laugh slips past my lips as I scrub the exhaustion from my face. But then, my fingers find my wedding band, and I give it a slow twirl. "And out of all this, I got Jules."

I'd run through hell and back again for my girl, no questions asked.

My Peach Pop.

My wife.

CHAPTER 49

Brian

It's only been a few days since I last saw my Jules, but it feels like forever.

I'm worn down to the bone, dragging with exhaustion, and all I can think about is a hot shower, a decent bed, and holding my wife for a straight week, no interruptions.

The second the wheels touch down in New York, it's like stepping into a storm. Reporters swarm us like locusts on a summer field. We exit the plane, and they're already shouting.

"Are you having an affair with Sydney Sun?"
"Is she pregnant?"
"Are you a throuple?"

A what?

"Is the divorce final?"

My heart seizes in my chest. *Divorce?*

What the fuck is going on?

My mind locks on the only thing that matters. *Jules.*

It takes less than a second to realize she won't be at the house. Mostly because if she were, the place would be swarming with press, and Jules dodges reporters like a pack of zombies circling the last fresh brain.

Out of pure habit, I check my pockets for my phone. No surprise, it's not there.

Colby pulls his out, tries to power it up. Dead, of course.

We finally, *finally*, manage to break free from the crowd, thanks to a friendly face in airport security—one of my former troops. He makes sure we're left alone and even grabs a brand-new, fully charged cell from the nearest vendor.

For which I'll happily owe him seats behind home plate for the next season's Yankees games.

I dial Jules's number. It rings. No answer.

Then I punch in the number I know by heart. "Tell me you've got a track on my wife."

"I do," Harrison says, his voice clipped. "She's at her place. I've already got three guards posted to keep the media out. But we got there a bit too late . . . Trent Mercer from Mercer Media slipped in."

My stomach drops. Trent Mercer? Of all people, that son of a bitch is with her? "And you didn't kick his ass out because . . . ?"

"From the window surveillance, they're just talking. She's not upset. If anything, they're chummy."

"Chummy? What the fuck does *chummy* mean?"

"It means we're handling it," Harrison says, way too calm for my liking. Then he adds, "Chopper and car are waiting. If you can get your ass out of JFK, we'll have you there ASAP."

I mutter a curse under my breath and say, "Thanks."

The ride is long, the drive even longer.

Harrison's getting me up to speed, firing off news articles and photos—each one a punch to the gut.

Jules was left all alone to fend for herself while I've been stuck wrestling with the living nightmare Angi becomes when her coke high crashes.

Goddamnit.

I've got enough anger simmering under the surface to burn the whole damn city down, and not just at the press. At me.

I left her.

Abandoned her without a word for days.

Fuck.

I should've been there to protect her. Or at the very least, stop hiding the truth and come clean.

But I gave her father my word. I swore on my parents' memories that I'd keep quiet—about the drugs, her fragile, spiraling mental state, the attempts to end her own life. Repeated ones.

How the hell do I go back on that now?

And how do I not tell my wife?

Jules, who had only just stepped out of her no-social-media bubble, is now a PR agent's worst nightmare. She's wearing a target a mile wide, and I'm the reason she's in the crosshairs.

By the time I pull up to her place, the frustration has built to a boiling point. I'm ready to bulldoze through that door like the Hulk.

But then it hits me—Trent Mercer, the guy who owns the largest global media empire on the planet, is on the other side of that door. Smashing in like a wrecking ball?

Bad idea. A *very* bad idea.

I suck in a slow, meditative breath.

Must. Calm. Down.

Just as I get close, the door swings open, and there he is—Trent Mercer. Expensive suit, power tie, stepping into the hall like he owns the damn place.

I pause, listening, because fuck, I don't know, old habits die hard.

Jules is still inside, and I have to strain to hear her. "I was thinking of blowing off some steam. Arcade World. Vintage games, junk food, zero booze. And spanking you at Pac-Man."

I freeze, my jaw locking. My *wife*—asking *him* on a date? Of all people, a sleazeball like Trent Mercer?

The second that smug smile spreads across his face, my fists clench, itching to wipe it off.

"I'd love to," he says, voice as smooth as cream.

I duck out of sight, behind a—what the hell? Ficus. My pulse is hammering in my ears, and I'm way too wired to face either of them right now. I can't lose my temper with Jules. Ever. She's not the kind of woman you win back by roaring like a caveman.

And Trent? Let's just say first-degree murder is a bad look. Not exactly the best move when I'm trying to fly under the radar at the Centurion Group.

So, instead of barging in on my wife or shopping for headstones for Trent, I stand there, rooted in place, fists clenching and unclenching.

My brain's spinning out, trying to figure out the next move when my new phone buzzes in my pocket.

I pull it out to see Harrison's name flash across the screen. "What?"

"If you need alone time with the Ficus, that's cool. But if you need a place to crash tonight, mi casa es su casa."

I let out a breath, half chuckle, half exasperated sigh and simply say, "I'll keep that in mind."

I know how Jules works. Coming at her full force, with all the charm of a bull in a china shop is the quickest way to lose her for good.

So, I go up to the door, and knock.

After a moment, it opens. Just barely. Taylor peeks out. "She doesn't want to speak to you."

The flimsy chain lock would be so easy to bust open, I could do it with a finger, but I don't.

"Let me in, Taylor."

"Um"—she pretends to think—"No."

Then she closes the door in my face. And now I'm banging on the door hard enough for the neighbors to hear. A few peek their heads out, then scurry back inside. Which pisses me off more, because what if I was an actual bad guy?

Finally, it opens, chain intact, Jules, with red, swollen eyes, looking up at me. She looks so defeated, it's taking everything in me not to kick in the door and scoop her up in my arms. "What do you want?" Her voice is small. So small.

"I, uh . . ." I notice people peeking their heads out again. This time with camera phones. I rub my neck to regain control. Any sudden moves are sure to go viral. "Can we talk?"

"No," she says softly. I can see she's barely holding it

together, and I slip a hand through the door, hoping she'll take it.

Miraculously, she does.

"I promise you, I can explain. It wasn't what it looked like, and—"

"Can we talk in the morning? I'm tired, and I just need a good night's rest."

"Sure. I'll be here. Bright and early. I'll even bring your favorite muffins," I add, hoping to sweeten the deal. I know she loves the peach ones with cream cheese frosting—bite-sized so she can eat them by the handful and still get that perfect cream-cheese-to-muffin ratio.

"Goodnight," she says, her voice quick and final as she slips her hand from mine. Abruptly, the door clicks shut like a slap, the kind that lingers long after the sting fades.

I make my way to the street, but every nerve in my body screams *Turn around, you idiot. Don't leave her. Not like this.* And just as I'm about to, I hear her, soft but firm. "Brian, wait."

I whip around, and then she's on me—lips crashing into mine with a kiss so fierce, it steals my breath, my sanity, my soul.

It's heat and want, deep and raw, pulling me under until I'm drowning in her. My hands grip her like she's the only thing tethering me to the world. And in that moment, she is.

Then, as fast as it started, it's over.

She's gone, and I'm left standing there, panting and stunned like I've been hit by a truck.

It takes a beat for me to notice the tiny weight in my hand. To open my palm and see it—her wedding ring, cold and final.

It isn't until a car pulls up that I blink from the fog. The window rolls down. Harrison hollers, "Get in."

I don't move. "What?"

"You've been standing there for half an hour, and it's about to rain. Get in."

With no more fight left in me, no more breath, and no more reasons to stand here, I do. I slide into the car, damn near certain I've just lost everything.

CHAPTER 50
Brian

The next morning, after a shower, six hours of sleep, and enough coffee to keep my homicidal tendencies at bay, I'm ready to tackle the day.

I need to let her call the shots. If there's one thing my Peach Pop will not appreciate, it's a big Alpha bull like me charging at her china shop of emotions.

But Trent Mercer?

Yeah, that bastard's on borrowed time.

Tick. Fucking. Tock.

By the time Trent Mercer strolls into his office, arrogance personified, I'm already there.

Sitting at his desk.

Enjoying the thought of how long it'll take him to find all the shrimp tails I've hidden in the back of every single drawer.

Still, it takes everything in me not to leap across the room and lunge at his throat.

His eyes widen for a split second, then his cool, practiced

smile returns. "Bishop." He clocks my death stare, my hands gripping the armrests. "Truce?"

"Depends. Got plans with my wife, do you?"

"She's free to do whatever she wants," Mercer replies, his voice infuriatingly steady as he slowly takes the seat across from me. The one meant for guests. "Look, I might be an asshole, but I'm not the one who fucked her over in front of five hundred reporters."

Shit. Is that what he saw? Of course, it is. That's what *everyone* saw.

"I don't give a damn if the whole world thinks that," I growl, my grip tightening on the armrest until it snaps with a sharp crack. I barely register the sound as I jab a finger toward his chest. "It'll be a cold day in hell before you date my wife."

"What?" He chuckles—*actually chuckles*—like he has absolutely no value for his life. "I'm not dating your wife." He blows out a breath. "I know what it's like to need a little space. And I like Jules." He quickly corrects, "Not like that. I felt a little responsible for what happened—with Richards and Voss on my books, and me asleep at the wheel. I figured I owed her."

I glare at him, my patience thin. "So, what? You spent an hour with her and gave her a pep talk?"

"I gave her a job. A writing job. In Korea."

I freeze. "She's going overseas? For how long?"

He blows out his cheeks, puffing air. "Six months."

"When does she leave?"

He glances at his watch, wincing like he knows the blow he's about to deal. "She'll be heading to the airport soon."

I get up in an eager rush to the door.

"You might want to drop by and chat with her social media

manager," Mercer calls after me. "She'll be in soon. On the third floor, keeping tabs on Jules's itinerary. Though she's a bit of a vault when it comes to your wife's whereabouts."

"Thanks," I mutter, already halfway out. Just as I pull the door shut behind me, I add, "And sorry about your chair. And the tails."

"The what?" I hear him sputter as the door clicks shut.

CHAPTER 51

Jules

"Can I help you with that?" the Uber driver asks the second I step outside, his eyes glued to the suitcase that's threatening to burst at the seams.

Wow, he got here fast.

I hand it over without a second thought. "Thanks."

The SUV he pulled up in is way bigger than I expected—far more space than I need, but considering I was on the phone with Eomma, Dad, and Halmeoni, being told to pack everything but the kitchen sink "just in case," I'm grateful for the room.

And yeah, I'm late.

I've also heard airport security is its own special brand of adventure, so the fact that I'm being limo-ed to the fresh side of hell in an ultra-plush vehicle? Count me in.

As he loads my suitcase into the trunk, I open the back door, and a tiny voice squeals, "Princess Peach Pop!"

I blink. Is that . . . the little girl from the restaurant?

"Sit next to me!" she insists.

Which, okay, since I'm not hauling some high-end purse, I slide in next to her.

I glance at the two boys in the third row—one glued to a comic, the other engrossed in a game on his phone. They both look up, give me a quick wave, then promptly go back to being boys.

My gaze shifts to the man in the driver's seat. The man's rugged looks and the way he carries himself tell me one thing: driving people around is definitely not his gig.

If I were to guess, military vet is high on the list of possibilities.

"You're not an Uber driver, are you?" I ask.

He holds out a hand. "Harrison. And I'm guessing you haven't formally met my kids—Connor, Ollie, and this little tornado is Sophia Hannah Evans, also known as Snooki Pie."

"Hi." I wave awkwardly, offering a smile to them all, but my stomach knots as realization dawns.

Brian sent him.

He sent all of them, which—using kids to pull at my heartstrings—feels like cheating.

And the truth is, I'm not ready to see him. Not yet.

"Where are we going?" I ask, my voice betraying the smallest quiver.

"Normally, hostages don't get clues," Harrison says with a smirk, smoothly merging into traffic. "But Brian didn't want you to worry. We're taking you straight to the airport. International terminal at JFK."

"I was worried you'd be taking me to Brian, and I'd have to tuck-and-roll," I say, only half kidding.

"Bolting from moving vehicles is strictly prohibited," Harrison says with a wink in the rearview mirror.

I let out a small sigh, a little relieved, until the other half of me wonders why I'm not the kind of woman worth chasing after.

"Do you know how to braid hair?" Snooki asks, already handing me a brush.

I nod confidently. "Champion braider. Three years running. Totally unofficial, but still, the title stands." She flips through an *Angelina Ballerina* book—a Spenser family favorite because of Angi's full name—and I get to work, taming her thick locks.

Soft music plays in the background, The Spinners, I think, and I catch Snooki bouncing her feet and humming along like she knows it by heart.

Working my way back to you, babe, with a burning love inside.

By this point, I can't hold it in any longer. "Is he going to try and stop me?"

"Brian?" Harrison glances at me in the mirror. "He'd never stop anyone from chasing a dream. Least of all someone he loves."

Loves.

The word lands on me, soft as a feather, lingering for just a second before I let it drift away. I refocus on the braid. "Her hair is amazing," I murmur, my fingers weaving through the silky strands.

"She got those incredible locks from her mother," he says, his voice tinged with sadness.

He said *got*. Past tense. And even though he's still wearing his wedding ring, I feel the weight of their loss.

"I'm sorry," I utter before I can stop myself.

He nods, his expression heavy with emotion, but he won't say more in front of the kids. And I don't press, though my heart aches for him. For all of them.

Three beautiful kids growing up without a mother. And a heartbroken father, carrying the unbearable weight of it all, silently strong, all on his own.

I can't imagine it.

"Never go to bed mad," he adds after a moment, his voice soft. "That's what she used to say. And for the record, with her Italian fire and my Irish temper, it wasn't exactly easy. But I'm so glad we never did."

My chest tightens as I take in his words. And the storyteller in me, the part that craves knowing people on a deep, human level, aches to hear more. "What else did she used to say?"

"Lots of things. That pasta is a staple. That tiramisu without espresso is sacrilege. That life's too short to drink bad wine. And that when you love, love with all your heart or not at all."

Funny, I've tried *not at all,* and it was a cold, empty wasteland I acclimated to, but never enjoyed being in. But *with all my heart*? Will I ever be ready for that?

Harrison continues, a small smile tugging at his lips. "She always said love is like a pretzel."

"A pretzel?"

"Yeah. It twists you up, bends you out of shape, makes you uncomfortable. But that's the only way it exists. And if, even through all of that, you still can't see yourself with anyone else . . . that's how you know."

"Know what?"

"That it's real. And the kind of love worth fighting for."

We pull up to the curb, and even though my feet are ready to step out, my heart isn't. I'm not sure I've fully processed everything—Brian, home, leaving it all behind.

But Snooki doesn't let me linger in my thoughts. She throws her arms around me, hugging me tight. "Thanks, Princess Peach Pop!"

I smile, squeezing her back. "Anytime, Princess Snooki."

As I start to leave, I catch Harrison's eyes in the mirror one last time. There's something deep in his gaze—sadness, maybe, but so much love, too. It's like he's showing me what it means to have love, to lose it, and keep it all together. Because he has to.

My heart squeezes. I want him to find that again.

"Thanks for the ride," I say softly.

"Anytime," he replies.

Once inside, I'm swallowed whole by noise and chaos. The airport hums with the frantic energy of travelers, people surging past in that *take-no-prisoners* stride reserved for Olympic speed walkers and New Yorkers.

I stand there, utterly turned around, so lost I can't even tell which way is up. I try to master the flight board. It pretty much looks like a giant Battleship screen, an endless blur of cities, airlines, and the ominous trifecta of statuses: on-time, delayed, canceled.

Please don't be canceled.

"Juliana Spenser?"

The woman is petite and pretty, but all business—sleek suit, hair in a tight bun, looking slightly harried, like she's done this six times already today.

"What gave it away? Is it the signature Spenser look of complete confusion in airports?"

Her giggle is genuine, but brief. "Mr. Bishop sent me. Your ticket's been upgraded. The valet will take your luggage, and I'm here to escort you to the lounge."

The lounge. I would protest, but at this point, I'll go anywhere to get away from this crowd.

Eagerly, I follow on autopilot as my nerves simmer beneath the surface. "Is Mr. Bishop in the lounge?" I ask.

"I don't believe so."

We breeze through two sets of glass doors, and bam—five-star luxury. Champagne flows like a river, and there's every kind of food imaginable, but I'm too anxious to eat.

I sink into a cushy seat by the window, feeling the tension in my shoulders start to ease. The woman hands me a small envelope. "Mr. Bishop asked me to give you this. But don't open it until you're in the air. Enjoy your flight."

"Thanks."

After a short while and three champagnes, boarding begins.

Doubt sinks in that much more, but still, I shuffle toward the gate, one slow step at a time.

I'm in first class, the seat so plush it could easily be a bed. I scan the cabin, hoping—no, expecting—to see him.

But he isn't here. And when an older woman with a MacBook settles into the loungey seat next to me, I know he's not coming.

The envelope in my hand feels like a live wire, begging to be torn open. My fingers twitch, but I do as I'm told, waiting until the plane lifts off.

His handwriting is bold, strong, and achingly familiar. My heart skips a beat as I read the words.

Jules,
Nae maeumeun dangsini issneun gose isseoyo.

Translation: *My heart is where you are.*

CHAPTER 52

Brian

"It's a custom desk," Trent says, his hand gesturing lazily toward the massive piece of furniture. We're all seated at the far end of the conference room—me, Mark, Zac, and Trent—waiting as he continues, like the world hinges on this piece of wood.

Or the future of our partnership.

His voice drips with admiration as he gives it a lingering glance.

I clasp my hands, offering an appreciative nod. "It's exceptional."

"It reeks of shrimp," Trent mutters, completely deadpan.

I stifle a laugh, barely holding it together. "I'm really sorry about that," I murmur low, clearing my throat. "Had a lot on my mind."

His gaze sharpens. "I counted eight." The flatness of his tone makes it clear he's not joking. "Did I get them all?"

Honestly, I have no idea. I mindlessly ate as Harrison's kids practically force-fed me, insisting I needed to eat.

But since we're about to forge one of the biggest business

alliances in the western hemisphere, I can't exactly say that. Instead, I clear my throat. "There might be one or two still lurking in the cigar box."

Mark pinches the bridge of his nose as Zac, as casual as ever, leans back and asks, "Cohibas?"

"Mayan Sicars," Trent mutters, shaking his head as if he's still mourning their loss. "Hand-rolled. Aged to perfection. And now . . ." He lets out a long, frustrated breath. "Shark chum." His gaze refocuses, sweeping across the table. "But I'm sure that's not why you're all here."

Mark leans forward, his voice calm but firm. "We need to get the spotlight off our company. Permanently. There's no shortage of news out there, so why not shift the focus?"

Trent arches a brow, intrigued. "And you have ideas on where we should aim our public opinion scepter?"

"Absolutely," I say definitely.

Trent's smirk grows, eyes flicking between us. "And you're offering to pay for this service?"

Mark shakes his head. "No, we want to buy the company outright. Quietly. That is, if we can reach an arrangement."

Zac slides a small note across the table, the number bold enough to make Trent's eyes flicker with excitement. The corner of his lips twitch, the hint of a grin threatening to break through before he schools his expression. "What kind of arrangement are we talking about?"

"You stay on as CEO, remain the public face. To the world, nothing changes. Behind the scenes, this piece of the puzzle falls under Excelsior Centurion," Mark says, his voice steady.

Trent leans back in his chair, weighing his options, dragging out the silence in what can only be described as a bullshit power move. The kind that would work if we weren't already three steps ahead. But the quiet stretches long enough for Mark to elbow me in the ribs. Hard.

I clear my throat, ignoring the sharp sting. "I'll throw in a case of those cigars you're so fond of," I say, my voice even, though I'm breathing through the pain.

Fucker always hits the same damned spot.

Finally, Trent sucks in a breath and waves his hand, all nonchalance. "If you want to buy my media company for twice its worth, bygones." His brow quirks, amused. "Anything else?"

I lean forward, my voice low. "Roxana Voss."

His grin fades, but only slightly. "I already fired her."

"Fired doesn't even scratch the surface of what I need."

"I feel a public shaming coming on," he smirks.

"And I want to know how she found Angi faster than my team could."

"You think Roxie Voss found your wife's sister?" Trent's lips curl into a slow, sly grin. "That walking migraine has the patience of a two-year-old and the intellectual depth of cheese. It takes every brain cell she's got just to figure out which end of her phone to speak into." He shakes his head, amused. "Wyld Richards did the digging." Trent presses a buzzer on his desk. "Send him in."

"Yes, sir," a sultry voice replies from the speaker.

A second later, Wyld steps into the room, his eyes locking onto mine, and I see it—the flash of panic, his body frozen like prey staring down a predator.

And I don't blame him. He should be scared out of his mind, especially with Zac's arm the only thing standing between my fist and his throat.

Slowly, Wyld turns to take a seat. Trent's voice cuts through the air, sharp as a blade. "Did I say you could sit?"

Wyld jerks upright. "No. No, sir," he stammers, standing in place.

"Tell us how you found Juliana Spenser's sister. And if you leave out a single detail, I'll let the bookies I've been holding off get their pound of flesh."

Wyld panics, vomiting every detail in under sixty seconds. "Her arrests are public. She's hit almost every precinct—5th, 19th, you name it. I offered a thousand bucks to every dealer from here to the Adirondacks to send her my way, promise her free hits for life."

By now, both Mark and Zac are on edge, ready to grab me because they know if I get a hold of him, I'll end this.

But instead, my voice drops to a quiet, chilling calm. "She had enough drugs in her system to drop a man twice her size. She was hanging by a thread. If I press this with the DA, you're looking at twenty to life for attempted murder."

Wyld's hands shoot up in surrender, eyes wide. "That was Roxie, not me. I just brought her in! Roxie wanted her primed for the big reveal at the awards show. I swear, it wasn't me. I'll do anything you want."

"I know you will," I say, my voice a low, dangerous rasp. "What I want is everything you've got on Roxie. Oh, and I want your left ear."

"Wha—" He barely gets the word out before Mark and Zac are on him. Zac pins him with brute force, and Mark moves in fast. The tag snaps onto his ear with a sharp metallic click, and Wyld lets out a guttural scream.

"OW! Fuck! What the hell did you just do?!"

I watch him squirm, gripping his ear like it's been ripped clean off, his face pale from the shock. "Tagged you, Wyld. Like the sewer animal you are. Now we know exactly where you are at all times. And the second you even think about running or screwing us over, I'll make sure every single one of your bookies knows how to find you, too."

He's still wailing, cradling his ear like a baby, the sound grating on my nerves.

Honestly, it's just an ear tag, like a piercing with a big ass earring. My vote was for a Prince Albert, but thankfully, the Bishop men drew the line at getting anywhere near his disease-ridden junk.

Mark and Zac's exact words? *Fuck no.*

Trent snaps a finger right in his face. "You've got one hour to hand over everything you've got on Roxana—ranked by what'll cause the biggest headlines."

By mid-afternoon, both traditional and social media are flooded with stories about Roxana Voss, but not for the reasons she ever imagined. Instead of making headlines as a star reporter, she found herself at the center of them.

In fact, the biggest splash came from none other than Alfred Walsh, famously known as Scoop, with a headline that sent shockwaves across every platform:

From Byline to Mugshot
The Fall of Roxana Voss: Journalist Turned Criminal

Scoop sits proudly at his desk, a smug grin on his face as Anabelle and Felix hand out slices of cake. Apparently, Roxana's downfall has been cause for celebration for everyone. Scoop catches my eye from across the room, holding up a slice in silent offering.

I shake my head. With Jules gone, eating is no longer a pleasure but a necessity. A chore. Every breath without her feels like a slow, torturous ache, and food has lost all its flavor.

Nothing feels right without her here.

"You're missing out," a familiar voice chirps behind me.

I turn and find Taylor, her smile as wide as Long Island. "You're speaking to me again?" I ask.

She shrugs, casually. "Trent told me what you did."

"Trent?" I raise a brow. "Is this future husband number three hundred?"

"Not necessarily." She pauses, thinking it through while savoring another spoonful of pure frosting. "For once in my life, I'm taking things slow. Though, he *is* cooking me dinner tonight."

"The fire department will breathe a collective sigh of relief it's not you," I tease.

She giggles, nudging my arm. "I only *almost* burned the building down once."

"Hey," I nudge her arm right back. "Good for you," I say, my tone softening. "You've been an amazing friend to Jules. You deserve the best. And if Trent gets out of hand—"

"Don't worry," she grins. "I've got a shrimp tail guy on speed dial."

Our laughter fades, leaving a stretch of silence between us.

Taylor, still smiling, takes another bite of cake. "You really should try it," she says, popping another forkful of icing into her mouth with a playful grin. "Buttercream with a hint of peach. Gee, I wonder who picked it out."

I laugh, but it's hollow, the ache still clawing at me. "Jules should be here. She earned that Trailblazer Award. And she was robbed of the chance to bask in it." My eyes catch Trent glancing our way—or more accurately, at Taylor. "Looks like someone's here for you."

She glances over and smiles. "That's my ride."

"Then I'd better let you go." The words catch in my throat, and I pause, feeling the weight of my heart grow heavier with every second. "But if you see Jules... tell her—" I hesitate, the ache sharpening. "Tell her I miss her."

She blinks, then smirks. "No."

My brow furrows, confusion flaring into *what the actual fuck* irritation. "No?"

"Look, poor little rich boy, I'm not your secretary." Her grin stretches wider as she pulls me into a soft, teasing side hug. She whispers, "Go tell her yourself."

CHAPTER 53
Jules

"*Dolaon geoseul hwanyeong habnida, Spenser-ssi,*" the barista greets me, her warm welcome back coupled with a smile, as she hands over my tea.

"*Kamsa habnida,*" I reply, thanking her with a small head bow. I love the chance to slip in and out of Korean every chance I get.

And it's taken some doing for me to switch from coffee to tea, but with a small *yakgwa* on the side, it's paradise. The little flower-shaped cookie is just enough to keep a certain macchiato with cinnamon stubbled face someone from dancing through my thoughts.

At least some of the time, anyway.

This is my life now, and with every day that passes, it feels a little more comfortable and a little less like I'm missing my right arm.

But if I thought Brian would just take goodbye for an answer, I was dead wrong.

Every evening, like clockwork, he sends me a message.

Sometimes in English, sometimes in Korean. Always quirky and sweet, like, *Shoved six peach muffins in my mouth. Thinking of you*, or something ridiculous like, *Halmeoni fed me extra strong kimchi. Not sure I'll survive.*

And every single one inflates my heart just a little bit more.

I've already pitched a four-part series to Trent, and when he heard it, he insisted it'd be a feature. I still can't quite wrap my head around it—my work, my story, front and center.

And everywhere I go, Taylor's already scouted the most picture-perfect spots for me. Little corners of Seoul where the light hits just right, where I can take selfies—my real face, no filters—for all the world to see under my new handle: @WithLoveJules.

It feels surreal, me constantly taking selfies. Like when I was slurping a mouthful of *jajangmyeon* noodles—who knew *that* would go viral?

And now, when I catch a smile from a random stranger, I don't hide. I smile back. For once, I'm being recognized for all the right reasons.

For just being goofy and campy and . . . me.

And next week . . . next week, my family will be here. Mom, Dad, Colby, Halmeoni—just thinking about it makes my heart hike right up my chest.

Mom even offered to stay behind with Angi, which I didn't expect. Somehow, Brian pulled some strings and got her sentence reduced to house arrest. A really long house arrest, but locked up at home, nonetheless.

And remarkably, Mom agreed, determined that as a family, we would help Angi through it. Because it's not about big expectations. Just little wins. *'Haru haru,'* she now says—day by day. Brian even had his own men watch over Angi around the clock, giving my family the chance to finally relax and enjoy their time away.

And knowing Brian's still tied to them, knotted up in the sweet, messy tangle that is my family, makes me miss him all the more.

And as Halmeoni says, any man who'd do this for our family? *He loves you more than a steaming bowl of bibimbap on a cold day.* Which, coming from our family, is saying a lot.

When the bright day drifts into a festive city evening, I feel the pull to reach out. I imagine his voice, steady and sure, telling me everything's okay. Other nights, I miss him so deeply it aches, like a piece of me is adrift, lost at sea, and he's the only one who can give it back to me.

But then the moment slips away, and eventually, I drift off, letting the distance hold. I go to sleep, wake up, rinse, repeat.

And I know it's not that I don't love him. I do. I love that man with every inch of me. But fear? That's always been my shadow—clinging on, refusing to let go, no matter how hard I try.

But slowly, surely, I know the day's coming. That moment where I shove aside all this worthless, stupid fear and take the damn leap my heart's been begging for.

That's why, maybe, just maybe, today's the day I stop being a coward and let him back in. Right where he's always belonged.

CHAPTER 54

Jules

"Look!" Halmeoni points ahead, leading Mom and Colby toward a stunning view of the distant temple. We're walking through this beautiful garden just outside Seoul, the soft wind carrying the scent of flowers and pine.

Eomma and Halmeoni chat away up ahead, their voices mingling with the rustle of leaves. Colby's trailing behind, his camera snapping away like he's on assignment, and I know the little drone in his backpack will make an appearance soon enough.

The backdrop is breathtaking—blue mountains rolling into a gold and green horizon, the temple standing proud and serene against it, like something out of a watercolor painting.

Dad lingers back as we walk, me tucked under his arm, his steady presence grounding me like it always does. He motions at a bench, and he nudges me gently. "Let's take a selfie here."

"Okay," I agree, settling in next to him, the perfect view behind us.

Camera in place, we pose, snapping one sentimental shot

and then one goofy one—eyes crossed, tongues sticking out. Laughter bubbles up between us, filling the space with a warmth only moments like this can create.

As Halmeoni snaps close-ups of flowers for her Instagram wall and Mom and Colby grab snacks from a cart, Dad and I fall into easy conversation. We cover everything under the sun—the food, the weather, how Halmeoni and Eomma can never agree on where to eat. Nothing is off the table.

Well, everything except the elephant in the room.

Brian.

Finally, Dad shifts, resting his hands on his lap, the way he always does when a serious talk is coming.

"Do you still love him?" he asks, his voice soft but probing.

I sigh, the question stirring up knots in my stomach and a flurry of butterflies in my chest. "Yes," I admit. No hesitation because it's the truth.

"Have you talked?"

My hands twist together in my lap. "No."

"You know all that was malarky. What the press said about Sydney Sun."

"I know," I say softly. "Colby told me it was Angi. And I know Brian had to do what he did. Colby would probably be rotting in a military jail if Brian hadn't stepped in."

Dad looks at me, his brow furrowing. "Then, why not?"

I sigh, feeling the weight of everything unspoken. "Why not? A million reasons . . . and none at all." My throat tightens. "I'm always going to be scared. All those years ago, one photo—me, vulnerable—he took it. And ripped the rug from under my world when he did. Yes, it was a long time ago, but I'll always have that sliver of doubt." That and he dated

Angi . . . though I don't bring it up. "Isn't that why you've hated him?"

He shakes his head slowly, a frown pulling at his lips. "I never hated Brian. I just . . ." Dad claps his hands on his lap, like he's about to rip off a Band-Aid. "Brian never dated Angi."

Confused, I blink. "What?"

"He never dated Angi. I hired him to watch her," Dad explains, his eyes locked on mine. "To keep her from getting too crazy. To keep you safe and shielded. I mean, the two of you in the same school and the same grade presented me with the equivalent of dad hell."

"He never dated Angi?" I still can't wrap my head around it. "So he was, what? Her babysitter?"

Dad blows out a long, exaggerated breath. "Yes."

I think back to every memory of Brian chasing after Angi, and I can't help but smile. For all the time we spent together—them together, me the third wheel—I never actually saw them kiss. Not once.

In fact, every time she tried, his exact words were, "Get off me." I laugh out loud. I just thought he hated PDA. The time she full-on attacked him at the bleachers and he fell backward? Priceless.

I'm still grinning when I notice Dad's little brow twitch—his tell when he's holding something back. Worst poker face ever. I give him a playful nudge. "What else?"

He takes a deep breath. "Brian never took that photo of you, Jules. Angi did."

It feels like the air's been sucked from my lungs. I stare at him, trying to process the words. "Dad! I've blamed him all these years."

"I know," he says helplessly.

"Why didn't he tell me?"

"Because I made him swear he wouldn't," Dad says, his voice thick with regret. "I didn't want you hating Angi. And Brian was about to deploy . . ." He blows out a long breath, the weight of it sagging his shoulders. "I was just trying to protect both my girls. The only way I knew how."

His words slowly sink in, and before I can stop myself, I pull him into a tight hug. And then I let go. Of him. Of all of it.

The flood of emotions hits me all at once—shock, anger, relief, guilt. Brian, my husband, has been looking out for me, for *us*—all of us—for so long. How could I have been so blind? How could I not have known?

My throat tightens, and for a moment, I can't find the words.

Then, it all comes rushing to the surface. "I need to call him," I finally say, standing up, already reaching for my phone.

"First," Dad says, gently stopping me. "Bring up your food."

"I think you mean *feed*."

"Yeah, that. You promised me you'd post the shot of us and show me all the pictures you've taken."

"Now?"

"You've kept the man waiting all this time, Jules. Another sixty seconds won't kill him."

"You don't know that," I tease, fishing out my phone.

My finger hovers, itching to dial, but I pause. Dad did just travel halfway across the world, battling jet lag like a champ. So, I nod and pull up my gallery.

I sit back down, showing him every shot I've taken since arriving in Korea—temples, street markets, the bustling crowds of Seoul. He studies each one carefully, a proud smile on his face.

Then I post the one of us with the hashtag *#DaddysLittleGirl*.

Dad pauses, squinting at it. "*Blech*, some wild Sasquatch photobombed us. You'll have to do it again."

I laugh, shaking my head. "Right. Like I'd be lucky enough to capture a Yeti in Korea. Which, if I do, will definitely get me a bazillion followers."

With a smirk, I zoom in.

And there he is. In the background, blurry but unmistakable.

Bigfoot.

Aka Brian.

My heart leaps into my throat because he's in another shot. And another. I swipe through, and there he is again. And again. I keep expanding the shots, and he is *everywhere*.

He's been here the whole time. I mean . . .

The.

Whole.

Time?

What in the world?

I whip around, only to find the lumberjack of my fantasies walking straight toward me. Broad shoulders strain against a fitted tee, dark hair tousled by the wind, and those eyes, intense and focused are locked right on me.

And I absolutely die.

Dad pats me on the back, his silent gesture of approval and

a subtle *you've got this*. He and Brian exchange a quick handshake before he walks off and Brian steps forward.

His movements are slow, cautious, like he's walking on razor-thin ice. He's nervous. And with every step that brings him closer, the tension in my stomach twists, winding tighter like a spring ready to snap. And suddenly, I'm nervous, too.

"Hi," he says.

"Hi," I reply, barely breathing.

The air swirls with electricity, wrapping around us, knotting us closer. I lick my dry lips. "How did you know everywhere I'd be?"

"Your social media manager isn't exactly a vault."

And when he smiles, I smile.

And then, I'm on him. All my restraint snaps like a rubber band. The flood of everything I've been holding back rushes through me, and I full-on leap into his arms, kissing him like crazy.

He kisses me back with a force that feels like it could rewrite the stars, shift the tides, and set the universe on absolute fire.

His hands grip me tight, like he's terrified I'll vanish if he lets go. For a long time, there's nothing but us, kissing like no one and nothing else exists.

Which they do.

And since we can't keep our hands off each other, and there's a very real chance of us getting arrested for public indecency by the Korean police, we head for my place.

Seriously, the last thing Brian needs is *another* mug shot.

We race to my tiny apartment, stumbling through the door, barely making it inside before our bodies crash together again, desperate and frantic.

Clothes hit the floor, and then it's nothing but skin against skin, quick, heated, and everything I need.

I'm so unbelievably wet that when he spreads my legs, lines himself up, he's in to the hilt before I can even blink. I gasp.

"Fuck, I've missed you," he breathes, gruff and deep.

And I've missed him, too.

He moves with hard, desperate thrusts, like he's trying to make up for all the time we've lost, until every wall in the room feels like it's rattling.

It's like we've been apart for two eternities, and when we finally come together, it's a wild, earth-shattering explosion of everything we've held back—two galaxies colliding in a brilliant blaze of heat and light . . . and love.

Afterward, we collapse in a tangle of limbs, our bodies panting, slick with sweat. Brian lies beside me, a satisfied grin tugging at his lips. He rolls onto his side, his fingers lazily tracing over my bare skin.

"You'll pay for putting me through hell," he says, voice low and teasing.

"Gladly," I pant, breathless. "Though, in my defense, I thought with that speech you made, you were totally gaga for Sydney Sun."

"I was."

"What?"

"Still am," he says, flashing that grin, as if his bold statement didn't just crack my heart wide open.

His hands cradle my face, his deep ocean-blue eyes locking with mine, pulling me in like they always do. "I knew you were Sydney Sun all along, Jules."

I blink, confused. "What?"

"From that very first shot of you. As if Taylor's enormous sunglasses could ever hide those full lips or that adorable little scar," he says, his thumb brushing lightly over the scar on my chin.

"You know my scar?"

"The one you got when you tested out your Wonder Woman cape by jumping from a tree? As if I could forget."

My mouth falls open. "You knew?"

"Knew?" His smile brushes against mine, teasing and familiar. "That it was you in the coffee shop? Like I wouldn't know your smile. Your hands. Your scent." He breathes me in, and I feel it everywhere. His kisses trail up my neck before his teeth graze my ear. "And you weren't exactly invisible ducking under your desk."

I bury my face in his shoulder, giggling. "You really knew. The whole time."

"The whole time," he murmurs, his voice low and soft, every word sinking into my soul. With a tenderness that unravels me, he slips the ring back onto my finger and presses a kiss to it. "It's you, Jules. It's always been you."

Tears prick my eyes as I stare at him, my heart swelling with so much love it hurts.

"Now, tell me you're mine, *wife*, and let the punishment begin."

"I'm yours," I whisper against his lips. "Always and forever yours."

Epilogue

BRIAN

"You made it!" Taylor squeals, throwing her arms around me in a hug so tight, it's basically a chokehold.

I laugh, gasping for air. "You literally saw me yesterday. And I'm pretty sure Trent is giving me the stink eye."

"It's my resting bitch face," he deadpans, sliding an arm around Taylor's waist and pulling her close. "That, and I'm a possessive twat."

Her grin practically lights up the room as she melts into him. They kiss, slow and sweet, and for a moment, I almost forget it's Taylor—the new Taylor—always conscious, always with an eye on making sure no one catches her guy in anything less than the best light.

The waiter swings by, and it's clear Taylor's latest PR campaign—*Sober Curious: Explore Your Options*—is catching fire. The tray's stacked, not just with the usual champagne but with Kir Royale Kombucha and alcohol-free cookies-and-cream espressotinis loaded with collagen and protein, a favorite among expecting mothers and athletes alike.

Judging by the buzz around the room, it's a hit. The Instagram-worthy shots are already making waves, one of the highlights of this year's Excellence Media Gala. We all have a glass in hand.

Trent swirls his drink, eyes fixed on the stage. "She's really in her element." It's been a year since we were last here, and everything has changed. Especially my girl.

I follow his gaze, watching Jules take the room by storm. No hesitation, no flinching from the cameras. This is her moment—her voice—and she fucking owns it.

"Damn right," I murmur, pride swelling in my chest. "She's a force."

Jules catches my eye, and that coy little smile is my undoing every damn time.

As she's gearing up for yet another photo op with a legion of admirers, I watch her refresh her lipstick—the red one.

My cue.

I know if I save her now, she'll make it worth my while later.

I send Harrison a quick text and turn to Trent and Taylor. "Excuse me."

Taylor giggles, taking my drink, already knowing we're about to attempt to slip out unnoticed. "Go rescue your woman."

I weave through the crowd. She's mid-conversation with some high-profile journalists when I step up, but the throngs of people around her barely notice me. They're too busy yammering about influencers and likes to even blink in my direction.

Do I love that none of them glances my way? Hell yes. I'm officially yesterday's news, and I couldn't be more thrilled.

My life is best lived in the shadows, behind the scenes, while Jules has fully embraced basking in the spotlight—on her terms.

Still, I puff out a breath, because I can only stand here and eye-fuck my wife for so long. Clearing my throat, I tap her bare shoulder, my finger subtly skimming the black spaghetti strap for a brief, teasing moment. "A word."

She flashes a polite smile to the group. "I'll be right back."

We walk off and I lean in close, whispering, "Liar."

"Desperate times," she mutters, draining the last of her virgin espressotini as we slip out the door.

The second we step outside, flashbulbs explode like a storm. Paparazzi swarm. "Ms. Sun! Congratulations on your win!"

Her win. Jules has rallied enough support to push a bill on pen name rights. It's a hell of a fight, but making sure writers can't have their pen names stripped or misused? She's changing the game, and I'm loving every second.

My little Peach Pop is out here taking names and kicking ass.

Her smile grows wider. "Thank you."

"When's the big day?" another reporter shouts.

Jules rubs her belly—barely visible, but unmistakable. "Five more months, give or take."

"Will you be taking time off?" a little voice asks, and I glance over. It's Snook, holding up Harrison's phone, eyes wide with curiosity.

Jules beams, lowers down, and waves directly at her dad's phone, speaking to the @Snook&Co Instagram Live. "I'll be doing a piece called *Balancing Act: The Art of Mommying, Daddying, Work, and Kids.*" She playfully bops Snook's nose and winks up at Harrison, who salutes from the car.

Taking Snook's hand in one of hers, I grab the other, and we make our way toward the waiting SUV.

Harrison's already got the door wide open. Connor's up front, typical teenager, probably lost in his phone, and Ollie's sprawled in the back.

Snook doesn't just climb in like a normal kid—she scrambles over the headrests, giggling the whole way as she tumbles into the third row, a ball of kid energy Jules swears she'll harness one day.

And Taylor's already got big plans to sell it on Etsy for $9.99.

Then we slide in, and Harrison pulls away smoothly. I pull Jules close, my lips brushing against her ear. "You're incredible, you know that, Mrs. Bishop?"

Before I can pull her closer, we both notice a little Angelina Ballerina book with a note tucked inside.

Jules picks it up, smoothing out the paper, and we both recognize the sweet, crooked letters.

It's from Snook.

Dear Momma,

I miss you so, so much.
Daddy does, too.
He's sad.
I'm seeing Princess Peach Pop tonight. She's nice.
Maybe one day, you'll send Daddy a princess to watch over him too?

xoxo,

Snooki

Jules presses the note to her chest, her eyes brimming with tears, and I can't help but smile softly. I glance back at Snook and Oliver, both already fast asleep. I slip my jacket over them, gently tucking them in, and pull Jules close.

For a long moment, we just sit there, hearts swelling, wrapped in the quiet hope of a little girl's wish. The rest of the drive passes in silence, with us holding each other, both of us staring so hard at the back of Harrison's head that we're practically burning a hole in it.

He glances in the rearview mirror, one thick auburn brow lifting in suspicion. "What?"

"What what?" I stall, as Jules discreetly tucks the note back into the book beside her.

I know what she's thinking—despite the years, Harrison's still deeply affected by the loss, and the last thing my Jules wants is to upset him.

But I also know my wife. Jules-the-fixer already has a dozen wheels turning in her head. The second she gets a chance, she'll be speed-dialing her mom, Halmeoni, Taylor, Jess, and Mrs. D. She'll rally the troops because, as my sister Jess always says, never underestimate the power of a wish.

Harrison eyes us again. "You're both staring at me."

"No, we aren't," I lie.

Harrison deadpans. "I'm a father of three and a former SEAL. I've got eyes in the back of my head."

Still, I look him square in the eye and say, "You're imagining things."

For a second, he gives me the parental *I know you're up to something* look. But when he yawns, I know we're in the clear. The guy's beat, and after staying this late in the city just for us, another hour on the road is the last thing he needs.

We pull up to the building, and he puts the SUV in park. We start making our way out of the car. "Why don't you all stay over?" I offer. The rooms are basically theirs anyway.

He nods, stifling another yawn. "No argument. Thanks."

Harrison grabs Snook, I scoop up Ollie, and Jules tucks the book into her purse. As for Connor—the hulk-boy wearing size 11 shoes is on his own.

After saying our goodnights and slipping into the bedroom, I need just one thing. My lips graze Jules's ear. "I've wanted you all night, Mrs. Bishop."

She leans in, voice soft and teasing. "It's Miss," she insists.

"Is it?" I ask, my dick already at full attention as I loosen my tie, wondering if this is my Peach Pop's way of being a very bad girl, craving a little punishment.

Casually, she pulls a pair of dark glasses from her purse, slipping them on with an intoxicating smile. "Call me Miss Sun."

And in an instant, our clothes are gone, and I'm standing there, basking in her glow—from every inch of her breathtaking body to all the love in her heart.

I shower her with kisses, enough to cover every part of Juliana Spenser-Bishop/Sydney Sun, and I lay her down,—the woman who's owned my heart for as long as I can remember—and take her, again and again.

Before Jules, I had sex, and I fucked. But until now, I've never made love.

And this—*this* is love. All of me loving all of her. Hard and frantic. Then soft and slow.

And when our world explodes, her screaming my name, and me emptying every last part of myself into her, I kiss her tenderly, until there's nothing left but me and her.

My Peach Pop.

My forever.

My wife.

***

Thank you for reading *Knotted!*

Ready for more angsty billionaire romance?

Eight years ago, I nearly died. She thinks I don't remember that kiss… but how could I forget?

1-Click Them Now

Book 1: MARKED
Book 2: CUFFED
Book 3: KNOTTED
Coming in 2025!! Preorder NOW!
Book 4: SEALED

Subscribe to my Newsletter for Updates
www.LexxiJames.com

***

Need more?

SINS of the Syndicate >> **1-CLICK HERE**

>> Keep scrolling to read NOW

The Alex Drake Collection >> **1-CLICK HERE**

Ruthless Billionaires Club >> **1-CLICK HERE**

Sinful Soldier's Series >> **1-CLICK HERE**

Sins of the Syndicate

BOOK ONE

CHAPTER 1

Ivy

"I'm here to see Ms. Palmer."

The man's voice is deep, with an authority that makes me wonder why he requested his tour of the assisted living center with me. His suit is expensive but not overly fitted. And the dark gray is a stark contrast to the clear blue of his eyes. The silvery accents in his well-trimmed salt-and-pepper hair give him the air of distinction, with professional charm brimming from behind what seems to be a practiced smile.

It's not unlike the smiles I'm used to from people clinging to their courtesy as they navigate a world of decisions. How will I care for my loved one? Will they be safe? Is this covered by insurance? How much will it cost?

If money is no object, the ones with the deepest pockets land here. Except for me. It took two years for me to work off my mom's debt, and it gave me a lifetime's worth of watching people in return. I remind myself that I'm here to ease them into a relationship of trust and support. Not to pressure them with a hard sell, despite those very words from my boss.

"I'm Ivy," I say, stepping out from behind the long reception desk. I hold out a hand, meeting his solemn smile with one of my own as he takes my hand for a brief shake. "And you're Mr.—"

"Sin," he says, scanning the lobby and halls. I can't tell if he's overwhelmed or underwhelmed, but he avoids meeting my eyes as he glances around. "Call me Sin."

"All right, *Sin*."

I've already seen the roster, noting that the tour request was made by a Bryce Jacob Sinclair, Esquire. The formal name suits him as equally as the nickname Sin. A gravity and authority harden the lines of his face, hiding whatever's lurking just below the surface.

The heaviness that drags him down threatens to pull me with it, an occupational hazard to a career dependent on emotional connection and empathy. When his expectant eyes meet mine, I snap back to work.

Handing him a visitor badge, I gesture down the north hall. "This way."

Along our tour, Sin asks the usual questions: How many occupants are there? What's the caregiver-to-resident ratio? If the staff live on the premises—which feels more like he's asking if *I* live on the premises.

No matter how many times I give this tour, I'm delighted when he asks about the one thing that always connects us, though it never seems to at first. Mr. Whiskers.

The small fluffy toy is weightless in my hand as I tug it from the pocket it's been peeking out from and hold it up.

I'm not the only one beaming at the sight of him. Even the stone-faced Sin cracks a smile, albeit a very small one. It creases his face enough that I peg him to be about sixty, which makes me wonder if he's looking at the facility for his mother or possibly his wife.

"This is Mr. Whiskers."

"Your stuffed animal?" Sin's studious eyes move from it to me, the intensity of his gaze so much harsher than is warranted by my crazy talk.

Unnerved, I take in a breath. "Mr. Whiskers is so much more than that. He's a therapy stuffed animal. You can even pop him in the microwave to warm him up."

I avoid talking about my past or that Mr. Whiskers has been my personal security blanket for nearly twenty years.

Sin nods. "Do all residents get a toy? Or just the bad ones?" His contempt doesn't bother me. He doesn't understand, and it's my job to help him understand.

"Sparrow Wellness and Assisted Living is unlike any facility you may have seen. Our occupants range in age from twenty to eighty-two. Sometimes, a little non-threatening toy is a great way for people to open up. I didn't have to say a word about him, and you asked."

His face is stone. No hint as to whether he's annoyed or amused. His eyes wander through the opening to a vacant room. "Continue."

"Even if they aren't interested in a little support from a cuddly friend, he's a big hit with the children who visit. We keep a small stockpile in the back."

"Trauma victims?" He mutters the question under his breath in a way that sounds less like distaste and more like hope.

"We cater to a wide range of conditions, trauma being just one of them. Some residents have degenerative conditions that require more care than their families can provide. Others don't have families, in which case we become their family if their physician recommends us."

Sin takes several steps into the room, moving his gaze from the warm cream walls and big bay window to me. "Looking for a family, Ms. Palmer?"

His tone is sharp and icy, with enough condescension that I have to remind myself that people in pain tend to inflict pain. He's just hurting, and I'm the closest target within striking distance. But it's not directed at me. *Even if it is the truth.*

"Just looking to help as many people as I can." I hold my smile as I step away, shooing off a flurry of emotions that I'll need to deal with later. For now, Sin is in his role of distrustful client. It's up to me to win him over.

His brisk footsteps close in quickly from behind.

We stop at the courtyard, where a few residents have opted to spend their morning lounging on lawn furniture, enjoying the sun. We walk in silence. He takes an interest in a resident, Angie, lost in the strokes of a painting she's creating. I use the time to take a closer look at his paperwork, only now noticing he's left several areas blank.

It's not uncommon. People tend to be guarded their first time walking through. It's a long way from *nice to meet you* to *I trust you with my loved one*, but it's a familiar road I've traveled many, many times.

"It's you," Sin says, and I look up.

Seeing the painting this close, I realize the resemblance is uncanny. I'd almost believe it was me if not for the elegance of the off-the-shoulder gown Angie has painted her in, or the delight in her eyes that could never radiate from mine. It's how I want to look. Confident. Complete. Happy. Instead, my heart is riddled with so many holes, half the time it feels like it's about to collapse under all the damage.

Taking a closer look, I see the white curl in her subject's curly black hair—identical to the one that inexplicably grows at my right temple. Angie nods, beaming with a grin as she silently lets me know it is me.

It's a version of me that could only happen in Angie's beautiful imagination.

Grateful, I hug Angie, being gentle to avoid overdoing it. Her muscles are weak. Every word from her lips is a fight, but they're always worth waiting for. Especially today as she sounds out two words.

"H-h-hap-p-py b-b-b-irth-d-day."

My heart leaps as she completes the short sentence. It's the most she's said in a week, and I find myself speechless, if not a bit teary-eyed.

"Sorry, do you mind if I steal Ivy for a second?"

Derrick interrupts, probably to keep me from outright blubbering. He's more than my boss, though no one would know it. We've been a couple for nearly a year but keeping our relationship under wraps was his idea as much as mine. Sort of.

I keep one eye on Sin, watching as he carries on a one-sided conversation with Angie. He doesn't seem concerned that she isn't responding. On the contrary, his smile is genuine, even though he receives nothing more than a few polite nods back. But I'm ready to jump in if he demands any more.

Derrick's hands stay pocketed, the way they always do when he's hiding something. Maybe it's a surprise. Like dinner at a fancy restaurant on the waterfront. Or cuddling together in front of a romantic bonfire on the beach.

Between his work schedule and mine—which is a result of his—it's been weeks since I've had any action. I'm bursting at the seams with sexual frustration, so if my birthday celebration is a beer, a grilled cheese, and twenty solid minutes of hitting it hard during whatever sci-fi show he can't live without, I'll take it.

I'm grinning like an idiot when he says low, "I really need you to bring this one home, babe. Seal the deal. The numbers need to look good. I've got a big meeting tonight."

"Tonight? But—"

His cell phone buzzes, and he takes it, mouthing, "Gotta go," as he winks and rushes back inside.

"Why are you in this, Ms. Palmer?" Sin asks as he sidles up to me.

"What?" I scoop my jaw up off the ground, realizing he isn't referring to my conversation with Derrick.

Sin means my work. Of course, he does. His thousand-yard stare roves across the lush grounds, taking it in while not focusing on anything at all.

"The same reason everyone works here. It's personal. We've all been here. Helping family members who need assistance."

He turns, narrowing his eyes. "Family?" The way he says the word is strained, as if he doesn't believe me.

It compels me to share more than I normally would. "My mother had a degenerative condition. There was a lot of pain in her last years of life. I did all I could."

I don't talk about the specifics. How by the time a doctor diagnosed her liver disease, nothing could be done. That it never stopped her from the drugs or the alcohol. Or that despite the unbearable pain she suffered every second of her last days of life, she pushed me away until she was too weak or too tired to put up a fight. There's no way I can explain how you can love a person with all your heart when they seem to hate you with all of theirs, so I don't try.

By the look on Sin's face, I've already given him an uncomfortable amount of information to unpack. So, I wrap it up, quickly finishing. "I did what I could to make her comfortable."

The hard lines of his face soften. "I'm sorry for what you've been through."

"Thank you." The practiced smile I use in times like these emerge, and I nod appreciatively, steering our discussion back where it belongs. On him. And not because Derrick wants me to close the deal, but because this man and his family need me. And that's why I'm here.

"The first steps are never easy," I say as a gentle reminder. "We have different levels of care and service. Can you tell me more about the person who brought you here today?"

He spends another moment looking me up and down, torment storming behind his eyes as they finally settle on mine.

I don't know what to make of it, but situations like these can be delicate. With all my encounters, I'm patient as I let the client drive the discussion, deciding for themselves if they'll tear the bandage off bit by bit, or rip it off all at once.

With an abrupt huff, he steps away, his large, determined strides taking him inside the facility and back toward the lobby. I rush after him, but don't shout out his name or make a scene, not wanting to draw attention from the residents or staff . . . especially Derrick.

Sin wastes no time depositing his visitor badge on the desk, and I nearly break into a jog to catch up to his mile-long stride. When he bolts out the front doors, I'm right behind him, struggling to catch my breath.

"Sin," I say, winded but compassionate. He stops but doesn't face me. "If I've said anything—"

"You haven't."

His reply is so matter-of-fact, I feel silly for suggesting it. So, I reclaim my smile, if only for my own benefit.

"I know trust takes time. My card," I say, holding it out and feeling doubly foolish when he doesn't take it.

Instead, he sneers.

This is the point where others might give up, but I don't. It's the people who push you off the most that are in the most pain. At least, that's the excuse I've always given myself.

He eyes the card, then casts an amused glance to the sky. After an awkward second of silent conversation between him and a few puffy white clouds, he faces me. The hand he places on my shoulder feels paternal. "I don't need your card, Ms. Palmer. The person who brought me here today was you."

Unbuttoning his blazer, he fishes a thin envelope from the inside pocket and hands it to me as a dark car with tinted windows pulls up beside him. "Someone recently told me the first steps are never easy, Ms. Palmer."

A well-dressed chauffeur rushes around to open the back door, and as soon as Sin is seated inside, the man returns to the driver's seat.

The darkened window rolls down, and Sin's smile widens. "Happy birthday."

He slides on a pair of sunglasses as the car rolls away.

CHAPTER 2
Ivy

The black town car makes a left at the end of the drive, disappearing behind a thicket of birch trees, and I'm left there scratching my head. What just happened? I take another look at the plain white envelope in my hand, ready to open it until I notice Derrick. He's been watching from the large window of his office, a practice of his I've come to accept.

There's an intensity to his expression, one I meet with a cheerful smile. It takes him a moment before he returns it, waving me over. Maybe there's a surprise waiting for me. Like gathering the staff over to sing "Happy Birthday." Or an intimate cupcake with a single candle for me to wish upon.

"Everything all right?" Derrick asks as I enter. It's just him and me and the ever-growing clusters of paperwork and folders covering his desk. My hopes for a cupcake are instantly dashed, and it's a wonder he can find anything in the small space. For every new meeting with his accountant, the mounds of paperwork are only getting worse. He closes in from behind me, though the door remains open.

"Yes. He's going to think it over," I say as I slip the envelope into the roomy pocket of my cardigan. I want to remind him that sales aren't made in a day. That trust must be earned. But the irony is enough for me to bite my tongue.

I should tell Derrick about the envelope. For once, trust him. Really let him in. It feels self-sabotaging not to.

As often as I repeat the usual mantra, *I should trust him,* over and over again in my head, I can't deny the parts of my mind and heart that don't . . . and it's not for a lack of trying. Or admitting to myself that I'm damaged goods, the byproduct of an absentee mother and father unknown.

But Derrick is my ticket to a normal relationship, even if things between us have felt a bit uncomfortable lately. It's just a hiccup, one every couple encounters. He's stable. Sweet. A bit of a workaholic, which means I haven't seen him much in the past three weeks. But at least he has a J-O-B, and that should count for something, right?

Still, I can't help but shove the envelope deeper into my oversized pocket, hiding it from both my boyfriend and my boss. No matter how hard I try, distrust slithers between us, threatening to pry us apart.

Let's face it, I have issues, and trust is just the tip of the iceberg.

One of his arms wraps around me. Instead of giving him the usual elbow to the ribs, I nuzzle into him, and it feels . . . nice. Warm and caring and . . . nice. That is, until he releases me. And just like that, I second-guess everything.

Am I like Goldilocks complaining that my man is too nice?

Derrick's shirt is perfectly fitted, the navy blue tapering over his chest and abs before disappearing into his slacks. It looks professional and sexy, though I still prefer his lucky polo. His sweet superstition is that whenever he wears it, luck lands in his lap. As if I was a manifestation of luck.

"Chase another one off?" he says, only half-teasing me.

With his half smile and adorable gaze, maybe he's ready to finally make it official. "Aren't you afraid someone will see us?" I playfully ask, wondering if we can finally stop hiding our status from coworkers and Facebook alike. Be a couple in the actual light of day.

I know I agreed to keep our relationship under wraps, but maybe this is a baby step in the right direction. Hope blooms from deep within my chest that maybe, just maybe, I'm finally learning to trust.

"You're probably right," he says, pulling away to bring us back to a proper boss-employee distance apart. When my frown catches his eye, he lowers his voice. "Hey, it's not forever. Just for now. Meeting you was my destiny."

His sweet words and wink revive my smile, but before I can slip him a kiss, he steps back.

Noticing the envelope, he asks, "What's that?"

It would be so easy to tell him about the tour with Sin. The strange encounter and Sin's bizarre escape. Why can't I take the envelope out and open it with Derrick? Share something, *anything*, with my boyfriend of nearly a year.

I slide the unmarked envelope from my pocket, flipping it aimlessly. "Just a letter."

"I'm running to the post office after work, then I've got a meeting. Need me to mail it for you?"

"I've got it," I say, forcing a smile. "Meeting?" On my birthday?

Derrick has taken several meetings this week away from the office. And another dinner meeting? This can't be good.

His nod is reluctant, and I know when to back off. But I offer him all the support he needs, cuddling Mr. Whiskers against his neck. And like Sin before him, Derrick can't help but crack a smile.

"You and that . . . cat."

I don't know what word he mentally used to fill in the blank between *that* and *cat*, and I don't care. I'm tired of being ruled by my stupid doubts. And they are stupid.

But I tuck Mr. Whiskers back into my pocket, leaning closer to Derrick's rigid stance. "I need something for luck. I mean, we can't all have a lucky polo."

CHAPTER 3
Ivy

"Table for two. Under Brooke Everly," my best friend says, rescuing me from a birthday dinner for one of mac and cheese.

"You reserved a table?" I ask as we're seated, surprised because we never get a table. We always sit at the bar.

"The strongest they have . . . so we can dance on it. It's your birthday!" She squeals loud enough that absolutely everyone is looking. "And just because your boyfriend has to work doesn't mean we celebrate less. After this, it's karaoke time."

Her elbow nudges mine, and I know she's serious. My throat dangerously tight, I choke down the ball of fear with a few sips of the chilled water our waiter has placed in front of me.

Brooke instantly demands two tequilas. Both for her. "And keep them coming," she tells the waiter.

We've plowed through our first basket of chips as she tosses back her second shot.

"So, let me get this straight," Brooke says as she taps her lip with her index finger. "Some mysterious good-looking guy books a tour with you just to deliver mail and check out your ass?" She slurs the word *ass* and motions for the waiter. "Tell me he at least offered you a lap dance."

"He did not."

"Fucker. So, what did the letter say?"

I shrug. "It's still in my pocket. I got busy, and—"

Her eyes widen. "You didn't want to open it in front of Derrick in case it's a dick pic."

I deadpan. "Who would print out a dick pic?"

"A man who fills the page. You can't open it until after dinner. Birthday present number one."

Laughing, I shrug and dunk another chip into hot, gooey cheese. "Good-looking, yes. But more than twice my age, at least. And we all know twice my age is my hard limit."

"Really? I'll bet he's still hotter than Derrick. You rarely spend the night at his place, and we both know he's never at yours. Plus, he never takes you out. Ever. What kind of eighty-year-old boyfriend is he?"

"For your information, he's thirty. And I'm trying to be supportive as he builds his career."

"For a year? And when's the last time you've had sex?" she shouts, trying to be heard above the lively Mexican music.

Our waiter refills my water, grinning broadly. Sweltering heat rises up my face as I melt into the seat and die of embarrassment. Brooke roars with laughter, planting herself facedown along the bench.

"This coming from a woman whose face is kissing an area where someone's ass has been. After they've eaten their weight in Mexican food."

I ball up my napkin and toss it at my drunk friend's head,

which does little good. If anything, it eggs her on, as she moves on from laughter to a perfect whale-song combination of howling, raucous heaving, and silent squeals.

She rubs the flood of hysterical tears from her face before pointing a finger straight up, conveying how she needs a moment to catch her breath.

Hushed, I lean over. "I've had sex," I say, arguing with the giddy drunk girl. "For your information, I have it regularly."

"Like as regularly as when the salmon swim upstream?"

The waiter brings our food—two shrimp quesadillas for me and a taco salad the size of my Honda Civic for Brooke. I glare at her over the rim of my water glass as she orders a margarita.

"Virgin?" she shouts, having lost all control over the volume of her voice.

I scowl at her until I realize she was talking about a drink. Which actually sounds good.

Turning to the waiter, I ask, "Can you do a pineapple margarita with no alcohol?"

He nods and heads off.

"And more nachos," Brooke hollers after him.

In an instant, her elated happy face drops. Despite the fact that she's a champion lush who can usually out-shot or out-chug any man, I'm almost afraid she's about to be sick.

"You okay?" I ask, ready to rush her to the ladies' room.

She merely points past me, and I turn to see whatever zapped every last drop of happy-go-lucky from her face.

Lo and behold, it's Derrick.

I'm elated that he made it to my birthday celebration after all, until I see he's not in the professional button-down shirt he was wearing earlier at work. And he's not alone.

This version of Derrick looks freshly showered, his hair still damp and curled in a pretty-boy style that actually makes him look younger. Wearing his faded jeans that are my favorite, he's seated at the bar, relaxed as his spread-eagle legs give easy access to let a sloppy blonde slide in between them. She's made herself perfectly comfortable, smoothing her fingers against his chest and shoulders and pretty much all over his lucky fucking polo.

I square my shoulders, and before I know it, I've crossed the length of room, vaguely aware of Brooke huffing, "Shit," as her footsteps stumble behind me. I'm seconds from yanking the blonde by the hair—southern style—when I come to my senses and realize it's not her I'm pissed at.

"Oh, fuck," Derrick says like a dumbass because that's what he is. A worthless, dickless dumbass. He fumbles his way from behind the body of a woman whose perfume smells way too familiar because, like the man she's draped all over, that's also mine.

"Is 'oh, fuck' all you have to say? I guess she's your destiny, too." I frantically search the bar for the biggest drink within reach to toss in his face.

"What's going on?"

When his companion turns to face me, I realize it's none other than his accountant. Which explains all those closed-door and after-work meetings.

"Hey. Iris, right?" she says with the charm of a pole dancer, and now I'm searching the bar for two of the biggest drinks I can find—preferably crammed full of ice.

"Don't make a scene, Ivy," Derrick says calmly like a total idiot. "We're hardly exclusive."

"Excuse me? You're the one who was talking marriage and

kids. You're the one who's always asking what cut of diamond I prefer and where our honeymoon should be."

His lips tighten, and his words come out cool. "You can't pin this on me. I need passion. Spontaneity. A woman who will throw caution to the wind. The most I got out of you was your toothbrush."

He means a girl who will throw condoms to the wind. "And that's my fault? You're the one who wanted to keep our relationship on the down-low, and now I know why."

"Grow up. You don't want exclusive. You want to roam fast and free and with whatever guy rolls up. Like Limo-man this afternoon. What was in that envelope he gave you? Cash? A hotel room key?"

"What the fuck, Derrick? No."

At least, I don't think so. Besides, Derrick's so-called accountant is two seconds from sucking him off at the bar, so why am I the one on trial?

Derrick crosses his arms over his chest. "Yeah? Prove it."

He casts an arrogant glance at the pocket of my cardigan because, unlike him, I didn't have time to shower and change clothes before going out. I was actually working.

"I have nothing to prove." Which now looks like I have everything to prove. *Dammit*.

When I feel a tug at the envelope, I whirl around.

Brooke waves Exhibit A suggestively in the air. "And what if she hasn't been cheating on your sorry ass, Dare-dick? What are you willing to wager?"

At least my ride-or-die has my back, though I feel a bead of perspiration trail down the nape of my neck at her suggestion.

And since there's no backing down now, I square my shoulders and pray to God that Derrick is wrong.

Derrick waves her off. "It's not like you didn't already destroy the evidence."

"It's still sealed," I say, not certain if I'm making the situation better or worse but not willing to let my friend hang in the wind.

His expression sours. "Fine. What do you want if I'm wrong?"

"Your fucking car, jackass," Brooke says.

Wow. Her balls get all kinds of big after that much tequila. And when my bestie dives in headfirst, demanding his shiny new Mercedes convertible, there's only one thing to say.

"Yeah, Dare-dick," I say, repeating her insult because it's kind of catchy and totally spot-on as he plays fast and loose with Sluts-R-Us over here.

That's not jealousy talking. That's his accountant's cherry red lips now printing a path up another guy's neck before her tongue lands in his ear. It sickens me to remember that you've had sex with everyone your partner's had sex with. Perhaps a few weeks of no action with Derrick is just enough time to avoid a collision course with a round of STDs.

"Fine," he says, bellying up and stepping into my space. I anchor myself in place, ready for whatever he's got. Until he says, "Then if I win, you quit."

"Quit?" I squeak out.

I can't quit. What I do isn't just a job. It's my life. For years, I've cared for every single person in the center. Working evenings. Weekends. Christmas fucking morning. And now he wants me to quit?

Derrick is going too far. I'm not quitting my job over a stupid bet or even a breakup. No way. Not a chance.

I'm about to tell him so when Brooke cracks open the seal of the envelope and pulls out an old-looking photograph. Who in the world has photos anymore?

She flips it around and trombones the square to and from her face in the booze-filled hope of reading it. "Who's Olivia?"

"What?" Carefully, I take the delicate photo from her hand, staring at it hard, as hard as I can. My heart pounds wildly against my ribs, and I stand there, stunned. I blink before I regain my senses and can move.

Brooke slaps the empty envelope on Derrick's chest. "Ivy doesn't need your job. She's an overqualified badass who's tired of taking your shit."

Oh. My. God. Brooke really needs to stop talking now.

"Fuck both of you," Derrick spits out. "I'm not giving you my car."

As Derrick storms off, Brooke shouts after him, "Way to be a bad loser, Dare-dick."

It isn't until she wipes my cheek that I realize I'm crying.

"Hey, don't cry. He doesn't deserve you," she says, stroking my hair.

"It's not that," I say, staring at the image of my mother. At least, I think it's my mother. It's as if Angie's magic wand has brushed alchemist strokes across her image. Her dark curls are thick and full, framing round cherub cheeks and a big, beautiful smile I've never seen her wear. I almost didn't recognize her.

Next to her stands a man I don't know. His dark wavy hair is the perfect crown to his tall stature and confident stance. His lips are a line that barely tips up, and his dimpled chin could have been molded to form mine. But it's his eyes that draw me in. Instantly I want to know him, and it bothers me that I don't.

On the back is a riddle, one I reread again and again . . . and again.

For
Olivia Ann Palmer.

"What is it?" Brooke asks with a side hug that wraps me tight and squeezes out my reply.

"It's me. I'm Olivia Ann Palmer."

∞

1-CLICK NOW >> SINS OF THE SYNDICATE

To the outside world, I'm known only as Z. The enforcer. A widower with nothing to lose. An ex-SEAL sworn to keep one vow: protect the D'Angelo's at all costs.

I'm not a good man, and I never claimed to be.
Protecting her was second nature. Nothing more.
Claiming her was just a one-night escape.

But she made one mistake ... a cardinal sin.
Slipping away on her terms. Not mine.

No strings.
No commitments.
No names?

No way.

There's just one price for my protection.
And it's her.

<u>GET SINS NOW!!</u>

~

LOOKING FOR ANOTHER SEXY BILLIONAIRE? MEET Davis R. Black ... aka Richard. Some know him as a tech mogul. To Jaclyn, he's the King of the A-holes. Which is why this billionaire is hiding *his* in plain sight. Check out the first book in the Ruthless Billionaires Club.

<u>Get RUTHLESS GAMES now!</u>

About the Author

As a USA Today Bestselling author, Lexxi James has hit the top 50 bestseller lists on Amazon, Apple Books, and Barnes & Noble, with books sold in over 26 countries. Best known for seductive romantic suspense, she loves matching smoking hot heroes with their soul mates. Her signature style is witty banter, high heat, and a whole lot of heart.

She proudly calls the Midwest home where she lives with the man of her dreams and the sweetest daughter in the universe. Her pastimes include reading, loading up on unhealthy quantities of caffeine, and binging Netflix and reality TV. She's a sucker for kids selling cookies and pretty much anything on Etsy.

www.LexxiJames.com

Printed in Great Britain
by Amazon